Reunion

"Inspired by events in Snelling's own life, REUNION is a beautiful story about characters discovering themselves as the foundation of their family comes apart at the seams. Readers may recognize themselves or someone they know within the pages of this book, which belongs on everyone's keeper shelf."

—*RT Book Reviews*

"REUNION is a captivating tale that will hook you from the very start...Fans of Christian fiction will love this touching story."

—FreshFiction.com

"Snelling's previous novels (*One Perfect Day*) have been popular with readers, and this one, loosely based on her own life, will be no exception."

—*Publishers Weekly*

On Hummingbird Wings

"Snelling can certainly charm."

—*Publishers Weekly*

One Perfect Day

Wake the Dawn

ALSO BY LAURAINE SNELLING

Reunion
On Hummingbird Wings
One Perfect Day
Breaking Free

Available from *FaithWords* wherever books are sold.

Wake the Dawn

A Novel

Lauraine Snelling

New York • Boston • Nashville

Copyright © 2013 by Lauraine Snelling
One Perfect Day excerpt copyright © 2008 by Lauraine Snelling

FaithWords
Hachette Book Group
1290 Avenue of the Americas
New York, NY 10104

www.faithwords.com

Printed in the United States of America

RRD-C

First Edition: August 2013
10 9 8 7 6 5 4

FaithWords is a division of Hachette Book Group, Inc.
The FaithWords name and logo are trademarks of Hachette Book Group, Inc.

The Hachette Speakers Bureau provides a wide range of authors for speaking events. To find out more, go to www.hachettespeakersbureau.com or call (866) 376-6591.

The publisher is not responsible for websites (or their content) that are not owned by the publisher.

Library of Congress Cataloging-in-Publication Data

Snelling, Lauraine.
Wake the dawn : a novel / Lauraine Snelling. — First edition.
     p. cm.
ISBN 978-0-89296-901-2 (trade pbk.) — ISBN 978-1-61969-658-7 (audio download) — ISBN 978-0-89296-905-0 (ebook)
1. Loss (Psychology)—Fiction. 2. Life change events—Fiction. 3. Abandoned children—Fiction. I. Title.
PS3569.N39W35 2013
813'.54—dc23

Wake the Dawn *is dedicated to all of our faithful and courageous Border Patrol men and women who work so hard to protect us all. You are unsung heroes for the most part. Hats off to you.*

Acknowledgments

Like every other book I've written, I've had help. So much to learn in so little time, and one often does not understand all that is needed until right in the middle. Speaking of unsung heroes, I include in that list Anne and Bobby, who answered my early questions and then answered more. Bobby introduced me to a big, black dog who became my model for Bo. Sandy: idea maker, with unknown wealths of knowledge and creativity. You constantly amaze me.

Google has certainly made research more accessible even though I still want to severely wound my computer, though not as often as I used to. Thanks to my Round Robin writer cohorts who have become more like favorite relatives and play many different roles, from counselors to plotters to encouragers and prayer warriors. Whoever would have dreamed of all we have become for each other? My friends in Drayton, North Dakota, got me interested in the border patrol and interest is a trigger to future ideas.

I thank God for all those who love and read my books. You and your messages bless me more than I can say.

Wake the Dawn

Prologue

Allie had said, "No presents this year, but I have a surprise for you. Please don't be late."

But he had to bring her something. What could he bring his wife for a fifth-anniversary present? Why did he leave it to the last minute—as usual? Ben James turned his US border patrol SUV toward the shopping district, rather than toward home. Flowers? Did that last year. And the year before that. Candy? Allie wasn't a real candy eater, although everyone said chocolate was the answer. At least he had found her a really perfect card a few weeks ago. He stopped in front of that new florist on Dearborn Street. The shop featured a display of pots of red, orange, yellow, white, and bronze chrysanthemums. That was it! A pot of chrysanthemums. She loved fall flowers. This way she could put it outside and it would bloom again.

He nestled a pot of fiery burgundy blooms in a box on the floor of his backseat so it wouldn't tip over and turned toward home. Barring anything unforeseen, he would get there before she did.

The handset on his dash played Allie's signal and he punched the button. "Hello sweetheart."

Static. He listened with every sense. Had to be Allie. "Where are you, I can hardly hear you."

"Ben." Her voice was weak. More static.

"I can't hear you. I'll call you back."

"No." That came through clear.

He fought to ignore the static.

"B—B—Ben. I—I—I love y—you."

"What's wrong?" He swerved right, pulled into a no-parking zone, and killed the ignition to cut the noise of his engine.

"Ben."

"I'm here, sweetheart. I..."

"I'm going home. Good-bye."

He heard the last line clearly. A siren wailed in the distance, coming from the phone. "Allie...!" He screamed into the phone. "Allie, where are you?"

Nothing. No response, but he could hear the siren drawing closer through the phone.

God, where is she? What's going on? He punched in 911. "Ada, this is Ben James. Did you send an ambulance out?"

"Yes, a couple of minutes ago."

"Where to?"

"Single-car accident on SR 48 north of town, just beyond milepost twenty-two. Someone called it in."

He pulled a U-turn, hit his lights, all of them, and two-wheeled the turn onto Forest, headed for 48. Boot to the floor, he muttered over and over, "God, let her live."

Chapter One

"Chief? Dr. Ho is here." That annoying buzz in the intercom was getting worse.

He tapped the button. "Thanks, Jenny." Chief Paul Harden, leader of the best team in border patrol, guardian of two hundred miles of the US-Canada border, grillmaster of the annual church fish fry, was so out of shape his receptionist could outrun him. He should get with an exercise program soon. Lose the belly, build some stamina.

He lurched erect and strolled out to reception. Even that left him a bit breathless. Yeah, he was going to have to get cracking on some self-improvement.

This Dr. Ho could probably outperform him, too. The wiry little man beside the reception desk smiled and extended a hand. "Chief Harden, thank you for seeing me on such short notice. This makes my job much easier."

"My pleasure, Doctor. Coffee? Tea?"

"No, thank you. I just came from lunch."

"Then let's go back and solve the world's problems." He led the way down the hall to a small conference room adjoining his office. "Have a seat, please, whatever looks comfortable."

Of a sofa and three armchairs, the doctor picked the velvet-upholstered shellback chair. He had a good eye; it was indeed the most comfortable. Chief settled into the Naugahyde chair beside him.

Dr. Ho leaned back. "You know that the doctor in your clinic here, Esther Hanson, is a physician's assistant. Although she performs nearly all the functions of a physician, she must be supervised by a board-licensed physician. That is I. If a question comes up, she calls me. And periodically, I come by to assess her work."

Chief nodded. "She's mentioned you often and I might add, in positive terms. Glad you came by; I can associate a face with the name."

The little man smiled. "I'm on my way to the clinic, but I understand you're the person who takes over in emergencies. I'd like to get your views on Esther's work performance."

Chief leaned back. How to explain this in terms a civilian would understand? "I'm not officially in charge in emergencies. The town has two constables and some volunteer firefighters, and there's no sheriff's substation near. State patrol's presence is not a large one; feel free to drive any speed you like. I'm the de facto person in charge during an emergency only because our office is right here; I'm on the scene, if you will. So it's not chain of command, it's geography. Our agencies cooperate splendidly. Work together well. I merely coordinate efforts."

The man nodded. The explanation must have worked.

Chief added, "But that's all just theory. Nothing ever happens around here."

"Barb! Grab me another hemostat! I can't control this bleeding!" Esther had the kid's blood inside her rubber gloves as well as outside now, and direct pressure just wasn't doing it. "Rob! Crank up the oxygen! Way up! He's turning gray!"

From the doorway, Gavin's mother was clasping her palms to her cheeks and moaning, "Oh, God!" Sure, she was distraught, Esther could understand that, but she was darn irritating.

Here was the bleeder. Barb slapped a stat into Esther's hand and she forced it down into Gavin's leg, tearing a few minor muscles. The stat clamped down. Barb slapped a second into her hand but she apparently didn't need it. She watched the site a few moments and straightened up. Her hunched shoulder muscles ached.

"Wow!" Rob sounded amazed. "Nice job, Esther."

"Thank you. I'll stitch the artery, but I don't want to close until we're sure there's no leaks."

"I'll get sutures." Barb crossed the mini surgery and started riffling through a drawer.

"Esther?" a familiar voice called from the door.

She wheeled. "Dr. Ho!" Grinning, she hurried over and extended a hand, withdrew it quickly; it was still in its bloody glove.

He crossed to the table, leaned over, and peered closely at Gavin's leg, his hands clasped behind his back. "Interesting." He peeked under Gavin's eyelid, stood erect, and looked at her.

She peeled off her gloves. "This is Gavin Herr, Dr. Ho. Rob and Dennis brought him in a couple of minutes ago. Apparently he was climbing over a barbed-wire fence—not your usual barbed wire or concertina wire, but that stuff with the big, hooked points. The boys with him had the presence of mind to call nine-one-one before they skedaddled. They also called his mom, but by the time she got there the aid van was scooping him up. We suspect drugs may be on board."

"That's not true!" Mrs. Herr wailed from the doorway. "My Gavin would *never* take drugs. Never!" Obviously she had forgotten that Esther had asked her to stay outside. She hustled over and planted herself in front of Dr. Ho. "This young woman is nice, and she has lovely blue eyes, but she's not competent! Gavin was perfectly all right when they brought him in. I should've taken him home like I wanted to, but no. And now look at him!" She paused, scowling. "Are you a doctor?"

Dr. Ho smiled. "Yes. I'm Dr. Hanson's supervisor, Warren Ho. How do you do?" He extended his hand.

She sputtered, stared at the hand a moment, and accepted the handshake.

Esther washed her hands and slipped into clean gloves. Of all the people to complain to about her competence, Esther's supervisor was absolutely the worst choice. What if he believed her?

Barb had the suturing materials out on a tray and the irrigation bottle poised. Mostly to distract herself, Esther picked up a suture and went to work. Barb had already irrigated the area. Esther must concentrate on what she was doing. That hideous woman. Incompetent? She forced the woman's yammering into the back of her mind. *Focus, Esther. Pay no attention to Gavin's mother. Just fix his leg. Focus!*

Dr. Ho's voice commanded her attention anyway. "Mrs. Herr. Herr, right? Your son is still young enough to compensate well. Compensation is a strategy the human body uses to cope with extreme trauma. Children are especially good at compensating. Your son's femoral artery is ripped and he was bleeding to death, so his body compensated for the loss of blood by closing down veins to keep his blood pressure up. Your child appeared normal. But that only works for a short time. When the system cannot do that anymore, it simply collapses. Craters. And the child dies immediately. Dr. Hanson managed to pull him back from the grave. Thank your lucky stars, or God, or whomever you wish, that she got to him in time. She just worked a miracle."

"M-miracle...But drugs...no!"

"His pupils are constricted, Mrs. Herr. Besides, do children without diminished mental capacity cheerfully climb over a razor-wire fence?"

"But he's only twelve!"

Esther glanced up.

Dr. Ho was nodding. "So very sad, isn't it. If you would, Mrs. Herr, come with me next door. There's a wall chart there of the human circulatory system. I can show you exactly where his injury is and what the possible complications are." And, an angel of mercy, Dr. Ho led the woman out of Esther's life. At least for the moment.

Rob and Dennis tossed replacement supplies on their gurney and wheeled it out the door. Dennis paused long enough to slap Esther's shoulder and smile.

It took her nearly ten minutes to complete what should have been a five- or six-minute procedure. She must be more rattled than she thought. He said she was a miracle worker. Maybe that meant he did not believe the ranting Mrs. Herr. Maybe he was just saying that so that Esther wouldn't get angrier and screw up the procedure.

That debilitating, free-floating anxiety that gripped her so often was boiling up. Dr. Ho didn't know the half of it, and she wasn't about to tell him.

And what was going to happen when, sooner or later, she did screw up?

If Chief Harden were a journaling man—he wasn't—he'd start the first entry, "Day One on my road to a buff bod." It was going to be one long, miserable road.

His deceased wife had claimed that in cities, mall walking was a favored sport of many oldsters, and they all got to know each other. Here in Pineville, with one strip mall anchored by a snowmobile dealership, folks went high-school-football-field walking—more precisely, the cinder track around the outside—and everybody already knew each other. He parked by the fieldhouse and entered the gate.

Chief jogged a couple of yards and decided that it was best to work up slowly and carefully to an optimal degree of buffness and stamina. So he walked. Strolled.

Avis Breeden passed him. "Hello, Paul! Glad you're out here. They say a storm's coming." Avis was a good ten years older. "Herb, you know Herb, lives across the street from me, he says that big storm down south is going to come right up here."

"Oh? The weatherman this morning said it would miss us and nail Michigan."

"Herb says when his joints ache like now, we're in for it. And I believe Herb's joints before I'll believe some weather forecaster." She chugged off at her normal speed.

When really old, crippled-up Denise Abrams passed him with a cheery greeting, he stepped up his pace.

For a couple of yards. Winded, he leaned against a goal-post, catching his breath. This was going to be one *very* miserable road to buffness, but by golly he would do it.

The goalpost was freshly painted. It was painted every August since back when he was in high school; its diameter was probably a couple of inches bigger now with all that paint.

And the smell of it. The smell of the whole place.

The blocking sleds crowded together over in the corner. There was a day when he could move a sled ten yards with his coach standing on it. Run the length of the field and then run right back. Play hard enough and tough enough to win championships.

Then he went off to law enforcement training and a new generation of football players took the field. He lurched erect and continued. The sky had lost its blue, replaced by a pasty gray overcast, but the field was still bright green, its lines white. He reveled in this. Why had he waited so long to start?

Ben James. Why did he come to mind just now? Probably, the past glories on this field. And that legendary game between Pineville and Fillmore was the most glorious. Fifty-six to six. Ben quarterbacked that game; he was the best quarterback Pineville ever had.

Ben. He was a puzzle in high school, a puzzle now. Made sure he was the best at anything he tried. Valedictorian. Football. Married a prom queen. Topped his class in the law enforcement academy. And now look at him. Drinking himself to oblivion nearly every night. If he was going to be a drunk, he was going to be the best. Give him credit, Ben might look a little scruffy when he showed up at eight, but he was never drunk on the job, never ever behind the wheel. Chief kept a close eye on that.

"Hi, Chief!" The sky might be lowering, but Beth Clemens was always a ray of sunshine. She waddled up beside him and slowed her pace. She looked thirty months' pregnant, but if Chief remembered correctly, it was only seven or eight. Her blond hair was pulled back in one of those little elastic thingies.

He grinned. "Out exercising?"

She giggled. "Ansel says no Zumba until the baby comes. He's right; all that jumping and turning." She sobered. "Chief, I know it's none of my business, but do you hear much from Amber lately?"

His beautiful, screwed-up daughter, as lovely as her mother had been. Beth was one of Amber's best friends. "No, not lately. Have you?"

"No. Not for maybe two years. A long time."

"How's Ansel doing? I hear he got promoted."

And she was instantly sunny bright again. How did women do that? "He's the general manager now and re-gional rep for Sno-Go. Big salary jump." That tinkly giggle again. "Well, better finish my mile and get back. They'll be home soon." She returned to her normal pace and left him in the dust, if cinder tracks raised dust.

Finishing her mile. He nearly killed himself finishing once-around-the-track, but he made it and headed back to his car. How long was the track around the field? He'd forgotten. But he'd gone once around and tomorrow he'd go twice around. He flopped down behind the wheel, grateful to sit. He pulled out of the stadium lot and headed for his office.

Herb's joints or Hank Oldman, the weatherman on channel five? Which should he believe? He decided to go with Hank, since he'd gone to school with Hank and he knew Herb only very casually. Besides, Herb tended to be pretty negative, and Hank didn't. He climbed stiffly out of the car and let himself into the building.

Ada the dispatcher glanced up from her little hole in

the wall. "What are you doing here on Sunday afternoon?"

"I want to build the next two months' schedules without constant distractions and interruptions."

She smiled. "Welcome to Peaceful Valley."

He nodded. "I'm not here, understand?"

It was nearly dark when he finished up. Ada had left and Greg was on dispatch. He let himself out and climbed into his car. From office chair to car seat, from sitting to sitting. No wonder he got out of breath just fluttering his eyelids.

He should work after hours more often. Then he could drive home in twilight, like this. There was a peace to this little burg after dark. The yellowish streetlights were the old-fashioned incandescent kind that didn't glare. Most of the town was residential, and most of the residents took pride in their homes. There is a peace in neatness. He drove past Ben James's place. The only light was a flicker in the living room—Sunday-night football, no doubt. And the dork had left his garage door open again. Good thing this was a low-crime town.

Three doors down from Ben's he passed Beth and Ansel's place. Last July the town council thought they should take down that gorgeous oak in Ansel's front yard. Pregnant Beth threatened to chain herself to the tree and Ansel filed an intent to sue if they touched it, and they reversed themselves. That kind of grassroots politics couldn't happen in a city. Chief was glad he lived here.

He rolled down his window. The town smelled clean and damp and autumny. A dog barked. A cat appeared out of nowhere, flowed swiftly across the street from gloom into gloom. His left wheels bounced into and out of a pothole just beyond Third and Taylor. He'd call Glenn in the morning and get the street crew to fill it. That was something else you couldn't do in the city.

He pulled into his driveway, pushed the garage door button, listened to the opener groan as it dragged the garage door up. Probably need replacing soon. He parked the car and strolled out into cool darkness.

He glanced up. The cloud cover was black and much thicker than he would've expected. No faint sunset glow, no light smudge to betray the moon.

What if Hank's multimillion-dollar weather service was wrong and Herb's joints were right?

Chapter Two

"**B**o! Shut up!"

His black shepherd paced beside the bed, stuck his cold wet nose into Ben's hand dangling over the side. He barked again, a short sharp demand.

"I already let you out!" Ben fought to open bleary eyes. A jackhammer at full speed pounded without ceasing. He realized the phone was ringing. His landline, not his cell. Who in bloody blazes would be calling now? The dog barked again, splitting Ben's head wide open. The taste in his mouth made him gag, or was it the headache? Or the booze he needed like a transfusion to be able to sleep at night.

He fumbled for the phone, trying to ignore the glint of light off the bottle sitting on his nightstand. Perhaps a slug of that would stop the jackhammer. He shoved the handset into the general area of his ear.

"Good morning to you, too, Ben." The bright cheery voice of Jenny the dispatcher glued his eyes shut. "Ben! Don't you dare hang up on me!"

Bo barked again and paced the length of the queen-size bed, bypassing the dirty clothes of who-knew-how-many days littering the floor.

Jenny's voice took on a hard edge. "Good thing that dog helps get through to you. Chief wants you heading north up 270 in thirty minutes, and if he doesn't see you drive by, he will personally come haul your sorry rear in and confine you to desk duty. Are you sober enough to drive?"

"I'm sober." Ben groped for the bottle.

"Don't you dare touch that bottle, either!"

What, did the woman have a camera on him? "Yes, Mother Teresa." Fortunately he swallowed and nearly choked on the words he would have preferred to say. Jenny did not tolerate the kind of language that had taken over his mouth—and soul, too, for that matter. He started to put down the phone but realized she was still speaking. She didn't handle being hung up on, either. He'd learned that lesson the hard way. She might sound sweet but only when and if she wanted to.

"Ben, you have to get help."

"Thanks. I need a shower first and some coffee." He rubbed his face with one hand and glared at his dog sitting before him, Bo's lolling pink tongue the only spot of color.

"And give Bo a treat. I know he heard the phone first."

"Yah." Now he could hang up without getting his neck stretched. Get help. Sure. Such a simple thing to say and humanly impossible. The only help would be to bring Allie back. He had help enough; his only help to sleep, to wake, to live was found in that bottle.

He turned the shower on cold and stepped in, letting out a yell that made his head shriek. Call a cold shower penance of a sort. Wearing only a waist-wrapped towel, he searched for clean clothes, found one set of underwear in the laundry basket, and pulled on the cleanest uniform he could find. Good thing tomorrow was Saturday. Wait.

No, Friday. He thumbed his phone to see the day. Monday. This week was going to be a year long! He could drop his uniforms off at the cleaners and pick them up Saturday, thanks to Ellie at Ace Cleaners, who laundered them personally rather than sending them out with the regular cleaning.

How would he get through this day?

He thrust a mug of day-old coffee in the microwave and checked the fridge for cream. He sniffed the carton and tossed it in the overflowing trash. Bo paced beside him, as if not trusting him not to go back to bed. He had been known to.

The microwave pinged. He slapped his chest to make sure he had his badge; if Chief caught him badgeless again he'd rip off another piece of his anatomy. The coffee burned his tongue.

Had he fed the dog? Bo would be nosing his dish if he hadn't been fed. Together they exited to the garage. He groaned. He'd not closed the garage door again. What new wildlife had taken up residence overnight? The skunk had been a real mess to dispose of.

Bo jumped in as soon as he opened the car door and settled on the passenger side.

Ben returned to the kitchen, tossed back two aspirin, and returned to his vehicle, mentally checking to make sure he had everything. The coffee and the aspirin hit his stomach with equal vengeance. He hadn't grabbed a food bar, probably because there were none.

He smacked the horn twice as he drove by headquarters. Thumbing a couple of clicks on his hand mike, he waited for Jenny to pick up.

No sweet voice. No greeting. Just, "Did you eat anything?"

"Now you sound like my mother."

"I'll call your order in; they should have it bagged by the time you get there."

"Yes, ma'am." He finally noticed the waving trees. "You heard the weather?" Jenny always kept track of the weather. That was part of her job.

"Not looking good, but not too bad, either. Hank Old-man says the main storm will pass east of us, but we'll get some edge effect. NOAA weather says winds gusting ten to fifteen, half an inch to an inch of rain." She paused. "If you'd been at the meeting, you'd have been briefed."

"Thanks." Sarcasm dripped from the single word.

Jenny's voice softened. "Ben, I know what day this is, and I . . ."

Ben hit the OFF button and gritted his teeth. He picked up his breakfast burrito and fries to go, stuffed some money through the drive-through window, and headed out of town. He hated breakfast burritos.

In the Southwest, guides who escorted illegal immigrants across the border were called coyotes. Around here mostly Asians were coming across, and their escorts were snakeheads. And why was he pondering this imponderable factoid, anyway? He fiddled around with the radio awhile, pushing buttons, but nothing appealed. He turned it off.

Straight as a bullet, Route 270 took him north out of town through some low hills and off across the muskegs all studded with heather and clumps of scrawny trees. The wind was picking up, the pointy spires on the firs lashing back and forth.

Having been warned by his favorite stoolie that there was a possible sneak going down, Ben drove more slowly than usual and turned onto the dirt road he usually turned onto, part of his patrol zone but one with almost no traffic. He slowed down more. Tamarack and lodgepole pine dotted islands of solid ground surrounded by cattails and marsh grasses. The welter of bogs seemed impenetrable, but illegals passed through all the time. Those guiding must know this land even better than he did. Hard to believe.

Maybe they only knew certain routes, because almost always, they passed through right here. A bloody highway, the way they stuck to it.

A deer burst out and bounded across in front of him. *Oh, Allie, if you'd only done what I tried to teach you to do, not swerve for a deer.* That had been her last decision. She had swerved and lost control. Two years ago today. He ignored the tears until they clouded his vision, then pulled a handkerchief from his back pocket to wipe his eyes.

He parked on his favorite copse, a low, wooded rise where his vehicle was concealed but he could see all around. It was his favorite lookout because it was productive; from here he apprehended smugglers every month or two, just by sitting and watching. So he waited. And waited and watched. As accustomed to waiting as he was, Bo curled up and snoozed.

He was hungry. Had he thought to bring along anything for lunch? Of course not. Did he have a spare candy bar in his glove box? Once upon a time, but not now.

Past two o'clock he gave it up. People on foot who'd crossed the border during darkness would have passed this way by now. His stomach growled. He drove down off the copse and continued along the dirt road for another couple of miles, watching for heads bobbing out there, seeing nothing. The wind was picking up. You could hear it whistle.

Bo popped to a sitting position and whined, dancing with his front feet.

"Not now. There's no shoulder here. Just hold it until the next turnout."

The dog exploded. He lunged at the door, the windshield, his barking filling the SUV, instantly elevating Ben's headache back into full jackhammer mode.

"Bo, shut up! Down, Bo, down!" Ben pointed at the floor, but the dog ignored him, lunging at the window. He spun and barked at Ben, demanding. Ordering. Pleading.

His dog never acted like this. What had he picked up on that Ben missed? He stopped and, leaning way over, opened the door. Bo shoved through and tore off, back the way they had come. Before Ben could get out of the truck and cradle his gun, the dog angled south into a stand of pine and birch.

Concern switched to fury. Cursing the dog, the day, the wind, the terrain, he punched his handheld to notify headquarters.

"Want backup?" Ada's crisp voice.

"To help me find my fool dog? I don't think so."

"What if he's on to something?"

"He better be. Every time I call his name he barks, but he quit obeying orders when he went nuts in the truck."

"Keep us posted."

He signed off. "Bo!"

The response was closer. If there were any illegals in this area, they'd sure as hell been warned. He held his gun at ready, trying not to step into holes. Was he wearing his flak jacket? No, that required forethought. The wind screamed through the trees now, breaking off branch tips and spinning them ahead. The storm Jenny thought would hit Michigan seemed to have made a wrong turn. He hated wind. Plenty of mess, no upside.

He blew his dog whistle. Bo yipped. Close, but where? At least they seemed to be on an island of hard ground in the bog. The moss was squishy, but the ground under it didn't give.

Another yip; he angled to the left toward the sound. Some partner this blasted dog had become. Whatever had possessed the mutt to go tearing off like this? He puffed the whistle. A whine this time. He stepped around a clump of fir to see Bo curled under a heath.

Gun ready, Ben moved closer. Was it a body? Bo was trained to find live people, not corpses. "Bo, leave it!"

The dog didn't move. Other than one lip that curled slightly. His dog, his partner, was acting almost menacing.

What in thunder...?

As if on cue, thunder grumbled off to the southwest. The wind was from the southwest, so it would soon be followed by rain—with Ben's luck, a deluge; he'd left his slicker home.

A voice from his radio: "Ben, come in. Ben." Sounded more like Jenny than Ada.

He ignored the voice. Keeping all his attention on the dog, he took a deep, cleansing breath to calm down. Why couldn't he respond correctly to a simple incident, the way he was trained to do? What was going so haywire with his judgment that even his dog, equally trained, was picking up on it? Maybe Bo was reacting to his rage. He lowered his voice. "What is it, boy? What have you found?"

The black tail quivered, black eyes drilled into his.

Something white or once white lay within the dog's protection. It wasn't big enough to be a person. But this dog was one of the best sniffers in the business. Other departments often borrowed the two of them in emergencies.

"Easy, Bo, let me see. I'm okay now." Ben eased forward, keeping his movements firm and slow. A blanket?

A bundle wrapped in a blanket. A bundle of what? Bait in a booby trap? He stood up quickly, looked around. If anyone else was in the area, Bo would know, hear, or smell. Ben knelt beside the bundle.

A baby.

Bo had just found a baby. Was it still alive?

Bo wagged his tail and whimpered again. "Good boy. Good job, good boy." When he reached out with his hand to touch the bundle, Bo licked his fingers. "Good boy, I'll take it from here."

"Ben, where are you? Are you all right? Ben! Respond!" Definitely Jenny.

He touched the baby's face. Still warm. He laid his hand on the chest. Still breathing. He thumbed his handheld and barked, "It's clear. I'll file the report later."

"Good. Chief says get back here, pronto. We need you."

No matter what you're doing, someone wants you to be doing something else. He was getting pretty tired of it. "Jenny? Where's Ada?"

"Had to go home. Hurry in, Ben."

He scooped the baby up and rose to his feet. "Come on, Bo, let's get out of here."

With Bo leading, Ben clutched the baby to his chest and staggered back toward the road. If the baby was bait in a trap, he was toast; he couldn't keep his sidearm ready and carry the baby and keep his balance. Bog-wise, Bo bounded from firm spot to firm spot and was soon out of sight. Ben was just as bog-wise but not nearly as agile.

He stumbled, splashed through puddles, hit a grass clump wrong and his foot slid down into mire. He stepped out into the open and a gust slammed him backward.

The rain struck in an instant downpour. No polite starting sprinkle, no lightning.

He didn't dare stop to check the baby he carried; the wind knifed through his wet shirt, reminding him how soaked the bundle was. At last he reached solid roadbed and scrambled up onto it. Bo barked off to the right, and there waited his truck a hundred yards away.

He grabbed an emergency blanket out of the box in the backseat and let the wind slam the back door closed while he wrestled one-handed with the driver's door. He held it open with his back while he snapped the blanket open and laid the baby on it. These goofy space-age blankets. Aluminum foil made out of plastic, for pete's sake; didn't deserve the name *blanket*. But apparently they worked, because every emergency kit had one, so thank God for space-age technology. He wrapped the baby up and belted it into the passenger seat.

The wind slapped the door against his hip and the backs of his legs. "In, Bo."

The dog leaped to the driver's seat and down to the floor to sit facing the passenger seat. Ben climbed in and the wind instantly slammed the door closed for him. It was getting just plain nasty out there.

For the first time since he'd scooped up the baby, he allowed himself to pause a moment and close his eyes. *God, help this baby.*

The irony of him now praying to the God he swore to ignore was lost in long-ago habits that came thundering back. He keyed his radio with one hand and rammed the key into the ignition with the other.

"Jenny?" He didn't wait for a response. "Call Esther and tell her a baby's en route. A tiny one. Alive but unresponsive." He roared off in the wrong direction, grabbed the hand brake, and did a perfectly executed moonshiner's turn—180 at forty miles an hour. He felt momentarily smug; it'd been years since he did that, and he still had the touch. On the other hand, if his tires had hooked up, they would have spit him into the ditch, and this was not the time to need a tow. He headed toward town code three. His lights flashed red off the wet trees; the blaring siren giving him hope he was actually doing something constructive.

"Bo, guard the baby. Take care of him, Bo."

The flailing wipers couldn't begin to keep the windshield clear. Like driving into a car wash. When he swung south onto 270, conditions seemed to let up a bit. Until a blast broadsided him, shoving him across into the northbound lane.

The baby shifted; Bo nosed it back into a safer position.

Ben swore at the storm, at the fear riding him like a sumo wrestler on a Shetland pony. He straightened back into his own lane, his arms and shoulders already tight from battling the bucking vehicle. Eight miles to go. He sped up, but now he was driving beyond his headlights. It appeared he was the only one on the road. Still...

"Where are you?" The radio crackled a little.

"Just passed Owens Road."

"Esther's ready."

He grunted and glanced in the rearview mirror to see a pine crash across the road, not a small one. While he knew the roar it should be making, between the siren and the rain drumming on his roof, the tree fell soundlessly.

"Trees are falling," the radio informed him helpfully.

"So I hear. Route 270 is fully blocked at the eight-mile marker."

Two miles farther.

He stood on the brake; a tree lay dead ahead. He shoved his rig into four-wheel drive, grateful that four-wheelers no longer had to get out and lock Warren hubs by hand. He shifted into low and pressed the deer guard through the branches, eased down on the gas pedal. The wheels threw branches behind him, but the tree moved. He cleared one lane, backed off, drove through the passage.

Less than half a mile farther, a tree had fallen across the power line to the Hostettlers' place. The wire danced, throwing sparks. He swung wide. And he finally let in the thought that he mightn't make it into town.

He roared into the outskirts. A power line hung on a broken pole, but it hadn't parted. A truck ahead moved to the side at the sight of his flashing lights.

Emergency lights approached northbound. An ambulance flashed headlights at him and kept on going.

He keyed his mike. "Did you tell that ambulance that the road is closed?"

"They aren't going that far. Just Hostettlers'. ETA?"

"Five minutes."

The one stoplight in town hung black overhead. He slowed in case of other traffic and finally wheeled into the clinic. He hit the brakes and had his door open almost before the vehicle stopped. Reaching across the seat, he unsnapped the seat belt and grabbed the bundle.

"Here." Esther Hanson took the bundle and raced into the clinic, Bo and Ben right behind her.

He'd made it.

Chapter Three

Stay, Bo." Ben paused outside the examining room. Bo ignored him and followed Esther into the mini surgery. The bright lights above the examining table reflected off the silver blanket. "Bo! He figures the baby's his. Shouldn't have told him to guard it."

"It's okay. Help me." She unwrapped the crackly blanket and stripped the baby, dropping things on the floor. Laying her stethoscope on the naked little chest, she listened, shaking her head. "This is a miracle."

"What?"

"That she's still alive. How long do you think she was out there?"

"Couldn't be too long. Overnight the animals would have gotten her." A girl.

"No trace of the mother?"

"We didn't look. Bo found her. Wasn't going to even let me touch her until I calmed down. He knows I don't do hectic real well."

"Neither do I. Get me a blanket out of the warmer." Even as she spoke, she was checking the baby's vitals.

The clinic's sole warmer was in the hall so everyone on

the corridor could access it conveniently. Of course, in the hall it was convenient to no one. Ben snatched out a blanket and returned to Esther. "When we were returning to the truck, Bo gave no indication of other people around."

"So the mother left her baby." She wagged her head.

"Or the snakehead forced her to leave it. She's Asian, no idea what country."

"Possibly three weeks old." She reached for an IV kit. "Don't go; I need you to help. How we'll start a drip into veins this tiny, I have no idea." She tapped hands, arms, feet, rapped the inside of the tiny elbow. "She's so dehydrated. Her veins are collapsed. Come on, baby, stay alive. Have you ever done one before?"

Ben shook his head. His EMT training included starting lines, but not in an infant so small. "Where's Barbara?"

"Had to go home to get her kids when the lights went out."

"You're on generator?"

"Kicked in automatically." She poked about, still wagging her head. "Okay, we're going in here, this vein. Find me a rubber band."

"Her *head*?" Rubber band. There, holding together a bundle of vials. He ripped it off; vials rolled everywhere.

"It's the best vein I see. Dig me out size twenty-four. Even that may be too large."

He found it; the needle was the size of a really thin wire.

"Hold her head completely still. That's it." She positioned the rubber band around the baby's skull above her eyes, laid one finger firmly against a place Ben would have thought was random, and pressed the tiny needle against the tiny scalp. The baby didn't move.

Esther swore, backed off, tried again. A teensy bubble of blood rose into the very bottom of the floor of the syringe. Esther cackled triumphantly. "Have that saline ready, and a hanger."

Okay, so Ben was in awe. A vein that small...He set up the IV rack and bag, handed her the end of the tubing, plugged male plugs into females, bled the bubbles out of the line. She released a little saline, checking for bulges with her fingertips, withdrew the needle. The catheter remained in place. Success!

She stood erect, stretched her shoulders back. Her face looked drawn, weary already. "I'll tape it down and cut off the band. Can you diaper her?"

"Where're the diapers?"

She nodded toward a cupboard.

Someone yelled from the ER entrance.

"Go see who it is, will you?"

Ben grabbed a diaper and laid it on the table as he left the room.

An old man with a bleeding head wound looked about to pass out. He was pressing a kitchen towel against his head, but it was doing nothing to stanch the flow. He would probably be a crumpled little puddle on the floor if his son weren't holding him up. Ben knew these two: Ernie Gilbertson, a volunteer EMT, and Jens.

"Ernie, this way." Ben led them into room three. "Get him up there."

Ernie helped his father onto the table. "Piece of roofing caught him."

Ben ripped open a pack of gauze and handed it to Ernie. "Hold this while I scrub. Did you call nine-one-one?"

"No. No bars on my cell."

Mr. Gilbertson moaned and tried to sit up.

"Dad, don't move."

The thin, wrinkled lips muttered, "Your mother, where is she?"

"She's home, Nancy is with her. She's okayer than you right now."

Ben knew Ernie's mother had recently had surgery but right now could not remember for what. *What is Esther doing with the baby?* He jerked his focus back to this room and this patient. At least he could handle this one, up until the stitches, that is. Head wounds always bled like a broken water main.

"I need more gauze. This is soaked."

Ben set the box on the table. "Help yourself. Oh, and don't throw away that gauze. Just add to it. Then we'll know how much blood was lost. We'll get a drip on him soon as we can."

He heard the buzzer and voices in the waiting room. Forget about washing up; the rain-rinse would do; he was still damp. Snapping on latex gloves, he moved to Jens Gilbertson's head and took over with the gauze. "Go see who is out there, would you please?" With gentle fingers he probed the area around the laceration. Solid, no mush, no bubble of swelling, no indication of deep-flesh injury. "Good thing you have a hard head, Jens; we'll get some stitches in here and you'll be right as rain." *Right as rain.* Not particularly apt in this storm. He checked the man's pupils. No dilation, no indication of further trauma.

An approaching ambulance siren reassured him. Now they would have more help.

Ernie came back. "Ambulance just pulled up."

"Okay, keep your father from moving. I'll be right back." He stuck his head in the mini surgery, where Es-

ther was diapering the baby. "You're amazing. Scalp laceration in room three when you get to it. Ernie is keeping
his father from running out the door before we get him
stitched up."

"Thanks."

He watched her a moment. She looked strange. "You
okay?"

Esther nodded as she stripped off her gloves. "I can't
leave her quite yet."

"The ambulance crew is here. We need to triage the waiting room. I'll call headquarters, see if we can get some more
help. Who do you want me to call?" Ben watched the table
where the infant lay. "She's alive, right?"

"For now. I can't find anything other than dehydration.
We need an incubator."

"We don't have one?"

"No. One of those many things on my list. Or a real
crib." She was bitter; it came through loud and clear.

Yvette, one of the ambulance EMTs, stopped in the
doorway. "We have a possible cardiac here. Where can we
put him?"

"IV in place?" Esther almost looked frightened; Ben
must be reading her wrong.

"Yes, and EKG. We gave him bicarb and started a
drip."

"Put him in room two." Esther paused. "Then come
back here and stay with this infant."

Yvette Carlin, the youngest member on the volunteer
crew, nodded and hurried off.

"Ben, can you triage the waiting room?"

"Will do, but..." He stared at her face. "You're dripping sweat and you're white as that sheet in there. Are
you all right?"

"I will be. Now go."

Ben glanced from her to the baby and down at Bo. "He might not let anyone else touch her." He motioned. "Bo, come. Duty's done. Come."

The dog whined, looking from one human to another. He looked up at the table and settled back on the floor, muzzle between his front feet. His tail brushed the floor.

"Leave him."

"Stupid mutt." Ben glared at the dog and exited down the hall, speaking into his handheld as he went. "Jenny, can you get us some help here at the clinic?"

"As soon as someone else comes in. We put out a general call for everyone to report for duty. How's the baby?"

"Hooked up to an IV, but we have no incubator or crib."

"Put her in a drawer."

"Good idea." He veered back and gave Esther the message. He left as she was dumping supplies out of a drawer onto the counter.

It was already standing room only in the waiting room. Ben caught his breath. What to do first? He raised his voice and arms at the same time. "Listen up, folks." When the hush fell, he started giving instructions, all the years of disaster preparedness training kicking into gear. "I need someone on the phone, someone else to follow me around taking notes. We'll see you all, but we'll take you in order of critical injury."

Mrs. Breeden, known by everyone as Avis, stepped over to the desk. "I can handle the phone. What do you want me to tell them?"

"Only critical care here. Otherwise, ask them to remain in their homes for now if it's safe."

Dennis Schumaker, the other EMT, returned from

wheeling his patient into room two. "Esther is with him now. Tell me what to do."

"Start on that side of the room and I'll start here. Critical first." A child off to his left screamed and went rigid in her mother's arms. He went to her.

"She has epilepsy. We know what to do. Do you know where a tongue depressor is?"

He pointed down the hall. "First door on the left. Jar on the counter. If no one is in there, take her."

The father leaped to his feet.

Avis appeared at Ben's elbow. "Another call for an ambulance."

Dennis nodded. "I'll get Yvette." He hustled out.

"Ben." Jenny's voice on his radio. "How bad over there?"

He keyed it. "Full up." He needed a beer. "Any news on the storm?"

"Taking up residence right here. Michigan got stood up."

"Thanks." He knew he sounded sarcastic but at this point that might help keep him sane, something along the line of gallows humor. "Where's Chief?"

"Responding to another emergency. I'm it for here for right now."

While they talked, Ben moved to the next family.

"I need help in here!" Esther hollered from room two.

"Be right back." He strode down the hall and stepped inside two. "What do you need?"

"Transport south; this is more than we can handle here."

The cardiac patient, tilted halfway to sitting on the gurney, looked panic-stricken.

Rob Lewis appeared in the doorway. "Where do you want me?"

"You help Esther and I'll go back to the waiting room."

Rob nodded. "I think the Lutheran church is receiving guests. Can we send any of these over there, do you think?"

"Not so far."

Ben paused in the room where the infant still lay without moving, Bo at guard. "Good boy." At least her color looked better. He touched her face. Not hot, but warmer than before. "Hang in there, little one." He left for the next crisis, battling the lump in his throat. How could a mother walk off and leave a sweet little baby lying in the muskegs, not even beside the road? How could a God of love allow all this to happen? No time to rage right now, that was for sure.

The din had grown in the waiting room, only because the number of people had. No one was screaming or demanding, and those who could were already helping those who needed it.

Ah! Barbara, the nurse who was Esther's right-hand woman, had returned. She waved him over and handed him a list of names. "I took over triage. These are put in the order I thought most necessary."

"Thanks." He started to call out the next name when an old woman clad only in her underpants followed someone else in through the door. She wove between those on the floor, plaintively calling for her husband. He didn't know her, but he knew about her. Her man had been gone for three years, and her dementia had grown worse. Usually her neighbors kept track of her. A man rose and draped his jacket around her, then leaned closer to say something in her ear. She nodded and sat down where he indicated, only to rise immediately and call "Harold?" again.

Ben turned to Barbara. "Get her a gown, please. Maybe

someone can run her over to St. Mark's. Bring out any more blankets, too. Anyone suffering from shock in here?"

"Most likely everyone, to one degree or another." She disappeared into the hall. The phone rang again. Avis? Avis must have gone somewhere.

A man leaning against the wall picked up the receiver. "Clinic. Dr. Esther is tied up right now. Can I take a message? No, ma'am, the room, well, the whole building is full. If you cannot stay in your home, or your neighbor's, go up to St. Mark's Lutheran. They've opened the Lutheran church."

Ben nodded his thanks and moved to the next victim. A little boy tugged his arm. "My momma can't talk to me no more."

"Where is your momma?"

"Home. She said me and Sissy had to come here." He indicated a girl at least a year younger than himself. "Then she took a nap."

Ben swallowed the bad feeling growing in his gut. "Can you tell me where you live?"

The boy reeled off his address and clutched his sister's hand. A bruise on her forehead was already swelling her right eye shut. "A board banged Sissy."

"What is your name?"

"Charlie. Momma says don't talk to strangers but you're a policeman, so that's all right."

"Charlie, what is your last name?"

"Stevenson. My daddy drives a big truck."

Ben knew where they lived, a new family in town, and Stevenson was probably on the road somewhere, frantic about his family. "Do you know how to call your daddy?"

Charlie nodded. "But our phone didn't work. Momma

said to come here. Can you please go wake my momma up now? Sissy is hungry and she messed her pants."

"How old are you, Charlie?"

He held up three fingers. "My birthday is tomorrow. Then I'll be this." He held up four.

Ben patted Charlie's knee. The child's skin was cold. "You wait right here and I'll see what I can do." He moved down the hallway to call Jenny.

"What do you need?"

"I need someone to go to the Stevenson house, that new family in town. The children are here, but Charlie says he couldn't wake his momma up."

"Oh, Lord, no. I'll call Chief, or—or someone. Anything else?"

"Tell whoever goes there to call me with the response. I'll tell the kids."

"I will. Ah, Ben, who knows how many have died already in this." She clicked off.

Barbara was handing out blankets, but when he beckoned her, she handed the pile to someone else and came over.

"See those two little kids there? Can you get someone to change the little girl and check them? I'm hoping they can go up to the church."

"Will do. That new couple that just came in, you better check them next. How's Esther doing?"

"Last I knew she was treating a cardiac in two. Rob is with her, I'll check. We need someone to clean the examining rooms between patients, too."

He left her and crossed to the middle-aged man and woman. He knew these people, too. Wait a minute. He paused in midstep. Barbara did not ask *what is Esther doing*, or *where is Esther*, but *how is Esther doing*. How?

Barbara knew Esther as well as anyone; what did she anticipate might be wrong with Esther?

But then the man before him, Roy Abrams, seized his attention. "I think Denise is bleeding internally."

"Let's get her in here, and I'll get help." He led them to three. At least the room where Ernie had his dad was cleaned up now, somewhat. The wrappers were picked up and the bloody gauze dumped in the hot bag. Judging from the crowd in the waiting room in this crisis, they were going to have to put up with semi-clean tonight. "Let's lay her down on the table. There should be a blanket in that cupboard there. What happened?"

"The power went out. I lit our Coleman lantern while she went out on the back porch to bring in some knitting. She can knit by lamplight. That's when the apple tree fell on the pantry and she got trapped under the rafters. Took me a while to get her out and the phone is dead so I couldn't call for help. We don't have a cell phone."

"Cell's dead, too. How long ago?"

"Might be half an hour. Took a while to get here. Trees are down, power lines; Ben, it's a horror out there."

It was a horror in here, too. Denise looked terrible, pasty and pained.

"Be right back." Ben headed down the hall. Suddenly he detoured. His boss, Chief Paul Harden, was coming in the side double doors. The milling crowd, all these people expecting him to make their problem go away right now, that abandoned baby... The fury in him rose and boiled over. He yelled, "Hey!"

Chief turned and looked at him.

Ben squared himself directly in front of this man. "Exactly why am I here?"

"You don't want to be out there. Nobody wants to be out in this hurricane-on-steroids."

Ben spaced his words out clearly, his fury seething now. "I am an experienced border patrol officer. My duties are to catch bad guys trying to sneak over the line and to work with equivalent Canadian officers. I am *not* a medic; I am certainly not a hospital administrator, nor do I want to be."

Chief Harden measured his words just as carefully. "You are here, *Officer* James, because you're the only EMT in the county who's on the national register, you did part of your ER time with Mayo, you're certified for invasive procedures, you're levelheaded in tight spots and when you have to you can ad-lib, and unless you're blotto, you're dependable, so—"

"Dependable!" Ben interrupted. "Not even my dog trusts me!"

"In short, you're here because we need you. It's where you were assigned."

"No one assigned me here!"

"I did. And if you'd been at the staff meeting yesterday at four, you would have known that. Next time don't start drinking until after six."

This was his supervisor, his boss, he must not—he didn't give a rip who this guy was. He was yelling now. "I can't do this job!"

"None of us can do the job we're doing. That's the way emergencies go. So hang in there and just keep doing what you can't do."

Yelling wasn't getting anywhere. Frustration equaled his anger now. So they wanted a hospital administrator, did they? By glory they'd get one. "We're gonna get some FEMA funds out of this, right?"

"We're in line for their whole fiscal budget. Did you see what it's like out there?"

"I drove back in it, remember? And it hadn't really gotten going yet."

"Then, Bucky, you ain't seen nothing yet." His voice was so soft and sad, so heavy with meaning, Ben's fury almost melted.

But not quite. Over there across the room. "Hey, you! Kid!" Ben crossed to a gangly teenager with acne. "Aren't you the Culpepper kid?"

The kid quailed. Almost whispered. "Yes, sir."

"You know how to mop a floor?"

"Sorta."

"Then you're about to learn. Follow me." He started off for the custodial closet, calling over his shoulder, "Ten dollars an hour cash for as long as we need you. You'll clean up the examination rooms and minor surgery between patients."

"I—I don't know how to..."

"Join the club, kid. All of us are doing jobs we don't know how to." He thrust the mop and squeeze bucket into the boy's hand, uncapped the disinfectant and showed him how much to pour in. They filled the bucket out of the slop sink. Ben handed it to him. The kid was strong enough to hold it without a problem. "We'll use three for practice."

Ben waved a hand as he entered three. "Kid, this is Roy and Denise Abrams. You're going to have to work around us sometimes." He put a cuff on Denise and grabbed a stethoscope out of the drawer. "First you pick up any litter. Wrappers mostly—anything sterile comes in a wrapper and we toss it when we're busy—blankets, everything." He pumped up the cuff, pressed the stethoscope bell to Denise's arm. "Then you mop the floor. When the table here is vacated, you go over it with a rag wet with disinfectant water. Go get a rag out of that closet we were in." He let the pressure down slowly, waiting, listening. Down. Down. Eighty-five. He pulled the stethoscope out of his ears and stood up straight. "I'll go get Esther."

Roy nodded. Denise vomited.

Ben left the room in a stately manner but broke into a run the moment he was out of sight of the door. He burst into two. "Esther, you better check this one quick."

The look on her face stopped him cold.

Chapter Four

I lost him." Her face; Ben had never seen a face that said—well, said all that. Esther looked stricken, absolutely stricken. But it was much more than that, infinitely more. She was tired. She was horrified. She was furious and terrified and heaven knew what else. She was at the end of her rope. Past the end of her rope.

"She didn't lose him, he was beyond help, at least here in our limited facilities." Rob pulled the sheet up over an older man's head. "I'm sorry, Esther, but you can't go blaming yourself. Right now we don't have time for that." He must not have looked at her face, or he would have known his words, intended for encouragement, were harsh.

Now what? If Ben was administrator he might as well administer. "Rob, will you see to a kid out there with a broken arm? He doesn't look bad now, but kids that age compensate, and he could crash. Ask Barbara."

Rob nodded and hustled out.

"I have another one out there, Esther. Her BP is eighty-five and I quit looking for the bottom. Her husband fears internal bleeding. I think he's right." Ben moved in closer, lowered his voice. "You look ready to check out on us. This isn't like you."

"Give me a minute." Esther took a deep breath, another, and shook her head. Her pasty white skin remained white. The sweat stood in beads on her forehead. "Nothing a little time won't cure. What do you think we should do with the body? I hate to be so callous, but it's taking up room and we have other lives out there we may be able to save. What did our emergency plan say to do?"

"Call the mortuary." He grimaced. "No one is out on the roads other than emergency vehicles. I suppose we can call over there and see what they say."

She was grimacing, too, staring vacantly at the floor. "If they have a phone. My cell can't get out, I suppose the tower's down. They say nearly all the landlines are down." She wagged her head. "Ben, I thought I had him stabilized, and all of a sudden his heart just quit." She was nearly shouting. "Just *quit*! Lord, what did I do wrong?"

"You don't have to do anything wrong for the world to go to crap." *Allie, gone.* "I know from experience."

She inhaled, shuddered, grabbed her elbows with her shaking hands. "Enough, Esther. That's enough! Get a grip. You have no time for a reaction like this." Another shudder. "Can you find me a cup of coffee?"

"If there's coffee in the building, it's yours. What do you put in it?"

"Nothing." She was taking deep, sobbing breaths. "I know; stash the body in the hall closet for now, where we store the backboards and water rescue stuff." She seemed to have clicked back into her professional mode. Her face softened, she stood straighter. "I'll check on the baby first and then we'll bring that woman in here. All the surgical instruments are here if we have to go in. Is there anyone out there who will clean up?"

"A kid named Culpepper is—"

She didn't seem to hear him. "We can't bring her in here like this." She gestured toward the wrappers on the floor, a spent syringe, vials of something scattered around the room. The place was a mess, agreed. But it was powerful testimony to her heroic efforts to save this guy. "I'm going to go look in on her; clean up in here." And she gestured toward the body as she left.

How strong was he? He could bench-press 250, but this was, literally, deadweight. He'd need the sheet; he whipped it off and threw it over his shoulder. He yanked the floppy corpse to sitting and twisted under the fellow, ruched the guy up on his shoulders in a fireman's carry, and schlepped him down the back hall. Ah! Here came the Culpepper kid out of the employees' men's room. "Open that closet door for me."

The kid's mouth dropped open and he stood stock-still a moment, then dived for the door. He swung it open and Ben carried the body inside. "Is—is that a dead man?"

Ben let his burden down and covered it with a sheet. The fellow was more knotted than laid out, but he probably didn't care anymore. "It is. We're likely going to lose a couple more, but we're doing the best we can." He stepped out and closed the door. "I don't want to go all night calling you 'the Culpepper kid.' What's your first name?"

"Gary."

Dang, he needed a beer! Might as well administrate some more. "Gary, Dr. Hanson is doing a magnificent job, but so are you. Cleaning up is just as vitally important as the rest of the operation. We really need you and you're coming through like a champ. We're grateful."

The kid seemed to soften a little. "Thank you, sir. I was just coming out to tell you I quit, but I guess I won't."

"Good man! Can you get the mini surgery right away? We need it."

"Yes, sir."

Yet another crisis averted. The kid wasn't Mr. Clean, but he was doing okay, and Ben wasn't lying about needing him.

He stopped by the break room to pause at the drawer that held their tiniest patient.

Esther was standing there gazing at her, too. "Still too far out to get dependable vitals. I slowed the drip a little more anyway. She's looking better."

The back of his hand touched her cheek. Baby soft as only a baby's cheek could be. "I thought so, too. She's not so cold anymore."

"She'd do even better if we could find someone to hold her."

Hold her? "I'll ask."

Esther headed off to the Abramses and their internal bleed, and Ben walked out into the waiting room. "Barbara? Can you start coffee? Esther was asking."

From over by the wall, Barbara called, "Sure."

This reception area was still totally stuffed full, still standing room only. He felt like he hit a wall, almost the way Esther's face had looked. So many injuries. He called, "We have a baby that needs to be held and kept warm. Will any of you volunteer?"

An elderly, heavyset woman in one of the clinic's wheelchairs raised her hand. "I can't walk, but I can hold a baby." She extended a trembling hand. "Hannah. Dr. Hanson knows me, but you don't."

"Ben. Thank you, Hannah." Ben wheeled her off to

the break room and set her brakes. Gently he picked up the infant and, trundling the IV pole with his other hand, brought her to the woman. "Sorry, Hannah, but the dog here is part of the package. His name's Bo. Long story, I'll tell you sometime."

"No problem as long as he doesn't need to be let out." Hannah reached out and gathered the baby into her generous bosom, murmuring gently as if she'd known the girl since birth.

"She's stable. Let us know if she wakes up or something changes."

"I will. Can you raise my right leg on this contraption? Getting mighty painful."

He dropped to one knee and fumbled the lock gizmo. "What happened?"

"Fell down the stairs trying to get to shelter in the basement. Tom brought me in, says he thinks it's broken. I think it's just a torn ligament. He had to get back home to take care of the others."

Ben nodded. "Have you been given anything for pain?"

"No, but you go take care of those others that need you worse. I'll keep on praying."

Ben finished adjusting the leg, flinched with her when she groaned as he lifted the leg rest. "Be right back." He grabbed some painkillers from a cabinet. No time to get an ice pack going or go searching for inflatable splints, but with a paper cup of water, he gave her the pills. "If you need something, tell Bo to find Ben. That's the command to use. Find Ben."

"I will, you go."

He heard the ambulance blip as he returned to room three.

Esther's 'scope was draped around her neck and she

was flicking and tapping possible sites on Denise, searching for a functional vein. Esther was known for her ease in finding veins—look how she'd tapped into the baby—but you wouldn't guess that by her lack of success just now. "Ben, you try." She unbuttoned the woman's blouse and plugged in her ears, listened to Denise's heart and lungs, probed the abdominal area desperately seeking the bleeder.

She glanced up at the woman's husband. "What happened?"

Ben would try the right side first. He tied a loop of rubber cannula around her upper arm to raise whatever veins were left.

Roy drooped, woebegone. "The dog was tied up out back. She went out to bring him in and a piece of something blew into her and knocked her down. Never seen wind like this. And rain. She's on Coumadin for her blood pressure and something else, I forget what. Sorry."

"Got one. Her right hand here." Ben fingered a barely discernible vein. "You want to take over?"

"No, you're doing fine. Go in with a butterfly. Mr. Abrams, do you know her blood type?"

"Uh, no . . . I guess I oughta, but I don't."

From her gurney, Denise murmured, "O positive."

"Good. We have no means here to type blood, so I'm very glad you know. Ever had an adverse reaction?"

Denise's voice dropped to a whisper. "Roy, where's Tuffy?"

"Safe in the house. It's okay."

Esther waved a hand. "Ben, there should be a defibrillator in the corner there, every room is supposed to have one."

In the corner there. It took him a moment; the defib

was stuffed between a cabinet and the wall. And it was dusty. He popped the case open and brought three electrode pads to the table. He applied them as Esther fiddled around with her 'scope. By shoving Denise over a few inches he made room to lay the machine on the bed beside her. He connected the leads. "Turn it on?"

"Yes. All we want it for is to monitor her heartbeat. What's the battery life?"

"Supposed to be four hours continuous use—at least that's the one I carry in my van—but there's a converter, so I'll plug it into the wall. Good forever."

Their cleanup guy had finished but was watching intently, then picked up his mop bucket and headed out. Ben called to him, "Thanks, Gary! Good job."

The kid bobbed his head and almost smiled.

In a cold, flat voice, the machine announced, "Reading." Moments later, "No shock indicated." Ben turned the volume down to mute.

Whatever was wrong with Esther before—and something very obviously was—it had apparently eased off. She seemed back to her normal crisp self. "Ben, I think we have a unit in the cupboard. Get one to start with, maybe we'll have to switch to dextran then, at least for a unit or so. Mrs. Abrams, where exactly were you struck? Can you show me?"

Ben finished setting up the transfusion, hanging the bag, setting the drip. With the IV up and the lifesaving fluid dripping into Denise's arm, Esther heaved a sigh and managed a smile at Roy. "We'll leave you two in here for now and check in frequently. If you see any change, holler. I mean that: Just start yelling. One of us will come."

Ben followed her out into the hall. "Know what we're missing?"

"I know a thousand things we're missing—enough blood, for starters. What?"

"Clipboards. With forms to fill out. I asked for someone to help take notes, but no one offered, and I forgot. We haven't the slightest idea how many we've treated so far."

She snorted. "Sure we do. What's the population of this county?"

They walked out into the waiting room. It was still packed.

Barbara was by the front door talking to a teenage girl with her arm wrapped in a dish towel. She'd know what was going on. She was telling the girl, "I'm sorry, Jennifer, we'll get to you as soon as we can." The kid nodded glumly and sat back down against the wall, holding her injured arm to her chest.

The front door blew open, sucking the fury of the storm in with it. Beside Ben, Esther jumped straight up and cried out. She sort of froze in place, got that terrified look on her face again, started breathing heavily. It was raining on her but she just stood there. Barbara leaped over and shoved the door shut again.

Ben grabbed Esther's elbow and led her forcibly back to the mini surgery. He closed the door behind them. "Okay, what's going on?"

She yanked her arm away and burst out, "Stop it! Stop treating me as if something was wrong with me! I'm fine! Do you understand that?"

"I understand you're yelling at me, and I didn't do anything wrong." *And not too long ago, I was doing exactly the same thing to Chief.*

She looked ready to light into him some more. Instead,

she said, "I'm just so frustrated! I begged them for years to get a working hospital in this area, showed them plans, tried to get it on the ballot, nothing! Now we have this and people are dying because they were so cheap and pig-headed! Let 'em die. Let 'em all die, the b—"

The doors slammed open and she yelped and jumped again.

Yvette and Dennis came in pushing a gurney. On it was a man maybe Ben's age.

"Something happened to our radio," Yvette said. "And I'm pretty sure it's our radio, because we can't pick up the local frequency. And there's no antenna on our roof anymore. Whatever knocked it off, boy, was that a loud clunk!"

Ben helped them transfer their patient to the operating table. They had a line going, but the fluid bag was already pretty low. The wound was obvious with all the bright red blood and the tourniquet above the rip on the inside of the man's leg. Femoral artery. You could bleed out in two minutes flat from a femoral artery. These two were pretty darn good at handling a potentially lethal situation.

Dennis's belt radio squawked a tone-out. "That's us. Here we go again."

Yvette waved good-bye as she followed him out, shoving the gurney ahead of her.

The fellow opened his eyes. "I'm gonna be okay, right?"

"Right. Ben, can you assist? They did a good job; bleeding is slowed enough the first thing is to get that tourniquet off, or he'll lose his leg." Esther was sweating so much it was dripping now. It wasn't that warm in here. "Loosen it a little, I'll tell you when to loosen it more."

"Hey, I put that on because I was bleeding so bad." The fellow looked panicked.

Ben pretended to smile. "We're controlling it now. It's all right."

She waved toward a cabinet as she plugged her 'scope into her ears. "Put on scrubs and scrub, hands and arms up past the elbows." She bent over the fellow, staring off into space as she listened to his lungs and heart. "Deep breath, please."

Scrubs. No bottoms here, so he slipped into a top and tied it behind. And to think some people put these on every workday. Washed up. The latex glove boxes were all empty; the only gloves left were some of those blue nitrile gloves in extra-large. When he slipped into them, a quarter inch of glove extended beyond his fingers. He hoped he wouldn't have to do anything delicate. He crossed back to her.

She was cutting the fellow's pants off. "I can't believe this. Second femoral artery accident in forty-eight hours. You know the Herr kid?"

"Gavin? Yeah. One of our pre-felons, runs around with the Barton delinquents."

She nodded. "You ever assisted in a surgery before?"

"Nothing like this."

"Can you handle the anesthesia?"

"If you tell me what to do."

"Wait a minute! You saying this guy doesn't know what he's doing?" The patient started to sit up.

She shoved him back, not gently. "I can stitch your femoral artery back together without any anesthesia if you wish. And cutting down in to work on it, of course."

"No, wait!" He struggled, so Ben pressed his shoulder to the table. "I don't want no small-town quack cutting me up!"

The small-town quack placed her face very close to

his and in a clear, firm, carefully modulated voice, said, "We do not have to treat you here, sir, and our resources are stretched dangerously thin already. If you prefer, we will gladly put you aside with your tourniquet in place, and when the storm passes we can transport you to a large city where non-quacks can work on whatever is left of you. Or, you can cooperate. Your choice." She put an edge on the words *your choice* sharp enough to cut steak.

He shrank back wide-eyed, and Ben felt suddenly, deliciously, absolutely delighted, the first such feeling that had washed over him in years. Behind, where the guy couldn't see him, he pumped his fist, grinning.

The guy went under promptly and Esther got right to work. She was stitching her way back out when the bag Yvette had plugged him into drained, so Ben hung a sack of normal saline up. It was the last unit they had.

Finally Esther stepped back. She looked totally drained as well, as limp and flaccid as that cast-off bag. "What's the drop-dead date on that saline they put in him?"

He picked the bag up off the floor and looked. "Last month. Six weeks."

"So the aid vans are running out of supplies, too. Ben, we're going to be out of everything soon at this rate." She stripped off her gloves.

He watched her face a few moments, assessing. "You look a little better. Are you feeling better?"

She went stone-hard instantly. "Better than what?"

He just shrugged.

No post-op room, but they put the man in a corner and dealt with three other patients while he recovered enough to respond drowsily to commands. They rolled him on a gurney to the break room, with Hannah to keep watch over him. Let him sleep.

Barbara or someone had made coffee in the break room. Esther poured herself a mug of it. It was black, as close to road tar as coffee got, the pot almost empty. She sagged against the wall.

No, she was not fine. She appeared to be very close to panic. Or fury. Or some other explosion. Ben couldn't read it clearly. She lurched erect and crossed to the vending machines.

Barbara came in. "Need a new pot yet?"

"Yes. Anyone have change for a five?" Esther studied the selection of junk food behind the glass door.

Fury rose up and danced in Ben's head. Esther was the sole medic holding this place together and she needed change for a five? The hospital administrator was about to administrate again. "Barbara, you have the key to open those coin-ops, don't you?"

"No. The supplier does."

"Esther, get back. Way back."

"What?" She moved over beside Barbara.

The iron caster base of the old office chair should do just fine. He picked up the chair and swung it, slamming it into the front of the soda-pop dispenser. The sheer violence pleased him immensely. The glass shattered inward. He broke open the snack dispenser, too. "Bon appétit, all." He chose a couple of candy bars and a can of soda. Dinner. Late, but dinner. How late? He glanced up at the clock. Almost eleven.

Chief Harden came in through the side double doors as Ben was exiting the break room. They walked together to the waiting room.

The chief sounded, if anything, even wearier than Ben. "Which are the children you called about?"

Ben pointed. Charlie and Sissy were sound asleep on the floor. "What'd you find?"

"Their momma won't be waking up again. I put out a call for their father but no idea where he is right now. I didn't have time to search their house thoroughly. Got another call."

"How bad is it out there?"

"The crews are pressing retired guys and high school kids into service. They're chain-sawing their little brains out, but we're cut off completely until they can clear the downed trees and power lines. Choppers can't fly in this—high wind, low visibility—but according to the weather service, the worst has passed, just barely. Doppler shows winds are dropping, but it doesn't feel that way when you're out in it. The river is going to flood if this rain keeps up, but so far..."

Ben grunted. "I sure hope to heaven we have plenty of fuel for that generator."

"I can handle the fuel part. Still plenty in the reserve tanks."

"What do you want us to do with the children?" Ben turned when he felt a tug on his pant leg. Bo tugged again. "Good boy, in a minute."

"We shouldn't take them out in this yet. Keep them here for the time being."

Ben nodded. "Be right back." *I can't tell those two babies that their mother died. I can do a lot of stuff, but not that.* Wait. He was border patrol, not Grim Reaper, the agent specifically trained to knock on people's doors with the ultimate bad news. *Not my job. Let the chief do it. He gets paid more.* He followed the dog to the break room.

Hannah was grinning. "She opened her eyes for a moment and squeaked. Not a real cry, but a squeak. Do we have something to feed her?"

Ben touched the baby's cheek and she turned her head, rooting for a nipple. "Will you look at that?" He swapped a look with Hannah that made him blink. "I'll tell Esther."

"Oh, and the man over there. He woke up for a bit and muttered something. I told him where he was but I think he went back to sleep before he heard me much."

"We'll attend your leg, too, shortly. Sorry about the long wait."

"You take care of the others. Me and the Lord are doing our part in here."

Ben ignored the last part of her statement and found Esther back with Denise. Patients were lining the hallway now, some sleeping, some waiting. "She's awake."

"Our baby?"

"Yes, do we have anything to feed her?"

"Formula in the pantry. There are bottles there, too."

Ben left the room. He'd never fixed a baby bottle. But surely Hannah would know. When he entered the break room, Bo sat right next to the wheelchair, his tail brushing the floor at Ben's entrance but his eyes never leaving the baby.

Hannah gave him a pat. "That's some dog you got there."

"He found her. I'm getting formula and bottles. Can you tell me what to do?"

"Guess you can read the instructions well as I can, but we'll do it. You better get someone in here now to watch that man. He's coming to."

"Right." Ben returned to the waiting room. Dennis and Yvette were hustling back out the door. Must be another call. Rob would be working in one of the other rooms. Ben went to the desk where Barbara was talking on the phone. At least a few of the landlines must still be up. "We need someone to watch that guy we operated on."

"Ask Ansel over there. He can wait in there good as out here."

"What is their problem?"

"Well, might not be a problem yet, but his wife's contractions are about four minutes apart. And this is her second baby. That child asleep in his arms is two and a half."

"I know." Ben crossed the room to where the small family sat. He'd known Ansel since grade school and Beth since her family moved to town when they were in junior high. They used to be in the same Bible study.

But that was before.

He crossed to them. "Glad to see you're okay. And Barbara told me your circumstances. I have a big favor. Could I please move you into the break room to watch a man who had surgery? Hannah is already in there taking care of a baby but she has a bad leg and can't walk. The good thing is, you'll be that much closer to one of the rooms if…"

He paused as Beth sucked in a huge breath and panted her way through a contraction. "How close?"

Ansel checked the clock. "Three minutes."

Ben stared from Beth to Ansel and back again. *Just what we need!* "Okay, we can lay your daughter on a pallet on the floor; hopefully she'll stay asleep." He shook his head. "We don't have another room right now. Come with me and let me go see what I can do. Wait. Beth, should I find you a wheelchair?"

"Thanks, Ben." She heaved herself to her feet. "Walking is better anyway."

Ben showed them into the break room. All he could find to lay Ansel's kid on was a stack of folded scrubs. With apologies, he arranged them in a corner.

"That's okay." Ansel laid his daughter down and tucked his jacket around her.

Ben tied their surgery patient down to the gurney with cannulas so he couldn't roll off. Or climb off or...the dummox. He checked the IV drip. The fellow was pale but breathing okay. He had gone back to sleep.

"Sorry, Hannah." He returned to the wheelchair. "Got sidetracked." *Again.*

"What do you need, Hannah?" Beth asked.

"A bottle fixed for this little one. Ben said the supplies are in the pantry."

"I can do that." Beth leaned her hands, stiff-armed, on the counter and panted again. When it passed, she waddled to the pantry and looked down the shelves until she saw the formula and bottles. "And the distilled water is...here." She hefted a jug.

"Easy, fella." Ansel walked over and patted the shoulder of the man, who was now rolling his head from side to side.

"Hurts. Really hurts."

"I'm sure it does. Hang on, I'll get help. Ben?"

"I'll ask and be right back." He found Esther stitching up another wound in two and told her the situation.

"Squirt some of that codeine in his IV. The big stuff, the joy juice. Dosage is on the vial. I've unlocked the drug cabinet so we can get to things more quickly. That should help within a minute or less." She returned to her stitching.

Ben did as instructed and sure enough, the man re-laxed within seconds. Mighty good stuff. He turned to see Beth hand the baby bottle to Hannah and go into her panting routine again.

"Two minutes apart." Ansel looked to Ben. "You ever delivered a baby?"

Ben shook his head. He'd done one with the plastic save-a-life dummy but not in real life. But then they were all doing things they'd never done before. Going on one A.M. And they still had no idea how bad the damage was outside.

Chapter Five

"We need a table," Ben whispered from the door to Esther.

"Be right there." She nodded to the husband—"Come get me if anything changes"—and stepped into the hall. "Now what?"

"Beth is dilating. Contractions are less than two minutes apart."

"At least on this one I know what to do. Ben, I can't find her bleed. I was praying the internal bleeding would stop by itself, but I just hung another saline on her IV. How many more units of saline do we have on hand?"

"Zero. I radioed all our fire apparatus and aid vans from my handheld, asking them for any IV equipment and units they have on board, told them we desperately need the stuff here; no one has anything. We are fresh out."

She looked grim. No fooling. "Okay, what's happening in the other rooms? Can we move someone to the hall to make room for our mommy?"

"Next to the break room, nada. The Culpepper kid is cleaning up two, but that's spoken for; the ambulance called to say they are nearly here with a head injury."

"Bleeding or fracture?"

He shook his head. "Not sure. The transmissions aren't clear. I'd planned on putting Beth in there."

"Room one?"

"Rob is working with someone there. I'll check; maybe he's done."

"And our internal bleed is in three. I'll go see about Beth. We can deliver a baby on the break room floor if we have to. You ever delivered before?"

"No, only a little practice with a Resusci Baby. We borrowed one of those dummies once that simulates birth. It ain't the same. Rob has and I think Dennis has. Chief has but he just left again."

Ben tapped on the door to one and looked inside. Other than a mess, the room was empty. And the Culpepper kid busy down the hall. Guess he'd clean this one up himself. Oops. Not empty. There was the old lady in her underwear, huddled in the corner, sound asleep. What had she done with the jacket she'd been loaned?

Well, at least she didn't go out on the street again by herself. Ben gently woke the woman. "Come with me, Mrs. Unfeld." He took her arm and waited when she drew back. "I have a better place for you to sleep."

"Is Harold here?"

"No, I'm sorry, but he's not."

"Then I'll wait here. He said he'd be right back. I'm cold." She drew her knees up and wrapped her arms around them.

Ben fought against the desire to just snatch her up and carry her to another room, but where? Who would watch out for her? "Barbara is waiting for you. You know Barbara, she's one of your neighbors."

Mrs. Unfeld shook her head. "No, I don't." She shrank back into the corner.

Esther appeared in the doorway. "Oh good, it's available. Leave her there and I'll get Beth while you clean up what you can."

Ben did as she instructed, grabbing a garbage bag from under the sink and stuffing detritus of an earlier examination and treatment into the white plastic bag. He grabbed the full one from the garbage can and dragged them both to the back door. No time to haul them out to the Dumpster, and the pile was growing.

He found a paper cover for the bed and was tugging it into place as Esther ushered Ansel and Beth in. They helped Beth up onto the table and set her feet into the stirrups.

"Is that you, Harold?" the quavering voice asked.

Beth groaned. "The baby is coming. I can't..."

"Well, don't cross your legs and try to hold it back. We're ready." Esther snapped her gloves into place; Ben noted she was wearing the extra-large nitrile gloves, too, and her fingers weren't as long as his. The flappy finger ends stuck out even farther. "Ben, there should be an OB kit on the top shelf over there."

He opened the cabinets in turn, exploring top shelves, pulled down and wagged a package about a foot long. "This?"

"That's it."

Beth made a weird wailing noise.

Esther announced, "The head is presenting. Beth, remember to breathe."

Remember to breathe? Ben tore open the pouch. "Hey, here's a pair of rubber gloves! We can use 'em. Towelettes. Absorbent pads. In fact, we can use most of this stuff."

"Slip one of those big pads under her."

He did so. And watched with something akin to awe. Esther was massaging the area around the tiny emerging head, keeping the perineum from tearing, working the opening larger, pressing. How could she do that in those oversize gloves, with those nitrile bobbles on the ends of her fingers constantly getting in the way? The baby's head popped out suddenly and flopped down.

"Suction."

Ben handed her the suction bulb from the kit. Expertly she drew the fluid from the tiny mouth, the minuscule nostrils.

"The shoulders are giving us a bit of trouble." She cupped one hand around the head, manipulated the area. The baby slid out, simply slid right into her hands like paste from a toothpaste tube. "Thank you, God. Some-one? The exact time."

Ben and Ansel both glanced at their watches. "One twenty-eight." "One twenty-seven," they reported simul-taneously.

"Close enough, I guess." She carefully gripped the tiny ankles between her fingers and raised the baby high, head down. This was a little boy. Wow, was he, with oversize purple equipment that, Ben knew, would turn right-size and normal shortly. Ben expected Esther to spank the lit-tle bottom, but she just rubbed the small of the baby's back, tapped the soles of his feet.

A gurgle, a cough; the little one filled his lungs with his first air and let out a wail. Beth pressed both hands over her mouth and she was sobbing; Ben realized it was joy, not sorrow in her weeping. Was there such a thing as real joy anymore? Beth thought so. And look at Ansel's face glow, way past just grinning.

Esther placed the infant facedown across his mother's bare chest, his head draped downward. "Ansel, lay your shirt on him, keep him warm."

Ansel did so instantly.

Ben would have cut the cord next, but Esther did not. Was she so weary she was starting to slip? He kept his mouth shut. Wiping her forehead with the back of her hand, she kneaded Beth's abdomen the way Allie used to knead a lump of bread dough. *Allie.* Ben's memories sabotaged him at weirdest times. Like a huge, most unappealing blue-black-gray sea worm of some sort, the afterbirth slid onto the paper.

"Scalpel." Esther held out her hand. "Then the clamps."

Scrambling, Ben found the scalpel in the OB kit and slapped it in her open palm with the sterile wrap still on; his hands were dirty. She popped it out of the paper as Ben found the clamps.

She handed the scalpel to Ansel. "This baby has been all Mommy's for nine months. Now, Ansel, it is appropriate for the father to cut the cord; provide your son with the first step of separation." She stroked the umbilical cord toward the baby a couple of times, then clamped it off. Ansel looked a little uncertain, looked at the clamps, at the scalpel, at the clamps. As if a fire were suddenly lighted in him, he gripped the cord tightly on the placenta side and gave his son his first lesson in independence.

And now Esther and Ansel were laying their hands on Beth and the baby, and Ansel began praying aloud for the life and safety of his son, for God's blessing on them all, Esther too. Ben should be there with them, his hands on Beth and the baby also, praying in mind and heart as Ansel gave voice.

He couldn't. He just plain couldn't. He couldn't touch them, couldn't pray. What the blazes was wrong with him that he couldn't pray in this situation, this only bright spot in a miserable night of pain and death? He wasn't normal anymore. Maybe he wasn't even human anymore. Chief and Jenny, they all said he should get help. Were they right?

Esther stood erect. "Blanket. Ben, can you do the placenta then?"

He unfolded the tightly wadded receiving blanket in the bottom of the kit, shook it out, handed it to her. Then he did what some EMTs simply could not bring themselves to do, squeamish women especially, and he could never understand that: He carefully examined every millimeter of the placenta to make certain it had not torn on the way out and left behind any little bit of itself to cause infection and death. The edges on the single tear in it fit together exactly. A gift of God, most of Ben's friends would say. He opened the plastic bag that the kit thoughtfully included for just that purpose and slid the gelatinous mass into it, closed it with a twist tie the kit also provided.

"Talk about a textbook delivery. Beth, you did really well." Esther closed her eyes for a moment. "Did you bring a diaper or gown?"

"Sorry, I was afraid the house was crashing down around our ears. It was. The big oak in our yard went down on it just as we backed out of the driveway. So, I guess you could say we are homeless."

Esther wagged her head sadly. "You're not the only ones." She turned to Ben. "We should still have diapers somewhere. See if you can find any."

"Is that a baby crying?" Mrs. Unfeld's quivery voice rose from the corner. Ben had forgotten all about her.

"Take her with you, please."

Ben stared at Esther. "But..."

"Take her to Barbara."

Nuts. "All right." He handled that dead man, he could handle this. He lifted the slight body and carried her from the room to the area behind the reception desk, nearly gagging on the odor. "Can you keep her here?" He didn't wait for a reply but put her down, still all curled up in her fetal position, behind Barbara's chair.

"I'll try." Barbara sighed and pushed her dark hair back from her forehead. "Mrs. Unfeld, Bessie, you stay here with me for a while so Ben can go looking for Harold. Okay?"

"She needs to be washed up and I don't know what happened to the jacket that guy loaned her. We found her in the corner behind the door of room one."

"Was that a baby cry I heard?"

"Yes, a very unhappy little boy and he's letting the whole world know about it. But mother and baby are doing fine and Ansel is, too."

"One ray of good in this mess."

"Yah, that big old oak tree took out their house, just as they backed out of the driveway."

"Dear Lord, thank you for keeping them safe."

Ben kept his response to himself. He was too tired to argue faith matters at the moment. "We need to get some food in here for these people." *And a nice stiff belt for me. And this time, I earned it.*

"I know. And we're out of coffee. I'll put out the call. Reception is so erratic. Sometimes I can get out, sometimes I can't."

The ambulance blipped outside.

"Here we go again." Ben detoured through the break

room. Hannah had the baby on her shoulder, burping her. The man on the gurney slept soundly and Ansel's toddler daughter did the same, except the kid didn't snore softly like that man did.

Hannah looked up. "Beth is all right?"

"Yes. I'll probably be bringing them back in here. What can we lay her on?"

Bo was staring at him. Of course. When Mrs. Unfeld had to go, she went. Bo was holding it. "Come on, Bo. Your legs must be crossed."

Almost eagerly, his dog abandoned his protective watch over the baby and followed Ben out through the back service door. Black dog in the black night, he disappeared instantly. When the hospital was on generator, it burned no outside lights.

In fact, no one was burning lights. Every power line in town must be down. The wind still screamed through the trees. Things still whipped past now and then—roofing shingles, small branches—but the wind was definitely tapering off. The rain was not.

Bo came back to the door soaking wet, stopped at Ben's knee, and shook. Stupid dog. They went back inside, out of chaos into chaos, back to reality. Bo resumed his post curled up at Hannah's feet.

Ben returned to the front reception area, but Barbara and Mrs. Unfeld were not there. Avis had taken Barbara's place at the desk again. The waiting room was still stuffed full, but now most people were curled up in the chairs or stretched out on the floor, sleeping. A short guy Ben knew only as Dominic consulted a list in his hand and looked around the room. He threaded his way to a couple sitting in a corner. They climbed stiffly to their feet and followed him out into the hall. The Culpepper kid was coming out of one and he didn't even look tired. He smiled at Ben. Ben smiled back.

Dominic led the couple into one. "Someone will be here shortly."

"Dominic?" Ben wiggled a finger. "Where is Hannah on that list?"

He frowned. "I don't have a Hannah on this list. Who's Hannah?"

That old familiar fury boiled up instantly. *She wasn't even on the list!* All night she'd been holding that helpless baby and she wasn't even on the list! And he...

"Ben!" Dennis and Yvette shoved a man in a wheelchair through the double doors. "Asthma! Our O_2 ran out. We gave him a shot of epinephrine, so his heart is racing."

The fury would just have to wait. This fellow looked terrified, fighting for breath, and he had turned blue. "Dominic, put Hannah on the list *now*! Dennis, maybe three is open again."

Behind him, Dominic was asking, "Yeah, but who is she?"

Three was a mess, but it was open. They lifted him onto the table Rob and his patient had just vacated. The Culpepper kid showed up in the doorway. Dennis adjusted the table to half sitting as Ben hooked the line from the nose prongs to the nozzle in the wall. How much oxygen remained in the big bottle in the supply closet? He set it while Dennis checked to make sure the life-giving air was flowing. The Culpepper kid started picking up.

"Surely we have albuterol," Ben muttered as he searched the cupboards; in all of his looking for stuff, he had not checked these cabinets. No meds of any kind.

He turned to the patient. "You have any sort of bronchodilators with you?"

No response.

Dennis said, "We didn't find any, but we didn't look far. Wanted to get him here."

"Dennis, go ask Esther. She's in the next room, or at least she was. If she's not, Barbara is in the restroom, cleaning up Mrs. Unfeld. Barbara will know." Barbara, a registered nurse, knew everything. Nurses knew more than doctors did, at least regarding the practical stuff. Might as well check under the sink; it was the only door left. "Oh, for pete's sake."

Who would stash a big plastic box of meds under the sink? But there it was, and rifling through it Ben found albuterol. He bit the cap off the vial so he could pour it into the nebulizer.

Dennis came back in. "Under the sink. And the clamp is over the sink."

He opened a cabinet door above the sink, dragged out a plastic bag of various gizmos, poked through it with one finger, found a clamp. "Now we get to find out whether this thing works." He slipped the little black clamp over the patient's middle finger, fiddled with it, studied it. "Okay; at least now we know his oxygen level. Up the saturation, can you?" Ben had no idea where his stethoscope had gotten to. "Need your ears." He pulled Dennis's 'scope off his neck and shoved the bell against the victim's chest. With the guy's shirt on he wasn't going to hear much, but the heartbeat was all he was looking for anyway.

Slowly but surely the man's breathing eased. At least they didn't have to do a tracheotomy. He'd done a couple of trachs in the past and dreaded attempting another.

The heart rhythm eased as the oxygen flowed more freely. The deathly blue pallor faded.

"Where's Yvette?" Ben had not even been aware she'd left the room.

"Someone needed another set of hands. Is there any coffee?"

"I'm not sure but if you find some, please bring me a cup, too. We need to get some food in here for these people."

Dennis took out his cell phone and thumbed buttons.

"Who you calling?"

"My mother heads the church ladies' group. They'll get some food in here. We can go pick it up with the ambulance if need be." He put his cell to his ear a couple of times and shook his head. "No signal. By the way, your house is still standing. Doesn't really look damaged, like the roof is still on. That birch out back went down."

"Thanks."

Dennis's radio howled his code. "Looks like we'll be on our way. Now I get to go look for Yvette."

"The place isn't that big. Probably the ladies' room." Ben checked their patient's vitals again. Here at least was one they'd been able to save. The man's eyelashes fluttered, and he started to sit up. Gently pushing him back down, Ben nodded. "Just take it easy, we're through the worst. What happened?"

"Power went out, no nebulizer, panic." His voice rasped.

"Well, they got to you in time. I'll be moving you out of this room because we need it, but you can rest here for a minute. Okay?"

The man nodded and let his eyes close again.

Ben turned at a knock on the door.

"How is he?" Yvette asked, handing him a cup of coffee.

"Good. Where did you find this?" Coffee, third on his list of beverages, behind beer and whiskey.

"Barbara said someone brought over a can of coffee."

"But no one is supposed to be out in this storm."

"Just say thank you and enjoy it." She turned away. "Oh, and mother and baby are sound asleep on some quilts someone else brought in." She raised a hand. "Don't ask. Call them our guardian angels."

Guardian angels. Where were they two years ago when Allie needed them, out having a beer?

Ben followed her down the hall, careful to not trip over sleepers. They'd need to start hanging hammocks next. He peeked into the break room. Ansel looked up from checking on the man on the gurney. "Everyone in here is sound asleep but him and me. Thank God for the quilts."

Beth was curled up near her daughter, the new son nestled in a quilt. Someone had slipped a sock over his head in lieu of a newborn cap. Hannah's head had dropped forward, but the baby slept in her arms.

Grateful for a moment of respite, Ben listened to his stomach growl and grumble from the coffee. Too bad, at least it would help him be alert again. Someone had swept up the glass from the vending machines at some point, but they were now empty of snacks and drinks. He left the break room and stopped behind the front desk. "What's the weather report?"

Barbara glanced up with a smile. "No letup on the rain, but the winds are now at strong breeze, not gale. You're familiar with the Beaufort scale, right?"

"Right. Twenty-five to thirty."

She smirked and continued. "You can be sure the power crews are out there. And the highway trucks, moving the trees off the roads. If they can get us clear one way, we could send the ambulances with our bad ones to the hospital. Perhaps the choppers can fly come daylight. We're all praying for that."

Ben felt his jaw tighten. Why waste your time praying to a God who kills women and babies? At the look on her face, he realized she'd guessed what he was thinking.

She laid a hand on his arm. "No easy answers, I know."

Ben turned away and thought about Mrs. Unfeld curled up on a quilt in the corner of the break room. Bessie Unfeld, a church leader for years, and look how God rewarded her. He almost said something but kept on going; he'd not seen Esther for how long? He opened the doors to the examining rooms, peeked in. Rob was cleaning two, apparently having just handled a case. Denise, the internal bleed, was sleeping on her table, Roy stretched out on the floor beside her. Culpepper was cleaning one, working around their asthma guy.

Here was Esther, in the mini surgery with a patient on the table. "I could use another pair of hands here."

"Scrub?"

"Get the gloves on." She wiped the sweat from her forehead with the back of her hand. Strange, it wasn't that hot in here.

Though she had snapped at him before, he decided to try again.

"What's wrong?"

"I can't keep the blood out of the field."

Ben didn't mean what was wrong with the patient, but he said nothing.

Ben looked from her to the child whose compound fracture of the tibia lay exposed under the lights. Sure there was blood, but not a bleeder, or else she had already stopped it. The man hovering at the head of the table looked up at Ben. He poured a bit of water on the wound, irrigating it, keeping the bone moist lest it die.

"Hi, Jensen." Ben turned to Esther. "You going to try to set that?"

Jensen nodded. "Hi, Ben. It was bleeding pretty bad, but she got that stopped."

"How's the rest of your family?"

"Safe. Down in the basement. With all this rain, that's starting to leak, but I got a pump and a generator."

"Okay, here we go. Jensen, you hang on to your son." She gave Ben orders and together they pulled the bone back into place. She picked out small bone fragments and blew out a breath. "Thank God for anesthetics. Clear the field for me again, and I'll go searching."

Ben recognized the gauze sponges as having come from the OB kit. They were using every bit of supplies, and now these were used up as well.

They placed a drain, Esther did some fancy sewing to close it up, they bandaged the wound. Slipping an inflatable splint onto the leg was the easy part. Ben blew it up by mouth, since he had no idea where the pump was. At least their supply of inflatables was still adequately stocked.

Jensen was smiling a sad, weary, grateful smile. "Just as good as the big city."

Ben chuckled mirthlessly. "That's what we told some other guy. He didn't want quacks working on him." That was long ago, so very, very long ago! Ben looked up at the clock. Seven A.M. He'd been on the go for twenty-four hours and he knew others were functioning on even less sleep. Dennis and Yvette, and...

Let's insert a ray of sunshine here, Ben, boy. "Barbara

thinks the choppers might be flying now that the wind has died some."

Esther stepped back and pulled off her gloves, the ones that had been in the OB kit. Or had she raided other OB kits to get more? "Please, God, I hope so. The woman..."

Ben knew she meant Denise. "I looked in on them a few moments ago. Want me to check again for you?"

"No, you stay here until the anesthetic wears off and I'll go see."

Ben watched her tilt and thump against the doorjamb as she went through the door, lurch erect, continue on out. How much longer could she keep functioning? Were the rest of them in as bad a shape as she was?

Chapter Six

E sther sagged against the wall behind her office door.
*Come on, woman, you know the tools to deal with
this. Stay with it. Breathe deep, again. Again! Shut it out!
Focus!*

The orders marched through her mind but for some
reason, they didn't connect with her body. She knew lack
of sleep and meals was part of the culprit, but since neither was available...

She sucked in another breath, shrugged her shoulders
to release some of the kinks, and rotated her head. Holding one hand out, she could tell from the reduction in
quivering that she was doing better. *As soon as you get
home, you can get back on your sertraline, but now you
just keep going. You know what'll happen if someone figures out what is wrong.*

She knew, all right. She couldn't shake the memory of
the night one of these attacks caught her in the middle
of an examination in the ER where she had worked some
weekends. She'd been working anywhere she could, anything to bring in enough money to keep going. Her dream
of med school started to die that night.

She dug a clean lab coat out of the nearly empty supply cupboard and headed back for the break room. At least in there she would find new life and hope. Two babies, one with two doting parents and one who would be given over to social services. Parents unknown.

She glanced toward the waiting room as she passed, checked her watch; after seven A.M. and the waiting room looked just as full. A small child whimpered and was shushed by a parent.

"But I'm hungry!" rose from a different part of the room. It seemed like a lifetime ago that Ben had picked up the chair and slammed it into the glass door of the drink and snack machines. The contents disappeared quickly after that. If there was a complaint from the vending company, so be it. But he hadn't signed the lease agreement for those machines; she had.

Ben. Intriguing in a way. Cute guy. Dark, though. Grumpy. A couple of people said he drank too much, but she had never seen him drunk at all, and those times he came in for his service-mandated physical, he tested out just fine. When she'd arrived in the Pineville clinic six years ago, the old women were still talking about the wedding over a year before. "Oh, Esther, you missed the wedding of the century!" "Loveliest wedding I've ever been to, and I've attended many a one." "Such a cute couple! Just perfect for each other." Ben and his Allie. The whole town, absolutely the whole town, had turned out for it. Chief Harden had proudly given the bride away, Allie's own father having died.

Esther only met Allie once and to her, the girl seemed a little vapid. Not real deep, not interested in weighty stuff, not much ambition. But Ben was obviously smitten with her and she with him. Then the whole town turned out for Allie's funeral, too, every person stunned, grief-stricken. Esther was handling the clinic full-time by then, and she was accustomed to the taciturn, easygoing nature of Pineville's citizens, so the outpouring of vivid grief surprised her.

She stepped around those on the floor, some sleeping, some with pain-glazed eyes. How long since the ambulances last arrived? She made her way down the short hall that felt like a mile. Was she really ricocheting off the sides of the doorway or did it just feel that way? She was afraid to stop in the restroom and look in the mirror. Some things were better left unknown, but since several people had asked if she was all right, it must be bad.

The ambulance siren wailed again; she was beginning to abhor the blip signal that they needed to be on the move. She tapped on the door to the room where Denise and Roy had spent the night. No answer. She peeked in; they were both still sound asleep. She hesitated. Disturb them or wait until...? Without entering, she looked over at the hanging bag. Empty. They had nothing left to give her. She shut the door so gently, it did not even click.

Rob came out of the break room. "Can we do Hannah next? She has to be in terrible pain, but she soldiers on."

"Is the mini surgery clear?"

"I think so."

She heard laughter and a rise in conversation coming from the waiting room. Now what? She continued on to the waiting room. With grins wide enough to stuff a controlled-substance report into, Dennis was carrying a big plastic bin and Yvette was shoving a gurney through the door. No patient, though—plastic and cardboard boxes took up the space, with a large coffee urn jiggling dangerously at the foot.

Behind them, Gerty Larson and Ellen Jackson came trooping in. Esther knew them, had treated them both. Why were they up at this hour and smiling?

Dennis called, "All you folks stay where you are, and these angels of mercy will bring this around. We have sandwiches, coffee, and juice for the children." He put his plastic bin down and popped the lid. Yvette opened the boxes on the gurney.

Ellen gestured with a plastic pitcher. "I'm doing the juice. Children first, and then adults can have what's left. We're preparing more over at the church, so don't worry about taking the last of anything."

Gerty pulled out a plastic tray, put a creamer and sugar jar on it, and began pouring coffee into paper cups.

Rob appeared in the hall entry, swore a very happy Anglo-Saxon epithet, and gathered juice and sandwiches in both hands. "For the Gustafsons in two!"

Esther let herself sag against the wall. Thank God for church women who would feed people no matter how the storm raged. How they had done this, she'd probably never know, but when Dennis handed her a sandwich she simply took it and thanked him.

Dennis wasn't losing that glorious smile. "They have that refugee shelter set up in our church basement. Really chugging along. Harry in the power truck went to the grocery store and stocked them up with food and stuff; grocery didn't even charge them. Thank God for their oversize generator; it's big enough to handle all this. We can move some of these people over fairly soon, I would think."

Esther bit into her sandwich and accepted the cup of coffee. *One more minute, if I can have just one more minute.* Seven forty-five. Maybe she was going to make it. Maybe they were all going to make it.

"Esther?" Ben beckoned her from the surgery. "We have Hannah ready."

"Did you take an X-ray?"

He shook his head. "I'm a border patrol officer and a hospital administrator, remember? I don't know how to use that machine."

"Wheel her down to radiology and we'll start there." Radiology. Sounded so big-city, and it was essentially a closet pressed into use because it was big enough to hold the machine.

Ben was asking, "No X-ray technician in this town?"

"One, but I haven't heard from her all night." Surely if all were well, Susan would have checked in.

Ben was sure chatty. Annoyingly so. She didn't need noise, not even his rat-a-tat monologue. "The repeater's down and our only radio communication is with each other. Local. The ham operators, though, they've been bouncing signals around and made contact with a friend of a friend...you know how they do. Minor miracles sometimes."

No, Esther did not know how they did or what they did. And she didn't want to. But she anticipated that she was about to find out.

Ben rolled on. "They made contact with Minneapolis, who put the word out. Choppers are lined up to come in as soon as the weather permits, and half a dozen ambulances are waiting until the roads are cleared enough for them to get here. And they told 'em we're out of blood and saline and everything else. So we have blood and bags coming, lots of units."

"Good." She finished her sandwich and tossed the plastic bag in the trash, then headed down the hall as Ben went off to fetch Hannah. Three people stirred from their places against the wall or on the floor.

"Is it morning?" one asked. The wrapping around her leg was bloody and she groaned when she tried to scoot back against the wall.

"It is. There is food available in the waiting room if you can make it down there. Or send someone and they'll come to you."

The others woke and hobbled or helped each other down the hall, two with obvious wounds and the third assisting.

Esther pushed open the door to the X-ray room, heaved a sigh, and turned on the machine. "What did you do with the baby?" she asked as Ben pushed Hannah's wheelchair into the room.

"Ansel is holding her. He said to tell you that the guy on the gurney needs to be knocked out again."

"Maybe we should just put him outside. Get a shower and clean up his act." Esther clamped her teeth. Talk about inappropriate. She heaved a heavy breath. "Sorry, Hannah, that just slipped out."

The woman rolled her lips together, laughter dancing in her eyes. "I thought just that. Makes me feel better that someone else feels the same."

"I think Ansel would rather take on a roomful of snakes than put up with the likes of him. The dude's not happy he's tied down." Ben studied their patient. "Hannah, we have to get you up on that table."

Esther closed her eyes. "Get some help in here." She pushed the machine on the overhead track into place and slapped two lead pads on the table.

"Sorry to be so much trouble."

"Oh, Hannah, you might be the one who saved that baby's life last night. We just have to work out some logistics here."

"Get me on my feet, er, foot, and let me lean on Ben. We'll manage."

Ben came through the door with Rob on his heels. Between the two of them they got Hannah prone on the table and stepped back when Esther told them to leave. "No, I mean outside the door." She slammed the negatives into place, positioned the overhead with the marks on the table, and stepped behind the shield. "Hold it; no movement, don't breathe." *Click.* "Okay, Hannah, breathe." By the time they took one more and got Hannah back in the chair, tears were streaming down her face.

"I'm sorry." She sniffed and patted her pockets for a tissue.

Esther handed her the box from the shelf by the door. "Let me check these. It will take a moment to develop them."

Develop X-ray films. That had gone out with buggy whips and horizontal-control knobs on TV sets. A good, modern, digital X-ray machine didn't cost all that much, provided a high-resolution picture, and she could have the results instantly with no trouble at all. Snap the shot and look at it, just like that. Snap another if you need a different angle. Then send it all to the monitor in the surgery. But no. The Frugal Fathers of this burg didn't want to buy an X-ray machine when the clinic already had one that still worked. She really, really wished she could strangle the Frugal Fathers.

Back in the mini surgery, she snapped the X-rays into the light box on the wall. Rob and Ben peered over Hannah's shoulder, so she explained to them all, pointing. "Here is an obvious break in the lower tibia."

"Not obvious to me," Rob interrupted.

"Well, it would be more obvious were the swelling not

so bad. This is going to require surgery, but by a good orthopedic surgeon, not us here. And it can't happen until
the swelling goes down. An inflatable splint might help,
but we don't have one of the appropriate size and shape.
We may try taping it. So, Hannah, we'll get you set up
with ice packs and more pain meds and..."

"And I can have my baby back?"

"Yes, you can, with all our gratitude." She looked to
Ben. "You can do this?"

"Taping it as in taping an athlete's ankle before the
game?"

"That kind of tape job."

"We'll take care of it. Can't be harder than diapering
that baby."

Hannah punched him on the arm. "Keep your priori-
ties right, son, or I'll sic my dog on you."

"Doctor!" The call came from down the hall.

Esther spun and headed out the door. Denise. There
must be a change. "Coming, Roy." She jogged instead of
running because a casual jog was the absolute greatest
speed she could muster anymore. She entered without
knocking.

Rob looked worried. "She's awake or at least conscious,
but...well, look at the machine there. It's different, sort of."

Loud and clear, the green line tracking across the
screen told the world that Denise's heart was struggling
desperately. Even Roy, probably untrained to read an
EKG, could see that. Some of the spikes were starting to
lose their sharp points, the wrong spikes you wanted doing that. And there was a short straight line where a line
of gentle wiggles should be.

A knock at the door. Barbara poked her head in and her
voice bubbled. "Choppers are on their way!"

Oh, thank God! For the first time in—well, in for-ever—a wave of happy relief washed across her. Esther smiled at Roy. "You heard her."

Roy closed his eyes and nodded. "Please, God, that she makes it."

"She'll make it now. Those birds are equipped with all kinds of fluids and better monitors than ours." Esther turned to see Ben at the doorway.

He was grinning. "Heard the news? Gimme your car keys. We're clearing the parking lot by the side doors for them to land."

"Good choice. No power lines there." She dug into her pocket and handed him her keys.

"No power lines anywhere." He jogged out.

The cleaning kid came in. "Did you hear?"

"We did! Go find me a gurney. This one will be first in line to go."

"I'll get one!" And out he raced.

Back with her patient, Esther listened to lungs and heart. Slow and heavy, definitely weaker. She prepared the IV site for transport.

"Roy? Unplug the machine, please."

"Don't we want to keep track—"

"We will. It has lots of battery, and they have a defib on board." She leaned over their patient. "Denise, can you hear me?"

A slight nod. Very slight.

"Hang in there. Help is nearly here."

Another nod, or was it only a flutter of eyelashes? Es-ther turned to Roy. "You been in a chopper before?"

He shook his head. "No. Will they let me go along?"

"We'll have to see if there's room, since you probably can't drive there yet." She ran through the list of patients in her mind. The only other one was the femoral artery. And Hannah. Hannah for sure before that guy. No one else, was there?

Ben came in shoving a gurney ahead of him, with the cleaning kid right behind.

"Ben? How many can ride in the chopper?"

"Lots. They brought in the Chinook. It's better in heavy weather. Sorry there's no sheet here, but we have none."

"Okay." She turned to Roy. "Pull out that roll of paper and put it down on the gurney. I was hoping to use a sheet to move her." She laid the defibrillator on Denise's chest; the abdomen felt drumhead-tight. The green line seemed to falter a bit as it tracked across. Bad connection?

Ben wiggled a finger. "Gary? You can help. We can do this. Stand there. We reach across the gurney, lift, slide her toward us. Don't have to elevate her any farther than just to get her on the gurney. Understand?"

"Yes, sir!" He appeared just plain eager.

"Roy, here." Ben lined them up, and Esther let him. He was doing fine, and she was too weary to think any farther than necessary. She'd do the head and the IV. Let them do the heavy lifting.

Ben instructed, "We all move on three. One; two—"

"Listen! I think I hear the chopper." Roy turned his head to hear better.

"Okay, three." They all lifted at approximately the same time and drew her over onto the gurney beside the examining table.

As if on cue, Rob called from the doorway, "Chopper's here."

Ben barked, "Tell 'em in here."

Roy leaned over his wife's face. "Hang in there, sweetheart. Come on, stay with us."

Esther happened to glance at the defib monitor. "Oh, my God!" Quickly she cranked the volume up. "*No!*"

The thin green line had gone flat.

The defibrillator's monotone took over, instructing them all to stand back, announcing the shock.

Denise's whole body jumped. The cleaning kid gasped. The green line made a wild spike, another, dropped to flat again. The defibrillator continued its dispassionate monotone, urging them all to stand clear for another try.

Esther's heart leaped. "Come on, Denise! You can't do this. Not now!"

The defibrillator jolted her again. The line blipped a couple of times and went flat.

Two men in jumpsuits came jogging into the room. "We've got her." They shoved the gurney out the door with Roy right behind. But Esther knew better.

Ben slammed his hand on the examining table—and swore.

Esther found herself sobbing, leaning on her stiffened arms against the bed. "We lost her."

Chapter Seven

You will not cry! No crying now, you hear? her mother's voice, harsh and critical, screamed at her. Mother the avid feminist didn't abide crying; liberated women didn't do that.

"Esther?" The voice came again as from a far, far distance. "Esther!"

Pay attention! Get back into it! Esther wanted to ignore that internal order but her sense of duty won out—finally. By this time, the voice had taken on a note of command or demand. Whichever wasn't important.

"Yes."

Barbara heaved a sigh of relief. "Chief is here, and he really wants to talk with you."

"All right." Esther straightened her shoulders to go to her office and realized she was already in her office. When had she come in here? What time was it? *Welcome back to the real world.* The voice in her head spoke in full-blown sarcasm now. How long had she been gone?

Chief loomed in the doorway. He looked as beaten down as she felt. She pointed to the chair, still trying to orient herself, to stabilize. "Are you all right?" Chief didn't take the chair, choosing instead to lean against the closed door frame.

Be honest? Cover up? She shook her head. "Are any of us all right after all this?"

"Ben said—"

"Said what?" she interrupted. "Look, we all had a bad time here and most of us got through it."

Chief nodded, his jaw firm to belie the warmth in his brown eyes. "You're right. We'll do our Monday-morning quarterbacking some other time. He was just concerned about you, and since it's been a long time since he showed concern for anyone else, I figured it must be pretty serious. You know that anytime you need to talk, I know how to keep a confidence."

"Thank you." Easy to say, not easy to do, especially if you think others might be at risk.

She glanced at her watch while trying not to be obvious about it.

"I know, there are still mountains to climb." He pulled himself away from the wall. "The supplies that first chopper brought are stacked in the hallway."

As far as she could tell, she'd only been gone five minutes or so. Had her watch stopped or something?

"They unloaded while moving Mrs. Abrams out. They worked on her, too, but they've not had any more success than you did."

"You heard from them?"

"Yes. They are calling it DOA. Esther, you did the best you could, you know that?"

She sniffed and nodded. *Let's change the subject.* "How soon until the next one lands?"

"About three minutes. Ben is taking care of the order. We haven't been able to go house-to-house yet, but the base was able to get us some trucks, so that's next up. Don't know how many injuries are still out there; there might be more who couldn't get in to the clinic. I know this sounds crazy, but is there anything you don't need here?"

She smirked, short of a smile. "Ask Ben, he's gone searching for supplies more than I have. The ambulances are out of everything, too. Critical stuff first." She paused. "How bad is it still out there?"

"Winds about twenty, gusting higher, pouring rain, river nearly to the banks. I've asked for help, but getting equipment in is another equation. The power company is doing all they can."

She heard a chopper, even above the banging of something that must have broken loose, or almost. "Thanks for your concern. We'll be all right."

He stared at her a moment longer, then opened the door. The folks in the waiting room were louder now, and she could hear Ben giving instructions. Back to the fray. She headed to the break room where Ansel and Ellen Jackson were caring for the babies.

Esther watched a moment. "You know, you four are the bright spots for all of us."

"They put Hannah on the first chopper. She was a bright spot."

"I know." At least she remembered giving that order. "Anything you need?"

"Other than a home to go back to, not immediately."

"You and half the town." For the first time Esther thought of her little house. Had it made it through? For the first time, too, she was grateful she had no pets to worry about. Denise had lost her life because of her attempt to rescue a dog. Esther knew she would have done the same thing, especially if her cat had still been alive.

Leaving the sanctuary of peace and back in the hall, she could hear a man giving orders—not Ben, a different voice. She made her way through those still lining the hallway, nodding her greetings and assessing distress as she went. They still had plenty of work to do here. And sure enough, that was the blip of the ambulance. She turned and headed back to the emergency entrance instead.

The double doors slid open. "Is the surgery clear?" Dennis asked from the rear of the gurney. Yvette trotted beside him, keeping pressure on the bright scarlet rag wrapped around Chickie's arm. Why had the Patersons named their boy Chick? And of course, at age thirteen he'd be Chickie. He looked pale, so he'd been losing blood awhile. He gave her a wan smile. She returned it. She had seen him through mumps, measles, and chicken pox so far. His parents were not big on immunization.

"Clear but…" Esther had no idea what was available.

A strong male voice called from the hall. "Bring that gurney right on through to the back door. We have better facilities on the chopper."

Esther turned to see who had spoken.

"Sorry, Doctor, but I just got here and we haven't met yet." A tall, skinny guy with graying temples extended a hand. "George Livingston. I head up ER over on the base."

She couldn't help it; the opportunity was just too ripe. "Dr. Livingston, I presume." She shook his hand.

His look made it obvious that he got that all the time.

A man with him signaled two others, all of them strapping young fellows in air force fatigues. Instead of trying to thread Chickie's gurney through the quagmire of needy people to the double doors, they simply hoisted it high, Chickie and all, and carried it down the hall and out the back door.

Dr. Livingston glanced at Dennis and Yvette as if they were privates and he the general. "You have anyone else out there, bring the ambulance back here. Oh, and we have supplies for you, so come anyway."

They didn't move, instead looking pointedly at Esther.

She nodded to them. "Do as he says. We need all the help we can get." It was clear that Dennis got the same vibes she did. She ignored for the moment her resentment at the man's high-handedness, but right now anything that anyone could do needed to be appreciated. She'd just have to pray her resentment didn't swell to explosion status. It could happen, especially with the state she was in.

"Who was that man, Mommy?" a small voice asked.

"I think that was Superman," the older boy beside her replied. "But he musta forgot his cape."

The titter that flitted around the room caught Esther, too. Leave it to children. Right now they sure could use a Superman or three. She checked the examination rooms to find Rob with an old man in the first. She knew the fellow. Cooper? Somebody Cooper. Her brain was turning to fuzz. "Need transport?"

"Yes," Rob said. "Possible heart."

"Okay. I'll tell them." She turned back into the hall and flagged down one of Dr. Livingston's EMTs. Or was the young man a paramedic? "Where is his wife?" she asked Rob.

He shook his head.

When she mouthed *gone*, he nodded. She couldn't bear to mouth *dead*.

He looked grim. "Mr. Cooper was found unconscious by a neighbor."

The new man appeared in the doorway and looked from Rob to Esther. "We'll take care of him." He stepped backward into the hall, waved, and returned. A young woman in fatigues pushed a gurney into the room, the man behind her carrying in a bag of gear.

The gurney was one of those lightweight aluminum jobs you see in supply catalogs and dream about. Top of the line. The pockets in the fatigues they all wore bulged with supplies to be whipped out on a moment's notice. Esther couldn't suppress her envy. They had all the best and latest. She had a clunker X-ray and commissioners who didn't want to spend any money.

They expertly slipped an oxygen mask in place and tucked the small oxygen canister against his side, splacked the electrode patches on his bared torso, and plugged a slim and tidy portable defibrillator onto them. "We'll hook him up in the chopper and leave this O2 with you." Away they went. Military precision.

The Coopers; Grace. Ernie. They were both my patients. Esther fought for control.

"They celebrated their sixtieth wedding anniversary last Sunday," Rob said softly.

Esther nodded. "I know. I was there."

"I'll clean up in here. I think Gary fell asleep."

"Thanks." She checked room two where Ben was adjusting a sling around a teen's neck, cradling her arm. For a border patrolman, he tied a nice sling. "Broken?"

"Yes. I put ice from the machine on it for now. We're out of ice packs and inflatables."

"It hurts so bad," the girl cried. "I mean über-bad."

Esther had never seen the girl, but the mother had

been in a couple of times for migraines. Esther asked Ben, "We have a slew of boxes. Are we unpacking them?"

"No time yet."

"What do we have left to give her?"

"Aspirin. Only because we had lots of it to start with."

"Please! I need something! It hurts so bad!"

Esther forced a grimace that was just going to have to pass for a smile. "We know, and we'll do the best we can for you."

"Don't you have anything stronger?" Her mom, either overweight or undertall, hovered at her side. "I gave her some Imitrex before we came. It didn't seem to do any good." Chase. The mother's name was Chase. Esther finally remembered.

"Sumatriptan is indicated for migraines. It doesn't work well on normal pain."

"This isn't normal!" the girl howled.

Everybody suffers pain, that's life. Get used to it. Esther had to either ignore the kid or blow up. She chose to ignore her and turned to Ben. "Take her back to Susan and let her get started. I'll meet you in X-ray. We can take time for that now." She didn't even try to smile at the mother. "An orthopedist needs to deal with this. Let me—" She cocked her head. "Is that another chopper leaving or coming?"

"Coming, ma'am," a young man with a Southern accent said with a smile. He stood in the doorway in clean, neat fatigues, looking at their patient. Ogling? Almost. "You heard our Huey leaving. What do you need?"

"Splint for a broken arm?"

"Yes, ma'am." From one of the leg pockets he pulled out a handful of little plastic packets, chose one, stuffed the others back in. "Got a small right here." He shook it out.

"What's that?" The girl looked alarmed. "It's not going to hurt worse, is it?"

"No, ma'am." The fellow was smiling even brighter. Esther and Ben both stepped back to let him do his thing. "On a break like yours, it will relieve the pain—not altogether, but a lot." Deftly, he untied that lovely sling and let it fall away. Supporting her arm with one hand, he slipped the clear plastic tube over her wrist and up to the elbow. That had to make the hurt worse, but she was gazing at him, her knight in shining fatigues. Esther had forgotten all about teen psych.

The knight leaned over and inflated it by mouth. The clear plastic tube expanded, tightened. He purred platitudes in a quiet Southern drawl as he shook out a triangular bandage and built a sling around her arm that was not nearly as neat or artful as Ben's. Then he pulled out another triangular bandage, whipped it into a swathe, and wrapped it around her upper body, snugging the sling against her chest. *It must be nice having enough triangular bandages to be able to use two on a patient.* "My name is Kyle. What's yours?"

"Tiffany. Tiffany Jane, but I like just Tiffany."

"So do I." And Kyle ushered Tiffany and her mother toward the door. "I sure hope riding in a helicopter was on your dream list, Tiffany, because that's what is going to happen."

The mother stopped. "No! Wait. Can I just drive her? The cost..."

In that smooth Southern accent, "Don't worry about the cost. We're military. There will be none."

From the hall, a starchy woman's voice asked, "How many?"

"Minor with her mother."

Esther and Ben just stood there looking at each other in the silent, empty room.

A middle-aged woman in fatigues paused in the doorway, a clipboard in hand. "We've got the cardiac loaded, the old man, and we'll take these two. We can handle two more. Do you have others ready to transport?" She studied her clipboard. No eye contact.

"I-I'm not sure." Esther hesitated. She should have a better handle on her patients. She didn't even know who had been transported and who had not. This was all getting away from her. "Check with Barbara on the front desk. She's been able to keep better track."

"I will do that." Without looking at either of them, the woman marched off.

And Esther was too tired to care. For the next hour she and her team worked with the new team as they dealt with those still in need of aid and put away the fresh supplies.

By ten o'clock the easily portable patients had been moved to the Lutheran church where they would be fed and looked after. The ambulances had been refueled and restocked, ready for their next runs. Everyone in the waiting room had been seen and were either waiting for transportation, watching television, or, in many cases, sleeping.

She needed...she needed...she needed everything. Food, sleep, comforting. Everything. Wait. Comforting? Why did that come to mind? And not just comforting, either; a man's hug. She was a liberated woman! She didn't need a man's hug! And she yearned for one.

She walked into the break room to find Ben digging baby supplies out of various boxes. "What are you doing?"

"Getting together some things to take the baby home with me."

"You can't do that."

He stood and glared at her. "Look, she needs a home and you know Bo isn't going to let her out of his sight, so we're going home. They say there's no damage to my house."

She could tell he was trying to sound reasonable, but the squared-off jaw showed his real feelings. No doubt he was at the end of his rope same as she was at the end of hers. "Ben, listen to me. You're in no condition to take care of this baby. You work a forty-hour week, you can't leave her alone, you can't be up all night, it wouldn't work, do you understand? She has to go into the social services system and be put in foster care."

"She has a foster home, with me and Bo."

"No." She pulled a deep breath. She wasn't getting through and her mind was becoming more befuddled by the minute. "No, listen. Social services would not release a newborn to a man living alone. Little babies need constant attention at first. And if a service rep caught wind of an alcohol problem, they'd scrub you instantly. I'm sorry."

"Okay, from this day forward no beer, no booze at all. I'm taking her."

"*Why?*" She had to control herself. And she couldn't. "Why are you so stubborn about this? It's not your child!"

"I gave her life. The world's worst mother tossed her under a bush and I—" His voice dropped. "I don't know. I feel this intense—I mean, I have this intense feeling that I'm the one she needs. I can't hand her off to strangers. She's *my* responsibility. But it's more than that. I can't explain it."

Esther knew there were probably more diplomatic ways of dealing with this, but all she could do was yell. She took a deep breath. "No, Ben, I won't sign off on this one. The law is very clear. No. I can't."

His eyes had narrowed until they were mere slits. He dropped his voice. "You think I would put her in danger after all she has been through already?" The words wore diamond-cutting edges.

"And you think I would?" She fought to keep her own voice under control.

Ansel interrupted. "We were thinking of calling her Dawn, Esther."

She knew he was trying to ease the tension, but it wasn't working. "Dawn. That's nice." *Actually, it is nice.*

"She's coming home with me." Ben made it sound final as he shoved a package of diapers in the box and grabbed another container of formula off the shelf. "What if you don't have distilled water?"

"Boil some." She grabbed his arm. "Listen to me!"

"You go ahead and fill out your paperwork to cover your..." He ground to a halt and stared at her hand clamped on his arm. With excruciating politeness, he removed her hand with his other and let it drop.

Dawn, who had been sleeping in Ansel's arms, whimpered and squeaked before settling into a real, genuine baby's cry.

"Now see what you did." Ansel raised her to his shoulder and patted her back. "I just got her to sleep."

"If she doesn't come with me, what are you going to do? Put her on that chopper and let them leave her alone in the hospital?" Ben shook his head and tucked the edges of the boxes into each other to close the top.

Good question. Esther shoved her hands in her back pockets and stared at the floor. She glanced up to see Ansel and Beth each cuddling a baby. *Life goes on.* "You know for sure your house is beyond living in?"

Ansel nodded. "That's what Chief said. And I saw

that oak tree topple in my rearview mirror. Structural damage for sure, and who knows how much water damage."

"Okay, I have an idea. Ben, are you listening?"

The glare he sent her could have melted a steel I-beam. He wheeled and went to the fridge.

She pressed on. "These people need a house, you have a house. You need help with Dawn, they have huge hearts to take care of you all. I can't fill out the paperwork for a few days at least, so what do you say we all work together on this one?"

Beth interrupted. "That would be wonderful! With three of us, we can take turns sleeping and there will always be someone to take care of the babies. Sleep is the one thing you don't get with a newborn." She smiled at the infant in her arms, and then to the little girl on the pallet. The child had been up that morning, Esther knew, but she was again sleeping soundly.

Ben put a baby bottle in the microwave and pushed buttons. It began to hum.

Beth looked over at Ben. "We should be able to do this, we've been friends for a long time."

Esther watched Ben and his internal war while trying not to seem obvious. She glanced down at Bo, who was watching each of them in turn, as if he understood every word they said. As well he might; she figured his vocabulary ranked pretty high on the dog charts. When Dawn didn't quiet back down, the pooch lurched to his feet and walked over to stand by Ansel, as if ready to do whatever was needed to make her stop crying.

She almost giggled. "It's all right, Bo. You know he's a friend."

"But I have his baby and he's not taking any chances."

Ansel took the warmed bottle that Ben handed him. "I think Bo and baby don't like loud noises."

Dawn latched onto the nipple and filled the silence with her sucking noises.

Bo laid back down, nose on his paws, and watched Ben to see what they were to do next.

Everyone watched Ben.

He tipped his head back and blew out a heavy breath. "All right, if this is what it takes, so be it. Dawn will *not* be going into the social services system. Period. End of discussion. We'd probably never see her again, and I need my dog."

Ansel nodded and turned to Esther. "Can we get enough diapers for two? Our store at home might be pretty wet by now."

Esther heaved a sigh of relief to match Ben's. "This will be good." *Please Lord, let it be so.*

Chapter Eight

W e appreciate this, Ben."

Ben nodded. They'd driven less than a mile and the destruction was beyond imagination. Roofless houses, collapsed garages, uprooted trees; were it not for the few remaining street signs, he'd hardly even know where they were. His tires whispered hoarsely through a heavy carpet of leaves, twigs, and branches.

"Someone said the west side of town was hit worst."

Ben nodded again, carefully navigating his SUV around the top of a downed tree. Someone had moved it enough to clear the road. How could his house still be standing? But he saw it ahead, since so many trees were stripped or knocked down. Three old houses still standing in a line as if the wind had sheared around them, like some capricious child at play.

"Oh, my..." Ansel's mouth hung open, his head shaking like a bobblehead figure.

Ben realized he was doing the same. The house his father had built those many years ago. He always said if you did it right, it would last; even he could not have predicted an anomaly like this. When he first moved back home Ben had buried the power lines from the street to the house, despite the long driveway. His father accused him of being mad. But if the entire town had buried the power lines, they might not be in the fix they were in. And if the entire town had chosen to push for the hospital, those who died in this might not have.

The rage that had been simmering ever since Allie was killed made him clench his teeth. His only panacea was now off limits. The fight made him churn, too, when it was time to sign Dawn out of the clinic, out of Esther's immediate care. How in heaven's name had she drawn that promise out of him, his word that he wouldn't drink at all while he had the baby, lest it get away from him? It could drive a man to drink.

He glanced in the rearview mirror where Beth held Dawn in her arms. Her own baby lay sound asleep, and their two-year-old sat in her child's seat, sucking her thumb. Perhaps that was what the grown-ups needed to do, too. He slowed and stopped in the street; a tree lay across his driveway. So close and yet so far.

"I think you can push through that." Ansel leaned forward to peer through the rain-rivered windshield. "You want me to get out and see?" He reached for the door handle.

"No, stay put." Ben shifted into four-wheel drive and eased forward. A branch scraped across the windshield, catching the wiper on the passenger side.

Bo whined from the back of the vehicle. He was not happy banished to behind the seats, but kept his nose on the seat next to Beth's shoulder, as close to his baby as possible.

The engine growled, but the elm gave in and let itself be pushed off to the side, so it now lay more or less beside the drive. Had they needed to, they could have hiked to the house, but now they'd be able to better protect the babies from the elements.

"Thank you, God," Beth murmured from the backseat.

If God had been protecting like He promised, Ben's life would not be as desolate as the destruction. Nor would the town look like this. A memory flicked through, of Esther disappearing into who knew where. Looked like PTSD to him; he'd seen it too often to not recognize it. But what could have gone on in her life to cause something like that? Far as he knew, she'd never been in the service.

He let himself in the side garage door and pulled the red rope disconnecting the electric opener. He shoved mightily, raising the door by hand. Ansel had taken the driver's seat. He pulled it in. Ben pulled the door down. They'd made it. "I'll go open the doors and make sure..."

"I'm coming with you."

Ben shrugged. "Let's go then. Bo, stay."

"Apparently he isn't interested in leaving." Beth stroked her daughter's hair.

"Daddy?" The panic in the child's voice was not surprising.

"Daddy will be right back, it's okay."

Without listening for more, Ben opened his door and then kept it from slamming. Beth didn't need three crying babies, that was for sure. Ansel came around the front of the vehicle and followed him to the back door.

Inside, only the pounding rain echoed in the empty house. He wouldn't have been surprised to find neighbors or strangers there, seeking asylum after their own houses disappeared.

Ben looked around. No water spots. "I'm going to start

the generator. If you want, start the fire in the stove, help take the cold out of here faster."

For use in case of power outages, especially winter power outages, Ben had installed a wood-burning stove in the living room. In fact, Ansel had helped him put it in. For a change he had done something right, always kept the wood box full and kindling, too, and the fire laid. All Ansel had to do was strike the match.

"Okay." Ansel sounded almost cheerful.

Another miracle. The basement was still dry. He'd been thinking he might have to wade through water, but no. Again, his father's fine building skills had done their job. Three tries and the generator kicked over, chattered—and died. He swallowed a choice curse word and hit the starter again. "Come on, come on." It ground, groaned, and sighed. He waited, hearing his father's voice, reminding him to be patient. Machines needed time to adjust. Ben stared around the basement. Had he been home, this was where he would have waited out the storm. He and Allie and that baby she'd been finally carrying. He slammed the flat of his hand against the concrete wall. The sting on his palm reminded him to not hit the starter but to push it in firmly yet gently, like he was supposed to. He held it in to the count of nine, when the engine coughed and settled into the steady thrum that almost made him cry. Something was finally going right.

His father would have said *thank you, Lord*. At one time, Ben would have, too. Leaving the generator and memories of his father down in the basement, he flipped the switch that would send power to the rest of the house. At the base of the stairs, he paused and listened for the freezer. While yesterday seemed an eternity long, the power had not been out long enough to defrost either that one or the refrigerator upstairs. They better check the milk, though.

When he returned to the kitchen, Ansel was helping Beth and the babies in from the SUV. Bo padded right beside Beth, watching her carefully. Ansel carried his brand-new son and shepherded Natalie with the other hand.

"Here, give me the baby and you help her." Ben wiggled a finger toward the two-year-old. He took the well-wrapped bundle of joy, and Ansel picked up his daughter.

"Go home, Daddy, wanna go home."

"I know baby, we all do, but right now we are going to stay with Uncle Ben."

"No! Go home."

Beth leaned her rear against the kitchen counter, the sink right behind her. "Power and all, how blessed we are. Thank you, Ben. So... how would you like us to do this?"

"First of all, why don't you sit down and we'll figure it out." Allie would have had a fit if she saw the state of their house right now, and company here. Not that Beth and Ansel were company, more like family. The two couples had done everything together.

"I don't have any baby things." He followed her into the living room. When she eased down on the sofa—she had to move some dirty clothes aside to make room—he started to hand her the bundle he was carrying, but she still had Dawn. Natalie climbed up next to her mother, all the while giving Ben the eye, as if this were all his fault. "You know the bedrooms are upstairs. I kept the downstairs one as the TV room." And it was the worst mess of all.

"Perhaps we could do the drawer thing for both of the babies. You have something like that?"

"Sure. The guest room has a queen-size bed and..."
The bundle in his arms started to squeak.

Beth laid Dawn on the sofa on her other side and reached for the baby. Bo sat with his nose next to the still-sleeping infant.

"I'll bring in the rest of the stuff." Ansel left.

"We'll need to figure out a way to keep Natalie from falling down those stairs." Beth looked around the room. "We could lay a couple of those dining room chairs, one at the top and one at the bottom." She yawned. "I know you need sleep desperately, Ben, and so do I. So I think we might give Ansel the first watch."

Ben caught the yawn from her and his nearly cracked his jaw. He ought to be the cheerful host. He was a zombie. "Ansel can find what you need, right? The linen closet is in the hall by the bathroom. That bed hasn't been changed since I don't know when, but no one's slept in it. Clean sheets and towels. Gas water heater, so we have hot water."

"Go to sleep, Ben. We'll be fine."

He recognized the tone of her voice as the same one she used to soothe her little daughter, but at the moment he was beyond caring. He stopped at the foot of the stairs. "Coming, Bo?"

Bo thumped his tail and, as if shrugging, turned back to his watch.

"Wake me when it's my shift." Ben used the railing to half pull himself up the stairs, fell on his bed, and knew no more.

When a cold nose flipped his palm up, waking him, he blinked and stared at the clock. Seven. But looking out the window, he had no idea if that was A.M. or P.M. "Good dog." He stroked Bo's head and waited for memories to return. For a change he did not have a thundering headache and the phone was not ringing. Should he be at work already or—? Or! He had a baby now. And people living here and two babies and...Yesterday rolled back through his mind like the nightmare it had been. Had Dawn needed him and he'd slept right through it? Wouldn't that prove to Esther he was not a fit father for her?

"Why'd you let me sleep like that?" He sat on the edge of the bed and scratched his head.

Bo cocked his head and gave him a doggy grin.

"Well, you're sure in a good mood. How's our baby?"

Bo headed for the doorway, then turned to look over his shoulder as if to make certain Ben was up.

"I'm coming."

He filled a basket with dirty laundry on the way to the kitchen. Wait. Shouldn't run the washing machine on the generator. He'd take the load down anyway. When he got to the head of the stairs, he heard laughter, both adults and a child's high-pitched giggle. He found them around the small table in the kitchen, with Natalie sitting on a stack of phone books. Lots of phone books; small town.

"The coffee is still hot." Beth smiled at him. "I hope you slept well."

"Slept. I think I died." Ben poured himself a mug of coffee and leaned back against the counter. "Sure smells good in here."

"I'll fix you a plate." Ansel pushed his chair back. "How do you like your eggs?"

"Over easy. But I can do my own."

"I know, but I'm getting to know your kitchen. Sit down."

Surprised, Ben did as he was told. "What happened to taking turns, shifts?"

Beth seemed cheerful, too. "Well, we did. I slept for a while, then while I fed Nathan here, who thinks his meal should be more than it is yet, Ansel went to sleep. Dawn was awake for a while. If she so much as kicks her feet, Bo will come and get you. He's worse than an old man."

"Is she sleeping now?"

"Just got her back down. Most babies take a morning nap."

"I not a baby." Natalie stared across the table at him, then gave her mother a line of gibberish that left Ben wondering if his hearing was going out.

Beth handed her daughter the last piece of bacon and Natalie munched away, never taking her gaze off Ben.

"Did anyone try to wake me?"

"Bo did, but when he came back down, I swear he was shaking his head."

"I don't even remember that. No one called from the office?"

"Nope. But then the phone lines are down, no dial tone. The tower is back in business. I used my cell to call my mother and make sure they were all right and let them know where we are."

If his cell had shrieked at him, surely he would have heard it. And Bo would have persisted. "I better call in." He pulled his cell out of the holster and groaned. Dead. He'd forgotten to plug it in.

Ansel shook his head. "We did the same. Plugged it in this morning so if you want, you can use it." He set a plate in front of Ben and his cell, too.

"Do we have power yet?"

Ansel frowned. "I don't remember. Is your generator set to shut down when the power comes on?"

"Yes, but there is a slight pause. A long flicker."

"Then no, at least I don't think so, but I haven't taken time to go down there and check. How big is your fuel tank?"

"Diesel and fifty gallons, so we're in good shape." Ben fell to eating and listened while Ansel brought him up to speed.

"They hope the river crested, it stopped raining about three A.M., no flooding so far, but the high water has cut pretty far into the bank on the other side, that bend on the far side downstream of the bridge. Talk of closing it."

"You've been on the police band?" Ben spread jam on his toast. He had his base radio set up in the living room, and thanks to the generator they had access to the news that way. He picked up Ansel's cell and punched in the numbers of the border patrol. He had to stop and think, since he had his phone set on speed dial and never dialed the number any longer. "Did anyone mention the WiFi towers?"

"They got the one across the river operational sometime during the night. The one in town took a hit, but repairs should move ahead now that the storm is leaving. We can only pray that the storm right behind the first bypasses us."

"There's another one on the way? Wasn't this one enough?"

Jenny's business-like voice. "Border patrol."

"Jenny, Ben here."

"Oh, good. We were about to send someone to your house to check on you. You all right?"

"I am. Ansel and Beth are here with me, since their

house isn't habitable." From the sound of the breath she exhaled, he figured she was afraid he was passed out, not just sleeping. And passed out for a different reason than exhaustion. "Jenny, listen. I am okay." He spoke slowly and with all the sincerity he could muster.

"Ah, good. That's real good. Chief said to tell you that for right now, you needn't come in. That baby is with you, right?"

"Yes, Esther gave her okay when Beth and Ansel needed a place to stay, too. Is there anything more I need to know right now?" Even he could detect the difference in his voice. He was feeling pushed again. Jenny cared, that's all; he mustn't let it get to him.

It wasn't her fault she was the first to hear the news. Well, often the second. Whoever was manning 911 heard the worst first, then border patrol, if at all.

"You're sure this is all right?" He lifted the cell away from his ear to look at the face. Two bars. "My phone should be recharged fairly soon."

Jenny was asking, "You have enough fuel for your generator?"

"Yes, ma'am."

"Now, don't get huffy. You have no idea how many calls we've had for diesel. They're about out at the Quick Stop. So, you better refill yours, just in case."

"Yes, Mother."

"Sorry."

Don't be a jerk, James. You've been one for far too long. "Are there still travel restrictions on the roads?"

"Yes, we're asking people to not drive unless absolutely necessary. The usual service trucks, emergency vehicles, and National Guard are excluded, of course."

"How is Esther doing?"

Jenny was silent a moment. "Let's just say...ah..."

"I take it the military are still over at the clinic?"

"Ah, yes, that would be affirmative."

"Is her house still standing and habitable?" He couldn't believe he was asking these questions, and from the sound of Jenny's voice, she was surprised, too.

"I—I think so."

"She's not sleeping at the clinic?"

"Not that I know of."

And if she didn't know, no one did, so he rather doubted. The grapevine in this small burg could relay information faster than the WiFi, although all those downed phones might slow it up a little.

"Thanks, Jenny."

Again, she sounded as though she was shocked and trying to conceal it. Had he really been as bad as all that? Or was she overreacting? She wasn't much of a drama queen, so he doubted she was overreacting.

Since he'd not stopped at the cleaner's, his uniforms were in the SUV. Better bring them in and hang them. They were probably pretty dank and a little smelly. On his way out the door, he caught a message on the scanner. The bridge was now officially closed.

Chapter Nine

Good thing her mother had trained her well in manners.

Esther managed to nod at Dr. Livingston's instructions, although she flunked smiling. At least she didn't think she was shooting daggers at him and his high-handedness, even though she most assuredly thought about it. *He is only doing his job*, she reminded herself for the umpteenth time. *And he is good at his job. Your job is to be thankful.*

The reminder to herself drummed deeper into her subconscious. Thankfulness was not normal when orders and questions were dipping and flying faster than bats in a cloud of mosquitoes. Her response with a "Yes, sir," caught her by surprise and earned her a narrow-eyed look.

Dr. Livingston stared at her a moment, then rolled his lips to keep from smiling, if the slight crease in his cheeks could be called a smile. "You are not one of my staff, are you?"

"Rhetorical question. But I do appreciate all that you have brought to us and all that you and your staff are doing."

"Thank you, Doctor. That was well said." He leaned his haunches against a counter. "Do you have any questions?"

"I understand you're pulling out before the next front hits."

He nodded. "Affirmative. The National Guard will still be on site but not medical help. I wish we had some roads open, but closing the bridge cuts off your closest route to Grand Forks, am I right?"

"Yes."

"But there is another?"

"Of sorts, an unmarked road up this side of the river. But at least all our supplies are restocked—and, thanks to you, some things we didn't have before."

"And you and your people got some rest?" With arms loosely crossed over his chest, he rubbed his chin with one finger.

"Yes, thank you."

He dug a card out of his chest pocket and handed it to her. "A direct line to me. If you get an emergency over your head, call me and perhaps we can talk you through it."

Esther mentally heaved a sigh of relief. "Thank you. I didn't see any way of helping our bleeder, short of going in, and we just weren't set up for that."

"I know. Our field hospitals are far better equipped than you are. I hear you've been lobbying for a regional hospital to go here."

She nodded. "Fat lot of good it has done."

"You've taken on the county, too?"

She shook her head. "But that's the next step. Hopefully this storm will change their minds." Like closing the barn door after the horse had hightailed it but better late than never. She must still be tired; she was even thinking in clichés.

"Why have you not gone back and gotten your MD?"

She hoped the flinch didn't show. "Personal things."

"How long have you suffered from PTSD and what are you doing about it?" When she started to say something, he held up a hand traffic-cop-style. "Don't try to BS me, I've been at this a long time and heard it all."

Esther pulled herself up short and reminded her shoulders to disengage from her earlobes. "I hoped I was dealing with it well enough."

"On meds?"

"And counseling. Have been for about three years."

"And?"

Esther heaved a sigh. "And this was hard to deal with." *Talk about understatement!*

"'This' meaning the storm and all the chaos?"

She nodded. "The pressures of med school sent me into full-blown attacks and so I dropped out—before they could kick me out."

"You are sure they would have kicked you out?"

"I guess."

"Or was it the paranoia of the disorder?"

"I—ah..." She stared down at her crossed arms and tongued her bottom lip. When she looked back up at him, she could feel her eyelashes near to fluttering, her throat drying, and one swallow wasn't sufficient. "I don't know." The words wrenched themselves from a dark place deep inside and flung themselves from her mouth. "I was afraid I might misdiagnose or mistreat a patient. I couldn't bear it if someone died or grew worse because I couldn't control what was going on in my head." *Or my whole body for that matter*—the tremors used to rack her entire body.

"But the diagnosis by someone other than yourself is solid and documented?"

She shook her head. "All of that would show up on my medical records. No bona fide med school would let me back in."

"I wouldn't give up on that if I were you. So you basically do everything any doctor would do in a clinic on the edge of nowhere. And it looks like without supervision?"

"We are an affiliate of the regional hospital in Grand Forks. They send various specialists up on a rotating schedule and I report to Dr. Ho, head of the satellite clinics."

"I see."

"Five minutes, Major." The call came from the hallway.

"I'm going to think on this and get back to you. There might be some other avenues."

"Thank you, sir." The rush of gratitude wobbled her knees. *Don't count on anything*, that insidious inner voice warned her. *After all, he doesn't know the whole story.* She chose as usual to ignore the voice. "And thank you for all your assistance here. Please thank your staff, too." She held out her right hand and shook his.

Barbara stuck her head in the door. "Sorry to interrupt, Esther, but the ambulance is on the way back in. They found a spinal injury in a nearly crushed house. ETA three minutes."

"Thanks, Barbara."

He paused. "Let us take this one with us."

"Thank you! We'll tell them to go to the choppers." She turned and left the room, realizing he was right behind her. That phrase that was getting hackneyed but was oh so powerful echoed in her mind. *I've got your back.* This man indeed had her back. *Does he see the difference he makes in people's lives? And not just on the operating table.*

She told Barbara, and Barbara told the aid van crew. Chain of command. Suddenly wearied, she headed for her office. No doubt the walk-in closets in Dr. Livingston's home were bigger than her office. Who knew: Maybe unlike her office they even had windows. And they probably didn't smell a little musty the way her office did. Rain must have gotten in somewhere, somehow, and a moldy, soggy spot was lurking behind a file cabinet or something.

How she was ever going to get all the paperwork caught up was beyond her. Where to start? No clue. How many did they treat? No record. What about the drug cabinet she'd opened and left open, making controlled substances, even the Schedule 1A's, available to the whole world? How to inventory what had been used or abused or stolen or borrowed or...How much had they spent on that Culpepper kid? He'd get at least minimum wage. Who would end up paying for the smashed soda and junk machines? Right now, right this moment, all she needed was a few quiet minutes to process the conversation with Dr. Livingston and gear up for the next wave. So far, the clinic was empty, her helpers were rested, and all the new supplies were put away. The weather report sounded like they'd made it through the worst.

What if I could go back to med school and finish the program?

She'd not allowed herself to even consider that for the last few years. Had she been Catholic, she might have referred to her job here as her penance. One way to right an unrightable wrong?

She sank down in her office chair and flipped open her phone. "Hi, Mom."

"Are you all right? We've heard terrible things about your town! It's all over the television. National television, too, not just the local news. We lost power for several hours, but we finally have the phone on again and power, too."

Esther smiled and shook her head. "I tried to call." She could hear pans rattling and could just picture her mother, receiver glued between ear and shoulder as she started the next meal in her shiny kitchen. Her mom, Madge Landauer Hanson of the Connecticut Landauers, never did one thing at a time when she could do three. "And yes, right now we are all right. The military sent help and they've restocked our supplies. The public safety people are saying that half the town has some kind of damage."

"That bad! Oh, my. Of course you never know with the TV, are they being realistic or sensationalist? Remember last year when that mini tornado dropped a tree on a trailer home in Mankato? One house trailer, but you'd have thought the whole south half of the state was ripped apart, to hear them talk."

"Well, this storm really pounded us." She closed her eyes for a moment as pictures flashed through her head of the folks they'd cared for here in the clinic. "I hope we've seen the final death toll. We have two little kids whose mother died and their father is a truck driver trying to get home." She didn't mention Denise. That one hurt too bad yet.

"We heard six for the county. They can't exaggerate the number of deaths, can they?"

"No, but they can underestimate. At least four here in town. The bridge is closed." She paused to listen as a chopper revved up and lifted off. It came clattering over the building, still very low, and its backwash rattled the loose shingles or whatever that was making noise on the roof. On the one hand, she hated to see them go, but on the other it was nice to be back in charge. She heard Chief's booming voice; he'd be here in a second. "I got company coming—border patrol chief. Do you need anything, Mom?"

"No, no, we're fine. We have the power back now. It looks like the brunt of the storm hit you instead of us. Call me when you can. Your father is worried about you."

"I will." She snapped it closed. And while her mother always said she was praying rather than worrying, Esther had long ago realized that while her father never said much, he lost sleep worrying over her. "In here, Chief."

He tapped on the door and entered, shaking his head. "Seems to me you could have more office space than this hole in the wall."

"Well, when we build our new facility, I'll make sure to put a real office on the blueprints. Shucks, maybe two. Get a good one for Barbara."

"You can bet they'll bring in a real doctor if we get a real hospital here. You thought about going back and finishing med school?"

"What's with everyone today and me finishing med school?" Esther didn't bother to keep the frown from her face.

"Oh?" His eyebrows rose. "Who else?"

"Dr. Livingston."

"Oh."

Esther studied him. She thought she could read him, well, most of the time. She turned her head slightly to the side and dropped her chin. "You weren't too impressed with the good doctor?"

"Typical know-it-all military officer."

"And what did he do to set you off?"

"Took over. And don't give me that look. I saw your re-action, he took your operation over, too."

"Can you believe he apologized for being so high-handed?"

Chief fell back in his chair in mock horror. The two shared a bit of a laugh and then settled into business.

He cleared his throat. "You and Ben worked well to-gether, the give-and-take. That doesn't always happen with Ben these days. How about I station him back here?"

She shrugged as nonchalantly as she could. "Fine with me."

"Don't get too enthusiastic." His voice dripped sar-casm.

"Sorry." She seemed to be saying that a lot lately. She glanced down at her hand, pen clenched and doodling hearts and dollar signs on the pad she kept handy for phone conversations. Change the subject. "Is this new weather front as bad as the other, and an ETA, please?"

"ETA is tomorrow, early afternoon, and predictions are less wind, more rain. The Doppler shows it slowed down. Still could veer away. North up into the bogs would be good. You need more staff?"

"Barbara is here; she's an RN, but I don't know where we could drum anyone else up. And Susan can't leave her mother right now."

"What if we got someone else in to take care of her mother?"

"If you can." Esther knew Barbara had called the other two part-timers who worked in the clinic, and their ex-cuses were valid. Hard to leave a baby with spina bifida, or three young teens when Dad was already called out with the border patrol.

Chief's belt radio squawked something unintelligible.

He thumbed the key and barked, "Be right there." He stood up and turned to Esther. "Anything else?"

Esther shrugged. "Oh, I know. Did you get through all the damaged houses yet?"

"In town, but not all in the county. Jenny is calling everyone in the phone book, at least all she can. A lot of lines are still down, though, and the power isn't all back on, either. Take care."

Esther heard him say something to Barbara on his way out. In her mind, the man looked like he'd aged ten years in the last three days. He even walked like he was carrying the whole town on his shoulders. Maybe she should have insisted he have a checkup. With something niggling at the back of her mind, she walked out to the records closet and pulled his file. Sure enough, his BP was elevated and she'd noticed an irregularity in his heartbeat, but he'd blown her off when she suggested he go in for tests. She checked the date. Two months ago. Sliding the file back in place, she closed her eyes for a moment, calling up the picture of him sitting across from her. Had there been changes caused by something other than weariness and pressure? . . . as if that weren't enough? How could she get him back in and clap a cuff on his arm? An EKG wouldn't be a bad idea, either.

She returned to her office and fired up her computer. She watched the screen change as the monster's innards did mysterious things, and planned how to attack the mass of reports and paperwork generated by the hideous storm.

Chapter Ten

This power outage business was getting old fast. No TV, not that there was any football on Thursday. No computer unless absolutely needed. No laundry. No dishwasher. No anything else that sucked amps out of the generator unnecessarily. Ben sighed and shuffled the deck yet again, laid out still another game of solitaire across the kitchen table.

Bo walked over to the back door and barked.

"Hey, shut up!" Ben whispered hoarsely. "Beth's asleep!" Either Bo needed a rest stop or someone was coming. He hopped up and opened the door. Both, apparently. Bo hastened outside, and Esther stood on the back stoop.

"Come in! Come in." He stepped aside and swung the door wide.

She wore the white jeans and colored shirt that she always wore under her I-am-a-doctor white jacket. With her hair pulled back into a French roll—Ben seemed to remember that was the name of that do—and her face relaxed, she was quite a pretty woman. She stepped inside.

Ben waved toward the table. "Coffee?"

"Thanks. I have no power at the house yet, so no coffee." She sat down.

"Then it sounds like no breakfast, either. What would you like? We have most everything." He waved a hand. "Propane stove."

"Really? What I like and what I usually eat are two different things. Usually I just grab a doughnut and run, but what I like is bacon and eggs. Never have time for it."

"Make time this morning. My treat. I assume you're on your way to work." Ben pulled down the cast-iron frying pan and got out the egg carton and bacon. She sat silent. He paused and looked at her. "Is that okay?"

She took a breath. "Yes. Yes, very okay. You surprised me, is all. I wasn't expecting...I was just going to stop by a minute...Yes. I really should be saying, *Oh please don't go to all that bother*, but it sounds so good. Thank you. I didn't even get the doughnut this morning."

"So what you're doing here is checking up on me and possibly administering a Breathalyzer test."

She turned pink. She actually blushed. "I didn't—"

He interrupted. "We're friends and colleagues. Let's be honest. Honestly, I'm happy to make breakfast for both of us, since I haven't eaten yet, and I assure you that so far, I've stayed off the sauce." He poured her a mug of coffee and set the creamer out beside the sugar bowl. "Real half-and-half."

"'So far.' Good answer. If you said *Absolutely not*, I'd be concerned. Are Ansel and Beth here?"

"Beth is asleep. She takes the night shift so she can feed Nathan. They finally agreed on the name Nathan. Bacon smells so good as it fries." He forked the bacon onto a paper towel and asked, "How do you want your eggs?"

"Over easy. Or scrambled. Whichever is easiest."

"I'll just scramble a bunch, for when Beth gets up."

She grew wide-eyed as he broke eggs into a bowl. "You can afford to use so many eggs?"

"Ansel is down the street at their house with the wheelbarrow, bringing over all their freezer and fridge stuff, pantry stock, baby stuff—this is his third run so far. As regards supplies, we're in tall clover." He dug his whisk out of the drawer.

"I am constantly amazed by—" She pursed her lips a moment in thought. "I guess, by the resiliency in this community. You people all act like this disaster is no big deal."

Now it was his turn to think. He drained off most of the bacon grease. "You say 'you people.' You've been here, what, six years? Why are we still 'you people' and not *us*?" He glanced at her.

She was sitting openmouthed.

Apparently she needed some time, so he gave her the space while he dug out the milk and sniffed it. Still good. He seasoned the eggs and started whisking.

"I never thought of that. I do feel like an outsider. Maybe because the city fathers won't listen to anything I say or try to do. Maybe because all the people I meet I only meet professionally, as a doctor to a patient. Besides, I'm not much of a schmoozer. Bit of introversion, you might say."

"Just a bit. But you grew up around here."

"About four hours away. We were closer to Bemidji, so if we drove somewhere, it was there. Not over this way, to Pineville. When I took this job I knew about where Pineville was, but I'd never been here." She watched him put the bacon in a warm oven. "However, when I was in high school my father rooted for Pineville, not my school."

"What was your school? Riverview?"

"Jefferson. My school had a lousy football record and Pineville was top of the pile. My father dwells heavily on success that you can measure."

He poured the eggs in the frying pan. "I think I hear you. A lot of our rooters don't measure Pineville by academic excellence. Can't see that on a scoreboard. Just football."

"Exactly. Mom's the same way. I'm not a resident at Mayo, so I haven't succeeded."

"I feel sorry for her."

"Sorry!" Silence. "Yeah, I guess that's true."

"You're successful. I watched you in action. But it doesn't show on a scoreboard."

"Or in the local paper in that column that crows about citizens who made good." She sipped her coffee.

Snuffling from the other room. He raised a finger. "Her Highness. At a count of five, you'll hear a cry. Three, four, five."

Dawn wailed. It was not her strident wail, just an I-woke-up-and-I'm-alone cry.

Esther stood up, grinning. "I'll take over the eggs."

"Thank you." He walked out into the formal dining room. It was a nursery now, one of two. He and Ansel had brought over their crib for Nathan, who slept upstairs, and their folding travel crib for Dawn down here. Resilient? Yeah. He scooped up Dawn and laid her down on the sideboard, which now served as a diapering table. She wasn't poopy, but she sure was soaked. That taken care of, he draped her on a shoulder and took her to the kitchen.

Esther broke into the brightest smile. "Oh, Ben! She is looking so good! Look at those plump, rosy little cheeks!"

They swapped chores, he back to his eggs, she to dandling the tiny child who a few days ago teetered on the rim of death.

The door flew open and Bo bounded inside. Ansel followed closely. "Esther! Good to see you! Ben, I brought some stuff over from the pantry. Esther, we're stocking Ben's pantry. Note I didn't say *restocking*."

She laughed. "But when she went there, the cupboard was bare, and so the poor dog had none."

"Oh, the dog had plenty. It's people food he was short on."

Ansel shoved bread into the toaster as Ben served the bacon and eggs. He sort of kept up with the light, idle chatter, but he was aching to ask her the big question: What about Dawn?

After they finished eating around seven forty-five Esther called the clinic. No appointments. No emergencies. Good. She could come in late.

Ansel hurried off to work. Dawn insisted on immediate attention, so Ben prepared her bottle.

Esther watched him a moment. "I'll clean up the dishes."

"Want to do something even more helpful?"

"Sure."

"Take Bo out for a walk. Maybe down by the pond or on that bike trail; half an hour or so. As soon as Beth gets up I'm going to the office to catch up on desk work, and Bo won't get any exercise."

"Neither will you."

"With me, exercise is optional. With Bo, well, you better not neglect his."

She giggled, a happy, relaxed giggle. It was the first he'd ever heard from her and it pleased him immensely. When she took the leash down from its hook by the door, Bo figured things out immediately. Eager wagging, eager jumping around. He went off with her without a backward glance.

Ben stuffed the bottle into Dawn's mouth and walked out to the front window to watch them go. Dawn slurped contentedly. Bo settled to the trail with élan. Esther was moving along with a spring to her step.

And that pleased him most of all.

Chapter Eleven

You gotta be kidding!"

Chief Harden shook his head. "How often have you seen me kid about assignments?"

"Never. But this is ridiculous! I'm not a medic." Ben knew why he'd not gone on for more emergency training when he was offered the chance. He just didn't feel he could do as good a job there as on patrol. Bringing in bad guys made his day. So here he stood in front of the chief's desk wishing he were somewhere else. Anywhere else. At least some sleep and some desk work had made him feel almost back to normal. Now he wanted to get completely back to normal.

Thoughts of tiny Dawn tickled his mind. She'd smiled at him that morning when he'd given her a second bottle after Esther left. Well, sort of smiled. Beth said it was gas bubble pains. He knew better. And she'd kept one small fist tangled in Bo's fur and waved the other at Ben.

Had they not been on patrol in that area, she would never have lasted a night.

"You did an exemplary job during the storm and we

have another one about to hit. The other detail is searching damaged buildings for more victims."

"Which is what Bo and I are trained for."

"True. And where is Bo?" Chief dropped his chin to
stare over his glasses.

"You said I could leave him home."

"I know. If you'd been going out on patrol, he would
have come in, too."

"So aren't we wasting his training?" Good point, but
Ben knew perfectly well that good points did no good
when arguing with Chief. Chief had made up his mind
and Ben knew changing it was more like trying to open
a bear trap rusted shut. Besides, he wasn't sure how to
get Bo away from his self-assigned duty as guardian of the
baby. Ben grimaced and started to turn away but stopped.
"Did you get any rest between these fronts?"

"Why?" The word barked out.

"Well, you look like you could use some sleep."

"Don't we all?"

Ben smirked. "Just doing my duty. You're the one who
assigned me to medic, so I'm being medical. To be honest,
you look like death in a slop bucket. Maybe you should
come to the clinic for a checkup." He raised his hands in
front of him, palms out, to fend off the burning scowl. "I
know, just doing my duty. I'm going, I'm going." He gave
a sort of salute, one more narrow-eyed look, and shut the
door behind him.

Jenny greeted him at the reception area. "You look better than I have seen you in a long time."

"Thank you for your concern." He let a hint of sarcasm
creep in. No sense letting her feel like she was always
right. Besides he didn't owe her just one debt of gratitude
but a whole dump-truck-load.

"How's our baby?"

Funny how Dawn had become the darling of not only the station but the clinic and probably part of the town. "She smiled at me." *Get a grip, James. No extra blinking allowed.* "When I fed her this morning."

"Our miracle baby."

One thought had awakened him early. What if Esther decided today was the day to put his baby into the social services system? No, that wasn't possible. There was no way to get her to Grand Forks and the offices. "In more ways than you know."

"Oh, I see a walkin', talkin' miracle right in front of me."

"Jenny, knock it off." He heard the hoarseness creep into his voice. If all the others were as close to the line as he, they were in bad shape. He glanced over his shoulder and leaned closer, dropping his voice. "Is he as bad off as he looks?"

"Chief? In a word, yes! But he won't listen to me, you, or anyone else, so put on your prayer armor that he can get through this." She shook her head. "Life with him was so much easier when his wife was still alive."

Ben nodded. He used to have a wife, too. He used to have prayer armor. Was it all rusted beyond use? Wasn't it enough that he'd quit drinking? Of course, how would she know that? Or any of them? Himself included. Esther had certainly put the fear of God into him if he wanted to keep that baby. The memory of that toothless smile, those crinkly dark eyes...no drinking allowed, no how, not any-more, no matter how much stress.

"I'm outta here before he comes out here and rips me into shreds. Thanks, Jenny."

"For what?"

But he was out the door. He paused under the roof of the entryway and just watched for a minute as Mother Nature girded herself to throw yet another fit. The wind was already swaying what trees and portions of trees they had left, occasionally ripping off leaves, and while the rain was still fairly light, the cold of it and the wind drove right into his bones. The black monster off to the west would fill the sky from about two o'clock on; the real storm. And its arrival was not far off.

He parked near the rear entrance of the clinic and flipped the hood of his rain jacket over his head. His vehicle seemed empty without his furry black buddy. He entered the building to find quiet. He hung up his wet jacket and went in search of Esther.

"She's in two with a patient." Barbara did not seem particularly cheerful today.

"And good morning to you, too." Ben smiled at the dark-haired woman. "So it has begun again?"

"We've had two patients in ten minutes. If she doesn't need you yet, how about moving that box of distilled water for me? It needs to be in the storage room rather than the kitchen break room."

"Of course. Anything else?"

"Start a pot of coffee."

"Sure." *For this I am here?* But he knew better than to say anything. He tapped on the door to two and stuck his head in. "Need me?"

"Not yet." Esther sent him a questioning look, then turned back to her patient, an elderly man.

"Hey there, Mr. Rustvold. How you doing?"

The older man had been a math teacher when Ben was in high school, retired a few years ago. To Ben, he had seemed ancient when he was still teaching. And despite the fellow's retirement, Ben could not bring himself to address Mr. Rustvold by his first name. He was *Mister*.

"Not too bad. Ran out of my prescription and they wouldn't renew it without I check in here. So here I am."

"Glad it's nothing more than that. Say hi to your wife for me." She'd been his history and US government teacher. The school lost some fine teachers when these two had retired. He shut the door and went on to the break room to perform his mundane, non-law-enforcement tasks.

One of their two ambulances wailed a few streets away. The other was still parked at the south end of the lot, mutely awaiting a call.

He stowed the distilled water in the closet and returned to the break room. His baby had spent hours here, surviving. He reached for the coffee filters. He should go ask for a report, but the need for a cup of coffee drove him to finish this task first. The other would come to him. He filled the coffeemaker well as he heard the door swoosh open. He headed for the ambulance entrance. "What do we have?"

"Cardiac."

"Room three." He looked down at the man on the gurney. "Mr. Aptos." A spidery hand reached for him and Ben clasped the cold hand between his warm ones. He glanced at Dennis, who was pushing. Dennis shrugged. They all knew the old gentleman who had been Ben's grandfather's best friend. The two had played dominoes every day down at the Drop In Café and bingo every Thursday at the veterans' hall. They had both walked in the parade on Veterans Day every year since he could remember. Dennis wheeled him into the examining room and they lifted him onto the table. He almost weighed less than the box of water. Ben wished they had a more comfortable bed for him.

He met Esther in the hall. "Mr. Aptos in three. Cardiac."

"Is he stabilized?"

"Appears so." He opened the door for her to enter.

"Hello, Mr. Aptos, not feeling too well right now, eh?" She automatically checked the monitor. Dennis had shifted to the clinic monitors. "No, please don't try to sit up. Let me see what is going on here." She patted his hand and put her stethoscope to his chest.

Dennis and Yvette stepped back and pulled their gurney out of the way. "We need to get back."

"I know. Have they shut down traffic on the streets yet?"

"No, but there aren't many cars out."

She checked the saline drip. "What have you given him?"

"Besides oxygen, Activase."

"Heparin?"

"Not yet. His heart rate seems to be settling down some. He wasn't fibrillating—we put the machine on him, of course—but he was having a hard time breathing."

"Was he unconscious?"

"Almost, mighty weak. Sitting in his chair in front of the dark TV." Dennis kept his voice low.

"I think he'd slept there, too. Blankets on the floor," Yvette added.

The old man shrugged. "No power. Had some cheese, slice of bread." His words were strung out, barely hanging together.

"Mr. Aptos, when did you eat last? Today, yesterday?"

"I-I'm not sure."

"Can you chew and swallow?"

"Can't find my teeth."

"I see." Esther looked to Dennis. "Was there power to his house?"

"No lights on, but I didn't check switches."

"Mr. Aptos, I'm going to give you some nutrition via the IV but I want you to eat something now, something soft you can masticate with your tongue. Can you sit up if we crank the bed up?"

"I-I think so."

"How about heating him some soup in the microwave?"

Ben nodded and patted the man's shoulder. "We'll get you ready to play dominoes again real soon."

"Thank you, son."

Soup. Ben fumbled around in the little cabinet where the staff kept emergency rations for when they were too busy to break away and eat. Chicken noodle. No, chunks. Cream of celery. Ben hated celery and wouldn't do that to anyone else. Cream of potato. That would do. He dumped it into a bowl and poked numbers on the microwave. Anything else? He looked in the refrigerator. Cheese. American cheese squares in wrappers. Could you handle that stuff without teeth? Sure.

He dug a spoon out of the junk drawer, rinsed it off to make sure, and headed back to three with his tray of delectable delights.

Esther met him on the way. "I think he's mostly dehydrated and weak from not eating and drinking. We can't keep him here, and he can't be left alone. What do we do?"

"According to Dennis, when in need call his mother. Is the Lutheran church taking in refugees again?" Ben felt like he'd been out of things for a week rather than a couple of days. "Or maybe someone in town will take the old man in for a few days."

"I'll ask Dennis." She headed to room one to check on her patients there.

Mr. Rustvold was leaving two as Ben entered three. "Mr. Aptos?" Ben set the tray on the counter and watched for a response.

The faded blue eyes struggled open, and the old man turned his head to see who was talking. "Ah, Ben. You take after your father, you know."

"Really? I brought soup, do you need help eating?" While he was talking, he cranked the head of the bed up. "That better?" But when he saw how the old hand shook, he dragged over a chair. "How about if I help you?"

"Do you by any chance have any coffee?"

"We do. Let's get through the soup and the cheese I brought, then I'll get you coffee." He waited for a nod. Had he ever fed someone like this before? Surely Barbara or someone could do better than he. He should be out chasing bad guys, not force-feeding an old man. The first spoonful dribbled down the man's chin. Ben mopped him with a tissue and tried again. "Sorry, my fault." After a few spoonfuls they got the rhythm and the soup disappeared. Ben unwrapped the square of cheese and handed it to his patient. "Can you manage that?"

Mr. Aptos nodded and with a shaky hand took a bite. "Coffee?"

"Coming right up." He left the room, trying to figure out how he could bring coffee that wouldn't spill. Barbara might know.

"Check the cupboard above the sink," Barbara said.

"Good, thanks."

At the same moment they heard the ambulance siren.

"Here we go again." Barbara answered the phone and waved him off with the other hand.

Sure enough, in the cupboard he found those travel mugs with accordion-pleated straws sticking out of the lid. Perfect. Ben pulled the first one his fingers reached, a turquoise job with a Hasty-Stop logo, poured the coffee, and added the sugar that for some odd reason he remembered from days with his father and his friend.

He carried it in to the old man. "I hope you still take sugar."

"I do. How did you ever remember that?" He took the cup with steadier hands.

"Is there anyone we might call who could stay with you for a few days?"

Mr. Aptos shook his head. "Just Harry. But his house was damaged, and they're going to live with his daughter. They came and told me they were leaving."

"Okay, we'll find someone."

"I don't want to be a bother, you know."

"I understand, but you can't live alone until we get your strength pumped back up. Enjoy your coffee."

He heard Esther say, "Okay, room two." So he headed for two. But wait. Someone was shouting out in the waiting room. He paused, sighed heavily. "Be right back."

Chapter Twelve

"Sir, I told you, you'll have to wait—" Barbara's voice was firm and loud enough for Ben to hear down the hall.

The man's reply was louder. "I don't have to—I need something. Show me your drugs. Now!"

The voice, blaring, shaky, desperate sounding, stopped Ben from slamming open the door and charging into the waiting room. He opened the door a crack. While he couldn't see the man, he could hear Barbara stammering a reply.

"I-I-I don't know. I'm just the receptionist."

From somewhere in the middle of the waiting area, a woman screamed. "Don't hurt my baby! Please! Not Robbie! Please!"

A man swore. A child somewhere close was screaming.

Ben opened the door a bit farther; how much could he see? Not much. A clean-cut man in an orange T-shirt, probably the child's father, was helping a sobbing, distraught woman to her feet out among the chairs. Barbara, terrified, was riveting her attention on a very ratty-looking fellow standing unsteadily, his feet braced wide, between Ben and her desk. Ben could smell him from here.

Good luck bit number one: His back was turned. Ben slipped into the room and shook his head when Barbara saw him. Her eyes continued past him. Still, the smelly guy shifted to the side to glance around the room. One arm clamped a shrieking little boy to his chest, while the other hand held a knife point to the boy's throat. He turned enough to catch a glimpse of Ben, who was silently moving closer. "Take another step and you'll see blood all over!" Grizzled stubble on his chin, oily hair straggling down to his collar, and clothes that hadn't felt the caress of laundry detergent for years. And he reeked penetratingly.

"Hold still, Robbie! Don't move!" the orange-shirted fellow pleaded, wrapping an arm around his wife's shoulders.

Ben stood still, raised both hands palms out. "Easy, fella. We'll get you what you want. Don't hurt the child. No drugs are worth injury to a child." Out of the corner of his eye, he saw someone coming up to the front entry door.

"Barbara, lock the door."

She half rose. "What? Don't you...?"

"There are people about to come in. We don't need..." Ben fought to keep his voice calm and even. "...them. Not right now."

"No!" Smelly guy was, if anything, growing wilder. "I mean it! She don't leave! Take me to where you keep your drugs, bitch."

An old man Ben had not even noticed at the back of the room hopped up and waddled to the door. He opened it a little and said something. The people outside ran away. The old man ran out the door, slammed it behind him.

It was obvious that life was moving faster than the smelly guy could handle it. Panicky, he looked all around, his eyes wide, their whites so bloodshot they were pink. Maybe if he was so addled he didn't know what to do, Ben could suggest something to do; maybe the guy would even do it.

Good luck bit number two: Ben had a stethoscope looped around his shoulders. "I am a doctor. Dr. Jones. I operate this clinic." He dipped his head toward Barbara. "Miss Funkmeyer, the prescription drugs. Please bring them."

"I will. Don't hurt the boy. I'm going to stand up now." Barbara pushed herself to her feet. "We'll help you."

Ben stepped back, his hands still clear. Scabs on the man's arms, the shaking. Crank, meth. What? He started to move forward. "Why don't we...?"

"*I said, don't move!*" The fellow jerked, and the point of the knife pierced the boy's skin. A trickle of blood sent the mother into a screaming, crying frenzy; her husband was wrapped around her tightly, doing all he could to comfort her.

"Now look what you did!" the smelly guy screamed. "I warned you! Don't anyone move, or my knife might slip again. What the..." A dark wet spot was spreading down his clothes. In his fear, the child had wet his pants. "I should just..." He inched his way to the door. It was closed. "You, open the door."

Ben nodded again. "Miss Funkmeyer, give him everything in the cabinet. As soon as he has our drugs, he will release the child."

Barbara nodded and moved to do as she was told, following "doctor's" orders.

No way could he get across the room in time to take

him down in here. He glanced toward the couple. The man kept his arms clamped around his wife.

As Barbara led their smelly drug addict into the hall, Ben slid back out through the side door. The mother wailed. He distinctly heard Barbara's, "Don't anyone come out of the exam rooms. Stay where you are!"

Hearing a horrendous crash and glass shattering, Ben surmised that Barbara had just opened the locked cabinet. Vials and bottles rattled. Sounds told him they were dumping everything into a bag.

Ben slipped into the storage area, lit eerily green by the EXIT sign. He paused beside a steel shelving unit, squeezed back against the wall, waited. Hardest thing in the world, just waiting. He'd burned up a third of his life on surveillance, sitting, watching, and waiting, but this was different. A child could die here.

His ears told him some of what was going on, but he dared not peek.

Barbara's voice: "... an exit over there that will take you out the back way. See it?"

Footsteps approached, staggering steps. He could clearly smell the guy. The little boy was crying. Getting louder. He kept his mind on task by rehearsing his next move.

The stench intensified, and now the fellow loomed into sight immediately in front of him, Robbie still pressed against his chest. Now!

Ben put his years of football training into use, combined with a bit of judo from the academy. His hands shot out; he seized the wrist with the knife, yanked it away from the child, kept moving, slammed the hand against the wall, and tackled the guy with a full body slam. The three of them crashed to the floor, but grabbing Smelly's wrist had twisted all three of them aside and they landed on Ben's left arm. All three of them. A white plastic kitchen bag fell open and spewed bottles and vials out across the floor. The clatter seemed magnified in this narrow passage. So did the stink.

Ben wrenched the man's arm behind his back—the hand no longer held the knife—and surged to his feet. But the fellow's other arm still wrapped firmly around Robbie. This worn old derelict, who seemed so compromised, turned out to be amazingly strong. Ben was in shape, and he was struggling.

"Let go of the child!" Ben dropped, both knees, onto the man's back and, grabbing his hair, slammed his face into the concrete floor.

Smelly said, "Oof," and his arm relaxed. *Let's hope the other arm is just as relaxed.* Ben could hear the child choking and coughing under there. If Ben's face were pressed that close to this mess of a human, he'd be coughing, too.

The boy's father burst into the passage.

Ben jerked the scabby perp to the side by his bent arm, earning a shriek of pain that reverberated. The fellow was getting his wind, spewing a volley of filthy names.

The father grabbed his son's legs and pulled him away.

Ben yanked the stethoscope off his neck, but the rubber tubes were too short. "Get me something to tie him with."

From right behind him, Barbara handed him a roll of gauze.

Ben could hear people moving around him in the narrow passage, but he kept his attention on the pile of manure before him as he bound both hands behind the man's back, wrapping the gauze in tight figure eights.

Really tight figure eights. He staggered to his feet and jerked the prisoner upright to sitting. "Someone call the highway patrol." He rubbed his left elbow.

"That old man who ran out the front door had a cell. They're on their way."

"Where's Esther?" Ben took a moment to simply inhale deeply. Smelly's stale odor put an end to that quickly.

Barbara stood beside him watching their would-be robber. And to think that the papers would refer to this as an "alleged" robber. "Working with that patient yet. I guess there are some complications. What more do you need? Our sweet old man here has a rather severe nosebleed. At least that's where I think it's coming from."

"What a shame." Ben fought to control his breathing, yearning for the impossible, to take on oxygen without taking in air. "Where can we stuff him until they get here?"

"Tie him to a chair?" Barbara poked him. "And what's this 'Funkmeyer' stuff, 'Doc'?"

"You wouldn't want the doctor to use your real name, would you?"

She smirked.

Ben swiveled to see the mother kneeling close, leaning forward, carefully checking over her son as he lay in his father's arms. The father was sitting spraddle-legged on the floor. Robbie's snuffling had stopped, but he still looked frightened.

Ben ignored the continuous line of threats and filth from the man he'd tackled and settled down close to the father's legs, watching the boy. The bleeding had already stopped from the knife stick and, occasional hiccuppy sobs aside, the child seemed to be breathing all right. His overall color was good, except for one side of his face. It was already turning pale yellow and starting to swell. The kid was going to have one beaut of a black eye. But he was alive.

He was alive. Wonderfully, vibrantly, alive.

Ben held both hands in front of the boy. "I promise I won't hurt you. I want to check your pulse. It's part of what we do." Carefully, he laid two fingers on the kid's carotid. Robbie watched him suspiciously, but he didn't move from the warm nest of his father's bosom. His pulse was firm, steady, about right for a kid his size.

A siren cut off outside that Ben had not even realized was hooting.

"State patrol. They're here." Barbara moved behind him and called, "Right in here. This way. It's under control. You can put your guns away."

Ben didn't bother to tell her that law officers never pay attention to suggestions to holster sidearms. Or were they carrying something heavier?

Heavier. Not AK-47s exactly, but some hefty firepower. Two uniformed highway patrolmen appeared, their guns pointed up and prepared to blow holes in the ceiling.

Ben gestured with his head, but he didn't move from his seat in front of the family. "He's all wrapped up and waiting for you."

"Any other weapons on him?"

"Didn't check. But he didn't go for any after he lost the knife."

The taller of the two, a solid hunk of a guy with LAR-RIMER on the cotton name tape on his shirt, walked over to Smelly. He leaned down to frisk the foul fellow and quickly stepped back. "You planning on cleaning him up some?"

"Probably not." Definitely not. Why spoil the kid's dream of taking in a clean perp?

Larrimer asked, "You have a holding cell or something in town here?"

Ben shrugged. "You might try city hall. There used to be a cell there down in the basement, remodeled janitor's closet."

Larrimer grunted, a sort of acknowledgment. "Four blocks south on the right?"

"That one, yeah. Look for a clock tower. Clock doesn't run right, so don't believe what it says." Obviously the officers had been brought in from some other part of the state. They didn't know the area, and Ben had not seen them before.

The shorter of the two, labeled OLSEN on his shirt, bagged their evidence, the knife, without touching it. Ben admired the professionalism.

The smelly one burst out with, "You can't treat me like this! I got rights! I'm a citizen, not one a them illegals."

Larrimer grimaced, actually a half smile. "Ya know, I think I've heard that line somewhere before."

"You hit me! I'm suin'!" It sounded more like *shoo-in*.

Ben rather enjoyed this now that it had ended happily ever after, except for his elbow. "I was making an official arrest."

"You're a doctor! You can't arrest me!"

Ben dragged his badge case out of his pocket. Dang, his left elbow hurt! He flipped it open where Larrimer could see it but their perp could not.

The fellow nodded. "This guy walk?"

"Not real steady, but he walks." Ben felt suddenly very, very weary. And the day was still young. "Just get him out of here. Please?" He climbed to his feet and helped the missus to hers. "Let's take your boy into one of the exam rooms and look him over."

"Come with me." Barbara took the mother's arm. "Let's

stop and get some coffee." Her soothing voice helped bring calm to the whole area.

"We'll come back later to get a statement." Officer Jensen moved forward to help haul their prisoner to his feet, reflexively stepped back, steeled himself, and grabbed one armpit. Smelly lurched upright, still breathing fire and smoke. The man was coming up with words Ben hadn't heard since high school.

Larrimer asked, "Gonna check this one out?"

Ben heaved a sigh. "Maybe." The concession was almost more than he could bear. The thought of even touching the scum again made his skin crawl. "After we take care of the boy."

"If we get a call…"

Ben raised his voice. "The boy comes first. Then Mr. Congeniality here, if I get to him. We're a very small facility. He should really be seen in a larger facility. Mayo, maybe. I hear LA has a nice hospital."

Larrimer shrugged and grinned. Jensen nodded. "Good for you."

"I'll bring you coffee if you like," Barbara offered. "No, wait. Why don't you all follow me to the break room and make yourselves comfortable? Coffee and maybe some bagels left. You're going to want to get information from witnesses anyway, right?"

"Thanks, ma'am. You have creamer?"

"Sure do. Real cream, too."

They trooped off toward the break room, and Ben led the boy and his father to the one empty examination room. "I am so sorry. That's the first time we've ever had an incident like that."

"Not your fault," the father answered. "Wish I'd a been able to help you."

Ben cranked the head of the examination table as up-right as he could. "Sir, sit up on the table here so I can see better, and just hold him, snuggle him; no need to try to lay him down. Poor little tyke, he's been through a lot. What were you coming in for?"

The fellow stretched himself out and leaned back to half sitting. "So long ago, I hardly remember."

"I know the feeling." *Boy, do I.* Ben paused to count the child's breaths. Normal. "So you're Robbie."

"Alstrup. Robert Mason Alstrup. I'm Joe. Joseph. His mother is Donna. He has a rash on his chest and belly and was running a temp. We were thinking impetigo at first, but that's mostly on the face, right? I've not seen some-thing like this before, so we tried to get here before the storm."

"Mommy?" It was the first word Ben had heard from the child, since screaming doesn't count. Robbie started to look frightened again.

"Your mommy's getting coffee and she'll be right back." Ben gently touched the swollen face, earning a shriek as Robbie jerked away. "Easy, Robbie, I need to see what's wrong so we can fix it. Let's get X-rays here, just to make sure his facial bones aren't damaged." The swelling was already closing one tear-filled eye.

He lifted the boy's little shirt. Sure enough, the rash his father mentioned. Ben checked the arms and legs. Clear. Only on the torso. And he'd seen it before. "Ever hear of Christmas tree rash?"

"No. Sounds seasonal."

Ben smiled. "Because it sometimes forms a pattern on the torso like a sort of Christmas tree. *Pityriasis rosea* is the medical term. My cousin Tom got it and my aunt was sure he was going to die. It looks gross, but it's harmless. It cures itself and almost never comes back. No good medication for it."

"When? When does it disappear?"

"Usually about three weeks, a little more."

Joe shifted a little. "His mother wants it to go away right now."

"So did my aunt." He checked for broken bones, and Robbie let him. He put on his ears—this stethoscope was coming in handy all kinds of ways today—and listened to the child's chest. Sounded clear.

Barbara entered with two coffee cups in hand and set them on the counter. Donna Alstrup came in right behind her and Robbie instantly stretched out his arms toward her. The momma took her child, and it was obvious that Robbie's world was back on its axis.

Barbara watched for a moment. "The staters are taking witness statements, then they'll take ours. You need cold packs?"

Ben picked up his coffee. "Yes. Is Susan here?"

Joe Alstrup stared at him. "In *coffee*?"

Ben rather liked this guy. Despite watching his son get kidnapped at knifepoint, he was handling the moment really well. "To minimize the swelling on your son's face. He may not like it, but we get better X-rays if there's less swelling." Digital imaging did just fine with swelling. This clunker equipment did not.

Barbara paused in the doorway. "Susan's here. I gave the officers their coffee, too. Our odorific visitor is out in their squad car. Apparently it's against protocols, but they have both front windows cranked clear open. Oh, and I apologized to everyone out front. We have two more patients out there, but they don't seem critical."

"Thanks. Help here, please, while I check on Esther."

He stepped out into the hall, blinked a few times, and blew out a breath before tipping his head back and sidewise.

He stood a moment at the door to the mini surgery before he stepped inside, surveying the mood of the place—more specifically, Esther's mood. She seemed to be doing all right.

An older woman lay on the table, pale, sort of shaking, perhaps Parkinson's.

Esther shook her head. "I could hear some of what was going on but I was busy here. I'm assuming no one was badly hurt. How's the boy?"

Ben gave her a rundown. "Sure glad you didn't try to come out."

"I could tell Barbara meant business when she hollered. I had plenty to do here."

"All by yourself. Sorry." He studied her awhile. She wasn't quite normal, not quite the firm, assured, efficient person he knew. She seemed distracted, hesitant, even frightened.

She tapped an inflatable splint, testing firmness. "She's been unconscious since they brought her in. Her poor body; I'm afraid it's going to give up on her. If only they had found her sooner, there might have been more hope."

"That's not your fault."

"My head knows that but somehow there's a break in communication between my head and my heart."

Maybe that was it. Maybe he was reading too much into her odd behavior, her appearance of fearfulness and sorrow. It made her seem vulnerable. Maybe she was vulnerable. This had been a heavy burden for a physician's assistant, and it wasn't over yet. It startled him to realize that this uncertainty, this vulnerability made her very beautiful. She was a pretty girl anyway, but now she seemed quite stunning.

The deep sadness in her voice made Ben want to wrap his arms around her and get her to cry. Like his mother had always said, God gave us tears to wash away the sorrow. Had God answered the prayers he shot heavenward or...? He moved toward her.

Apparently without thinking what she was doing, she spontaneously moved away from him, keeping the distance. "Dennis keeps telling me this could have been so much worse."

"Yeah, I know." Not that that was any real help right now. "Get you anything?"

"No, but I can't leave her on the table like this without restraints. She might roll off. And what if I need the table for someone else?" She turned her head slightly, frowning. A worried frown. "The ambulance again?"

"We'll see." He let himself out of the room and headed back the hall.

The officers in the break room had finished their coffee and were packing up their laptops. Larrimer said, "Border patrol, huh?"

"And the bad guys tremble in their boots. Where you two from?"

"South of St. Paul. We're part of the emergency forces sent up here to help you folks out."

"Thanks. From all of us. At least the Drop In Café is back in business, so you have a place to eat." He made himself mental note to remind the Alstrups about the café. They must be starved by now.

"We're good. Emergency services has taken over the school, so all us emergency people have food and a place to sleep. School cafeteria food and squeaky cots. What more could we ask for?"

"Lucky you." The whole world could be falling down out there and he'd not have known. He hadn't even called home since arriving at the clinic. *Please Lord, let them be safe.* While the house had withstood the first storm, it could have been damaged enough to... *Don't even think that*, he ordered himself. *Get out to the waiting room and see who needs what.*

"Thanks for your help here." He watched them leave and turned to the next patient as the ambulance burped its arrival announcement.

The place was nearly full again. Where would they put the new patients?

Chapter Thirteen

Flicker.
 Flicker.
Black.

Well, not black everywhere—it was only going on five in the afternoon—but black in Esther's office.

More flickers, the generators coughed and kicked in, and the light came on again. Her computer was dark, of course; it had died with the first flicker. She pushed the START button and sat back, fidgeting impatiently. This desktop had to be at least ten years old, and it took forever to boot up. Clunky computer, clunky generators, clunky X-ray apparatus. She'd had a terrible time getting satisfactory images of little Robbie's bruised head.

The only tiny bright spot, if you could call it that, was that she noticed Ben James repeatedly rubbing his left elbow. So when the Alstrups were taken care of, she made him stick his arm under the beam and get it X-rayed. Bruised, but nothing broken, same as Robbie's skull. But of course, pain was another matter.

Someone thumped on her door and entered before she

could say *Come in*. Chief flopped down in the chair beside her desk.

She nodded. "Chief Harden."

"Esther."

And then she found herself saying, "Paul, you look like death in a thunder mug." She raised her hand to fend off objections and added, "I don't want to check you out. I want real doctors in a real hospital to check you out. And quickly."

"You gave me a physical a couple of weeks ago."

"It was over two months ago, and you had elevated BP and irregular pulse then. It hasn't improved; I can tell by your skin tone."

"Hey, look. If I want to get badgered, I'll go back to my office and let Jenny do it. She's better at it than you."

"So she wants you to get your health looked into, too."

"And Ben James. And Barbara. I'm getting a little sick of it. More than a little. What I came over to ask was, your power just now failed, right, so you're on generator? How's your diesel supply?"

"Good."

"Do you need anything else so far?"

"Not yet, but the night is young. What's going down out there?"

"Usual. Wind, lotsa rain. Incidentally, before you hear it on the grapevine, one fatality so far: George Jacobson, age seventy-one, tree fell on him."

She gasped. "He's my patient! Was. Diabetic; I had him on insulin therapy and an exercise regimen and he was responding beautifully. I'm so sorry to hear that."

"We're all sorry. He left behind a lot of friends. Life-long resident, he and his wife owned Ace Cleaners."

"The one on the mall?" Mall. Five stores and a snow-mobile dealership.

"Yeah." He stood up by leaning on her desk and lurching forward. His skin looked pasty.

"Paul, let me check you now. I mean right now. Things are going—"

"Esther, knock it off! I'm tired, understand? Two killer storms practically in tandem harness. Call us when you need something." He left.

She heard Ben's voice in the hall. The chief shouted, "Will you people cut it out!" so Ben must have remarked on his health, too.

And then Ben cried, "No! Not George!" The chief must have just told him. She got up and hurried out into the hall.

They were standing near the waiting room. The radio on the chief's belt squawked. Esther had trouble understanding radio chatter even when the chatterers spoke plainly, and this radio talk sounded garbled to her. She could not even follow what was going on from the chief's side of the conversation.

"No." He was scowling, and Ben, standing close to the radio with his head cocked, was scowling as well. "No, tell her she mustn't touch the car door. If she touches the metal car door it could fry her. Did you?" Gabble gabble. "No. Ask Jeff; I think he's on. Where's Harry?" Gabble gabble. "No." Gabble. "I'll be there as quick as I can. No, no one else around to take it. Thanks, Jenny." Gabble gabble.

Ben pulled the stethoscope off from around his neck. "I'll go."

"I want you to stay here. I think we need a doctor on this one. Sick kid. Esther, get your traveling bag."

Esther gasped. "I can't leave here! Injured are going to start coming in, like the last time, and—"

"There's no crises here right now and Ben can handle it until you get back. Come on."

Ben spread both hands and took a step back. She interpreted that as "Not worth trying to argue." Ben knew Chief better than she did.

She caved and got her kit. It was stocked. She always kept it stocked, basic medicines, inflatable splints, even a toothbrush, in case she got pinned down somewhere overnight. She followed Chief out to his squad car, the heavy overcast obscuring the border patrol insignia decal on the door. When she tossed her bag in back and slid into the passenger seat, she was wet already, and she hadn't been out in it but for a few seconds. The wind was whistling above the building, thumping something in the rooftop air handler.

They left the lee of the building and the wind hit them full-force, actually moving the car sideways a couple of inches. The windshield wipers splacked frantically and couldn't keep up with it. And the old, familiar horror boiled up inside her as if it were brand new. She was going to have another episode, she just knew it. This was not the time, not the place with a major law enforcement figure seated beside her.

She must focus. But on what? "What's going on?"

"A woman and kid trapped in a car with power lines draped across it. Still sparks and dancing, so they haven't been able to cut the power to it yet. She was told to stay in the car and not touch anything. Always a dicey situation." He fumbled in his shirt pocket, brought out a fresh roll of antacid mints, opened the roll to extract one, and popped it. "She was headed for the clinic. Her kid is having some kind of sickness episode."

I can relate to that. "Did she give any of the child's symptoms?"

"Don't think anyone asked." He turned off onto Sayre Street past a gorgeous little house that Esther always wished she could afford. It was a picture-perfect bungalow with a picket fence and a huge, stately oak tree in the front yard. So cozy, comfortable, inviting. She longed for such a safe retreat where she could withdraw from everything and everybody. But as they passed, she saw a ragged, torn-off oak limb sticking out of the front picture window. It struck her like a punch in the stomach. People injured and dying in these storms, but a tree branch in a window slammed her! How stupid was that?

The chief poked buttons on his radio and picked up the mike. "Hey, Jenny?"

But Esther's mind was now flying in all directions like a flock of frightened birds. George Jacobson. Dead. A former couch potato, he was getting out and walking every day like she had suggested, saying he felt so much better. But what if he was out walking, according to her orders, when the tree fell on him and crushed him? What if she sent him to his death? What if...? Her heart was beating so hard it threatened to bounce out of her chest.

What if Robbie Alstrup's bump on the head caused a brain injury she hadn't caught on the X-ray? Tamponade, contrecoup fracture, all sorts of things go wrong; she could have missed it. What if the olecranon in Ben's elbow was cracked? He could really mess up his arm, permanently mess it up, if it wasn't taken care of. But then, he was able to flex the elbow. He couldn't if it was broken. On the other hand he was one tough dude, maybe he'd just kiss off the pain because he had a job to do. She shouldn't even be practicing when she was this tired, this addled, this terrified. And here she was, out in driving rain and howling wind that threatened to break right through the windshield and attack her, beat her to a pulp, drown her...

Chief roared, "I said, 'Do you think so?'"

"What?" She swallowed. They were miles away from her damaged little dream bungalow, somewhere out along the river road, with trees slamming around overhead. "I—I'm sorry. I was thinking of other things. What?"

To their left, the river was rushing along up to its very brim, thundering and plunging. It threatened to overtop the banks any minute, to swirl out across the road to engulf their car.

"Why someone with Illinois license plates would be out here. It's not even a numbered route. Any guesses?" He popped the last antacid in the roll and tossed the empty foil on the floor.

Something to focus on. "Uh...uh..." *Focus, Esther!* "The bridge on the main road has been out for hours; maybe they were looking for another crossing. Maybe they're just lost."

"Lost! Would you drive a remote, unpaved country road during a storm?"

"Uh...I guess, but only if I knew the area well. But you said Illinois tags. You said they were headed for our little clinic in town here? How would they know about that? Why not the other direction, toward the Cities?"

"Hm." The chief lapsed into sudden, uncharacteristic silence. He swung the car wide of a tree limb on the road, crashed and crunched through its end branches, driving almost automatically.

The river. Look at it! Rushing, roaring, right here. She wanted to curl up in the foot well, to hide from this insanity. Make it quit happening! Make it end! *I can't do this!*

Ahead there, one headlight. A motorcycle? Lightning

flashed. No, not lightning; it was a loose wire flailing and arcing. The tip end of it sparked again, out on the road surface this time.

From the radio speaker, "Chief? She says she sees headlights ahead of her. Could that be you?"

"I only see one headlight in front of me."

"She says her right front wheel is in the ditch."

"Then we're there. Ask her about the kid. And call my cell. I'm hanging up the mike." His eye on the wires along the road, he stopped and parked. His headlights illuminated a little gray car tilted off to the right with its whole right side buried in grass and brush. The hot wire, still flapping wildly about, thunked on its car roof and bounced away. Esther could hear it hit.

His cell phone rang; he already had it out and in his hand. "Jenny!" he barked.

Jenny's voice on the cell was distant but audible and understandable. "She says the child is strapped in the backseat and unresponsive. She can't see the boy and it's dark, she says, except for lightning."

He turned to Esther. "Sit with your heels up on the seat and wrap your arms around your legs. Don't let your elbow touch the door and don't touch the dashboard or anything." He spoke to the phone. "Jenny? She's under a live wire and it's dancing all over. The power is down on our side; the live wire is being powered from the Cotter Crossing substation. Get someone out there now—and I mean *now*—to shut it down. Shut down the whole station!"

"That's not in our county!"

"I don't care if it's in Iraq! Shut it down!" He was sweating and he looked just plain frantic. Suddenly he leaned forward and vomited; he got the steering wheel, his side of the dashboard, and the floor between his feet.

Esther was ready to lose her stomach, too. "What is it? What's wrong!"

He wagged his head. Took deep breaths. Straightened back against the seat. If you didn't notice the roar of the swollen river, or the howling wind, or the stage whisper of wind-thrashed trees, or the rain drumming on the roof, it was quiet. Peaceful, almost.

He took another breath. "My daughter, Amber. Amber Marie. Beautiful girl. Beautiful young woman. Graduated with honors, all set to go to college, be a doctor or something. Loved kids. Then she got tied in with a bunch of yay-hoos over in Duluth. Quit college in the middle of her first semester to run around with them. Here I am heading up an agency where interdiction is a priority, and my own daughter's a drug addict. I told her, 'You're not going to live here until you clean up your act,' trying to force her. Know what she said? 'That's for sure.' Walked out."

"I'm sorry." What else could she say?

His voice was shaky, very unlike him. "I'm law enforcement. I have resources. Traced her car. She sold it in Duluth. Did a trace on her. Last known address is the house where I live." He smirked. "That's what comes of talking shop at dinner, Esther; your kid knows all your methods by the time she grows up. She knew how to disappear."

Esther asked the question she really should not have. "Are you certain she's still alive?"

"Almost got a finger on her in Chicago, but the lead dried up. That was a little over a year ago. No option. I have to assume she's still alive."

"Chica—" Two and two suddenly made four. Chicago. Illinois plates.

He sounded so plaintive, so vulnerable. "That could be her, right there."

Jenny's voice broke the unsilence. "She says she has to get out of the car and come to you. Her baby's having trouble breathing."

"Tell her not to!"

Esther squirmed around and pulled her bag out of the backseat. "Have you noticed that when that live wire jumps, it never comes down in the same place? I'm going to try to get there. Tell Jenny to make sure the woman's doors are unlocked."

He was going to refuse to let her; she could tell. Instead he said, "God be with you."

She grabbed her door and propelled herself out quickly. Driving rain instantly struck her in the face, the drops coming so fast they stung. The wire beside their car lay still. She watched the other, the dancing one, the sparking tip end of it, approached the car in the ditch, still watching.

The car's single working headlight shone pretty much along the roadway, but it was turning yellow as the battery died.

The wire rose ten feet up, like a striking cobra, and slammed down. Esther screamed and leaped straight back. It danced around a bit, sparking. Her rubber-soled shoes were still dry. If they got wet, she could be electrocuted during the next dance. Or if that wire touched her.

She bolted forward, grabbed the door to the backseat, and flung herself into the car. The door slammed behind her. "I'm a doctor."

The driver cried out, "Oh, thank God!" She was sitting on the passenger side.

So well prepared was Esther that she also had a flashlight, one of those little LED things. She flicked it on to see the child. It was a beautiful child, winsome, maybe three years old. He was wheezing so badly he was barely wheezing at all. Even in the sallow LED light, she could see he was blue from lack of air. "Is this a chronic problem?"

"Asthma. Yes. I've never seen it this bad. Is he going to die?"

"Not if I can help it. When did—"

The end of the wire struck the car hood, cannon-loud. Esther screamed and went straight up.

She grabbed a couple of deep breaths. "Sorry. I don't do sudden noises well. When did this episode begin?"

"I don't know. I'm sorry. I just don't know. I've lost track of time and everything else. Hours, but I really can't say how many hours. I'm a bad mother, aren't I?"

"You're a good mother!" She pulled an ampoule of epinephrine and loaded a syringe. "Does the child have a nebulizer?"

"In the trunk. I should have had it up here. But he'd been so good these last few months, no problems; I didn't even think I'd need it, I just keep it in the trunk as a precaution."

"Good foresight. We'll get it later."

Esther's nerves were shot, her mind a train wreck. Could she even do this? She must, so she would. She'd go for subcutaneous first, and if she couldn't manage that, go for intramuscular. She poised the needle, took a deep breath, and pushed. It slid in beneath the skin and she closed the syringe down slowly, slowly, watching; she deliberately inhaled when she realized she'd been holding her breath.

Success.

The mother called, "I can't hear him breathing! Did he die? *Did he die?* Oh, God!"

"God is taking good care of him so far. Yes, he's breathing."

Reason would suggest no one wanted to hear wheezing in a three-year-old, but when the child drew a deep, wheezy breath, Esther rejoiced. He had been so far gone, this was an improvement. He coughed. He spit up. He wheezed some more. Esther whipped out her stethoscope to get vitals.

The driver's voice seemed firmer now, less shrill. "I didn't see that broken line until I was right on top of it almost. It was bouncing around on the road right in front of me and I swerved to miss it. Right into the ditch. I tried to back out and couldn't. Tried driving forward. When I realized I was permanently stuck, I tried my cell. Two bars, enough of a signal to get out. The woman on the desk said she was sending help and told me to stay away from anything metal. Sit on the passenger side; you know, because of the steering wheel. But he was wheezing worse and worse, and I got scareder and scareder. I was about ready to jump out and run with him when your headlights appeared."

And Esther asked what was none of her business. "Is your name Amber Marie?"

"Why did you ask that?" It was a demand more than a question, and a harsh one.

"Just a guess. You heard that the bridge into town was out, so you crossed the river down at Centennial Bridge and came north by the back roads on this side. Then your son had an unexpected asthmatic attack and you had to get to a clinic. Your father last heard of you in Chicago. And here you are with Illinois plates on an unpaved back

road no one but a local would know about; and only a local
would know it's a good way to town on this side."

"So you think you know my father."

"If your father is Paul Harden, yes, I do. He brought
me; he's sitting in that patrol car."

She gasped, drawing in enough air to implode the windows. "Who are you?"

"The clinician. A border patrolman, Ben James, is
minding the store while I'm out here."

"Ben..." She buried her face in her hands. "I should
never have come. This was so wrong. I shouldn't have returned."

The little boy started squirming, so Esther released
him from his car seat. She curled him up and passed him
across the seat back to his mother. She wrapped around
him and he clung to her, wheezing and coughing and crying. The crying eased off. The dancing wire slapped the
car roof. Esther jumped. Her shriek was even louder than
the boy's. He began crying again, sucking in great breaths,
breathing vigorously without realizing what he was doing.

Esther leaned over the backseat and turned the flashlight on him. "Good. He's getting his color back. All the
same, I want him to spend the night at the clinic, please,
just to make sure he's doing well."

"I was going to stay at the Sunrise Motel. That's close
enough to the clinic that I can get there if I have to."

"The Sunrise Motel burned down two years ago. Sus-
pected arson, but never proven."

"Oh." She looked crushed. "Things just keep getting
worse and worse."

Half a mile up the road, the sheets of wild-flying rain
began to glow in streaky flashing red. Esther pointed.
"Look! Reinforcements!"

As the ambulance approached, the rain-blurred flash-ing red lights turned into regular flashing red lights.

That dancing wire lay limp on the road. Dead? Or about to leap up any second to zap someone?

The driver's-side door of Chief's vehicle opened, cream-colored in the yellowing headlight of this car. He stepped out and stood in the road, gripping the door, looking their way. He held his cell to his ear; it made a glowing blue mark on his cheek. He flipped the cell shut; the glow disappeared.

He took two steps forward, hesitated, hung on to the car door. "Amber?"

Esther had guessed it right.

The driver cried out, shoved on her door. It unlatched but wouldn't move, blocked shut by the ditch berm. Frus-trated, she swore and butt-scooted up the seat to the driver's-side door. She shoved it open. "Daddy!" She leaned on the door to keep it open as she crawled out, let it slam shut behind her. "Daddy! Oh, Daddy!"

Leave the child in the car or bring him? Esther thought a moment and decided to bring him. They could tend him in the ambulance. She left her bag in the car, scooped up the little boy, and squirmed out. She ran toward Chief as Amber was also running to him, but not for the same reason. He hung on to the car door without moving, looking ready to fall over. Min-utes ago he had vomited. That said much. Too much. He was in deeper trouble than the child right now, cardiac trouble, Esther was certain, and the big oaf wouldn't even admit it.

Yvette and Dennis tumbled out of the ambulance and they were coming toward Chief, too. At least they had their rain gear on. Esther should tell them to bring a gurney. Esther was instantly soaked to the skin on the windward side; her leeward side was hardly damp.

Amber was soaked through, too, her clothes clinging, her hair stringing down over her shoulders. She sobbed, "Oh, Daddy! I'm so sorry!" And she hugged tightly around him.

He had abandoned the car door and was wrapped around her, both arms. He pressed his head down against hers. "Amber, Amber, I was afraid you were gone. I'm sorry I drove you away, baby. I'm sorry! Please forgive me! Please don't go!"

She said something that Esther didn't hear because she could see Chief's face turned toward her and it seized her full attention. Highly emotional, yes, the facial expression one would expect. But it changed to a shocked expression. He exhaled loudly. His eyes went wide. He sucked air in, a What-in-blazes look on his face. His eyelids dropped to half-mast, his face lost all expression. As if his very bones had suddenly melted, he slid gracelessly down through his daughter's hug, collapsing in a pile on the ground.

Did Esther set the little boy down or simply toss him aside? She didn't remember, she didn't care. She darted forward—"Cardiac! Get the defib! The defib!" She grabbed Chief's ankles and straightened him out, rolled him to his back, ripped his soaked shirt away, the buttons flying. "No!" She screamed it as she tapped his xiphoid process to locate it, centered her palms on his sternum, leaned directly over him to keep his heart going with CPR compressions.

He would not die! He would not! Not now! This was too much! The rain slammed his face, hit his half-open eyes, and he did not close them.

His daughter was screaming "Daddy," shrieking hysterically. Now the little boy was screaming somewhere behind her. Yvette was screaming. Dennis was screaming. She kept up the compressions. She would save him!

He must not die now! Esther must save him. She must! The chest compressions would save him. Dennis was drying off the chief's bare skin over his ribs enough to slap on the patches. He was telling Esther to back off, let the defibrillator do its thing. She must save him!

The mechanical voice was telling them shock was indicated, telling them to stand clear. No! The compressions would save him! She must...!

Dennis had wrapped his arms around her waist; he was physically pulling her off Chief, keeping her from saving him. She fought him. He dragged her back, away, where the pelting rain slammed her and she could not reach Chief to save him. No! No! No! No!

As if at the other end of a tunnel she heard the harsh mechanical voice, the hysterical daughter, the screaming child. She kicked, she fought. He was dying. She had to save him. The rain. The wind. The roaring river. The flashing lights. No!

Her feet touched the ground. She lowered herself, wrapped around herself, pulled everything together, curled up in a tiny knot that the noise and rain and wind could not get into.

"Esther?" Ben's voice. Firm hands held her shoulders; their warmth penetrated her sopping-wet shirt and lab coat.

She was sobbing. She was curled up in the middle of the dirt road in the rain with all the storm noise still around her.

"Esther."

Yes, it was Ben. She uncurled, straightened a bit.

She looked up at his wet face. He was sitting up against her, his legs going in the other direction from hers, his right side pressed close against her right side.

She shuddered and let her head drop against his shoulder. "Why are you out here?"

"Dennis said abandon what I'm doing and get out here now. I'm glad I did."

"But where are they? That's his daughter, did you know that?"

"I know. They're taking Amber and the boy back in the ambulance. You're getting kudos for risking your life—huge risk—to get to the boy in time to save him. They did some blood work on him; he was checking out when you shot him the epinephrine."

"Chief."

"Nothing you or I or anyone in the world could do to save him. Had he been in the emergency room at Mayo when he went down, they couldn't have saved him."

"I'm not going back there. I don't want to go back if Chief's not there." She shuddered again, clear down to the soles of her feet.

"You have to." His voice was steady and very, very sad. "You're the only doctor. No medical examiner. You have to officially pronounce him dead."

Chapter Fourteen

I should have just—just..." Ben wagged his head.

"Just what? Tackled him like you did the meth jerk? We all tried to tell him! He wouldn't listen." Jenny blew her nose again.

Ben stopped his pacing to stare up at the ceiling, hoping to stop the tears. This was almost worse than when his dad died. Chief had been like a father to him, ever since he joined the border patrol. What would they do without him?

"Go on home. Hug that baby." The baby. The bright spot in a black moment.

"What is Amber going to do?"

"Stay at her dad's house. That's what she was hoping to do anyway. How someone as lovely and decent as her got so messed up, I'll never understand. The two of you dated for a while, didn't you?"

Ben nodded. The heady pride of dating the prettiest girl in school burst over him again, of being chosen homecoming king and queen, she with her pretty dress, he still in his football uniform, dirt and all. He'd been the one to break it off, well not really, but when he joined the marines they wrote and emailed for a while, and then he deployed and the relationship faded away. He'd heard she quit school and got married, that she was shooting meth in Duluth, that she was an A student at North Dakota State, that she was hiding from her daddy, that she was traveling. He was halfway around the world with his own things to worry about—like staying alive, for instance, as his comrades in arms died around him. Wondering when the next roadside bomb would go off, whether he would return from his next patrol. He heaved a heart-wrenching sigh. "Make sure someone lets me know if…"

"We will."

"Is someone there with Amber?"

"Her aunt came from out in the country; I think she lives over near Bemidji somewhere."

"And Esther?"

"That shot you gave her knocked her out. I tucked her into bed with her cell phone at hand. I'll spend the rest of the night in her guest room, me and the cat."

"Jenny, you help hold this town together."

"Get outta here." She paused. "You're okay, aren't you?"

Ben snorted. "If you mean will all this knock me back to the bottle, you needn't worry. There's none at the house and if Esther heard I fell off the wagon, she'd take Dawn away from me faster than I could blink."

Jenny shook her head slowly. "Guess that is one of the many things we can be thankful for in all this storm. You are back among the land of the living."

"Yes, Mother."

She threw a pencil at him. "Just make sure you show up at seven A.M. and keep your phone handy. Maybe I should be telling Bo this."

Ben touched two fingers to his forehead in a casual salute and headed for his truck. While it was still raining hard enough that he needed the wipers on high speed, the wind had died to fitful gusts. Doppler showed the storm heading east to torment some other region but lacking the power it had used to slam Pineville.

Why had God taken Chief? But then why did God pick and choose so randomly? That's what it seemed like. Like Allie? But this time the thought of her didn't send him into a towering rage. That was another change. He knew plenty of people were praying the change would be permanent. Instead of driving straight to his house, he turned onto the street that led by Esther's. The porch light was on and a lamp in the living room, but otherwise the house was dark. Should he go check on her? Or leave it for Jenny? He parked across the street to think a moment. She should sleep for four to six hours at least. He checked his watch. Two hours already gone.

Headlights came up behind him and the small SUV turned into Esther's drive, parking. Jenny climbed out, reached back in for a bag, and waved at him.

Ben blinked his headlights and drove on home. Beth had left the light on in the mud room and the light above the stove. Bo met him at the door, tail whipping, and whimpered his delight.

"Yes, I am home, big boy." He leaned over for the requisite face washing and rubbed the dog's ears the way he liked best. "You been taking care of things here?"

"I'm in here, Ben." Beth's voice came from the living room.

Ben hung up his slicker and bent over to unlace his boots, giving Bo's tongue access to his ears. "Okay, that's enough. I'm here." Together they padded into the kitchen, where he glanced at the note on the table.

"Supper wrapped in fridge, just microwave. B."

Ben followed the instructions, feeling the tension of the last hours drain away and quiet peace settling over him. Thank God he still had his home to come back to. So many didn't. Beth and Ansel didn't. Leaning against the doorjamb, he smiled at the picture before him. Beth with a baby blanket thrown over her shoulder and the sounds of a nursing baby loud in the quiet room.

"Everything okay here?"

She nodded. "All is well. Ansel brought a few more things from our house, so that makes it better. They got tarps over most of the damaged roof. He's been out all day volunteering with half of the town. Your sister called, I left a list of messages by the phone."

The microwave pinged, so Ben went for his meal and returned to sit on the sofa near the rocking chair that had been his mother's. "Thanks." He lifted his plate.

"Least I could do."

"Dawn sleeping?"

Beth nodded. "Fed her first. She gets real unhappy when she is hungry and nothing shows up—immediately." She rested her head against the back of the chair. "So what's the news of today?"

Ben flinched. Beth didn't know. "It's bad. A druggie came looking for a fix, held a little boy hostage. We took him down; the highway patrol has him. Various illnesses and injuries, and..." He had to swallow and blink. "And Chief Harden collapsed and Esther couldn't revive him."

"He *died*?" She gaped at him.

"Hugging his daughter."

"*Amber?*" She clapped her free hand over her mouth.

"She was coming back to her daddy and got stuck in a ditch. Not her fault. I mean, not bad driving. She has a son, Beth. Cute little kid. When—"

"Chief Harden has a grandson." She sobbed. "Had one."

"Yeah. When the boy got a severe asthma attack, she nine-one-oned and headed for the clinic. Chief responded, took Esther with him because of the medical emergency. I'm getting all this secondhand from Dennis, but apparently the chief and Amber were in the middle of reconciling when he went down right on the street. And Esther risked her life running past a live wire to get to the boy. Saved him."

Beth was wagging her head. Her newborn squirmed and she mindlessly put the baby to her shoulder and patted, staring at Ben.

"It gets uglier. Esther was giving him CPR when the van got there with a defib, and Dennis had to pull her off him. She went ballistic, then catatonic."

"Esther! Ben, she's so strong and competent...look how she did! And delivered Nathan here. But then, I suppose, losing Chief...Is there something wrong with her?"

"I don't know." He knew, but that wasn't a topic of conversation yet. "I brought her in, shot her with a good sleep aid, and Jenny and Yvette took her home."

Tears bubbled up over the rim of Beth's eyelids and trickled down her cheek. She mopped her face with the corner of the blanket. "He wasn't that old."

"Sixty-four. He'd talked about retirement but we all knew that after his wife died, he'd stay until they kicked him out."

"And Amber came back."

"Apparently, to make things right with her father."

"And you said he died when they were hugging? How awful for Amber!"

"I'll know more when I can talk with Esther." Ben forced himself to eat more of his supper and then took his plate to the kitchen.

She called after him, "Just put it in the sink. I'll take care of it later. When do you report in tomorrow?"

"Seven." He stiffened his elbows, propping himself on the counter's edge. The world was happening way too fast. "Thanks, Beth. Is there anything I can do for you?"

"You already did."

Bo informed him just before the alarm went off that he needed to go outside, so Ben pulled on his bathrobe and complied, and while he was in the kitchen he started the coffeepot. No matter how quiet he was, he seemed to wake Ansel. The temporary housemate blinked his way into the dimly lit room.

"Morning." A yawn split his face. "I didn't even hear you come in last night."

"Making it despite everything."

"Beth told me after she fed the babies. I'm so sorry, Ben. The destruction is bad enough, but to lose Harden this way. Remember when he coached football?"

"And when he took his scout troop on a twenty-mile hike that about killed them." Ben snorted. "We were too tired to sit around the campfire. Soon as the tents were up, we crashed. And I suspect that was his idea all along. He never did like s'mores."

Ansel chuckled, nodding.

Ben leaned at the counter, staring out the kitchen window to see a strip of pale morning on the horizon. It was still raining lightly here, but the front had nearly passed.

"Storm's about over." He paused. It was still too raw. "That man made more of a difference in my life than anyone but my dad. First as a kid, then getting me into the patrol. He never let up."

"Thank God."

"I am, my friend, I am." He opened the window a little to hear better. "Choppers."

"More help?"

"Most likely." A sharp bark at the back door said Bo was ready to come back in. While Ansel went to the door, the coffeepot pinged and Ben poured two cups. Bo parked close beside him and shook. Stupid dog.

"I need to get dressed." He handed one mug to Ansel and took the other with him upstairs. Grateful he'd put in an extra bathroom during one of his renovating times, he showered, shaved, and found two clean and pressed uniforms hanging in the closet. Beth again. One more thing he owed her for.

Having a woman in the house sure made a difference. As he descended the steps, he heard a baby cry, not the newborn from the sound of the wail. Bo appeared at the bottom of the stairs and gave a sharp bark, then hightailed it back to the dining room. Ben headed downstairs just in time to see Ansel picking Dawn up. "I'll feed her."

"You have time?"

Ben nodded. "I'll make time."

"You change her, I'll warm her bottle." They both whispered in the hopes of letting Beth and Natalie sleep.

Jiggling the baby in one arm, Ben headed for the highboy. Bo watched as if making sure he did nothing wrong. This one took a while to clean up.

Ansel handed him a bottle. "Anything else?"

Ben settled himself in the rocker, set the bottle on

the end table between the rocker and the sofa, and got Dawn cradled in his arm, all the while shushing her in a singy kind of voice, one that worked with animals and seemed effective with a baby, too. She latched onto the bottle like she'd not eaten for a day rather than a few hours. "Look at you, beautiful baby. Take it easy so you don't choke."

"Beth says to take it out of her mouth every couple of minutes so she has to slow down. Otherwise, she has been known to puke all over you. If I were you, I'd cover that nice clean uniform with a towel. Hang on, I'll be right back." He returned with the towel and draped it over Ben's chest and knees. "I learned this the hard way."

Ben's phone rang, and he dug it out of his breast pocket. Doing normally two-handed things with only one created a bit of a problem, especially when the hand had to not hold the bottle. He clamped that under his chin, and Dawn wiggled to get the nipple back.

Ansel's laugh didn't help.

He barked at his phone, "Ben James."

"Hope you're all dressed and ready to roll, because we need you here as soon as you can get in."

"Good morning to you, too, Jenny. I'm feeding Dawn but Ansel here can take over. Do I bring Bo?"

"Not right away, but we may need him later. You want me to order you breakfast?"

"Yes, please."

Ansel took the baby from his arms and sat down in the rocker as soon as Ben stood up. "The store's closed. I'll be reporting into the disaster center. Let me know if you want me to bring Bo over."

"Thanks. And tell Beth thank you, too, will you?"

Once in the SUV, Ben hauled in a deep breath. How

would he do all this if he didn't have Beth and Ansel there?

How would the whole town cope? Some of the trees that made it through the first storm had succumbed to the second, the waterlogged ground too soft to hold their roots in place. Houses gaped without windows, and roof shingles lay all over yards and streets. A big oak limb had plowed through the front window of that cute little house on the corner of Sayre Street. Had the river gone over the sandbags lining its banks out through Cherry Valley?

He'd been so tired last night, he'd not listened to the police scanner on the way home. He rather regretted that now. He had no idea what was happening in his world.

But today the skies were clearing, and the golden sun was rising as if the storm had never happened. Rising to remind him that God was still in charge and making sure life continued. Thoughts like that used to come to his mind, but not since the day Allie died. What had happened to him had to be a miracle. Well, that's what his mother would have said. "At least in heaven you don't endure storms like this," he whispered. "You were spared."

Still caught in morning amazement, he swung by the drive-in, grabbed his breakfast in a bag, and drove on to the office. Dread wrapped slimy fingers around his neck. Nothing would be the same without Chief there. Who would take over?

You would think Jordan, the assistant chief, would whether he wanted to or not. He'd only taken his position because Chief badgered him into it. Or would the higher-ups send in someone new? Ben chewed on the last of his potato cake while he parked.

The low brick building had withstood the wind and rain assault, but some of the prettiest trees surrounding the parking lot hadn't. Puddles that looked more like ponds covered half of the asphalt part and most of the graveled section. He thought of driving by the disaster relief center set up at the school but knew he'd better get inside. The tone of Jenny's voice had spelled trouble. Two big Hueys came in low, headed for the temporary landing at the school.

His phone sang the marine hymn, and he recognized Esther's number. "Ben here."

"I should hope so, it's your phone." Gravel peppered her voice. "What in Hades did you hit me with last night? You said it was a muscle relaxant because I was so tense!"

He told her and waited for the explosion. Giving her that sleep aid was a medical no-no. He wasn't qualified to prescribe, not qualified to administer it. He deserved any blistering he got.

No explosion. "Did it really happen?" Her voice rode over the tears he could hear swimming below them. "I mean—it seems exactly like a flashback, not reality."

Ben cleared his throat, hoping to sound firm. "It did. You at the clinic yet?"

"No. I just woke up."

Breakfast sack in hand, he bailed out of his truck and headed around the corner of the building for the front door. He wasn't sure why he didn't enter the back door by the offices, but his feet carried him this direction. "You still there, Esther?"

A big sniff, nose blowing, and she answered. Her *yes* sounded more like a little girl than a grown woman, one who'd saved lives and handled crises; if it wasn't with ease, at least she'd handled them. Despite what was going on in her head. One of these days they would have to talk about that.

The little-girl voice firmed up a bit. "Where are you?"

"Entering headquarters."

"If anyone asks, tell them I'm awake and will be in to the clinic as soon as I shower and dress."

"And eat breakfast and drink some coffee. Lots of coffee."

"Tell Jenny thanks for the fresh coffeepot. And spending the night."

"I will. In fact I just walked in the front door and she's glaring at me now. Bye." He flipped his phone shut and crossed the room.

"Everything all right?" Jenny asked from behind the front counter.

He nodded. "That was Esther." Interesting, she'd never called him before, at least not for a long time. "She's not happy with my medical decision."

"Didn't figure she would be. But ultimately, good decision. I woke up during the night and looked in on her. She looked good. She was sleeping soundly when I left." She raised a finger telling him to wait while she answered a call. She nodded, as if the caller could see her assent. She hung up. "They're gathering in the briefing room, waiting for someone. Go ahead and finish your breakfast." She stopped. "How's our baby?"

His eyebrows climbed up his forehead. This felt amazingly like a normal day in here where nothing looked changed. But there would never again be the normal they had known. "Ansel called her a little pig because she eats so fast. She has the most beautiful eyes." He plopped down on the sofa beside her desk and unwrapped the rest of his breakfast. Bacon egg cheese croissant. Someday he would order his own breakfast—not a bacon egg cheese croissant—but this would do.

"You're getting too attached to her."

"I'm already permanently attached to her. You feed her, change her, dandle her, and you're attached. Trust me on this."

The phone rang and she answered it. What would she have said, had she not been diverted?

Actually, the croissant wasn't bad. He heard the back door slam and people talking as he wiped grease off his fingers with the inadequate little enclosed napkin. He headed down the hall to the conference room with a heavy heart bordering on fear. What would this day bring?

Chapter Fifteen

Esther rifled through a closet even tinier than the one she called her office, looking for a decent lab coat. Nothing. The best she could come up with was blue scrubs. She slipped into the top of a set so that she'd look halfway like a medical person, but she would not wear the baggy pants. She hated those one-size-fits-nobody scrub pants.

More or less in uniform, she walked out to the waiting room. Barbara at the desk was handing forms across to an angry woman. She waved a hand. "Mrs. Applegate and Sarah here are our only patients at the moment."

Time to put on her public face. She smiled. "Hello, Gladys, Sarah." They both scowled at her, but then Gladys Applegate scowled at everyone all the time. She sighed. So it was going to be one of those days. "Show them back to one then, please."

Barbara handed her the folder as she went out. Coffee should be ready. On the way down the hall to the break room, she opened the folder. She was to give fifteen-year-old Sarah a female examination and test for sexually transmitted diseases. That was worth another sigh. She'd rather thought Sarah kept her nose clean.

She swilled some coffee and walked down to one, tapped, and went in. Sarah sat on the exam table with her legs dangling, and scowling Gladys perched rigidly on the front half of the chair.

The world was upside down and skewed, Esther's nerves were on edge despite a night's sleep, and she did not, absolutely did not need Gladys Applegate just now. "Gladys..." She licked her lips. "I'm going to have to ask you to wait out in the waiting room. I'm sure—"

"This is my daughter, and I will remain. I want to know."

"You will know. Your daughter turned fifteen two months ago. Do you remember when you were fifteen?" She did not add, *it was so long ago*. "You would have felt mortified if your mother watched over the doctor's shoulder as she examined your most private parts. I will spare Sarah that embarrassment. Please wait outside. We will then sit down in my office together and discuss the visit."

It would seem that Gladys's world was no closer to upright than Esther's, but with total grumpiness, she left.

Sarah watched the door close. "Thank you."

"Sarah, I'm sorry, but I do have to do the exam. Would you undress, please? Can you tell me why your mother brought you in here?" She pulled on gloves.

"She thinks I'm having sex, why else?" She squirmed out of her top.

"Wait. Let me look at your top half and you can put that back on." No hickeys, no bite marks, nothing sordid whatever. Clean. "Why does she think that?"

Sarah slipped back into her bra. "I got a text message from a boy who wants to date me. She saw it and wigged out. I guess she took it seriously." She pulled her top back on and stood up to remove her panties. "Skirt too?"

"No. Incidentally, it's a really cute skirt. I love that print."

"It's my favorite." Sarah hopped back up on the table with the ease and flexibility only a fifteen-year-old could muster.

"Scoot down a little." Esther guided her heels into the stirrups. She took swabs and labeled them because legally she was obliged to, but it didn't take long. "Thank you, Sarah. You can sit up."

"That's all?"

"The law requires that I must also take blood and urine samples, so I will. But that will be all." Esther stepped back and crossed her arms, suddenly immensely relieved. "Sarah, you are still a virgin. Did you lead your mother on that you were involved with a boy?"

She laughed mirthlessly. "I didn't have to lead her on, Dr. Esther, that's for sure. She assumes stuff, whatever stuff she wants to assume. I don't know how she saw my text message, but that's all she needed. I'm mud now. Dirt. Less than dirt. I'm grounded for the rest of my natural life."

"I'm so sorry for you." Esther peeled off her gloves. "Do boys really text that explicitly?"

Sarah looked at her as if she had just arrived on the planet. "Sure. They want you to get all hot and excited so you go out with them and say yes. They don't know what a big fat turn-off it is. Boys are so dumb."

"And not just little ones, either. Come on. Let's get the fluid samples over with." The boys she had to work with, too. Dennis, calling Ben in, Ben putting her to sleep against her will, so to speak. Chief dying against her wishes. All of them.

"Dr. Esther? What does Mom mean, she's sure that the rabbit died?"

Fifteen minutes later, Esther ushered Sarah and the scowling Gladys Applegate into her office and closed the door. Ever since the first storm arrived and she managed to intubate Ben's baby, she had felt intense terror, worry, frustration, doubt—you name it, she carried it. But her burden seemed to be congealing now into a single big blob of intense anger. Was that good or bad? Who knew. But she was furious at her co-workers, and angry now at Gladys. She knew all about Gladys's negativity; her own mother was too much like that. And she no longer cared about making nice.

"Please be seated."

Gladys plopped into Esther's chair. "She's pregnant, isn't she!"

Esther perched on the desk corner. "Are you familiar with the term *anointing the stick*, Gladys? It replaced dying rabbits thirty years ago. Today's pregnancy tests are quite accurate, and I can tell you positively, your daughter is not pregnant. I'll tell you something else: She has never had sexual intercourse. Never. Her hymen is intact; rather tight, actually; her first few times will be painful."

Sarah turned a bit pink and tried to hide her smile. She was obviously relishing this. Curiously, so was Esther.

Gladys fumed, "You can't say that for certain!"

"I can! I just did. Now let me tell you something else. My own mother accused me of things I did not do, and then she assumed I did them. I know what my feelings were, the deep sadness and anger at my own mother's distrust, the injustice. Injustice is especially painful to young girls. I cannot imagine that you would hurt your child that badly, to cause those feelings in her. She is a delightful young woman worthy of your trust, and you do this to her! I'm furious with you. I'm sure that's not what you came here to hear, and that is exactly why I am furious. Please go home and figure out how to apologize to your daughter. It wouldn't hurt to take her out for ice cream, either. Let her explain to you about today's teenagers, and sexting."

Gladys leaped to her feet and Esther braced for the howling diatribe sure to follow. Instead, the office door popped open.

Dennis stood there and his face went blank. "Oops! I'm sorry; didn't know it was a conference. Esther, people here to see you."

"And I want to see you. Gladys, Sarah, will you excuse me, please?"

She marched out, grabbed Dennis by the arm, piloted him into the break room, and shut the door. "Why did you call Ben last night? You should never have done that!"

"Because I was scared!" He came right back at her, nose-to-nose. "Really scared! Here you are, pumping away with CPR and I'm trying to get the defib on him, and you knew darn well if the defibrillator jolted him while you were touching him, you'd get zapped, too. You knew that! Especially in the rain! And when I pulled you off him, you curled up on me. Plop! I didn't know what to do. Nobody knew what to do, so I called Ben. Even if he didn't know what to do, he can think on his feet." His voice rose. "Esther, nobody knew how to help you!"

Nobody knew how to help you. That fury that tasted so delicious instantly evaporated.

From the hallway, Yvette called, "They're here!"

She frowned. "Who's here?"

"Dr. Livingston and Dr. Ho."

"What do they want? Why now? It's over..."

"You'll have to ask them." Dennis even held the door for her.

They were setting up something in the mini surgery, she couldn't tell what. Several large white metal cases on wheels stood open. Dr. Ho was frowning as he looked around. "There she is. Hello, Esther. I didn't realize your facilities were so primitive."

"And this is our most modern room. Hello, Dr. Ho. It's good to see you." She extended her hand for a shake. *Maybe it's good.* "And Dr. Livingston. Welcome back." She shook with the military hospital director also.

"Here's the buckets." Dennis sat half a dozen big white plastic painters' buckets inside the door and left.

The doctors returned to their busyness, laying instruments out on the counter beside the table. Heavy-duty instruments—a big, coarse bone saw, some chisels, big scalpels and scissors, and nothing sterilized. Germs up the kazoo and apparently no one cared. She was about to ask what was going on, but for some reason, she suddenly knew. Her stomach did a little flip, and that feeling of terror snuck back in.

Dr. Ho slid his arms into a smock, so she tied the strings in back for him as he tied Dr. Livingston's. Neither put on a surgical mask.

She looked from face to face. "Why?"

Dr. Ho studied the floor a moment. "Esther, you're a brilliant woman. You excelled in medical school, top of your class as a PA. You're quick and analytical. For example, we didn't have to tell you just now why we're here. You know."

"But I don't know why."

"That's what I'm telling you. You're too good a doctor to lose. I phoned your assistant, Barbara, on a routine matter, and we talked about you some. You see, Dr. Livingston and I both understand about PTSD. We've seen it a hundred times."

"A thousand times, in my case; I'm a military doctor," Dr. Livingston chimed in.

Dr. Ho nodded. "A common part of post-traumatic stress disorder is the feeling that it's your fault. Had you acted differently, done differently, tragedy would not have happened. The chief of the local border patrol facility died in front of you last night. We want to find out why."

All the thoughts and images came flashing back. "Why here?"

"This is not a formal autopsy, nor will it be thorough. And it's easiest done here, since the funeral is scheduled for tomorrow."

"Sort of off-the-cuff?" She watched them nod. "And your reason for wanting to know...?"

"If it were negligence on your part, we want to know that, of course. But we don't think it is. We want to be able tell you authoritatively that it was not your fault, and there was nothing you could have done. To do that requires an autopsy."

Yvette stuck her head in the door. "He's here."

"Thank you." Dr. Livingston smiled at her. The door closed.

He continued, "Esther, I was very positively impressed by your handling of this facility under combat conditions. And the grace with which you let me step in to help. I called Dr. Ho here to congratulate him on his brilliant PA and we got to talking about you. We've decided between us that you have some serious problems, but they're not insurmountable. Get you past them, and you'll not only be a splendid doctor, you'll be a much happier person."

"All that from an off-the-cuff autopsy."

"This is step one." Dr. Ho smiled. "Besides, I'd like to know. It's actually fairly rare that someone just drops like that."

Obviously, this was all going to go down whether she wanted it to or not. People higher and stronger and more authoritative than she had just taken over her domain, her life, her destiny. She was not in control anymore, not that she'd ever been.

She opened her mouth to speak but her thoughts were too weird, too jumbled. "I don't know what to say."

"For starters, tell us whether you want to be present when we work on him."

She thought about that a moment, and they gave her the space. "I've worked with people doing autopsies, and I've studied cadavers. But no one I knew. But...close. The whole town was close to Chief. We all worked so closely with him. I—I don't think so. Too close." Why did she keep saying *close*? Why couldn't she be more articulate?

Dr. Livingston nodded. "Right choice, I suggest. But we wanted it to be your choice, not ours."

"What do you want me to do?"

"Go have a cup of tea, or a sandwich with Barbara, or wander down to the pool hall and shoot a few rounds of snooker. Kick back, if you can."

Right. Just relax. "Thank you." She stepped outside and closed the door. Their beloved Chief was about to be hacked up in an autopsy and she was told to relax.

Yvette and Dennis were standing back by the double doors. They watched her leave and wheeled a covered gurney into the hall. Outside under the roof, the funeral home's only hearse was parked.

She was going to slip past the waiting room, but Barbara called her name.

As she detoured to Barbara's desk, she saw Mr. Aptos come hobbling up the front walk toward the door.

Barbara was smiling broadly. "Sarah Applegate asked me to tell you you're the coolest doctor in the whole world, and she's going to go to medical school and become one like you."

Esther smiled despite herself. "When you see her, tell her I'm flattered." She strolled back to the break room and the coffeepot. The junk-food and soft-drink dispensers had not yet been replaced. They stood smashed and mute and quite dead. But someone had left a big, open box of doughnuts on the counter; on the lid was scribbled FREE TO A GOOD HOME.

She replenished her coffee mug and chose a maple bar. It was fresh and soft and puffy and oh, so tasty. She savored that first big bite.

"In here." Barbara opened the door, and in came Mr. Aptos. He was just as shaky and spidery as ever, but there seemed to be a grim determination about him that Esther had not seen during the storm.

He smiled. "Mornin', Doc." He raised a hand. "Not here as a patient this time. Feeling good for once."

"Glad to hear it." Esther stood quickly and put on her please-the-people smile. "Would you like coffee? And we have doughnuts."

"Sure. May I sit?"

"Of course!" Esther poured him a mug of coffee. "Milk? Sugar?"

"Sugar. You wouldn't know that, of course. But when I

was in here during the storm, Ben brought me coffee, and
he remembered about the sugar. From years ago."

She set the coffee and sugar before him. Not exactly
fancy: a cottage cheese carton. But sugar. She simply set
the whole doughnut box on the table. Let him choose.
She sat back down across from him.

He picked a maple bar, too. He too seemed to relish
that first heavenly bite. "Fine young man, Ben James.
His grandpappy and me were best friends, I watched him
grow up. He joined the marines; changed some when he
got back, seemed darker. But still the fine, caring fellow
he'd always been. So sad about his Allie."

And his chief. But she said nothing. *Yes, I suppose Ben's
a fine man. His dog likes him. And so do I.* That unexpected thought struck her oddly.

"You only been here what, couple years? I lived here
my whole life, except two years in the army and four years
in teachers' college. Never ever saw a storm like this one,
and then another hard on its heels." He wagged his head.

What to say? "Many people are saying that."

He nodded. "A doozy, all right. Double doozy. You
don't know this, I'm sure; not many people know this.
Not even Ben, I don't think. But after I retired, everyone
said I oughta get a hobby, so I took up investing. Figured
out what the *Wall Street Journal* is saying when it quotes
stock, you know, those pages of tiny print." He snickered.
"Bought myself a pretty strong magnifying glass, too.
Picked out some stuff I figured might grow—none of
that dot-com baloney. Real companies. Worked out pretty
well. Got myself a nice little nest egg. But then my lady
died and I kinda lost interest."

"It sounds like a good hobby, though." That sounded
lame even as she said it.

"Well, here's this power outage, and I'm sitting in my chair and the TV set's black, and I'm thinking, I'm old, my lady, she's gone. Why not just lie there and let death take me? Not something I'm afraid of. But then a neighbor dropped by and called an ambulance. And once I started feeling better I saw the conditions you people were working in. It's a disgrace!"

"I've rather thought that, too."

"I know. You've put together all the plans, the paperwork, we all—the whole town—know how hard you worked to get a decent hospital in here. Maybe not a hospital exactly, but a sound building with good equipment, plenty of supplies, and room to work. Even in a major emergency. A fine clinic people can be proud of."

She nodded. "That's my dream."

"Mine too. I'm asking you to gather them all up, the plans and prospectuses you think will work best, and have them ready. You know, I didn't think much about it until those kids—you know, Genevieve Schumacher's boy— with the ambulance hauled me in and you people took such good care of me even when you didn't have anything decent to work with." He straightened, beamed. "And that, Miss Hanson, is why I'm going to sue the town."

They held Chief's funeral in the almost-new St. Mark's Episcopal Church, not because he was Episcopalian—he was not—but because it was the biggest sanctuary for miles around and could hold the most people. Also, it had a dandy closed-circuit television system that could carry the service to overflow crowds in the parish hall and to the Lutheran church right next door. Still, the seating space was not enough, and mourners filled the Lutheran church and stood out in the courtyard.

When Jenny mentioned the viewing beforehand, Esther came early just to see; yep, his casket was open. How... She paused before him far longer than expected, searching for marks from the autopsy. There were none. Wait. Above his hairline there, the skin had been laid back and reattached with staples. You would never notice if you didn't know. And with a demure silk coverlet up to his armpits, his hands neatly folded, they didn't have to be careful about breaking apart his rib cage. She hurried out back, barely making it to the peony bushes before she threw up.

She really should go back in. She walked around to the front in order to enter the back of the sanctuary and just stand there against the wall near the door, not letting all those people crowd in too close to her.

She paused out front, for here came Ben, dressed in his class A uniform, military creases in his shirt and his real gold badge (probably brass, but it looked gold), not the fabric sew-on of the field uniform. She found herself thinking, *Oh, man, he looks good!* She didn't say it aloud.

He stepped up beside her. "You doing okay so far?"

"So far."

"I heard about the autopsy. Dennis called me and I came in, talked to the two doctors awhile. They're calling it medical research. I guess it is."

"At least we know how he died." She could feel the terror mounting. She desperately wanted to get out of here and she desperately wanted to stay.

"And I hope you realize now that there was not a thing you could have done to prevent his death or delay it. Nada. Scientifically proven; autopsy by two qualified doctors."

She nodded. Why did people keep harping on that? "You told me that on the night he died, remember? When you sat with me. How did you know? Or did you just guess?"

"Almost always, when a person just drops like that, he's gone. I didn't know then, no. Guessed. I was saying anything I could think of to keep you from blaming yourself."

"How did you know I'd blame myself?"

"'Cause I do it all the time."

She snorted. "Well, I still do. If only I'd insisted he come in for a check."

He gripped her upper arms and turned her to him, eye-to-eye. "Read my lips. He had two simultaneous events going on, a coronary occlusion *and* an aortic aneurysm. The aneurysm took that moment to burst. End of story. Unless you had big-city imaging equipment, there was no way you could have found them ahead of time. They are completely invisible to external examination." He spaced his words carefully. "There is nothing you or I could have done, even if we had gotten him onto the examination table." He stepped back.

She was on the verge of losing it, she just knew.

His voice softened. "Barbara mentioned Bill Aptos was in to chat."

A change of subject, and just in time! She nodded. "He's going to sue the town and the clinic."

Ben's mouth dropped open. "What...why..." He licked his lips. "So what did you say?"

"Nothing, as it turned out. I gasped so loud I sucked in some doughnut crumbs along with the air and couldn't quit coughing."

He laughed, a welcome, delighted laugh, and then the organ began its soothing dirge, so they walked inside. Part of her wish was granted. Standing room only and they couldn't even move aside from the aisle.

Some patients, many strangers. Well, strangers to her, but probably not to Ben. He nodded recognition to several in the immediate neighborhood.

The huge room was furnished with many curved rows of pews that focused on a broad stage one riser high, low enough to be easy to step onto, but high enough to elevate the speaker or choir or whatever was up there. The casket was up there now, covered in sprays of flowers with more flowers and potted palms artfully placed all around.

The funeral proceeded as such things do, she supposed; Esther had not been to many. Three pastors presided, the chief's border patrol chaplain, a rickety old fellow who was apparently a former pastor, and a fellow whom the program described as his current pastor.

And then the current pastor, whose name she forgot, made a dreadful mistake. He opened the mike to the audience. Young men in black suits ran up and down the aisles with cordless mikes, passing them to people here and there who stood up to extol the chief's virtues, as if no one knew about them.

And there was spidery old Mr. Aptos down near the front row, and he was handed the mike. He turned and stepped onto the stage. "Harry!" He pointed to one of the councilmen. "Sam!" To another. He loudly named all five. "If you had acted when Dr. Hanson first started pressing this medical clinic thing, a dozen people would still be alive now, possibly including Paul Harden here. But no. You didn't want to spend the money. Well, folks, you're going to spend money now, because I am suing you and this town for negligence, breach of trust, and culpability in the death of Chief Harden. There's one way you can avoid paying legal costs for the next ten years. You can build a hospital now, and I mean now, no stalling. Now!

I am hereby donating the first million dollars toward its construction, but only if the foundation is laid in the next ninety days."

One of the councilmen leaped to his feet. "You're a retired teacher! You don't have a million dollars! This is a funeral for a respected friend and you're trying to turn it into a political rally."

Mr. Aptos pointed. "Lars, you're the bank manager. Do I have a million dollars?"

He stood, his voice loud and clear. "You have far more than a million dollars, Bill." Then the fellow identified as Fred jumped up. "Don't you threaten us, you old coot! It's the county's responsibility."

Mr. Rustvold stood up. Esther knew he had been a math teacher or some such. And he was at the clinic during the storm, she remembered. "County be hanged. They have their regional hospital in Bemidji and they aren't interested in us. I say it's past time for us to do something, and the proof of it is lying in that casket."

"Well, lawsuits aren't going to help anything." Esther couldn't see who that was. "It just lines the lawyers' pockets!"

Someone else shouted, and others called out, waving their arms to be heard. The noise was reaching cast-of-thousands proportions.

And then Ben suddenly changed. Esther could not explain it, even to herself, but one moment he was a gentle, caring man and highly attractive escort, and the next he was a formidable law enforcement officer ready to quell a riot. He stood straight and tall, and he went for his baton at the small of his back. He was nodding toward another border patrolman nearby. The fellow nodded back and they moved forward down the aisle, pushing aside people who stood in the way. And there were two other officers in the next aisle, and...

Esther wheeled and shoved her way out the glass doors. She ran down the walkway, away from the screaming, shouting, yelling hubbub of the funeral of the man she had held so dear.

Chapter Sixteen

"Those old codgers certainly went at it." Ansel didn't sound like he was too thrilled with old codgers. He tossed some popcorn in his mouth and picked up his drink.

Ben nodded. What could he say? What should have been a time of remembering Chief's life and service to the town had turned into a screaming match.

"Can you believe that Mr. Aptos? Suing?" Beth chimed in. She kept her rocker moving with one foot while nursing Nathan and joining in the conversation.

Ansel shook his head. "I had no idea he had that kind of money stashed. A million bucks to give away? They were teachers, for pete's sake. And Rustvold's almost as wealthy. How did they do that?"

"Maybe we should have him take us all back to school, this time on life and wealth management." Ben shifted Dawn from his shoulder to the crook of his arm, who now that she had a full belly was half asleep. So was he. This had been some day.

"Ben, something's been bothering me. I hate to bring it up but..." Beth who rarely appeared hesitant, was.

Ben shrugged. "Put it on the table and let's deal with it."

"Has Esther said anything to you about Dawn and social services?"

That slimy hand he was coming to know so well clenched his stomach. "Why? She said I could have Dawn if I didn't drink anymore."

"That sounds wonderful, but when we looked into maybe becoming foster parents, I learned quite a bit about the system. I think she, as a medical person, is legally bound to notify social services if a baby is abandoned and she learns of it."

"What can they do to her?" Ansel asked.

"Do you mean Dawn or Esther?" At his shrug, she continued. "They might be able to revoke her license. This ward-of-the-court thing is pretty serious in case the mother ever shows up demanding her baby back."

"But the mother abandoned her. She didn't even give her to someone, just left her in the woods. What kind of a mother was she?" Ben's voice rose; Bo's ears pricked, and he looked about to rise. "It's okay, fella, some things just get under my collar." Bo laid his muzzle back on his front paws.

"Like you said in the beginning, she probably was given no choice." Ansel always had been a voice of calm, even when they were growing up.

Right now calm was not on Ben's list. He was living up to his part of the bargain. He wasn't drinking and he had help. "Who would I talk to?"

"I guess if it were me, I would wait it out. Maybe I'm barking up a tree that got blown down in the storm. It's just been on my mind. Far as I'm concerned, she's part of the family. I know God has a plan for this but..." Beth wagged her head.

"But He's not given you written instructions—personal ones?" Ben's comment brought back youth group discussions from when they were all teens. Amazing how they thought they knew all the answers then. Until life got in the way.

"No, but He does promise to guide all our steps if we seek His will."

He wished she'd left off the end of that sentence. Ben knew when he quit trusting God. The day Allie last said she loved him. She went home. How many times he wished he could have gone, too. "I better get to bed. I'll put her down first." He stood up with the baby he considered his daughter and held her close, safe, hands cupping her head. Beth had tied a tiny pink bow in Dawn's sparse hair, right on top of her head. Her little round face with the tiny nose, the dark eyes that sparkled when she was happy, but were now softly closed in sleep, made him want to protect her from anything else happening to her. What a miracle that she was alive. He laid her down in her crib and covered her with the fleecy blanket Jenny had bought for her. *He must love you an awful lot to keep you alive, little one. Or have great plans for you.*

Bo sat right at his leg, looking from the baby to Ben and back again.

"Yeah, you take care of her, big dog." Ben rubbed the black ears, and Bo leaned against his leg. "Like Mom used to say, 'God only knows what's coming next.' That's for sure." He turned and left the room, hitting the switch on his way out and leaving the door partially open. "Lord God, please don't let anyone take her away. You can't be such a cruel jokester as that."

Of course, evidence such as Chief's death and Allie's might suggest otherwise. Friday morning he had to force himself into the office—for two reasons—first of all, no Chief, and second Samuel Perowsky, the man they'd sent as a temporary replacement. He had better be a short temporary before everyone threatened to walk out. Any other "Samuel" would be "Sam" five minutes into his job. Not this one. He wasn't even Perowsky. He was *Chief* Perowsky, pronounced *per-OAV-skee*, not *per-OW-skee*. Maybe he just needed to be taken down a peg or two. Acting like he'd been sent to the armpit of the border patrol wasn't scoring him any points. Within an hour of arriving, he had made no secret of the fact that he wanted to be back at headquarters and away from here. *May his wish be granted.*

Why they'd not given the job to John Jordan, the second in command while Chief was here, was beyond Ben.

He was still pondering this mystery as he and the others gathered to be given the day's assignments. No one was asked if he or she had a preference. The jobs were dished out arbitrarily without regard to anyone's strengths or weaknesses. His duty regarding morning assignments completed, Perowsky left the room and the rest of them swapped eyebrow-raised looks. Half of them would go out on patrol, and half would assist the local public safety agencies in checking on farms and houses outside of town, since everyone within the town limits was now accounted for.

Ben was on the assistance half. He loved patrolling.

He asked no one in particular, "Has anyone talked with the Army Corps of Engineers lately?" and got a chorus of responses.

"Not since I heard they were going to install a temporary bridge."

"That sure will make life easier."

"I hear they're doing it because the corps boys need the practice, not because they want to make our lives easier."

"Gonna be a pontoon bridge. Any of you guys ever cross a floating bridge?"

"I hear they got floating bridges around Seattle someplace. Sounds kinda wobbly to me."

Ben left the others to their speculations and stopped by Jenny's station to see what she'd been hearing, not just about bridges, but about everything. Their regular dispatcher, Ada, was working 911, and Jenny seemed to be on the phone a lot taking calls from people checking in or asking questions. Ben waited until she finished a call. "Anything we need to know?"

That seemed to be one of Chief Perowsky's favorite sayings: "A need-to-know basis." Stark contrast with Chief's "Let's throw it all out here and brainstorm." Far as Ben was concerned, anything going on in town should be everyone's need to know. Well, mostly.

She sat back. "You can cross the Rusteads out on Timber Road off your list. That was him just now, and he says they are fine. Lots to repair, but people and animals secure. He said he surely won't lack firewood this year and I should let him know if I hear that anyone's looking for some. Here's the list of folks we heard from." She handed him two pages.

Ben tapped his upper lip with a finger. "All that wood getting cut up. Not just Rustead's. I mean everyone in town seems to have at least one tree down. Who gets it?"

"They'll dispose of it somehow, I'm sure. Landfill, I guess. The big question is who's going to cut up all those trees. The line crews don't have time, and the town maintenance crews are busy doing things like reinventing washed-out streets."

"The football team is always looking for moneymakers.

What if they do the cutting and sell the firewood? They could take truckloads down to Grand Forks and sell it there."

"And cheap to anyone in town here who wants to buy it." She cackled with delight. "Not only that, our football heroes want strong muscles, and that'll sure build muscles. Great idea!"

"I'll call Coach and suggest it."

"And I'll call Andy Anders, head of the parent support group."

Ben gave her a thumbs-up sign. "Any other changes on this list?"

"Not that I know of. Will call if I hear."

"You heard from Esther?"

"Not yet this A.M. You want her to call you?"

He shook his head. He should probably drop by Chief's house and see how Amber was managing. She'd looked pretty frazzled, not to mention angry, after that fiasco during her father's service. But then she looked kind of worn anyway, as if she'd aged twenty years instead of the ten or so since he'd last seen her. If half of what he'd heard about the way she was living was true, no wonder she looked so old and worn.

Missing his furry partner, he headed east of town to his assigned area. Stop at farms, knock on doors, chat with the folks, leave notes on kitchen tables when no one was home. Remarkable how few people locked their doors.

He had two more farms to check, but instead of turning south as per assignment, he stayed on the main road to the river and the no-longer-functional bridge, and he had no idea why. As he left the road and pulled up near the shore, men in fatigues and hard hats were standing on the bank, pointing to something in the flood and gesturing.

Ben parked his SUV and climbed out. "What's up?"

One of the men turned, but Ben could see it, too, the mud-covered roof of a van. It had drifted against a fallen tree, trapped in the waving limbs. Only the roof stuck out; water swirled past it almost to the tops of the windows. "Someone's car got washed away? Hello, Abe."

"Ben. Good to see you again." The stocky fellow snickered and added, "In a non-competitive environment." They shook. Abe Higgins. Seeing him took Ben way back.

One of the others asked, "You two know each other?"

"Casually," Ben explained. "Players on rival football teams. I quarterbacked the victorious Pineville Eleven, and he scored the only touchdown for the Fillmore Eagles."

The former tight end grunted. "Crooked refs, or we woulda won. I called the highway patrol. We'll need a tow truck to winch it out."

"Or something bigger. If it's full of water it'll weigh a ton. Anyone been out to see if someone is in it?"

"Not yet. We just spotted it half an hour or so ago. Probably been in the water since the storm, think? Maybe came downriver before the water rose too high to let it go under the bridge."

"Hm." Ben shook his head. "The patrol office hasn't received any reports of someone going off the bridge." *But then, we are now on a need-to-know basis. We might not have needed that tidbit of information.*

"Think the river current could have moved it clear down from Baker's Ford?"

"Floods do strange things."

A state trooper stopped on the other side of the river and got out. Ben knew him. He flipped his radio to local. "Hey, Leroy? I'm surprised you're still here."

Leroy Larrimer radioed back, "So am I, but there's still a lot to do here. Another week at least, the boss says. Your tow truck is on the way."

"We're glad to have you." Ben meant it, too. He turned to Abe. "We should go out there. If there's anyone in it, we'll need to call in forensics."

Warren nodded. "I'm way ahead of you, hotshot. Called a fishing buddy; he's bringing his inflatable. Uses it for walleye fishing. Billy can catch walleyes like you wouldn't believe. You want fresh walleye, just ask Billy; he'll get you some in no time, in season or out of season." He stared at the roiling brown water awhile. "Never seen the river this high or for this long."

"Me neither." Why did that submerged van hold such fascination for him? Ben was not sure, but he couldn't pull himself away. Crazy. Or God speaking?

Behind them, a dark red pickup left the road and came lurching over to the riverbank. The bulging sides of an inflatable boat stuck out of the bed. The driver got out. Were he from the Deep South he would be the perfect Good Ole Boy, complete in overalls. He grinned hello to Abe, grasped his boat by a built-in loop in the bow, and hauled it out. It plopped to the ground with a bouncy *fwupp*, and he dragged it down to the water. He returned to the truck bed and lifted out a small electric fishing motor.

From across the river, Leroy radioed, "Hey, James. You know this river?"

Ben thumbed his radio. "I was born and grew up here. This was our playground."

"So did I," said Abe. He looked at Ben. "Wanna go out with us?"

"In a word, yes." Ben whipped out his cell and pushed

the speed dial for the office. When Jenny answered, he told her what he was doing and where.

She responded, "A drowned vehicle. We haven't had any missing persons calls. If there's someone in it..." Her voice trailed off.

"I'm going out with some others in a Zodiac, so I'll let you know. It's closer to the other bank than to our side, hung up in a sifter. Highway patrol is there."

"Be careful!"

He was going to say, *Yes, Mother*, but he didn't. With the river running this fast and high, there was in fact a strong element of danger.

Billy mounted his little trolling motor, and Abe and Ben climbed in. They each took an oar, Abe on the right (starboard, Ben knew, but no one used *port* and *starboard* around here) and Ben on the left. The puny electric motor screamed, maxed out, but it could not keep the inflatable going in the right direction. Grimly, Billy turned and headed upstream, hugging shore on this side. "You guys steer."

He sure knew his boat. He kept going against the current, close to shore, for what Ben would have thought was way too far a distance upstream. Then he headed out toward the middle. The motor howled, trying unsuccessfully to make way upstream. The best it could do was slow their downstream slide. As the inflatable strained to go forward and instead drifted back, Ben and Abe dipped their oars, twisting them, plunging them, sculling, keeping the front end headed upstream, edging the boat closer to the other shore. Ben was sweating profusely and his shoulders ached. If they missed the van they'd have to do this all over again, and he—

"Got it!" Abe yelled triumphantly. He was leaning over

the side, gripping the van's roof. "The driver's-side window's wide open. Slipperier'n snot! Gimme your anchor, Billy!"

He hooked the anchor into the steering wheel, and the inflatable and van were firmly attached to each other. "Now what?" He looked at Ben.

"Sit and breathe awhile. That was some heavy lifting."

Two highway patrol cars were parked on the bank now, and Ben could hear the tow truck coming. Billy cut his motor and handed Abe a big sponge. Warren began wiping mud off the driver's side of the windshield.

Ben grabbed onto the van's door frame, fighting to keep the Zodiac steady. "See anything?"

Abe shook his head. "Not yet. Billy? Got a flashlight? Too dark to see in there. Once we get it closer to shore and get a door open, we can drain out some water."

"Hey! Can one of you hook the winch on?" Larrimer called.

"Not without getting real wet and muddy," Billy grumbled. "Be nice if they'd call for a diver. Prob'ly didn't."

Ben felt an urgency that matched his fascination. What was going on here? He yelled, "Gimme the winch!"

Larrimer paid out twenty feet of cable, arched back, and tossed with all his might. The winch hook thunked on the van roof and Warren grabbed it. He passed it to Ben.

Ben wrapped the other end of Billy's anchor line firmly around his wrist, a casual and probably useless safety gesture, and slid into the muddy, clammy water. The current pulled on him, but he worked his way forward. Why was he doing this? *Wait for a diver, stupid.* He couldn't wait. He managed to hook into the front bumper. The truck winch groaned, made all the weird, grinding noises winches make, but it drew the van a third out.

Ben waved *stop!* He repositioned the hook around the axle and sloshed up onto the bank. Larrimer reached out a hand and pulled him to standing. Together they watched the mud-coated van rise by jerks out of the river, an inert, slimy, unthinking monster.

"We've not had any missing persons reported." Ben watched the monster come to a soggy halt, dragging Billy and his boat along with it. "You?"

Leroy shook his head. "None here. You border patrol guys would be seeing more unidentified persons than the rest of us."

"True, we do, but they usually don't come floating down the river to us."

"Gift-wrapped in mud." Leroy scowled. "I got a bad feeling about this."

"Sure hope there ain't anybody in there." Billy stared rapt at the van.

The ugly-sweet smell of putrefaction dashed Billy's hopes, his and everyone else's. Abe the former football player managed to wrench a back door open. He leaped aside as water cascaded out, then Larrimer looked inside.

Pale and shaken, he stepped in beside Ben. "Three bloated bodies. Nothing worse than dead bodies soaked in water for days. Nothing. I'll call in forensics." But the other patrolman was already on the radio to his headquarters.

Ben walked over and used Billy's sponge to clear off the license plate. "Want to run it or shall I?"

"I can do it."

There was nothing in the whole wide world that Ben wanted to do less, but he crossed to the open door to look more closely, and in the process learned that he could be soaked to his armpits in muddy water and his flashlight still worked. Larrimer peeked over his shoulder.

He turned away before he lost his stomach.

Larrimer mused, "Two Asian women in the backseat still have their seat belts on. Looks like the third tried to climb over the seat back into the backseat. Why would she do that? No driver." He scowled at Ben. "Speculations?"

Ben's head was as upset as his stomach. But the picture became clear. "Remember the pictures of that Sendai tsunami, and the cars floating?"

"Can't forget it." Larrimer took on an *aha!* look. "They floated slanting, nose down; the motor weighed the nose down. This van was carried away in the flood. It floated for a short time but slanting down in front. She was climbing into the backseat because water was filling up the front. So she must have been the driver."

"I doubt it. If she rolled down the window, she'd escape that way. I vote for a snakehead and his load."

Leroy wagged his head slowly. "The driver rolls down the window and gets out before it sinks, leaving the women behind. No, Ben! Can anyone be that callous?"

But Ben was overcome with a dozen emotions at once. The timing was about right. The van floated down from the direction where he found Dawn. And yes, a man who would force a woman to abandon her tiny baby would be that callous.

Was one of those bloated, rotting women Dawn's mother?

Chapter Seventeen

Ben watched Esther lay aside her pen. She was signing printouts, stacks of them.

She asked, "So, why call a town meeting right now?"

"Because everyone is passing the buck. The city fathers turned the hospital needs over to the county and the county said gee, sorry, they already have a regional hospital so it is not their problem." Ever since he heard the news, Ben felt like shaking a few people. He, they, everyone understood that the storm had cost the town far more than was budgeted for the year for cleanup. More than for three years. If it weren't for the National Guard shouldering much of the work, and border patrol taking some of it, they'd be so far in debt they'd never crawl out. The county and state both promised to assist with the cleanup, and FEMA would come in eventually.

But when? Ben thought of the help Minot had received for all their flooding. Slow response and basically inadequate. Repairs would take who knew how long, and winter was already breathing down their necks. There was an urgency here that most places wouldn't have.

Esther heaved another sigh, her third since they'd

started talking. "Bill Aptos certainly lit a short fuse when he made his threat at Chief's funeral."

Ben nodded. "True."

"Is this meeting sanctioned, or is it closed?"

"I talked to Lars over at the bank and he assured me that it's sanctioned and open. It's a meeting to get ready for the town meeting. You want to go with me?"

"Yeah, about like I want a hole drilled into my head."

Ben knew that feeling. "Sorry, can't help you there, but you understand our medical needs far more than I do. Besides, this is a planning session. Mr. Aptos suggested we do it this way so there can be no one screaming about being railroaded."

"Someone will scream no matter what, you know that." She stacked the papers, rapped them on edge to line them up, and laid them in her wire inbox. "Do you realize how many planning meetings I've been to in the last few years?" A sigh again. "Yes, I'll go."

"Good, let's go get hamburgers and eat on our way."

"We could walk."

"No idea how long this meeting will take."

"Who's going to be chairing this planning meeting for the future planning meeting?"

"I guess Lars will. He's the mayor, after all."

Esther shucked off her lab coat and tossed it in the hamper, then pulled her purse from the drawer she kept it locked in. "Let's go. Your truck or my car?"

"Let's drop your car off at your house so it's not left in the parking lot. Someone might think you were here alone."

She wagged her head. "That druggie jerk sure set us all on edge."

"And yet, people still leave their doors unlocked." He

stepped aside to let her to go ahead of him and held the door for her. He glanced around the lighted parking lot as Esther locked up. The debris had been cleared off, and if it weren't for the broken-off tree stumps you wouldn't have known all they'd been through. "Have you heard anything yet on the DNA samples?"

"No. Three weeks minimum."

He opened the driver's door on her mini and waited for her to get in. "Meet you in front of your house." Here they'd been talking like easy friends when all he wanted to know was what she was going to do about social services and Dawn.

So ask her. Why was it so hard to obey that suggestion? He had no answers. He climbed into his own rig. *Just spit it out.*

"So, the drive-in or the café?" he asked a couple of minutes later as she buckled the seat belt on his truck's passenger side and he eased back onto Main Street.

"Café, or do we have time for a sit-down?"

Ben checked the clock on the dash. "Half an hour. We can tell them to put a rush on it. However, at the drive-in, no one will stop by to comment or ask questions."

"Oh, never thought of that. The drive-in."

"Good." After they had their order, Ben drove to city hall and parked toward the back of the lot so they could eat in peace.

Ask her. No, I don't want to destroy this meal. Or mess with my mind for the meeting. With that decided, Ben took a drink of his chocolate milk shake. No one made shakes as good as drive-ins did, and especially this particular one.

He wallowed a fry around in ketchup and popped it in his mouth. "You thought about getting an artist's rendering of the finished hospital made?"

She frowned. "How can we do that before the plans are drawn up?"

"I'm thinking if there was something concrete to show people, they would begin to believe it really might happen. People buy what they see, not what they hear about. That's why physical evidence weighs so heavily in court. Wouldn't even have to be the actual one, but something they could see. I was thinking of having the drafting class and art department at the high school do this for us."

"What a great idea." She laid her hamburger down and reached for her drink. "We could come up with a rough draft. I've got pictures I've been collecting."

"I'll call and set up a meeting with the teacher." He watched as a couple of cars parked near the brick building. Mr. Aptos had a briefcase with him, probably all the paperwork Esther had already given him. Her years of collecting. He glanced over to see Esther with her eyes closed, head against the seat back. "Tired?"

"Yeah, you gotta admit life around here hasn't been exactly normal. Did you read today's paper?"

"Not yet." The *Pineville News* came out on a weekly basis, except for the storm week as it was being referred to. Printing a paper was impossible with no power, so they were trying to make up for missing the news now with a special storm edition. He'd glanced at it, but somehow the day had disappeared with half of what he'd planned still undone.

He made sure all the wrappings were in the bag and grabbed his jacket. "You ready?"

"What are my choices?"

"You don't have to go to the meeting."

"That would surely be a stupid move on my part." She grabbed her coat and reached for the door handle.

"Wait, I'll get that." He was surprised she waited as he opened the door for her. "I have a feeling we might have some surprises tonight."

"I really don't need any shocks, so I'll pray for good surprises."

He ushered her inside. They could hear the rumble of conversation as they neared the meeting room. Someone laughed; that was a good sign. About fifteen people sat around the tables set up in a U configuration. Coffee aroma rose from the shiny pot on the table by the wall as they entered, with the ubiquitous plate of cookies and bars. There would never be a meeting in Pineville without the requisite sustenance.

While greetings flew back and forth, Ben poured himself a cup of coffee and snagged his favorite bar with coconut, nuts, and chocolate chips. He nodded to Gertie Larson, who always made these just for him, and mouthed his thanks.

"You two sit up here." Lars, longtime mayor of Pineville, pointed to two chairs.

"Looks like that's the hot seat," Ben answered. "Good evening, Lars."

"Not tonight. No hot seats at this meeting. Besides, you two have gone way beyond your duty the last weeks. You're heroes in my book."

Esther took one chair and looked up with a grin. "Shouldn't that be hero and heroine?"

As the chuckle flitted around the tables, Ben nodded with a smile. "Just doing our jobs." He glanced around the table at those gathered and settled into a folding chair.

"Know of anyone else who was figuring on coming? Then let's get started." Hizzonor Mayor Benson, Lars to everyone in town, looked around, then continued. "You all know we are here to get the general town meeting planned for next week. Since we are on such a tight time frame, first off I think we need to talk about publicity. How will we notify the people around here, especially since the paper just came out today, Monday?"

"I'll print up posters and get them up around town."

"Word of mouth travels faster here than the Internet. If we all make ten phone calls, and ask others to do the same..."

"You'll head that up?"

A nod from a faded redhead brought out answering nods.

"I'll post it on Twitter and Facebook."

"Rushing it like this might be a bad idea."

"Need to strike while the iron is hot. People forget too dang fast. Besides, we've a ninety-day deadline, remember?"

Ben sat quietly, listening to all the comments. They were all right, no matter which side of the question they were on.

"Let's get back to order." Lars paused until quiet resumed. "Bill here has requested time to share some thoughts he has collected."

The frail-appearing, white-haired gentleman stood and removed papers from his briefcase. "I have here some notes for all of you..."

"Ever the teacher," someone commented, causing a ripple of chuckles.

Everyone sure seemed in a good mood, Ben thought as he watched the papers being passed around the table. One contained a pie chart and the other a list and several paragraphs. Leave it to Mr. Aptos to come prepared like this.

Aptos looked to Esther. "The goals page is based on what you and I talked about that time when we first started dreaming about a modern medical facility. I don't think anyone realized we would be cut off like that. Were it not for Esther and her crew, more people would have died, and if we had a decent facility here, fewer might have.

"I know for a fact that attorneys have been calling Roy Abrams and telling him he has a right to sue the town because his wife died of internal bleeding. They are calling it an unnecessary death, and I tend to believe them. 'Course, they're just ambulance chasers, but the lawyer Roy and Denise used for their wills says the same thing. Denise dying like that was a shock to everyone. I been talking to Roy. He has opted instead to use this as an opportunity to help the town get a hospital. I know that the odds of such a storm as that happening again aren't real high, but..."

Someone piped up, "And the chief collapsing like that. Perhaps better facilities would have prevented that, too."

Out of the corner of his eye, Ben caught the shake of Esther's head. He knew what a struggle she'd been having with that exact question: Had she done enough? Would she refute the comment?

When she didn't, he motioned to Lars. "Could I add something here?"

"Don't," Esther whispered.

He ignored her and stood up. "Just so everyone knows the facts. Chief Harden had a severe coronary occlusion, but it's an aortic aneurysm that killed him. No one could have saved him, even if he were in an operating room when it burst."

Someone interrupted. "Can't you get a pacemaker?"

"An aneurysm," Ben explained, "is a weak spot in the wall of a blood vessel; in Chief's case, the main vessel leaving the heart. The weak spot bulges out and may, at some unpredictable moment, literally explode. Rip open. In a major vessel like the aorta, your blood pressure drops catastrophically and you die immediately. I'm telling you this because we need to keep the facts straight, or those who think we're crazy will latch onto a mistake and take the focus off the real problem and solution. We see that going on with politics all the time. Let's not make that mistake." He sat down, leery of even looking at Esther.

"Thank you, Ben. Your comment about making sure our facts are straight is so true." Lars turned to the rest of those at the meeting. "We all need to be very careful of this so that our efforts aren't blown apart. We all know the opposition would like to do just that."

Bill Aptos nodded. "I stand corrected. Thank you, Ben." His eyes twinkled. "Guess we taught you well." He shifted his attention back to the papers he handed out. "As you can see, this plan needs to involve everyone. I figure some of us oldsters can call on our friends and challenge them to take part in this. I plan to contact Burt Humphrey and see about grant money; his company does a lot for our area. Anyone here excellent on writing grants in general? I have a list here of grant opportunities I have researched, but grant writing is a real art if you want to seriously be considered." He stopped and looked around the table. "Or do you know someone who is good at this?"

"But grants take forever," someone said.

"True, but we'll need lots of money over the next probably two years to get this up and operating." He smiled at Esther. "No pun intended."

"But it was a good one." Was Kathy Myers, assistant

manager of Lars's bank, just buttering him? She wasn't smiling. But then Kathy was something of a strange bird.

Ben watched and listened to the proceedings, grateful for the lack of animosity that had erupted at the funeral. The next meeting promised to be a battlefield.

By the end of the evening, a time line and list of volunteer assignments were ready. The coffeepot was empty and the refreshments consisted of half a dozen crumbs on the edges of the plates. Nine o'clock had come and gone. Lars closed the meeting, and everyone rose to leave.

"Thanks for coming, Ben, Esther." He shook their hands. "Life sure changes at times, doesn't it?"

"Thanks for all the information you gave me." Mr. Aptos snapped the latches on a briefcase that was probably the one he'd used to carry papers back and forth from school. "Big job ahead. Hopefully by next meeting I can guilt-trip some guys into contributing more than they think they should. 'Bout time some of us who've lived here so many years, and the town's been good to us, put our money where our mouths are." He stopped and rolled his eyes. "My wife would have said I massacred the English language with that sentence. Oh well, you know what I mean."

Ben and Esther walked out with him and saw him into his car.

"Are you sure he should still be driving?" Esther asked as they made their way to Ben's truck.

"Most likely only around town here. His mind is still plenty sharp."

"True, but not so sure about the rest of him." Esther shook her head. "If someone had told me he'd be spearheading the hospital drive when we started working on him during the storm, I'd have declared you loco. The human body sure can surprise us all, even the old ones."

"Now he has a reason to keep on going." Ben opened the truck door for her. The voice started up again. *Ask her.* "Ninety days to pour the footings? Surely he can't mean that."

"We can't get permits that quickly, let alone plans. I've never worked with an architect before, but we don't even have one yet. Do any architects live in Pineville or nearby?"

"I'll ask Jenny; she knows everything. And someone better talk with Mr. Aptos and see if he will change his mind on the qualifications. Losing a million dollars would be sad." He drove the dark streets to Esther's house. "Sure seems strange without the streetlights."

"A million dollars. And he seems to think there are others that can do the same." She turned to Ben. "Are there really people in this town with that kind of money?"

"Probably the ones we'd least expect." *Ask her.* "I'll walk you to the door."

"Don't be silly."

"My mother said a man never lets a woman out of a truck to walk to a dark house by herself."

"She didn't really?"

He got out and opened the door on her side. "She had rather strict rules on manners." *And besides, I need to ask you a question.* They walked to the front door, and he waited as she unlocked it.

"Night." Turning back to his truck he called himself all kinds of names, primarily coward. But the bottom line, he'd enjoyed not sparring with her for a change. A welcome change.

Chapter Eighteen

"Amber and her son Paulie are here."

Esther looked up from the paperwork that still hung over her head since the storm. Amber...Paulie... huh? Her brain stuttered.

"You know, you saved the little boy's life in the car?" Barbara paused to give Esther time to shift gears.

"Okay, thanks, sorry for the blank-out there. The death of the medical profession is paperwork. How come they didn't tell us about this dreadful disease in med school?"

"No idea, maybe they figured learning to deliver babies and repair bones was more important. Silly them."

Esther shoved her chair back; good thing it had casters. Today was proving to be a bit slower than normal, with few appointments and fewer walk-ins, so she was using the time to try to make a dent in the stack. "What is the child's name?"

"Paul. Paulie. Named after her father. According to him, just talking to him on some occasion, she was still in the drug scene, but it doesn't appear that way now. Not that I've had a lot of time to observe, but..." Barbara shrugged.

Esther checked her pockets for fancy Band-Aids and treats, snagged her stethoscope off the hook by the door and looped it around her neck, and followed Barbara to room two, where a file now filled the slot by the door.

"I had her fill out all the new-patient forms for both of them."

"Good, thanks." Esther forced herself to take a deep breath, let it out, and paste a smile on her face before opening the door. Chief's daughter and the grandson he never met. *Please God, she wasn't doing drugs when she got pregnant.* Hopefully she'd gotten her life straightened out first. "Good morning, Amber, right?"

The blond young woman sitting in the chair with her son on her lap nodded. "And Paulie. Thank you for saving his life."

"One of God's miracles."

"If I had just gone the ten miles farther out to Sven's Crossing and the main road. But that would have taken at least twenty minutes longer, plus there was a tree blocking and they hadn't gotten to it yet, but I knew about that back road, and..."

"My father always told me that we can't change the past, only the future. I've learned he was right."

"Sounds like something my dad would say."

"I probably heard it from him, too." Fighting to keep the tears from flooding back, Esther smiled at the boy. "How you feeling, Paulie?"

He nodded and looked up at his mother.

"You can talk with her, she's our doctor now, just like Dr. Peters." Amber looked up at Esther who had stood up again, with a crackle in her knee. "I've taught him he can't talk to strangers."

And today I feel like a real stranger. "Good." Esther

leaned against the examining table. "Which of you am I seeing today?"

"Paulie. We're out of his asthma medications, and we need a new prescription."

Esther flipped to the page in the file and read off the meds. "How long has he been on these?"

"He was diagnosed two years ago, after he had pneumonia and then bronchitis."

"Do you smoke?" At the head shake, Esther continued. "Any regular smokers in your house?"

"No. When I turned my back on my former life..." She paused. "Were you and my dad friends?"

"Yes, good friends. Your mother helped me feel at home here in Pineville and after she died, we kept up the friendship. So, yes, I think the question you are really asking is how much did your dad, and in this case your mother, too, tell me about you?"

Amber nodded and stared down at her son's dark hair. "Knowing everyone knew me, and what a mess I'd made of my life, made coming back here even more difficult. But I wanted Paulie to grow up knowing his grandpa, that he had a family." She wiped the tears from her eyes with one finger.

"I come from a small town, too. Ya gotta love 'em or they'll drive you crazy. Too many long memories." Esther quelled some memories of her own, then nodded and smiled at Paulie. "Well, young man, how about if I listen to your chest? Afterward, if you like, you can listen to your heartbeat with my special earphones."

He nodded but shortened the small distance between him and his mother. "My grandpa's gone to live with Jesus."

"I know that, and I know he is very happy there. Can

you unbutton your shirt for me?" As he did that, she warmed the scope's bell and diaphragm in her hands while she watched him fight the buttons. Normal gross co-ordination for a child that age. Good sign. "Okay now, you breathe in real deep and blow it all out."

She checked all four quadrants in back and moved to the front, asking him to breathe deeply again each time, then removed the earpieces from her ears. "You want to hear now?" At his slow nod, she put the earpieces in his ears and pressed the diaphragm over his heart. A grin split his face.

"I'm going *thump, thump*." He deepened his voice to sound like a heart.

Esther took the stethoscope back and slipped the bell into her breast pocket. "You sure are, and you have a good strong heart." She checked his pulse, the lymph nodes in his neck, and then his ears and throat, introducing her equipment each time. "One other thing." She went to a drawer and pulled out a clamp. "Let's check your oxygen levels, too."

She put the clamp on her own finger to demonstrate. She put the clamp on Amber's finger. When she slipped it on his finger, his eyes grew wide as the red numerals glowed. Good attention, normal reactions; also good signs.

Esther recalled Amber saying in the car that Paulie had been good for weeks, so she saw no reason to second-guess the medication levels.

"Anything else, Amber?"

"No, I can't think of anything."

Esther wrote the same prescriptions Paulie had been taking and gave them to her.

Amber looked a little harried—no surprise there—but

she smiled. "Thank you. Is Don's drugstore still there? I haven't had a chance to go down that street."

"It is, but it's not a Rexall anymore. And it still makes killer malted milks. Paulie might like to try one."

"So would I." Amber stood up and helped Paulie button his shirt.

Esther almost didn't do it, but her better self prevailed. She pulled a business card out of her pocket and handed it to Amber. "If you want someone to talk to, call me. We'll get together. That's my personal cell."

"Thank you." Amber glanced at it and slipped it into her purse. She took a deep breath and asked, so painfully casually that it was obviously not casual, "Say, do you happen to know if Ben James is thick with anyone at the moment; you know, dating?"

"I know you two dated in high school." *And right now he's all in love with a month-old baby, but you're not going to know about that.* "I don't know what his status is right now; I don't hear too much scuttlebutt."

"Just curious. Like you say, we used to see each other, but that was long ago."

Not long enough. What was wrong with Esther that she suddenly got this ridiculous jealous streak? She pasted on the old smile and saw them to the waiting room.

"Back to the paperwork," she told Barbara. "You know, I still haven't sorted out the mess from the first storm. Any word about the soft-drink and junk-food dispensers?"

"Not since the email message that he'd be here in a day or two."

"That was last week."

"We're not one of his bigger accounts. I have candy bars in my desk drawer if you get desperate."

Esther smiled. "I'll keep it in mind. Thanks." She

crossed to her office, closed the door, and locked it. *Why
did you do that, silly?* She flopped into her chair, leaving
the door locked. Chief Harden's grandson and daughter.
Treating them was a lot tougher than she would have expected. Chief insisted his daughter had not cleaned up
the booze and drugs, but so far Paulie showed no obvious
signs of fetal alcohol syndrome.

She leaned way back, scooting her butt to the front of
the seat, stretched out in the chair, closed her eyes, shut
herself away. So much ugliness was happening, ugly with
little streaks of light. Not all bad but hardly any good, and
most of it not—

The phone blared. She jumped, every nerve in her
body vibrating. She should have asked Barbara to hold
calls. Maybe she had; she couldn't remember. Picking up
the phone as if it might jolt her with a bezillion volts, she
said, "Hello?"

"Ben James. You sound sleepy. Did I just wake you up?
I'm sorry."

"No." *Ben James, for heaven's sake! He never calls.
Why . . . ?* "No, you didn't wake me. Not at all. I'm working
on the records yet, still working on that miserable storm
and trying to reconstruct records. It's horrible. No, you
didn't wake me up." And just for emphasis, she added another, "No." She was babbling. What was wrong with her?

"I can imagine it's horrible. If you want sometime, we can
sit down and sift through each other's memories, see who
we come up with." Ben's voice sounded a little tentative. "I
probably know more people by name than you do."

"That might be helpful. Uh, what can I do for you?"
Shock. That's what it was. She was just plain shocked that
he should call.

"Well, two things. First one. I apologize for dragging

you along to that meeting. Even the best meetings are dismal, and that one was a real moaner. It seemed like a good idea at the time, but the more I thought about it afterward, the worse it sounded. Anyway, sorry."

"Oh, please don't apologize!" In an odd way, his apology charmed her. "I've been going to these meetings for years, and it was good that I went to this one. Keeps me in the loop. I appreciate that you took me."

"You're gracious. Number two, I'd like to make up for it, at least in part, by taking you along to the football game tonight. The Loggers, also known as the mighty Pineville Eleven, versus Bemidji North's semi-fierce Wolverines."

She found herself laughing. When was the last time she'd truly laughed?

"Home game," he continued. "We can walk over to the high school."

"I really should try to get a grip on this backlog."

"Hasn't it been gripped enough for a day?"

Why was she hesitating? It promised to be interesting, sort of—she wasn't into football, didn't even understand it, but a diversion might be helpful. Help her get her wildly flailing emotions back under control. "All right, if you like. Sounds fun. When?"

"Ansel says he might come. Beth is staying home, but she's sending along a picnic supper. Tailgate party preceding the game. I'd come by your place around five thirty, we meet Ansel, eat, get our adrenaline running as the mighty Pineville Eleven defend their turf."

Barbara rapped on the door. "Patient in three."

Esther had forgotten it was locked. She raised her voice, "Coming," lowered her voice, "Sounds good. Thank you, Ben!"

Her stethoscope was still around her neck. She unlocked the door and walked down to three in a sort of daze. Not dazed exactly, just lost in thought. She, Esther Marie Hanson, was going out on a date with a cute guy. Who could have imagined it? Well, not a date exactly, if Ansel was coming. And certainly not a formal date; rather, a payback for a perceived wrong. Still...

She entered three. "Why good afternoon, Mrs. Breeden."

"Oh, I do wish you would just call me Avis, like everyone else."

Esther painted on her make-nice smile. "If you really wish, but I apologize in advance if I forget. It's not the way I was raised. What's your problem today?" She began her routine task of taking vitals.

"This shoulder, same as always. When I move it, it's as if I hit it with a hammer, only one that's vibrating very fast, like this—" She wiggled her hand. "Only faster."

Blood pressure, temperature, pulse, lung action, all normal; well, Avis's version of normal. "The last time you were in, we injected the joint area with a steroid medicine. How long did the effects of the medicine last?"

"Oh, three or four days is all, and then it started to act up again. Herbert—he's my son, Herbert, a very nice young man and not married yet—Herbert says I'm taking too many pain pills, and he's worried."

"I see. What other doctors are you going to?"

And the sweet little old lady's cheeks, which were pale white, flushed pink. "Well, uh. You know..." She scowled. "Has Herbert been talking to you?"

"No." Esther sat back. "I did not prescribe enough pain meds to worry your son, so if he is concerned, I surmise that you must be getting prescriptions from other physicians." She shrugged. "Which is fine, but we should write them down on my chart here—and the other physicians' charts—so that we can all keep track of them."

"There aren't *that* many."

"It's important, Mis—Avis. You'll recall the first level of treatment for your problem is mild, over-the-counter pain meds. When they don't do anything, we try the shots. The most drastic phase is orthopedic surgery."

"That's what Herbert said. 'Go to an orthopedist, Mom.'"

"A wise recommendation. Shall I make you an appointment with a good orthopedist in Grand Forks? There is also a good one at the county hospital in Bemidji." *And I have been fighting for years to get one here. You see how far that's gotten.* "Would you take off your blouse, please? I'd like to look at it for discoloration or swelling."

Reluctantly, the lady unbuttoned. If Avis was this modest for a female doctor, she must hide under a blanket for a male. Esther examined the shoulder—a little warmer to the touch than the other shoulder, but not visibly swollen—as Avis chattered on.

"Do you know, Paul Harden's daughter is back in town! I saw her in the grocery store with the sweetest baby. She's just as beautiful as ever. You know, she and that Ben James were a couple in high school, and so handsome. Just perfect, the two of them together. Everyone was so disappointed when he went into the marines instead of just marrying her and going to teachers' college. Of course, his Allie was very nice, too, and also a high school queen, but not the movie-star beauty that Amber is." And on and on she went.

Movie-star beauty? Esther definitely wouldn't say that. Amber, in fact, looked rather trailworn, as if life had not treated her well; or she had not treated life well.

"Thank you, Avis. You may button up." Esther was going to say, *Your problem is getting worse, and pain pills aren't going to do much* when she got an idea. "Uh, did you say if your Herbert is seeing anyone?"

"No. No he's not. He dates a little, but no. Would you like his phone number? I understand that these days, girls call boys as often as boys call girls."

"Yes. Yes, I would."

Quickly, eagerly, Avis wrote a number on a scrap of paper and handed it to Esther. This was excellent. Esther would talk to Herbert and get his take on his mother's condition. And she'd give him the orthopedists' names.

"I will write you a pain prescription, Avis, but only for one week. Two a day, maximum. By next week, I expect you to have an appointment with an orthopedist."

It took Esther another five minutes to get the yakkity Avis Breeden to leave; she might not have gotten it done at all, but Dennis and Yvette brought in a BLS Difficulty Breathing from the assisted living center and Esther was able to shoo Avis out the door.

Dennis was downright cheery as he wheeled in Mr. Lamont. "Home game tonight, Esther. Biggie, Bemidji North. Going?"

"As a matter of fact, Dennis, I am. Mr. Lamont." Esther plugged in her ears. "I'd love to say it's good to see you, but not with this labored breathing. Let me listen here."

Mr. Lamont muttered something muffled through his oxygen mask.

Yvette sort of sneered, "Dennis is a sports nut. He can get all excited about beginners' league bowling. High score, hundred and thirty-five; yay!"

Esther let the two of them transfer Mr. Lamont to the exam table. They were good at it, and this afternoon she felt very weary and wrung-out.

Dennis bubbled, "Hey! Neither team has lost yet, isn't that right, Mr. Lamont?"

Mr. Lamont muttered.

"Well, yeah, I know it's pretty early in the season." Dennis undid the restraints.

Yvette plugged the oxygen mask into the wall valve. "Esther, you may not know that twenty years ago, Mr. Lamont coached high school lacrosse."

"Really!" Esther slipped an oxygen perfusion clamp onto the man's finger. "I played in high school, but I was never very good at it. Mr. Lamont, your O_2 is way down. Have you been using your oxygen equipment consistently?"

He lifted the mask away. "Not on bridge days. Rest of the time."

"And today was a bridge day, right?"

Yvette wagged her head. "You should see them play bridge. Pirates are kinder-hearted than those cutthroats; I mean real pirates. Trash talk like you wouldn't believe."

Esther grimaced. "I see. Would you two please hang out with him while I talk to his on-call nurse over at his center? Just a few minutes."

"Sure." They waved her off, so she returned to her office. She and the nurse, whom she knew casually, compared notes and agreed that his COPD needed greater attention than he could receive locally, so Esther authorized a transfer.

They wheeled him out the door. Oh, if only Avis could be rolled away so easily.

Esther glanced in the empty waiting room and announced to Barbara, "Got a hot date. I'm going home."

"How hot?"

"Ben James, and probably Ansel. Lukewarm?"

"Oh, no! Boiling!" Barbara smiled, and her voice softened. "Esther, you know how Ben has been having such a really tough time since his wife died, and this is the first he's starting to act like a human being again. I'm so glad you two are going out. Thank you for saying yes to him."

"Hm. Now my hot date is a therapeutic intervention. Oh well. Good night."

Barbara giggled. "Good night."

She had never been to a tailgate party for the simple reason that she did not ever want to go to a tailgate party. So here she went off to her very first tailgate party, squeezed into the cab of Ansel's little pickup truck between Ansel and Ben. They parked in the high school lot with maybe a hundred other vehicles, all the people laughing and mingling and apparently enjoying it.

Ansel dragged three Eskimo coolers to the back of the truck bed as Ben popped open three folding canvas directors' chairs. He unfolded a resin table. From an open carton he plunked down flatware, paper plates and napkins, big bottles of mustard and ketchup. Ansel put the food out, a bowl of potato salad, fried chicken, corn-on-the-cob, and Esther could tell it was all homemade.

One cooler was beverages. Probably, alcohol was not permitted on the school grounds, but beer flowed freely, with people nearby surreptitiously drinking from paper cups. She watched Ben, curious to see if he would do likewise. He did not. So he was serious about keeping his act cleaned up for the baby's sake.

She made mental note to ask him tonight if he'd sent in the forms for Dawn.

The conversation was fast, light, fun. Esther enjoyed the talk and the food. These two men were both good company. Several people who obviously knew them well stopped by, congratulated Ansel on the new arrival, insisted the baby should be named Storm, not Nathan. Ansel vowed to stick with Nathan because the original, King David's spiritual mentor, was an upright and pious role model, and also because Ansel's uncle Nathan, childless, had amassed a fortune, and well, you know…

Ben smirked and told her as an aside, "He has no such uncle. He'll die penniless, same as the rest of us."

Ansel glanced at his watch and clapped his hands. "I'm headed home. Little Natalie just found out a baby brother takes lots of Mommy's time, and her nose is out of joint. So I'll go spend some time with her before bed. Enjoy. Lemme know who wins."

In moments, he and Ben had folded the table and chairs and put the food away; and their comfortable encampment disappeared into the back of the truck. Ansel drove off, and Ben and Esther walked over to the ticket window. Just the two of them. So this actually was a date.

"Tailgate parties are a whole lot more fun than I expected. Thanks!"

"Glad you enjoyed it. Busy day today?"

"Quite light, actually. I got a little headway on that mountain of paper."

Ben wagged his head. "We should at least have kept a list. I never thought of it until afterward."

"It wouldn't have been kept up. The cases were coming in faster than we could handle them." Esther expected them to climb up into the bleachers the way the rest of the crowd was doing. Instead, he led her to a box of seats on the fifty-yard line, ten rows above the field.

"Nice." She settled into a bucket seat to Ben's right. "I had assumed you bought general admission."

"I like to watch the players, not ants running around on the field. You follow football much?"

"Not at all."

"You are about to learn the game."

They rose for the national anthem as executed by the brass section of the high school band. They cheered politely and briefly as the visiting team took the field; they cheered lustily and exuberantly for the home team. Obviously, white with blue trim figured prominently in the home team's attire, and the opposing team was decked out in black and golden yellow. And all the while, Esther tried to analyze this situation as if she were undergoing an out-of-body experience.

This was Ben's natural habitat, a football field. He fit here comfortably. And yet he fit comfortably in the clinic during the storms, and he seemed to be fitting comfortably as a surrogate father. Which man was he, or was he all of them?

Which woman was she? A physician's assistant, tantamount to a doctor in this small town, but she did not fit comfortably. A Christian, but she rarely went to church. She enjoyed children but had no burning desire for one of her own. She found the whole thing confusing and in a large way, saddening.

Ben leaned toward her to be heard above the hubbub. "Each team tries to keep the enemy from getting close enough to the goalposts on its end of the field to score. They're tossing a coin to determine who has the ball first. Chance also determines which set of goalposts will be defended by which team first. At the half, they switch ends."

He went on, "It's especially important for the first few games of the season. The sun is going down, and it's in the eyes of the team trying to get to those goalposts."

She nodded. "Blinding. Very difficult see, with the sun low in your eyes." She would not have thought of that. She watched the players line up and crouch. A disembodied announcer crowed enthusiastically, "There's the snap. Conner to Wilkes, Wilkes takes it for five. Nice play."

She should have brought a jacket. She had forgotten how quickly it got cool this time of year. Most of the people here were getting out blue-and-white jackets or sweatshirts. The bleachers on the other side were turning black and gold as their people bundled up.

She jumped and gasped as a warm jacket dropped over her shoulders. Ben had just loaned her his own jacket. "Thank you, but you take it. I can—"

He grinned. "I'm good. I wore a sweatshirt under it, just in case."

He explained the next play as it was happening, as if he knew already what they would do. She realized, he probably did.

"Ben! It is so good to see you here!" Amber! She plopped into the only seat left in this box, the one to Ben's left.

"Good to see you!" He flashed her a bright grin. "Welcome home." He turned back to Esther. "You see which one's the quarterback?" She nodded. He pointed. "Watch the backfield, those guys there. One of them just dropped behind the enemy lines. The one way back is the target; he's clear of enemy players."

The quarterback threw the ball mightily; it arced over the players, and that lone fellow grabbed the ball and started running. The enemy players quickly brought him down.

"Ben!" Amber sounded astonished. "She surely isn't that dumb about football, is she? I mean, that's first-grader stuff."

Esther definitely felt her feathers ruffling. She turned

her attention back to the field. The players churned around a little, lined up, paused, suddenly burst into action. Now that she could see what they were trying to do, it was beginning to make a little sense. And now she knew about downs and yards. This was quite a complex game.

Amber pushed in against Ben's left side, rather hard to do with these bucket seats. "I love these Friday-night football games, don't you?"

Kind of a stupid question. Esther chalked it up to that's-just-Amber. Maybe the lady had trouble making small talk. Esther often did. Ben muttered something.

Amber pushed tightly against him, wrapped her right arm into his left. "Yes, this sure brings back old memories, doesn't it?"

The announcer called, "Myer picked up seven yards there. Second and goal."

Esther asked Ben, "So that's the line the player has to cross, right?"

"Right. Properly speaking, the ball has to cross it and be in the physical control of the player. That's a touchdown."

Amber purred, "It gets cold out here too quick. Ben, could I borrow your jacket awhile?"

Esther could hardly believe it. *Sheesh, Amber! That is so high school!*

Ben seemed not to notice. "Sorry. It's already loaned out."

Amber leaned way forward, looked squarely at Esther, and asked, "I don't suppose I could borrow for a while."

And the way Amber was looking at her, and the way she said that, Esther knew for sure she wasn't talking about the jacket.

Chapter Nineteen

Having a day with her family had seemed like a good idea.

Until it was time to go there, and now all Esther wanted to do was call and say she wasn't coming. Or couldn't come. But for what reason? That was where she drew a blank. She'd told her mother she'd leave right after church and if she was going to get to church on time, she'd better step on it.

Pastor was making the announcements before the start of the service when she found a seat on the outside end of the last row—easier to get up and leave if she couldn't handle the sitting any longer. Settling her purse under the pew in front of her, she turned her attention toward the front, at the same time taking a deep breath and slowly letting it out again. There was no need to have tension in her neck and shoulders when she was here. Another thought floated through. As sporadic as her attendance had been the last few months, why was something inside her so insistent that she needed to be here this Sunday?

The organist played the prelude to the hymn and everyone rose to sing. The voice in front of her sure sounded familiar. A man with a baby in his arms. It couldn't be. Ben! All these years she'd been coming here and she'd never seen him in church since his wife died. Beth and Ansel and their two sat beside Ben, Beth with the baby, Ansel with his daughter in his lap.

Why had she chosen to sit here? Now she'd be caught in a conversation afterward, unless she snuck out right after communion. She tried to keep her mind on the service, but questions kept bombarding her. She'd forgotten to ask him Friday night if he had sent in the paperwork on Dawn like she'd asked him to. Did she ask him to or was that only in her imagination? Tired as they'd all been, it was miraculous that more things hadn't fallen through the cracks. Or else she just didn't know it yet.

Trying to pay attention took so much energy, she settled into her corner and started listing things to be thankful for. Until everyone rose and turned to those around and behind them for the greeting. Pasting a smile on her face, she said good morning and she sure looks wonderful and how are you, Beth and... And the one she didn't ask was, *Should you have Dawn out in public where someone might start asking questions?*

But her concern let up when he told the people in front of him that he was taking care of the baby for now and that Beth was really doing all the work. As everyone sat back down to prepare for the sermon, Esther sucked in a deep breath and wished she could put her hand on Ben's shoulder.

What? Where had that come from? She'd like to hold little Dawn, too. Now, that was understandable, but what brought about the former? Yes, they'd had a good time at the game, until Amber joined them.

The minister's voice broke through her fog. "Let us pray."

That part she could do. With his words on one ear and her own petitions floating through her mind, she hoped God could sort it all out. She prayed for healing for herself, safety for Dawn, and an answer to the social services monster that had yet to rear its ugly head. So far, unless Ben had filed the forms, no one even knew there was a baby here.

She glanced at the bulletin. Sermon title: Love One Another.

"Let me ask you a question this morning. Jesus tells us to love one another—but how do we go about that?"

She'd learned the verses in Sunday school and sang all the kiddy songs. "Jesus Loves the Little Children," "Jesus Loves Me," "God Loves You, God Loves Me," all with actions to remind them.

What did truly loving mean? What did it look like? What did it feel like? According to the Bible she was supposed to love everyone. Right. Friends and family. Check. So how about loving her mother when she was at her most irritating? Instead of staying as far away as possible. What about the man who made the mother leave Dawn to die in the woods? What about Amber last night? Love her, cow's bells, she didn't even particularly like her. And yet she'd given Amber her business card and said she could call. How would she deal with that? If Amber called? Which she doubted she would.

Why did she care if Amber was hitting on Ben?

She jerked her runaway mind back to the time and place. Worship. *Focus, Esther!*

"It's not easy but God never commands us to do something without providing the tools to do so. Our excuses run rampant. *When I get around to it. Maybe next week. Perhaps after they make the first move.*" He paused, slightly nodding and looking around at the congregation. "Love is a choice, not a feeling. Folks, we are on an adventure called Learning to Love. Let's all learn together. Over the next weeks we'll be studying this commandment: Love one another, even as I have loved you. Amen."

He bowed his head to pray. All Esther wanted to do was leave right that instant. When they stood to sing another hymn, all her flight symptoms overrode her stay commands and she left.

Out in the car, she fought the tears that seemed omnipresent lately. Was she still that tired? What was causing her weepy state? Not that stress could cause this or anything. After blowing her nose, she turned right to the highway, rather than left toward the little house she loved and called home. She pulled into the drive-in for an extra-large cup of coffee with one cream and headed south. Refusing to allow her mind to take off on tracks where she did not want it to go, she turned the radio on louder than usual and focused on a discussion between an avowed atheist and a Jewish priest or rabbi or something. Anything to keep her mind away from the topics eating at her, and her mind was always free to float with music.

The devastation of the countryside eased up about fifteen miles outside Pineville. There were still a few downed trees as she drew closer to her parents' farm. It had been in the family now for three generations. Her brother Kenneth was farming with their dad and planned to take over more as the years passed. Esther knew that right now, her father had no intention of relinquishing the farm yet.

A new dog ran beside their basset Artie as he came to meet her when she parked in front of the garage. "I see you have a friend," she murmured to the aging dog

as he leaned against her legs. The younger basset hesitated, barked at her, then when Artie was happy came up
for pats. "When did you come to live here and how come
no one told me?" Artie whined and pushed the youngster
out of the way. "Obviously you are top dog, which is as it
should be." She knew she was prolonging the entrance to
the house. So many questions, comments on how she was
looking mighty tired, all the while she would be fighting
to keep her public mask firmly in place.

And staying away from her father's hugs. That would do
her in for sure. Keep it light, keep it general, and get out.
Those were her personal orders.

Dogs at her heels, she strolled up the steps to the
wraparound porch. The door opened to frame her grandmother, Alma Hanson. Arms wide, she waited for Esther
to come in.

"I am so happy to see you." The hug brought a boulder
to Esther's throat. Of course Gramma would be here,
Sunday dinner and she lived in a small cottage right behind the old farmhouse.

"Thank you." Esther hugged her back. She swallowed
and cleared her throat. "You look as good as always."

"Oh, phfff, stuff and nonsense." She locked her arm
through Esther's. "You and I are going to do some catching up, but right now I'll grudgingly share you with the
rest."

Esther stopped in the arched doorway to the family
room where the men were watching football. She could
hear her mother and Joan in the kitchen.

Her brother Kenneth held up one finger, meaning
"hold on," until the play was complete and he leaped to
his feet. "Told you they would take it." He crossed the
room to hug his sister. "Took you long enough."

"You know I don't drive fast."

"Not what I meant and you know it."

Her father, Peter, waited right behind him, then elbowed him aside. "My turn." He hugged Esther and whispered in her ear. "So glad you could come."

"Me, too." And she realized she meant it. "Sorry your team lost."

He snorted. "They didn't just lose, they rolled over, paws in the air. Pathetic."

"Where are the others?"

Kenneth grumbled, "Jill has school, and Andrea's kids have the mumps."

"Mumps! You mean they were never vaccinated?"

"Hey. When did Andrea ever do anything right?" Kenneth turned back to the TV remote.

Andrea did lots of things right. Esther bristled. In fact, Kenneth was all too often the screwup.

"So, you're stuck with the rest of us." Kenneth put down the remote and picked up the little blond toddler clutching his father's pant leg. "This is Auntie Esther. Been awhile since you saw her, I think you were just crawling the last time she was here."

Esther shook her head. "Knew you'd get the barbs in somehow. I was here the week before the storm hit."

"No, you weren't." Her mother, Madge, wearing her normal slight frown, came through the arch. "Been more than two months since you were here, but who's counting?" She'd tried to lighten her criticism but it was too late as far as Esther was concerned. It never failed. Her mother always had something negative to say. Even when Esther visited, it wasn't enough. Wasn't quite perfect.

For a change Esther chose not to respond. She gave her mother a big Brownie smile and glanced to see the woman behind her. "Well, Joanie, look at you!" She turned away from her mother to hug her sister-in-law. It was difficult; the closest she could get to Joanie's shoulders was about three feet. "When are you due?"

"March. I wanted to tell you in person, not over the phone."

"What a wonderful surprise. Do you know the sex of the baby yet?"

"No, the ultrasound was inconclusive. But that's okay. Johnny will have a playmate no matter which. I just want a healthy baby."

Esther knew they had lost a baby before Johnny and then one after. "You're taking it easy?"

"Yes, Doctor."

"Sorry, can't help it." She dug in the purse still hanging on her shoulder and pulled out a sucker. "This isn't enough to ruin an appetite and it's sugar-free."

"Tell Auntie Esther thank you," Kenneth instructed his son, who was instantly picking at the wrapping.

"Tank you." He handed his dad the sucker. "Pwease."

"You want me to eat your sucker?"

The little boy shook his head. "No! Mine. Open."

Esther rolled her lips together to keep from laughing out loud. "He's sure learned a lot of words."

"*No* was the first one."

Her mother barked, "Dinner is ready. We'll dish things up while the rest of you come to the table. Johnny's chair is by yours, Kenneth."

When they were all seated, Dad bowed his head and waited for the rest to become quiet. "Lord God, we thank you for this day, for our family, for bringing Esther home for a visit, for healing our grandchildren. And for the food that is always delicious. Amen."

Johnny echoed "Men," making everyone chuckle.

Esther dodged questions until the coffee cups were re-filled, after the apple pie had disappeared.

"Mom, your apple pie is the best anywhere."

"She won the top ribbon again at the county fair, too; I heard talk that one should not be able to enter having won more than three times. Or was it five?" Her dad wrinkled his brow trying to remember.

"Mom wouldn't be able to enter any baked goods with that kind of stipulation." Kenneth used the side of his fork to scrape up the last smidgeon of pie juice from his plate. "You're going to have to teach Joanie to make pie like this."

"She's tried. I'm hopeless." She looked to Esther. "Did you learn how?"

"I bake a mean pie, but no one can touch Mom's."

"Tell us about the storm!" her mother asked.

"What did you read in the newspapers?"

"It was bad."

"Doesn't begin to cover it. We ran out of all our sup-plies at the clinic, two people with fatal injuries just in the clinic, a baby was born, another found out in the woods, a man still might lose his leg, and too many other tales. Right now one of the old men in town has offered a mil-lion dollars to help build a clinic if we can not only break ground but start the foundations in ninety days."

"That's impossible."

"I thought so, too, but he has an ingenuous plan. Make it privately or municipally owned, funded by Pineville it-self, starting with his gift and what he can convince others to add to it. Last I heard he had grants or donations of two million more. All these years some of us have been fight-ing for an up-to-date clinic and now we might get one."

"I heard you even had a druggie attack!" Yes, Mom would be up on all the bad news.

"We did. Ben James took him down single-handedly. You remember Ben James, quarterback on the Pineville team the two years they went to state?"

"That boy could sure throw that ball." Kenneth had been a couple of years behind Ben. "I'm surprised he didn't try for pro ball."

"He certainly performs well under pressure. He's with border patrol now, has EMT training, and worked at the clinic all through both storms. You know we had a second storm on the heels of the first? I couldn't have made it without him." She started to tell them about Chief but changed tack when she realized that was not a good idea—too difficult for her to handle yet.

"But good will come of it, when you get the new clinic." Gramma Alma left off playing with Johnny and joined the conversation. "God sure is good at that."

"We paid a high price and the town meeting is this week. Wood chips will fly in the devil's workshop, of that I am sure."

Alma shook her head. "How could anyone be against that? You said two died."

"Change. There is a large percentage of people, especially in the local government, who don't want change. And frankly, a lot of skinflints, too. They don't like to spend money for anything if they can get by with something less. Our X-ray machine, for instance—"

"I don't like to spend money, either." Alma scowled. "You don't toss the old away just because something new's come out."

Esther almost had to smile. Gramma Alma still popped corn by vigorously shaking a pan on the stove. "We don't even have a real estimate yet on what it is going to cost. The estimate I gave them years ago isn't good anymore. Or recent plans drawn up. I'm sure we'll form a committee to do that, but that takes time, too."

"That's an impossible restriction; nothing can happen in ninety days." Dad snorted, the snort he used to declare *end of discussion*.

Kenneth asked, "You have a location in mind yet?"

"Yes, the city owns the land that the present clinic is on and several undeveloped acres beyond the parking lot."

Her dad shook his head. "You pull this off and it will indeed go down in history as a bona fide miracle."

"Along with the military bringing in and installing a pontoon bridge until they can get our bridge repaired?" She thought of telling them about her conversations with the two doctors, but figured that would lead to more questions. She glanced across the table to see that Gramma had taken the little guy on her lap and he was sound asleep in her arms. Leave it to Gramma. Esther couldn't help but smile. That little boy got plenty of attention for sure, living that close to grandparents and a great-grandma.

Joanie rose and brought the coffeepot back into the table. "Anyone for more?" She filled Kenneth's cup and then Peter's. "I'm drinking tea, Esther, if you would rather have that. There's both herb tea and regular."

With a smile, Esther shook her head.

"So, what are your plans for Thanksgiving?" her mother asked. "I assume you can join us this year."

Feeling like Bambi in the headlights, Esther made herself take in a breath before answering. Why did she take everything her mother said as an accusation? It was the tone of voice, she realized. True, she'd missed the last two holidays, but she'd not given this year a moment's thought yet. That was months away.

"Less than a month till then." Mom could even correct her thoughts.

"I'm not sure, Mom. All I'm trying to do is get caught up on the paperwork from that storm. During the worst of it we treated nearly a hundred people and didn't keep any records—it was coming at us too fast. And dealing with this clinic thing." She glanced at her watch. "Speaking of which, I need to get home before long. I've not been grocery shopping since before the storm."

"How long were you without power?" Kenneth asked.

"Two days or so. Good thing I had so little in the refrigerator. That meant I only lost milk and some leftovers. Since I wasn't there to open it, the freezer stayed pretty near cold enough. Some things got soft but nothing was rotten."

"You were lucky."

"I know." She pushed back her chair. "How about I help with the dishes?"

"How about you sit down and visit? We can always do the dishes later. They won't go anywhere." Her mother's reply caught her by surprise. The dishes were always at the top of her list.

Esther shot her father a glance only to get a slight nod in return. Since when was she company and not expected to help with the chores?

"When did you get the new dog?" Should be a safe topic.

"A month or so ago. He showed up here one day, someone must have dumped him along the woods road. We asked around but no one claimed him. Arthur growled a bit but then decided he liked having another dog here." Her dad smiled at her mother. "Your mother named him.

Since we have an Arthur, she said we needed a Lancelot. So he's Lance."

"You need to come home more often to keep up on the news." There it was again. Thanks, Ma.

"You know, the road goes both ways." Esther also knew how hard it was to be away when no matter what, chores time rolled around. Her father ran Black Angus cattle along with farming hay, beans, and sunflowers. "I have a perfectly fine guest room if you wanted to spend the night." *Besides, it is only about four hours away. You can't drive a few hours to come see me?*

Esther could feel the restlessness coming at her again. Why didn't she invite them more often? Because she didn't want to get into an argument. And if she was around her mother much longer, that would happen. She pushed back her chair. She had set her phone on vibrate and felt it going off. "Excuse me, I better check on this." Checking the screen, she walked into the family room to go stand by the front window. She'd not recognized the number.

"Hello, this is Dr. Hanson."

"Esther, this is Amber Harden. You said I could call, is this a bad time?"

"I'm at my parents' house. Do you need something?"

"It's not that important. If you would call me back when it is convenient?"

"Sure. Perhaps on the way home."

"Thank you. Enjoy your family." She hung up and Esther clicked her phone shut.

She analyzed the voice. Frightened? Anxious? No. Bored. Amber was lonesome. So she'd stop at the crossroad and pull over, talk to Amber, and then pretend she was needed elsewhere. Had she made a major error giving Amber her business card?

Back in the dining room, the table was cleared, and in the kitchen Joanie was loading the dishwasher while Mom was putting food in cottage cheese containers and such, what they laughingly referred to as Norwegian Tupperware.

"I'm fixing these for you to take. That way you won't have to cook tomorrow."

"Thank you. I need to be going." She waved her cell as if the call had been important.

"I'll walk you to your car." Dad grabbed her jacket, held it for her, then hand-hugged her shoulders. The burning started behind her eyes.

"Thanks." Esther stepped out the door, her father right behind. The sun stained the sky with vermillion and glorious pinks, gilding the clouds. Esther paused. "That is one of the things I think of when I think of home. The sunsets we always saw from this porch." Her father matched her step for step, their shoulders brushing.

"Now that it is just us, how are you holding up—really?"

Esther swallowed once and then again. How easy it would be to turn and collapse into her father's arms. "I-I'm fine." *As long as I don't have to confess the meltdown and what is causing the post-traumatic stress I'm fighting.* If he only knew. If only she knew, at least knew for sure. She could no longer keep track of what was memory and what was imagination. She set the sack of cartons on the floor in the back and slid into the front seat while her father held the door open.

He leaned in and kissed her cheek. "When you decide you can talk to me or the load gets too heavy, I have a shoulder and a ready ear."

"Thanks, Dad." *But if you ever learn my secret, you will hate me.*

Chapter Twenty

He hated meetings. That's one of the things Chief chewed on him the most about: being late to meetings. And those were border patrol meetings with only six or seven people. He hated town meetings a thousand times worse. There had to be 300 people milling around here, in a room the fire marshal thought ought to hold 176.

Ben poured himself a second cup of coffee and parked close to the refreshment trays, the better to grab Mrs. Peterson's fresh, moist, peanut butter cookies with the crosshatching on top; there was no cookie finer. Even Lars irritated Ben tonight. Hizzonor the mayor took a chair in the middle of the big long table at the front of the room, but he didn't sit in it. He shuffled papers and answered questions, smiling and nodding a lot. A whole lot. That meant he would probably try to please everybody, and that wasn't going to happen. Not tonight.

Esther entered from the kitchen door, way too wide-eyed and wary. She was shown a chair about three from the mayor's left. For as long as she'd been working on this we-need-a-good-medical-facility project, years, they ought to sit her at the mayor's immediate right. Or hand her the gavel. She seemed really squirrelly, but then that's how Ben felt, too.

"There you are!" A terribly cheery female voice. "I knew you'd be somewhere around here tonight."

Ben cringed. "Hello, Amber."

She pouted. Like a high schooler. "You don't sound happy to see me."

"I'm happy to see you. I'm happy to see everyone here. It's a very important meeting."

"That's what everybody says. So what are you doing afterward?"

She would ask that. His mind raced, looking for an excuse. Finally, "Sorry. I have plans already."

"What are they?" She pressed in close, and she was wearing a flowery sort of perfume.

He surprised himself by realizing that she was embarrassing him in public like this, and that was pretty high schoolish, too. Mildly embarrassed, but embarrassed all the same. He glanced over at Esther. If she was watching Amber and him, the embarrassment wouldn't be mild.

But she was just sitting there, apparently looking at nothing in particular. Suddenly her eyes opened wider and her jaw dropped open. She was staring toward the door.

Ben turned to look. Here came Dr. Livingston from the military clinic, and with him Dr. Ho from Grand Forks! No wonder her mouth dropped open. "'Scuse me." He brushed past Amber and headed for the door. Was he too abrupt with her? Who cared?

Pushing through the crowd, he reached them six feet inside the door. "Gentlemen?" He extended his hand.

"Good to see you again." Dr. Livingston shook. He

wore his class A dress uniform tonight. The only reason to wear class A's was to impress folks that you were brass.

Dr. Ho, in a well-tailored suit and tie, extended his hand. "Good evening, Mr. James. Quite a crowd."

"Quite an important meeting. Good evening." He started for the head table, and they followed.

Esther stood and shook with them. She smiled, but the smile didn't appear genuine. She looked confused, same as Ben felt. Kindred souls, Ben and Esther.

"Lars?" Lars was talking to an older lady Ben knew by sight but not by name.

Lars glanced toward him with a look of relief. One would think he wasn't eager to stand around yakking with this woman.

Ben flashed a smile at the lady, a sort of apology. "Lars, I want you to meet Dr. Livingston from the base and Dr. Ho from the hospital in Grand Forks. Dr. Ho is Esther's supervising physician. Gentlemen, this is our mayor, Lars Benson. His day job is banking."

And then he backed off and let them chat, before the lady decided to talk to him instead. Because he now re-membered her if not her name; she talked to people in grocery aisles, in the pharmacy line, on the street, waiting for the bus, on the bus, anywhere she found an ear. She told the world about a son who was an important lawyer in Davenport and a daughter who was going to transform the world of social sciences. Ben had Googled the daugh-ter once, out of curiosity. She had her own website, and from what Ben could tell, she was unemployed.

Now Lars was bumping Esther down two chairs farther away from him. Wrong move! And now he was seating the two doctors between him and Esther. Right move.

Ben glanced at his watch. A few minutes past time to get started.

A moment later Lars rapped his gavel and called for people to be seated. Ben glanced at Esther. Her face was white and she was gripping the table edge. He looked at the two doctors. They had noticed. The question now was, how much had they noticed?

The hubbub dissipated from loud roar to gentle roar to general titter. Lars stood sternly watching. The titter quieted. "Ladies and gentlemen, I believe you all know the subject of tonight's town meeting. If we can get moving on a medical facility in ninety days, we will be a million dollars richer. But before we get into that, even to decide whether to do that, I would like to introduce two guests.

"Because their time is limited, I will ask them to speak first so they can go. Understand they are not outsiders simply being brought in to push one side. They are a crucial part of this community, and of the matter of our medical readiness. Let me introduce Dr. George Livingston from the air force base. Many of you met him during our storms, when he came in from the base hospital to help us in the clinic and handle air transport. Dr. Livingston?" He sat down.

Dr. Livingston stood. Ben admired the way he could take control of a roomful simply by standing up and looking official. Chief had had that gift as well. "Ladies and gentlemen, I have a few brief words that are pertinent to your situation. But first I want to publicly commend, with the highest accolades, Esther Hanson. She served far beyond the call of duty, saved many lives and eased the suffering of countless others, and she did it most graciously." With an enthusiastic smile, he began the applause, and the whole crowd clapped loudly.

Pale and shaking, Esther forced a smile.

The smile left his face. Dr. Livingston cleared his throat. "In this recent emergency, just about all traffic ground to a halt. We could not get to Pineville. You could not get to us. The choppers couldn't fly. And there will be other situations like this, with increasing frequency. As most of you know if you watch the news at all, extreme weather is happening more often, and it is more extreme. Wind, rain, heavy snow. We hope it will all settle down shortly, but we can't depend on that. More important, you can't depend on us. We came in on the tail end of these storms because we couldn't come any sooner, and because the worst of the storm missed the base, so we didn't have emergency conditions tying up our personnel there. Put plainly, we cannot promise we'll be there for you." He turned to the mayor. "Do you have snowplows?"

Lars looked confused. "Of course."

"And highway crews."

"They did a splendid job, beyond the call of duty, too. Yes."

Dr. Livingston nodded. "Well, friends, you need a good medical facility for exactly the same reason you have snowplows and emergency crews always on the ready. Smooth service during little events, and adequate service during extreme events. Thank you for your attention." He sat down.

Lars stood up. "Any questions?"

Burt Yakov stood up. Ben sighed. Burt was one of the world's great contrarians. Tell him don't eat yellow snow and he'd insist it is good for you. "How much did these people pay you to come here and say that?"

And to Ben's delight Dr. Livingston, bless him, rose to the curmudgeon's challenge. "To answer your question,

Dr. Ho and I have been paid nothing. Rather, it is costing us money. Our travel expenses to come here will not be remunerated. Neither will our lieu costs. You see, sir, supervisors are on call twenty-four-seven. If we leave the area, we must pay someone out of our own pockets to be on call in our absence. I don't mind adding, sir, that I consider your question insulting."

A wave of cackles and titters rolled around the room. If there were other questions, apparently the questioners thought twice.

Lars stood. "We are grateful, Dr. Livingston. Thank you. Our other guest is Dr. Warren Ho. He supervises Esther, who is not a fully accredited doctor but rather a physician's assistant. Dr. Ho handles outpatient resources in Grand Forks. Dr. Ho?"

The man stood. He looked very natty in his suit, not really one with most of the people here in their T-shirts and jeans. He smiled. "Good evening. I echo George's sentiments and multiply them. Esther Hanson has done an outstanding job, just outstanding, better than anyone could ever expect of a PA. George and I apologize for having to speak and run. We are on our way down to Rochester to a symposium at Mayo on satellite and rural medicine. That is, medicine practiced outside major metro areas. There is an immense shortage of doctors who are willing to practice out in the sticks, if you will. Most want to specialize, and only major medical facilities can employ specialists. At the symposium we will be discussing ways to ease that shortage. While I am there I will bring to the board at Mayo Clinic a request to help with staffing a formal medical clinic here in Pineville."

Burt leaped to his feet. "What we have works just fine ninety-nine percent of the time. We don't need—"

Lars slammed his gavel down. "Burt, sit down! Let the man finish and then comment."

Burt opened his mouth and started to speak. But Ben had reached him. He laid his hand on Burt's shoulder, squeezed just the right place. Burt sat.

Dr. Ho continued, "A plan using rotating residencies has been working in other parts of the country. I want to put you on the list early, so you're near the top if you decide to expand your medical facility. Grand Forks is ready to help, and we can take a fair number of emergency cases. *If* the roads are open. When you can't reach us, you have to have something here that will meet your immediate needs. You have a real need here, and there will never be a better chance to meet it." He glanced down at his watch. "I'm sorry; we have to get to the airport. I wish you the very best as you deliberate." He backed away from the table as Dr. Livingston stood up. They headed for the kitchen door, where, Ben noticed, a driver in air force fatigues was waiting at parade rest.

Lars rose and led the applause. "To expand on their answer to Burt's question, we did not know they would be coming."

"Now it's my turn." The frail and spidery Mr. Aptos stood up in the front row, doddered over to the head table, and laid a check on it. The check was an enlarged version of an ordinary check, a good three feet wide, with the lettering writ large, ONE MILLION DOLLARS. $1,000,000.00, over his signature. It was postdated ninety days. "Break ground by then and it's yours."

Ben happened to know that as long as it was a legitimate check, you could make it any size you want. This one was valid. He'd never seen that much in one place, let alone on one piece of paper. And he would bet there weren't half a dozen people here who could see that much on their bank statement.

Gladys Applegate barked but did not stand. "You think you can get away with bribing us, Bill?"

"Ain't a bribe. It's a threat. Diddle away the time and you face a lawsuit. And you notice, I'll have a million dollars to pay for that lawsuit. I'll do it, too. You ready to plunk down that kind of money to fight it?"

Walt Jackson stood up. "So he's saying we don't have time to waste. I move we take a straw vote right off the bat, see how much discussion we need."

Ben called, "I second."

Lars nodded. "Straw vote moved and seconded. Show of hands. In favor?"

A sea of hands went up.

"Against?"

A sea of hands went up.

Lars sat down. "I didn't count, but it looks pretty even. Gonna be a long night. Who's taking notes?" He glanced around. "Amy? Good. Since Bill Aptos is mounting the challenge, let him tell us exactly what the challenge is. We'll go from there."

Ben should have been paying better attention, but Esther seized his interest and held it. It was obvious to him that she was fighting valiantly to maintain her composure. They should let her present whatever she was going to say and then leave, but of course, that sure wasn't going to happen. How long could she hold on?

He left Burt and worked his way back to the coffee station. Mrs. Peterson was putting out more cookies. He murmured "Bless you!" and snatched up another peanut butter cookie. The arguments raged behind him.

"I'm the township treasurer and I can tell you, we don't

have anywhere near the kind of money a lawsuit would cost us—or a hospital. Either one."

"But lots of money to waste, right? Lawyers don't come free."

Mr. Rustvold's voice roared, "Well, mine does. She's so sure it's a critical need she's working pro bono. Now, Mr. Bigmouth, where's your money?"

The yelling was getting hostile, personal, raucous. He was getting sick of this whole mess, and it was the short-sighted yokels mouthing off loudest. Why hadn't Perowsky assigned a couple of officers to the meeting, just to prevent this sort of escalation? Ben poured himself another mug of coffee. There were rational reasons both pro and con. Why wasn't anyone voicing the real reasons instead of all this fulminating?

That's what it was. Fulminating. He had had to learn the word for a high school English spelling test. When he missed it, scoring a ninety-six instead of one hundred, he protested that he would never ever use it, so why must he learn to spell it?

Well, he just used it. He owed his old English teacher, Mrs. McElhenny, an apology.

He wondered what had happened to the woman. Someone claimed she was widowed and remarried. He could not imagine that harpy finding one husband, let alone two.

The person he was most worried about in all this was Esther. In the last few weeks, she'd been slammed with lots of work, stress, sorrow. That would tip a stable person over, and she wasn't stable. Barbara said it: *how* is she doing, not what is she is doing.

What kind of family did Esther come out of, he wondered. Someone who taught her good manners. She was a people pleaser, polite, gracious. Yearned to be liked. Sometimes too much so for her own good. Esther.

His mind was wandering. He must bring it back to the room here and keep tabs on what was happening.

Who was yelling now? Sounded like Burt. He turned and looked out across the room. Yep. Burt. The old guy was on his feet shaking a fist. He was hollering at Lars about not being permitted to have his say, and in the time it took him to complain, he could have just said it three times, at least. He marched up toward the head table. Might as well put a lid on this. Ben started toward him.

Burt shouted "jackanapes" or something and banged his fist on the table right in front of Lars. The whole resin table gave a little bounce and tipped a coffee mug.

Esther screamed and leaped to her feet. She stared a brief moment at Burt, wheeled, and bolted for the kitchen door.

How could Burt do that? Because *he* was the jack-anapes! Ben rounded the end of the head table in hot pursuit of the woman who had just gotten one jolt too many. Would the scene behind him deteriorate into a free-for-all? He didn't care. Let Perowsky worry about it, on a need-to-know basis. Instantly he squeezed one eye shut and kept it shut. He was going to need night vision in a moment.

She skirted the butcher block in the kitchen and darted out the back door without closing it. He ran out into the night thirty feet behind her and, even with one eye a few seconds closer to night vision, almost lost her. He saw movement at the far end of the parking lot and then a *whup*! With night vision no better than his, she had run into a car. He raced off in that direction, trying to keep in the middle of the lane between parking slots.

This was a fine time to realize that two years of hard drinking, feeling sorry for himself, and slacking off had pretty much wiped out his stamina. Border patrolmen were supposed to keep in great shape so they could run down the bad guys. He wasn't in good enough shape to outrun a slip of a girl.

"Esther! Stop!"

"Go away!" In the glow of a streetlight she slowed and turned slightly to look his way, turned back and kept going.

Sheeze she was fast! He was keeping up, but he wasn't closing the distance very quickly.

This was getting personal now; his pride was at stake here, and be dipped if he was going to let her outrun him! She crossed Maple against the light and Howard with the light. Was she going home or leaving town? She didn't turn on Cherry, so she wasn't going home.

Aha! That's what she was doing, following the white fog line on the main route out of town. All he had to do was call for backup and—no. No, he couldn't do that to her. Flashing lights, maybe even a siren if someone wanted to play road cowboy...no. This was a job he must do, the quieter the better. And right now he really, really needed Bo. Bo could outrun a horse, take down a person without breaking skin. Bo even had the delightful little trick of tripping the person he was chasing.

She was flagging. Without slowing much, she called over her shoulder, "Please! No!" And she was breathless. Good news!

Of course, so was he.

Whoa! She was headed toward the river! She wasn't going to do something stupid, was she? Like jump in or something? In this darkness he'd never find her if she jumped.

The Corps of Engineers had their floating bridge in place already, a tidy two-lane creation with great, heavy cables laced along the pontoons to keep them in place. The bridge was apparently sturdy enough to support concrete Jersey barriers on each side.

She ran out onto the span, half stumbling, half walking. He wasn't doing much better. The hero of the border patrol finally caught up to his quarry halfway across the bridge. He flung both arms forward, wrapped around her upper arms, dragged her aside against the barrier, and then let friction keep him pinned against the wall as he gulped air that was never enough.

She screamed; she struggled. She flung her head and tried to conk him with it. But the fight was gone. He could feel it leave her.

The shrieking dissolved into sobbing. Then she screamed, "Help me! Someone help me!"

He broke into a profuse sweat. "Yell your lungs. Out. I'm not. Letting go."

"Someone. Will. Will hear me"—gasp—"and. Rescue me."

He breathed heavily until he could get a full sentence out. "I'll flash my badge. Tell them it's a takedown. You can get arrested—" Pause. "—for interfering in an arrest." He hung on.

"Please leave me alone. Just. Let me go." Her voice was softening. "Please."

"No. You're too precious to lose."

She was sobbing in earnest now. She covered her face with both hands.

"Esther, I understand what your problem is, and I—"
"No you don't!"

He stayed wrapped around her. "Esther, I was in the

marines six years! I know post-traumatic stress when I see it! I've dealt with it. In me." He tried to take the harsh edge off his own voice. "Now are you ready to talk?"

"No. I don't. I can't..." She shuddered. "No."

"Do you want to jump?"

"No. I'm not—that far gone."

He loosened his hold and was surprised when she sagged against him. Surprised and delighted. Maybe they were finally getting somewhere with this. He asked, "Did you hear what Dr. Ho was saying tonight?" No answer. He continued, "They have real trouble finding doctors to man rural clinics."

"So?"

"So you're a shoo-in. Get your degree and come back to Pineville, run the clinic. You had your trial by fire and proved you're capable. More than capable. Ho wants you here. He won't leave you hanging out in the breeze."

"I'd run up fifty thousand in student loans that I could never pay off if I worked in Pineville. Forget it."

"I'm pretty sure you'll get the financial help you need."

"Then I'd be obligated. I'd *have* to practice here. No."

She lurched erect and started a slow walk back toward town, so he strolled beside her, poised to grab her if she made a break for it. "You work here now."

That run had really wiped her. He was recovering somewhat, but she was still shaky. They left the bridge, followed the white fog line in silence awhile, walking in darkness through darkness beside silent darkness.

She shook her head. "No. Mom wouldn't forgive me."

"For what? Following your heart? You told me that was your dream, to get the full degree."

"For not being a famous, expensive ob-gyn in the city. And by city she means Minneapolis, not Duluth, or even

St. Paul. That's what she thinks I should be, what she wants me to be. Not a podunk general practitioner."

"Mm." He thought about her finding that tiny vein in Dawn's scalp, inserting that tiny line, saving the baby girl's life. What would be so wrong with obstetrics? She'd be a natural. He kept his thoughts to himself for now. "And what do you want to be?"

"I don't care anymore. Something, anything, that she'll praise for once. Just once." Another shudder. "It hasn't happened yet."

Chapter Twenty-One

Some days, dragging yourself out of bed was difficult; other days, like this one, standing on your feet was a miraculous feat.

Esther glared at the phone that rang at the same time as the fiftieth buzz of her alarm. One she could ignore, two—not. "Dr. Hanson."

"You running late today or...?" Barbara's voice sounded distant, as if even her ears weren't awake yet.

"Do I have a choice on the *or*?"

Barbara snorted. "That kind of morning, eh?"

"Anything important, or can it wait until I get in?" Esther headed for the bathroom as they talked. While a cold shower sounded agonizing, warm or hot water might send her back into dreamland. Surely you could not drown in a shower.

"Oh, it'll wait. I put the report on your desk."

"What report?" She turned on the shower. The effort made her arm weigh twenty pounds.

"The autopsy from the drowning victims."

"I'll be there ASAP." She clicked off her phone, clamped her hair up, and stepped into the shower to let out a bloodcurdling shriek. The cold water did the trick, or had the report of the autopsies already accomplished the jolt?

Within twenty minutes she had her full stainless-steel coffee mug in hand and was locking the door from the garage into the kitchen, while the garage door groaned open. "Hey, you even look like your socks match," Barbara said as Esther strode through the front door.

"They better, I own all white."

"Ever the practical." She paused. "Are you all right?"

"After that meeting last night how can anyone be all right?" Esther inhaled a slug of coffee, no cream or sugar to dilute the effects this time.

"I heard you left the meeting in rather a hurry, Ben hot on your heels."

"Is there no mercy in this town?"

"Care to tell me what happened?"

"One of these days we'll have a heart-to-heart."

"I could cancel your appointments for the day."

"You could but you won't. I'm better off here."

Barbara gave her a long silent look, then heaved a sigh. "I'll hold you to that. The report is on your desk."

"You read it?"

"Yes." Barbara picked up the phone. "Pineville Clinic. How can I help you?"

Esther strode down the hall and flipped on the office light as soon as she'd opened the door. In her nightmare last night the office had been full of dead bodies, stacked floor-to-ceiling, like lumber in a warehouse. The papers appeared to be waiting for her, those and the stack of pink notes of calls to return. Eyes on the report as if it had fangs like a rattler, Esther sank into her chair, dropping her purse on the floor.

After reading it once and then again, she looked up Ben's cell number and stabbed in the numbers.

"You in town or out on patrol?"

"Good morning to you, too. On patrol. What's up?"

"The autopsy report is here."

"So, read it to me." His voice went up a notch. Excitement. Concern. Understandable.

"No, you can read it when you get in."

"Four thirty or so. Come on, Esther, don't prolong the agony." When she didn't answer, he slid into his work voice. "Are you all right?"

She knew he was referring to the episode last night. "Bad night, but not surprising."

"If Chief were here, I'd come right now, but with Perowsky, he'd tack my hide to the barn wall, all nice and proper of course."

"I understand." What had she expected? What was he supposed to do? She had far more questions than answers. "See you when you get here." A memory intruded. The warmth of his arms last night when he held her close and she soaked his shoulder. Why all the tears lately? What had caused her wild exit last night? The people shouting to be heard, the pressure-cooker feel of the auditorium. They'd started at the city hall but as people kept streaming in, they'd moved to the auditorium at the high school. When that filled to standing room only, they opened the doors and put speakers out in the hall. Could sheer claustrophobia have kicked it off?

A knock at her door and Barbara stuck her head in. "Your first patients are in room one and I'll be showing another to room two. You need some more time?"

A sigh and Esther shook her head. "Just another minute and I'll be there." She leaned back in her chair, sipped from her coffee mug, and ordered her mind to stop spinning.

I am here, floated through the room like an apple pie fragrance. She held her breath, listening with every sense. Nothing else, but her shoulders had dropped back to their normal position and even without taking her pulse, she knew her heart rate had slowed. "Thanks. Don't leave, okay?" She could swear she heard a heavenly chuckle.

When she walked into room one she had a smile on her face and a spring back in her step. Glancing at the file in her hands, she greeted the young woman with a toddler at her side because her belly had taken over her lap.

"Well, Lonnie, how are you feeling? You look marvelous."

"Thanks, Esther. This baby can't come soon enough for me." The sturdy woman laid a hand on the mound she carried.

"Let's see, three weeks to go. Can you get up on the table so we can give that baby a listen?"

"With help. Are you sure I'm not having twins?"

Esther assisted her and after checking her vitals, helped her lie back down.

"Mommy?"

"Yes, Toddy."

"Hungry."

"There's a Baggie in the front pocket of my purse."

Esther glanced over while the towheaded little boy dug out the plastic bag with O's of oats and sat down on the floor to open it.

"From all I've seen, you have one bright child there."

"Keeping ahead of him keeps me on my toes. Are kids just smarter these days or what?" While she asked, she pulled up her top and pushed down her soft pants with the stretchy baby panel in front.

"I think they are." Esther moved the bell of the stethoscope around on the woman's belly, listening carefully. When she finished, she smiled. "Not two, one heartbeat, but all the sounds say healthy baby, healthy momma. How much have you gained now?"

"Twenty-eight pounds and I know where every one of them are."

"A little high. And she'll gain at least another five before your due date. I hate to induce her but..." Esther thought a minute. "I want to see you next week and we'll do some tests. You have someone to take care of Toddy?"

When Lonnie nodded, Esther continued. "We'll make a decision then. She's not dropped down yet, so she's in no hurry." She gave Lonnie a hand to sit upright again.

"Remember, Toddy did the same thing and he came a week late."

"True." Esther picked up the chart and flipped pages. "But he wasn't this big this soon. The larger the baby, the harder the birthing."

"My sister calls me rubber bottom since that first one was so easy. Not that I thought it easy." She huffed out a breath and stepped down. "Thanks."

"You're taking your supplements, too, right?"

"I am doing everything like you and that manual said. I might kill soon for a cup of coffee. Real coffee with every molecule of caffeine."

"I hear you. But it won't be long."

Esther left the room grateful for the reprieve. Delivering babies was one of her chief joys. Especially healthy babies.

As she saw her other patients, her good mood stayed

with her. *I am here* hovered in her head. Three people said they were so excited about the new clinic, one older man grumbled about that meeting lasting so long. When they closed for the lunch hour, she shut the door, took a salad out of her pack, and, after adding dressing, put her feet up on her desk with the chair tilting back. Again she reminded herself to relax as she ate her salad and nibbled the crackers she kept in the lower drawer. She could go into the break room, but then she'd be tempted by the goodies in the machine. The repairman had finally shown up last Friday. They now had functional vending machines again.

The phone rang, but she let it go to the answering service. Barbara had gone shopping and the front door was locked. When her cell sang, she checked the screen and let that go, too. Her mother. She would call her back later. Waves of weariness rolled over her, so she let her eyes close and actually fell asleep. At a tap at the door, she jolted awake and slammed her feet on the floor. "Yes!"

"Your next patients are here, but they're early. We have a drop-in, so I'm putting her in one, okay? You want some coffee?" At the nod, Barbara headed for the door. "I'll get it going. The patient is filling out the forms. She and her grandson are new to the clinic. She said they recently moved to a place south of town."

"Thank you, Barbara." Drop-ins were usually of three categories: old people with difficulty breathing, young people with asthma, and amateur carpenters who'd just smashed their thumbs. Which would this be?

She entered one with a smile. "Hello, I'm Dr. Hanson. Mostly I go by Dr. Esther."

The older woman extended her left hand to shake. "Sorry, my right hand is the reason I am here. And to meet you. I am Clara Holmgren and this is my grandson, Jefferson." She indicated the boy sitting in the wheel-chair.

Esther held out her hand to the boy then, after a bit of a pause, she simply took his hand in hers. It was limp. "Hi, Jefferson. I'm Dr. Esther."

He didn't smile or flinch but simply stared back at her. No, stared beyond her. Dark curly hair, a face that needed more sun, and slim to the point of skinny. He wore jeans and a T-shirt with a hoodie sweatshirt like 90 percent of the teens she knew.

"We need to find us a new doctor since we moved, and your clinic was the closest. Our daughter recommended it, said you did a wonderful job in that storm."

"I hope I can be what you need." Esther glanced down through the filled-in sheets. "Cognitive problems and spinal cord injury." She watched the boy's movement, what little there was. "Lumbar-sacral?"

"Yes."

"Can you fill in some history to flesh out what's on this form?"

"Jefferson is my grandson. He came to live with me when he was three. We lived on Eglund Road, it's over by Bemidji but not real close."

Eglund Road. So close to her family's home. "What brought you up here?"

"My other daughter, my older daughter, lives here and wants us closer so she can help me more. As Jefferson has grown, I can no longer give him all the care he needs."

"How long has Jefferson been in a wheelchair?"

"Since he was five. Car accident. I was driving one night and my car died. We were on our way home from visiting my daughter up here. I was just about to get out to flag down help when a car struck us from behind. The driver tried to miss us but we were right in the road lane. His car caught the passenger side rear. Jeffy's spine was damaged and he's never walked again."

"I'm so sorry."

"The hardest part is that the driver never stopped. Just spun around and tore off into the night. Good thing for us a patrolman came along and called the ambulance. How could someone hit and run like that?"

"I—I . . ." Esther's stomach tied itself in knots. "You said you need help with your arm?" *Work on something you perhaps can fix. Don't think! Above all, don't think.* "What happened?"

"I fell, and I thought sprained it, but the swelling won't go away and the pain is getting worse. I have to be able to use both hands to take care of Jefferson."

"So, you've not had this x-rayed yet?"

"No. We were right in the middle of the move, and I figured it would get better on its own. But it hasn't."

"We'll get that x-rayed then. Do I need to check Jefferson for anything?"

"All we need is a renewal of his prescription for his medications." She dug a worn piece of paper from her purse. "He takes these."

"Let me listen to his lungs. When did he last have a checkup?" Esther glanced at Jefferson. *Were there brain injuries, too? Why was he not tracking?*

"Well, uh, not for a while. But I suppose we should."

"Hey, Jefferson, what grade are you in?"

While he looked at her when she said his name, he didn't answer. "Okay, I need to check your lungs. Will you lift up your shirt?" *Surely he could hear. What was she dealing with here?*

His grandmother pulled up his shirt and Esther listened to his lungs front and back. She checked his pulse, which was normal also. "How long has he been on those meds?"

"Years. Since he was three."

"Any problems with them?"

"Not with his behavior. It's like always, for him."

"But he's not been reevaluated since ... ?" Esther looked at the lady.

"Well, we know what's wrong, so why spend money on doctors?"

"I'll write you refills for these, but I want you to have him evaluated. Children's physiology changes as they grow, especially their response to medications. Too, some children become sensitized, others become tolerant. Adjusting his medications may well bring marked improvement, but I'm not qualified to do that. You need a good pediatrician, ideally, one who specializes in special-needs children."

"What kind of improvement?"

"More responsive, more alert. Possibly not—as I say, I'm not qualified—but it's worth trying."

Esther wrote out the prescriptions and handed them to her. "Jefferson, do you want to go out and watch TV while we x-ray your grandmother's arm?"

No response.

"I'll push him out there."

"With that arm?"

"Sometimes he takes over and wheels himself."

Esther made a mental list of questions. "Let me do that." She pushed the wheelchair out into the waiting room and positioned it so he could watch TV, which caught his attention immediately. She returned to the room.

"So, he is twelve, right?"

"Yes. He was five when the accident happened, but he has always been real slow. The doctor said there was brain damage when he was born. That was the problem, you see. His mother—my younger daughter—his mother disappeared as soon as she realized he would never be—you know, normal—and left him for me to raise. It was far easier before my husband died, because he helped with Jefferson."

While they talked Esther ran the antiquated machine and then developed the images while Clara sat waiting, sat talking. And talking. Esther kept her focus on the older woman and refused to allow her mind to go where it wanted to. Back to the accident. Had the memories that kept intruding been of this very accident? Were these two the victims of her fears and incompetence?

Clara rambled on. "It's still hard to fathom, after all these years. I mean: My car was white. Surely it would show up in the driver's headlights, even if the taillights weren't working, don't you think?"

No, I don't want to think.

"And there's those red reflectors in back besides the taillights. We tried Jefferson in public school a couple of years, but it didn't work. They have to take special-needs children—it's the law, you know—but they couldn't help him. So we just gave up."

Esther clipped the images onto the viewer and studied the arm. "Yes, Mrs. Holmgren, there had been a break, and now it's not healing well at all, thus the pain and swelling. See this here?" She traced the break line.

"Yes. But what does that mean?"

"That means you need to see an orthopedic specialist. I can set you up with an appointment in Grand Forks.

We don't have specialists like that here. I know you won't want to do this, but there is no other option. They will most likely rebreak the arm, pin it or insert a plate, and watch awhile to make sure it is healing correctly."

"But what about Jefferson?"

"Can your other daughter take him awhile?"

"I suppose she'll have to." Clara slowly shook her head. "I should have gone in earlier, right?"

"Hindsight is always twenty/twenty." Esther swallowed. "Were you injured in the accident?"

"Not really, bruised and shook up, but Jefferson took the brunt of it."

"How are you dealing with your feelings toward the driver of the other vehicle?"

"I pray for that driver every day. The guilt that person must carry. I wish I could tell him—her or him—that we forgive. I understand running away from something beyond our control, how often I've wanted to do the same. But our actions always have consequences and often they involve others. That's just the way life is."

"You are very gracious."

"I live by God's grace every day." She rubbed her tender arm. "Thank you for your help. I have to be able to take care of Jefferson."

"If there is something I can do..."

She patted Esther's arm. "Thank you for becoming our new doctor. I feel there is something special about you."

Esther forced her mouth into a smile. "Thank you. I'll call you as soon as we can set that up. Let me wheel Jefferson out for you. Can he transfer himself to the car?"

"No, we have a lift in the back of the van."

"But he can wheel himself?"

"Sometimes."

Esther watched as the lift lowered and then raised the wheelchair. Jefferson did wheel himself in. Was he more capable than he was letting on and just letting his grand-mother do all the work? Or what?

"Thanks again." Clara settled into the driver's seat.

Esther returned to the next patient waiting for her. Good thing she had her lunch along.

The moment the second patient left, she flipped on her computer and went searching for accident reports, by area and date. Sure enough, there it was, in the *Bemidji Pioneer* archives.

She read through the report, keeping in mind the two people she had just met, both of them victims. The ac-cident was an accident, but leaving the scene—that was unforgivable. How could she have done such a thing? And to not know for all these years what was causing the PTSD? Even with all the counseling with Dr. Phillips, this had remained hidden. What were the legalities of such a crime? For it was a crime. Surely this would keep her out of medical school. Not to mention send her to jail.

She stared at the screen until the tears blurred it com-pletely. Hadn't she cried enough?

Barbara rapped at the door. "Difficulty breathing in room one. I'll set up a bronchodilator."

"Thanks."

Finally, four thirty rolled around and she stopped in the break room for coffee. Cold. Much as she hated to, she poured a cup and stuck it in the microwave.

"Sorry, I didn't get time to make fresh." Barbara sank down on a chair by the round table. "I've put out the CLOSED sign and called Ben to tell him to come to the side door. Said he'd be here by five." She stretched her arms over her head and yawned. "Consensus for the day regarding the meeting. Four glad the plans are moving ahead. Two think the townspeople are being railroaded. One can't figure what all the fuss is about. I guess things got a bit hot over at the café this morning."

The microwave *bing*ed and Esther added sugar and cream to make the sludge bearable. "Interesting the idea that we are railroading this through. Not like we've not mentioned it all these years." Esther stopped in front of the snack machine. Something chocolate sounded real good about now. "You want anything?" Pulling out the dollar bill she kept for times such as this, she inserted it, and pushed the numbers. A Baby Ruth bar dropped into the compartment, and her change tinkled into the cup. "You want part of this?"

"Oh, you talked me into it."

Esther smiled, crossed to the counter, and cut the bar in half. "Here."

They were each taking their first bite when a rap came on the side door.

Barbara rose and went to let Ben in, following them to Esther's office.

No greeting; Ben went right to the point. "What do you have?"

Her mouth full of peanuts, chocolate, and caramel, Esther handed him the folder with the report and took her chair behind the desk, pointing at the other.

Ben chose instead to lean against the door frame.

Was he being careful about being too close to her? She ignored the inner turmoil and watched him read, flip through the pages, and go back to read it again. After the scene last night, she'd just as soon not look him in the eye anyway.

"That could be Dawn's mother." He tapped a page titled *Jane Doe 3*. "'Indications of parturition within four weeks of death.' And no sign of a baby in the van. Not even a diaper bag."

Barbara nodded. "That's what I was thinking. A DNA test would make sure. What will they do with the bodies?"

Esther could answer that one. "John Does—and Janes—are kept in the morgue pending identification. We can draw a blood sample from Dawn for matching, or just swab the roof of her mouth. That works, too, but I'd rather go with the blood."

Ben slapped the papers onto Esther's desk with such force she jumped. "If it matches, Dawn will go into the social services system and be moved into a foster home."

Barbara asked, "But Ben can still be the foster parent, right?"

"Doubtful. They look for two-parent homes; ideally, families already cleared to provide foster care. It's quite a long and complex process." Esther kept her voice on a professional level, just giving out the facts.

"I see. So step one is get a DNA sample off." He snatched up the folder to stare again at the page with Jane Doe 3. Esther hated to see him so agitated. He tapped the page with a finger. "So what if we do nothing?"

"Have you filed those papers I asked you to?"

"What papers?" A frown connected his eyebrows.

"I'm sure I asked you to file the forms with social services." He was already shaking his head. Esther tipped her head back. "Oh, my. I was waiting for you to..."

"I was waiting for you to tell me what they said. I figured you were going to file them, since you're the designated medical person here. Been meaning to ask you about it." He scowled at whatever was in front of him, in this case, her desk.

Esther couldn't even see any straws to snatch at. "Okay. This is one of those things that fell through the cracks in all the mayhem. So far no one outside the few of us knows where she came from or anything about this."

Ben was wagging his head. "Yeah, but we won't be the only ones to connect two and two and figure it out. With the probable mother found, the cat is out of the bag. We have no more time. With Chief, we'd work something out. With Perowsky, she'll be on her way back to China or wherever. A charcoal briquette has more sympathy."

She sighed. "The only bright spot I can see, not filing with social services will look like a simple mistake made when our situation was in chaos. You assumed I would, and I gave her temporarily to an authorized law enforcement officer assuming that officer would. We get each other off the hook." Easy to say, but the guilt snuck in again and jabbed her. If she were doing her job correctly, she should have followed up on the paperwork immediately.

"Right. She is a gift that just fell out of the sky and Bo found her. I say, don't tell social services she exists until we absolutely have to." He shut the folder and laid it back on her desk. "Let's get the DNA thing going and see what happens next. I can go get her and bring her here."

"Or I can go with you, do the draw, and make sure all is done just right."

"I'll lock up here. You two go on." Barbara stood up.

"Thank you, Barbara." She dug her purse out of the drawer, grabbed her medical bag, and got a Styrofoam cold-box out of the mini surgery. She scooped ice into it and followed Ben out the side door to where their vehicles waited side by side.

"You can ride with me; I'll bring you back in."

"Thanks but no thanks. This way I have the cooler and everything I'll need, and...no, thanks, I'll drive separately." She knew she was rambling, but being in the same vehicle as Ben this evening was beyond her. She plopped her bag and the cold-box on the seat beside her and followed the border patrol van to Ben's home. A law enforcement officer, of all people. And she a—*forget it, Esther!*

He held the door for her at the house, and she walked into the kitchen ahead of him.

"Well, Dr. Esther, what a nice surprise!" Beth turned from the sink and smiled wide. "You two are just in time for supper. Ansel can set one more plate."

She hadn't counted on this. She should have. "No, really, that's all right. I'll just get the sample and get on home."

"I don't think so. I made a huge meat loaf and something prompted me to put in an extra potato to bake. Surely whatever you need to do can wait long enough for us to eat."

Ansel came into the kitchen. "Well, what a nice surprise! You're staying, I hope." He reached up in the cupboard for another plate and plunked it on the table. "Come see our little girl." He moved to the dining room, beckoning Esther to follow him. "See what we rigged up today." A baby jumper hung from a spring clamped onto the lintel of the dining room doorway. Tiny Dawn was wedged into it amid pillows, her feet barely poking out the edges of the leg holes. "When she gets bigger, she'll like it better, but look at her smile when I move this." He gently pulled on the contraption and the dark-eyed baby broke into a grin. She waved her arms in delight at the movement.

"Oh, my, how she is growing." Esther squatted down in front of the swing. "Hi, sweet baby. Look at you. Isn't she just beautiful!"

"You won't get an argument from any of us here." From the kitchen, Beth slid the meat loaf onto a platter and set the potatoes around it. "Come on, let's eat."

"I need to wash my hands first."

"The kitchen sink or the bathroom." Beth poured cooked, sliced carrots into another bowl, sprinkled them with salt and pepper, and added a generous pat of butter. Down-home cooking, like Esther's mom and aunts did.

Esther washed her hands at the kitchen sink and joined the others in the dining room, where she took the seat Beth pointed her to. When the others bowed their heads, she did likewise and Ansel said grace. His prayer for wisdom let her know that Ben had probably called ahead.

Once everyone was served, including little Natalie in her high chair between her mother and father, Ansel asked, "Ben told us about a DNA test. Logical. So what will the process be?"

Esther explained, "We'll get the sample tonight. I'll keep it on ice and send it in tomorrow. DNA usually takes about three weeks. Actually, they can do it in twenty-four hours or so, but they always have a backlog. And there's always people who are certain they're too important to wait in the queue."

"I'm sure you both realize that this will put our sweet Dawn into the social services system unless we have a way around that." Beth crumbled some meat loaf and laid it on the tray of the high chair, along with a few bits of potato and carrots.

Natalie started plucking up food bits. Apparently she was what one would call an eager eater.

Esther casually glanced at Ben. He had served himself man-size helpings, but he wasn't eating anything with man-size enthusiasm. In fact, he looked downright glum.

"She wants to feed herself, but she just can't handle a spoon yet," Beth explained. Once Natalie was attended to, she looked at Esther. "Ben, Esther, I may have a temporary solution. I think you need to know that Ansel and I are cleared as foster parents. We've done all the paperwork, the inquiries and all. So we can petition for her to be left with us. We thought of doing that for a while, and once our house is repaired and I'm no longer nursing His Highness, I would like to have another baby to care for. I love babies, and this way we can make a difference."

Ben stared at her. "Ah, Beth. Would that ever take a load off my shoulders."

Ansel bobbed his head. "All of our shoulders. We no more want her into the system than you do. But this will make her eligible for adoption."

Esther loved the atmosphere in this home. Good friends, good food, peace and quiet, no one looking for some little thing to disapprove of, no carping—most of all, everyone looking for the best solution to a desperate problem. So unlike her home.

"I'll start the paperwork for that as soon as I can." Ben looked to Esther. "You don't think Bo would let her go, do you?"

"Ben," Esther said patiently, "almost always the courts are looking for two-parent families." Why couldn't he see that? *Two parents, Ben. Read my lips.*

He shrugged. "I read about a woman who was finally able to adopt two little sisters she'd been fostering."

"No matter how good a father you will be, this will not be as easy as you seem to think."

"I never said it would be easy. I just said Bo and I will not let her leave us." He stood and went over to pick up Dawn, who'd begun to fuss, putting her up against his shoulder. She quieted immediately.

Esther shook her head at the picture they made. The big black dog looking up to make sure all was well, the man in a border patrol field uniform, toughness personified, holding a tiny little head with black hair that stuck out every which way, nestled against his shoulder. The hand patting the baby's back brought down a drug addict, used a gun with expertise, but for now comforted a hungry baby girl. Esther's heart stopped beating. Only for a moment before she could squash the thought. This feeling she had was fast becoming more than just a casual attraction for Ben James.

Chapter Twenty-Two

"Sorry! Bo, you have to come with me today." Ben kissed Dawn on the top of her head, handed her back to Ansel, and headed for the carport. Bo looked over his shoulder and whined. "Bo, come." Head down, the dog did as ordered.

"I'll be working on my house today," Ansel said, "so if you need anything I'm close by."

"Like what?" Ben paused in the act of getting in the SUV. Bo was already sitting in the passenger seat.

"I don't know. Just a feeling I have."

"I'll keep it in mind. I'm sure he's sending me out on patrol again, since he said to make sure and bring my partner in today. I don't think he has much respect for our K-9 officers."

"He won't last long here. He's managed to offend half the town already with his attitude."

"Anything I need to know about?"

"Nope." Ansel stepped back and waved.

Ben backed into the turnaround and pulled out to head for the street. He needed a real weekend at home to get some of the cleanup done on his own place. But come

Saturday he was sure he'd be over helping Ansel. Hard to believe it was already November, but the frost that glinted in the rising sunlight told its own tale. Winter would soon be roaring down their backs, and they needed to get Ansel's house sealed in again. Everyone was fighting the same kinds of things, so there were no extra hands to borrow.

Lots of cars in the parking lot at work; was something going on?

"Morning, Ben." Jenny leaned forward. "You better hustle. He's got another burr under his saddle."

"Seems to be a permanent condition." Ben rolled his eyes and headed down the hall to the meeting room. He was still five minutes early, but a glance at those gathered told him he was the last one in.

"Good of you to make it." Perowsky was already standing at the head of the room, clipboard in hand.

Ben just nodded and didn't even mention his earliness. A barb like that needed no response. He took a chair and nodded to those around him. This used to be a time of camaraderie, but not any longer. No one smiled or cracked a joke, or even really greeted each other. Ah, the things they had taken for granted. But then under Chief Harden, they had been a team. Now they were just a group of men and women waiting for orders.

Right at seven thirty the man in front looked up from studying his notes. "I'll post the assignments for today. It has been brought to my attention that some of you are heavily involved in this drive to fund and build the clinic. That is your volunteer time, it is not to be confused with work time. You are being paid to protect our borders and both keep out aliens and find the ones that have already entered. Do you understand?" He looked around the room and then stared directly at Ben. "Any questions?"

When no one spoke, he continued. "I have a rather unusual announcement here. The autopsy report is back on the bodies found in the van in the river. One woman was lactating and the condition of her uterus indicates that she had given birth within the month. The authorities have requested that we keep watch for an infant body that they believe might have floated out of the van via an open window."

Ben studied his hands. How many would put two and two together and realize the baby he had brought in might be that baby? But then he'd never talked much about Dawn here, although in a town like Pineville the news would have gotten around anyway.

"If there are no further questions, this meeting is dismissed." Perowsky strutted from the room without a nod or smile or any recognition to his team. Not that he believed for an instant that they were *his team*.

Ben joined the others around the board to read what he already figured. He was assigned the northernmost zone, but while Perowsky, no doubt, would think this was punishment, that was Ben's favorite place to prowl. It was the area where he and Bo found the baby. Most likely that emigrant trail was abandoned—though on the other hand, the smugglers wouldn't know they'd found the baby.

Ben turned to Jonas, the man next to him. "Where will you be?"

"East of you."

"Keep your eyes peeled. They've been using that area. You have your K-9 partner?" He put the slur on the term the way Perowsky had done.

"You think I'd go without my K-9 partner?" And Jonas used exactly the same inflection.

Ben nodded. He and Jonas were the only two with patrol dogs in their region. "Maybe today will be our lucky day. Let's keep in contact."

Carol, one of the two women on their team, sidled closer. "You just be grateful you are far away from this office."

"Bad, eh?" Jonas had developed the skill of hardly moving his mouth while talking.

"I sent in a grievance."

"Wow. For what?"

"Asking the higher-ups to find us a human being for our new chief. Surely this man is an android."

It was all Ben could do to not laugh out loud. Instead he headed for his SUV and his waiting K-9 partner.

As soon as his vehicle cleared the outskirts of town, Ben's mind flitted to Esther and her behavior of the last couple of days. Why could she not admit she suffered from PTSD? It wasn't like a contagious disease, nor was it something she chose. If she would just talk with him about it, talk to anyone about it, she might get some relief.

After all, he'd been there, too, but probably nothing as severe as hers. *Or maybe women react differently than men do.* Wondering what had caused the disorder to attack her, he became aware of the warm glow that seemed to visit him when he allowed himself to think about her. Yes, they were friends, but he was beginning to realize he wanted their relationship to be more than that. After Allie died he'd been sure he'd never feel this way again.

On the way north, Ben spoke notes and reminders into his cell's recorder. While he used to be able to call Jenny and ask her to set things up for him, now he didn't want to get her in trouble, either. "Call Lars and have him set up an appointment with Aptos and Esther—see if we can get him to extend the ninety days. Two: Talk to art department and drafting class re exterior of new clinic. Three: Thank-you notes to Livingston and Ho. Four:..." Bo's whining stopped his taping.

"You're right, big dog, we're almost there." Ever since they'd turned onto the dirt road, Bo had left off snoozing and kept his nose pressed to the window. It would seem this was his favorite zone as well. Ben slowed the SUV, watching both sides of the road for anything odd. The storm had created a disaster scene that, were it in town, would take years to clean up. Some trees were snapped off ten feet above the ground; others were only held up by the limbs of the surrounding trees. The water table was even higher than usual, leaving more open water than he had ever seen before in this area. No longer did this qualify as a bog. It was now a lake bed.

Chief Harden had believed that their very presence, driving the roads without any schedule, was a deterrent. Surely that would discourage smugglers of any kind. And now they'd need a boat to get through.

At one point he stopped, thinking this was where he'd parked before, but everything was changed and Bo didn't react. He hit Jonas's number. "See anything?"

"Water water everywhere."

"Yah, the water's almost up to the roadbed here. No wonder the river is still flowing high. Let me know if you see anything."

"I'm turning around," Jonas called. "The bottom is going out on the road."

"We need to get in here on horseback or ATVs." He

didn't want to turn around and get stuck in the soft shoulders. Now what?

Ben spotted something snagged on low bushes just off the road—a red plastic bag or something. "I'm stopping." He stepped out of the vehicle and Bo bounded to the gravel, his nose to the ground immediately. Tail waving like a flag, he veered off the road and right to the crimson bit. He sniffed at it and shot Ben a hurry-up look over his shoulder.

"I'm coming." Once again Ben wished he were in better shape. He'd nearly blown his lungs out keeping up with a woman who spent even less effort to keep in shape than he did. Early-morning runs had ceased to exist, the more he drank. But that was over. He really did have to get back into fighting shape again.

He pulled a plastic bag from the pouch on his vest and scooped the silk scarf into it. He'd bet anything it was foreign-made—but then, what wasn't anymore? No one with this kind of scarf wore it out into the brush like this, even if it was hunting season. Bo stopped sniffing at the water's edge and stared out across the lake.

If only Ben had some idea where they could pick up the trail again. He eyeballed the expanse of water. Diagonal would be the most direct; if they had a boat with a shallow draft, they could go a long way. He called into the office. "Jenny, how about asking His Lordship if he could request a flyover, chopper to keep it low. Perhaps some interagency assistance with the air force base?"

"You found something?"

"I did, or rather Bo did. A bright red silk scarf snagged on a low bush. Nothing else in the area. Bo tracked someone to the water's edge, then sat and stared across the water. I'd sure like to know every place on the shoreline where people have walked since the storm."

"I'll make the suggestion, but..."

"I know, the cost. Wish we had some of those drones they have in Afghanistan. Silent and can fly at night."

"Right. I'll try."

"Or I'll talk with him when I get back."

"Or both."

Ben shook his head as he clicked off. "Come on, Bo." Interagency cooperation? How about a little cooperation within the station?

"But, sir..."

"So you found a red silk scarf caught on a bush. It probably blew out of a car window. Women all over the country wear red silk scarves made in China or wherever. That's not enough to go on."

Out a car window? On a dirt road that went nowhere, except to the border. Then another thought struck. Had Perowsky read the reports and heard that Bo found the baby in that same area? A baby, a scarf, other than catching a snakehead with his cargo in tow, what did he expect? Ben realized it was a good thing he had learned to keep his face from revealing his emotions, thanks to the marines.

"Have you ever driven up there, sir?"

"No, that's your job."

Ben nodded. "Yes, sir. That it is."

Perowsky leaned forward, loosely clasped hands on the desk blotter. "Look, James, this whole sector was way, way over budget before and it's not going to happen on my watch, so just do as you're told, and we'll all get along better."

Ben stared at the man behind the desk, who had not a wrinkle in his class A uniform. He started to say something then nearly bit his tongue, clamping his teeth so hard and fast. His heart almost jumped out of his chest; the fight-or-flight adrenaline kicked in instantly. His eyes slitted, but he raised his chin and gave a curt nod.

Once out in the hall, he kept himself from sending a fist through the wallboard and strode on out the front doors, straight-arming the latch bar. He threw his jacket on the seat, called Bo out, and the two of them took off running down the street. Anything to work off the adrenaline.

When he was still shaking after a mile or so, he slowed to catch his breath, resolving that from now until it was too cold to breathe safely, he would run every day. Heck, a kindergartner could outlast him.

Back in his rig and officially off the clock, he made the phone calls he'd put on his prompts list when driving.

Yes, the art and drafting departments would be delighted to produce the building workup.

Lars was not nearly as delighted. "It's gonna be a waste of time, but I'll set up a meeting for the first possible date. You realize, Ben, that Aptos is badgering his cronies to commit to large amounts of money also?"

"I know. Even though Hazel was real cautious about revealing financial assets, I got the feeling there is more money right here in Pineville than anyone realizes."

Lars snickered. "Not sure what some of them are saving it for, but we can be real thankful old Aptos is spearheading this. Who'd have thought that nearly dying would make such a change in that man? Far as he's concerned, Esther walks on water and the clinic earned every dime he can raise. He and his wife were both altruistic, but most of the town doesn't even know all they did. They were always adamant about not being recognized. Strange isn't it?"

Ben nodded and then realized Lars couldn't see him. "That's for sure."

Ben sat at the meeting table feeling frustrated. Esther on his right looked just as frustrated. Lars sat at his left with an I-told-you-so smugness. Behind them, maybe twenty or thirty people sat around listening. This was an open meeting, but not too many people seemed interested this time around.

Across from them, the spidery Mr. Aptos sat back, adamant. "The challenge stays. If I was to take the pressure off, this might just slide right back into the apathy we've seen for years. People understand a challenge, and I don't see nothing wrong with it."

Ben and Esther swapped looks.

Aptos even looked rather pleased. "Some of them are hoppin' mad, but that's good, too. Gets 'em charged up to do something, you see, and the energy keeps building. Pineville folks are real good at getting hot and bothered and then doing the right thing. I should know; I've lived here all my life. I'd say I've become an expert on Pineville." He leaned forward and smacked the flat of his hand on the table. "Let's just do this and let the Lord lead as the ninety days draw to a close." His grin closely resembled that of a leprechaun Ben had seen in a picture. But the light in his eyes held nary a hint of deviltry.

"Do we have any choice?" Lars asked, his tone dry as pine needles.

Aptos paused. "Lars, you know me. You know I try to let God lead, sometimes more so than others. But I've been praying on this. The way that young woman there brought me back to not only living but wanting to really live again, I do believe that was her being willing to be used of our God. He has blessed me beyond measure and many others in this town. Now it is our turn."

Ben blinked and blew out a breath. He glanced at Esther, who appeared to be even more shocked than he was. Lars muttered something, obviously struggling to come up with a comment, but finally just threw up his hands. "What can I say?"

"You can say praise the Lord and pass the ammunition." Mr. Aptos stood up again. "I have another idea, too, so that more of our people can take part in this. I talked to Hazel, and she said it can be done. We sell bonds of various amounts that will be redeemed at staggered times. That way we will have the cash up front and people here will get a return on their investments." He studied each of those in the room, nodding all the while. "Another God idea. I never would have come up with that one on my own." He puffed out a breath. "Any questions?"

"Not right now, but I'm sure you'll have answers when I do. Did I hear you right that you said we'll let God do the deciding as the ninety days draw to a close?"

"You did. I believe He will come up with whatever extensions, if we need them."

Lars nodded. "I remember when one of the churches held a bond sale like this for their building fund. They found it very successful. But I don't remember them having such a tight time line." He wiped his glistening forehead with a white handkerchief. "Why do I feel like I've just been run over by a Great Northern train?"

Aptos sat down, a chuckle drifting into the corners of the room. "How do you think I feel? This wasn't exactly what I had planned for these next months, either. I thought to go visit some friends in Florida, and now I'm trapped here to see this through, and winter at the door. By the way, we have two more commitments of a million each. Any idea how much this clinic is going to cost?"

Esther nearly choked on her snort, which morphed into a coughing laugh. "No, none. I move we name it the Aptos Memorial Clinic."

"No. It will be the Paul Harden Memorial Clinic. He made a world of difference in this town through the years, an impact on everyone, one way or another."

And I miss him more than I ever dreamed possible. Lord this is all in your hands. "I'd say we best get the committees appointed and get this ball rolling." Ben pushed back his chair and stood. He checked his cell and saw Amber's name on the screen. What could she be wanting? He thought he knew. And it wasn't going to happen.

Chapter Twenty-Three

To call or not to call was more a dilemma than a simple question.

Esther took her cell out of her shirt pocket—again—and sucked in a deep breath. Ben was a friend; girls could call friends. Still, her mother's dictates rang in her head. *Nice girls do not call boys.* Even back then her mother had been hopelessly out of date. But Esther had believed her whether she planned on that or not. *You are a grown woman now, Ben is a friend, and it is okay to call him.* She flipped to contacts and tapped Ben James's cell number. After all, he was still at work. As the phone rang she nearly hung up. His comment about the new super being death on calls or anything during work time that was not work-related made her feel guilty. Not a difficult thing to do.

"Hi, Esther, what's up?"

She had to swallow to find her voice.

"Esther, are you all right?"

"Yes. Pardon me." She coughed and cleared her throat. "Sorry, swallowed wrong. I'm calling to invite you to come with me to my parents' house for Thanksgiving." She knew she was speaking too fast but better that than dropping the phone or something stupid. "I've put them off for the last couple of years and...you could bring Dawn. My mother loves babies."

"Yes."

"And we don't have to stay through all the football games if you don't want to."

"Esther, hold it."

"And...oh sorry." *You crazy woman. What's come over you?* "I'm holding."

His chuckle sounded even better than she remembered. Not that she'd been thinking about him unduly or any such thing. "Sorry." Her mind made a screeching halt. "What did you say?"

"I said yes."

How to make a fool of yourself in three easy steps. Not that she even needed three. "You will?"

"Yes, if you are sure that they are expecting you plus two others."

Esther heaved a sigh of relief. "Thank you. My mother and father love to have a big crowd on Thanksgiving. My baby sister Jill is going home with her college roommate and my other sister, Andrea, has to go to her in-laws this year so Mom was disappointed. There will be my brother Kenneth and family, Gramma, and us." She was babbling. Taking a deep breath she shook her head. "Sometimes my aunt and uncle come, too. They remember you from your football days."

"What time do we need to be there?"

"Anytime, maybe noon. It's a little more than four hours' drive."

"From something you said, I thought you grew up nearer to Thief River Falls."

"Nope. Sorry to bust into your day like this. You won't get in trouble?"

"I doubt it. Bo and I are scouting the backwoods."

"Find anything else since the scarf?" He'd told her about that before the meeting with Lars and Mr. Aptos.

"No so far. Helped a farmer out of a ditch. Said he swerved for a raccoon and nearly ended up in the lake. The shoulders are still soft from all that rain."

Barbara tapped on the door. "Phone for you."

"Gotta go. More later." She paused only long enough for his good-bye and snapped her phone shut before picking up the office line. "Dr. Hanson." The day was truly under way, but at least she had accomplished the most difficult thing first.

Thanksgiving was less than two weeks away. She needed to call her mother and find out what she was supposed to bring. "No, thank you. We aren't in need of any of those right now. No. Really. I'm sorry. No." How had that vendor slipped past Barbara's method of screening calls?

She left the building at three for her regularly scheduled appointment with her counselor. Halfway there, her phone chimed and she was told that Dr. Phillips had a last-minute emergency and she would need to reschedule. Puffing out a sigh, she turned around at the next driveway and headed back to Pineville. Since she had no scheduled appointments, perhaps she could get to the bottom of the catch-up pile.

"What are you doing here?" she asked Barbara after letting herself in through the side door.

"Same as you, catching up. I put some more paperwork on your desk, things that I needed to figure out first."

"Thanks heaps and bunches."

"Anytime."

Back in her office, she called and rescheduled her appointment, then attacked the stack that had grown larger in her absence. She was sure that two sheets of paper touching each other bred more during the night. In the daytime, the stack had Barbara's help. When the outbox was nearly full and the inbox empty, Esther leaned back in her chair. The files on patients treated during the storm were woefully inadequate. Those treated by others, like Ben and Rob, needed their input. Barbara had put sticky notes on the pages with the name of the one who'd given the immediate treatment.

Esther sorted the remaining stack into separate stacks so that the correct person could go over the file before Barbara consigned them to the file cabinets along the walls. Whatever could not be remembered or filled in—well, that was the way it was. Her concern was those who weren't documented. She pushed the button for the front desk.

"What do you need?"

"I thought you went home hours ago. Flipping through these I remembered those two little kids who came to us, the ones whose mother had died. What happened with them?"

"Yvette took them over to the church to the shelter and their father picked them up two days later. The women at the church made sure they were taken care of."

"And their mother's body?"

"Dennis and Yvette took it to the morgue as soon as they could. We didn't want that poor man to have to deal with her decomposing body when he walked in the door."

"Thank you. What other things fell through the cracks that I am not aware of?"

"Well, old Mrs. Unfeld, the one with dementia, as soon as her daughter could get her, she took her home with her. Again, the ladies at the church made sure she was cared for."

"The unsung heroes?"

"There are many of them in this town. Nothing gets people pulling together better than a natural disaster. But you know, people here have always taken care of each other."

"I guess. I've started piles here for Ben, Dennis, and Rob. How about giving them a call tomorrow and ask them to come when they can and see if they can fill in any of the blanks?"

"All right. Now go home."

"Yes, Mother. Night." Esther hung up and dug out her purse from the drawer. The stack was gone. The relief that washed over her threatened to carry her out with the tide if she didn't just give up and get some rest.

The next brisk November days flew by with talk of the clinic overshadowing everything except the football team, first with its league victory, then on to district. Despite the time they'd lost due to the storm and recovery, the team was charging forward. When you thought about it, the whole town was. Esther came in one day to find blue and white balloons that said ON TO STATE tethered to the underside of the reception counter and bobbing in the draft.

"And who do we thank for the new decorations? Don't they have to win district first?"

"That's this weekend. They're playing Fillmore, I think." Barbara snickered. "You know the old fifties movies where something horrible happens to the quarterback the day before the Big Game? Always the Big Game. Well, this one's the Big Game, capital letters."

"Wouldn't the state championship be the Big Game?"

"Normally, yes. Pineville has to get past the Fillmore Eagles to go to the finals. But beating Fillmore is almost more important than the championship. Certainly more important than life and death."

"Wow. Okay."

"Are you going?"

Esther kept from making a face. She'd been off to college when her brother played and didn't mind missing the games. Like she'd told Ben when he tried to teach her, she'd not cared much for the sport. "I doubt it."

The next day Beth called and invited her over for a girls-only party while the guys were gone to the division game. "I've invited Yvette, too, since her hubby went with Ben and Ansel."

"What can I bring?"

"Yourself. I'm making an apple crisp and I have chips and dip. Nothing fancy."

"I could bring a cheese ball and crackers."

"All right. But don't expect a whole lot."

When Esther arrived at Ben's house, Beth handed her Dawn and went to pick up Nathan, who had decided he was now hungry. "He's adopted a trait of Dawn's, wanting to be fed immediately. I thought they'd be down before company arrived." With Nathan on one arm, she sent her nightgown-clad little daughter for a blanket and settled in the rocking chair. "Thank you, sweetie." She flipped the blanket over her shoulder, settled her son to a noisy nursing, and heaved a sigh. "Not quite the way I had planned it."

The doorbell rang. "Could you get that please?"

Esther nodded and, Dawn in one arm, invited Yvette in. "Welcome to feed-the-babies hour."

"I can see what it would take to raise twins," Esther said a bit later when the three children were sound asleep in their respective beds. "How do you stay so cheerful and on top of things?"

"I guess because I love doing this. I have always loved babies, and watching these two grow and change is pure delight." Beth reached for a the knife to add cheese to her cracker. "This is so good."

"Thank you." Beth smiled. "A recipe I tried so that I could make it for Thanksgiving. My mother asked me to bring three kinds of hors d'oeuvres. I agree that it is yummy."

They talked recipes and life in Pineville, the funding drive for the clinic, and the arguments going on wherever folks congregated.

Yvette's beeper went off; she groaned and flicked it open. "I'm needed on a run. I told them I'd be on call." She grabbed her coat. "See you. Thanks, Beth."

"I'd better be ready just in case. Thanks for having us and for letting me hold Dawn for a while. This has been a delightful evening. And to think, we never even brought up football." She drove to the clinic and listened to the police band. They were bringing the patient to the clinic parking lot to meet air evac.

At the same moment, she heard the chopper coming in. What a shame that patients needed to be airlifted out because their clinic was so insufficient. She watched the smooth exchange and the chopper lifting off again. Who was it and what had they needed? So many of the elderly in Pineville needed closer care. Why was there so much arguing going on about the proposed clinic?

Thanksgiving Day came quickly. From long experi-ence with the big friendly gang wars that her mom

called "family getting together," Esther packed the perishables in the cooler and the nons in a basket, so when
Ben drove up, she was ready. She met him at the door,
handed him the cooler handle, and carried the basket.
He had left the SUV running, with Bo watching over the
infant seat strapped into the seat right behind the driver.
He wagged his tail and sat back down. Ben settled the
food things in the rear.

"You're not concerned Bo might have a snack?"

"He'd never touch that without permission. He's been
trained to not take food from anyone but me." He opened
the passenger door for her.

"What if something happened to you? Would he never
eat again?" She climbed in and glanced over her shoulder.
Dawn lay sound asleep, a pink fleece hood cupping her
round little face.

Ben slid behind the steering wheel. "Good question. If
someone else put kibble in his dish, he'd eat that. But no
hand-feeding."

"I assume there's a reason."

"So the bad guys can't distract him with a steak while
they do their badness. Or worse, feed him poison or
something." He smiled at Esther. "You ready?"

"As I'll ever be."

"Is this really so hard for you?"

Esther could feel him glancing at her. Trying to figure
her out. How could he figure her out when she couldn't
figure herself out? But if she forced herself to look inside,
she knew what the problem was. Plain old guilt. Guilt and
resentment. Two of those things God said to let go of. Resentment that her mother always had to find something
to criticize in her eldest daughter. Was she that way with
the others? If so, they didn't let it bother them. Kenneth

was the golden boy in their mother's eyes. He could do no wrong. So was it not only guilt and resentment but envy, too?

Why not look at 'em all? No wonder her mother constantly found something to harp on. Esther figured she brought it on herself.

With a sigh, Esther answered. "Probably only as hard as I make it. The others seem to get along just fine. I've always felt like the odd man out. Or woman in this case."

"And of course you are not an overachiever at all."

She stared at him wide-eyed. "Ya think? Whatever gave you that idea?"

"I think it is that eldest-child syndrome. Our parents expect a lot of us and so we expect even more. Something worth growing out of, wouldn't you think?"

"You excelled in football, earned straight A's, and could have gone to any number of universities. Why didn't you?"

"I had always wanted to be a marine, thought I would stay in and retire with a bunch of stars on my shoulders or something. But during my first hitch, my folks needed me at home, and I had lost my desire to fight. There had to be other ways to handle problems, nationally and internationally. So I finished my tour and came home. Took me one more year to graduate with a BS and I went to work for the border patrol, grateful to be stationed right here in my hometown."

"You ever thought of going back to school? You did a good job there at the clinic."

"I took the advanced EMT training. By then I was married and I didn't want to pull up stakes and go back to school. Allie and I moved into my folks' house to help take care of Dad; Mom had already gone. I've done some remodeling on the place and I thought we would raise our family there." He paused and cleared his throat. "Besides, I like what I do. Most of the time."

Esther heard squeaking from the backseat. She looked over her shoulder to see Dawn stretching and looking around. Bo whined.

"I know, big dog. I hear her. How much farther to your house?"

"Not long."

"Dawn probably won't make too good a first impression if she decides she is hungry. I tell you, she has a hefty set of lungs."

Esther giggled. "You watch. My mother will take her over before you can blink. Babies settle right down when she takes care of them. Turn right at the next crossroad."

The familiar farmland glided by out there—not a sunny day but not heavily overcast, either. Brown oaks, orange maples. Eventually, they pulled into the drive.

When he stopped the vehicle, Dawn was fussing and Bo was whimpering. Ben opened the side door and Bo leaped out.

Esther gathered the food baskets. Let Ben take the baby. She led the way.

The door swung open as she reached it. Time to put on her smiley face. "Hi, Mom. Dad. I want you to meet Ben James, and that pink bundle is Dawn."

"Glad to meet you." Ben untangled one hand enough to shake theirs. "Mr. and Mrs. Hanson, thanks for inviting us."

"May I hold her?" Mom reached for the baby. "And please call me Madge."

"She's probably going to start screaming any moment now. When she decides it is mealtime, she means right now." Ben handed his baby over, and Esther was privately grateful that Bo couldn't see him giving Dawn to a stranger.

"Then we better get right on that. Esther, introduce Ben around. Is her bottle in that diaper bag?" Without waiting for an answer, Mom snatched away the diaper bag and marched inside.

Ben held the door for her and Esther led him into the house. In the flurry and busyness of introductions and greetings, Esther almost started to relax. With all the hub-bub going on, she might be exempt from her mother's attention. Ben got sucked away into the living room, so Esther wandered into the kitchen.

"Esther, she is a darling," Gramma Alma crowed. She frowned. "I listened to all the news reports, but I didn't hear anything about a baby."

"We're trying to protect her." Esther arranged her con-tribution on platters.

"Doesn't that look pretty?" Her mom appeared, Dawn tucked comfortably into the crook of her arm, and stopped at the table. "Do you need more cocktail nap-kins? I have more in the drawer, that one down there. I'm going to feed little Dawn. What an angel."

Ben strolled into the room and caught the last of that. He watched her mom disappear into the family room and grinned at Esther. "You were so right. Dawn never goes to strangers without a fuss." He smeared cheese ball on a cracker. "Oh, my gosh, this is so good."

Kenneth joined him at the table, took a sample of each, and raised his voice. "You guys better get in here, or Ben's going to eat all of these." He wiggled a finger toward their houseguest. "This guy's a genuine hero, Esther, I guess you know. Single-handedly trounced the Fillmore Eagles twice. Walks on water."

Granny frowned at Ben. "Didn't you lead our team to a state championship?"

"Two championships." Kenneth licked his fingers. "But Fillmore's the biggie."

Barbara's Big Game. Esther almost laughed out loud.

By the time they all had their fill of the turkey and vast array of trimmings, Ben had settled in as if he'd been a longtime friend of the family. How much of that was Ben's easy personality, and how much was Football Hero worship? At first Esther would have guessed hero worship, knowing her dad and brother, but it looked like Ben would've been gold even if his victories had been in intramural volleyball. She watched and listened as they discussed the game that had just ended and the one about to begin. She wagged her head. What had started out as a holiday set aside to give thanks to God had now deteriorated to a day to pig out on food and football. Nationally, of course, not just in the Hanson home.

Being non-football-enthusiasts, Esther and Gramma boned out the turkey, put the food away, and returned the kitchen to its normal sparkle. Then Esther ambled into the family room, where Kenneth was divulging all the family stories.

He was just finishing the one about the time Esther was aiming her camera for a shot and stepped backward into a neighbor's backyard swimming pool. Maybe bringing Ben here was not quite the greatest of ideas.

"You should have seen her! Mad as a wet hen." Kenneth laughed.

"I thought you guys were watching football." She nodded toward the television set. They didn't seem to be paying much attention to it.

"Aaa, lousy game. You'd think both teams would be

sharp on their toes. But they're both making more mis-
takes than a kindergartner at a spelling bee." Kenneth
waved a hand dismissively. "How many turnovers already?
And it's still the first quarter."

*So that gives him the time and the privilege to make fun
of me, does it?*

"Oh, stop pouting, Esther." Mom smiled wickedly.
"You know, when you're mad, you're really funny. So don't
be so sensitive."

"Sensitive!" Kenneth laughed. "Remember that time
she hit a stupid deer? Talk about upset." He grinned up
at Esther. "You remember that? Just a couple of days after you graduated from college. You'da thought it was the
end of the world."

"I never hit a deer!" An acid fountain erupted in her
stomach.

"Sure you did. Really fell apart. I thought you were going to cry for three days."

"*No!* No, I never hit a deer. Why do you make up stories like that?" She was yelling. She didn't mean to, but
she was.

"Dad, you remind her." Kenneth looked at his father.
"It's no big deal."

Stop shaking! But yelling at herself did no good.

"What is it, Esther?" Her father's gentle voice only
made it worse.

The tremor in her hands ran through her knees and
down to her feet. Her throat dried up, and yet at the same
time she felt like throwing up. The flashback brought her
to her knees.

The darkness. Pitch dark. Unholy dark! Her car lights
hitting the reflectors of a car dead in the road, black car,
black night—it's too late. Too late! She slammed on the

brakes, nearly driving the pedal through the floorboards, but it did no good. She pulled the steering wheel hard to the right. *Miss them! Lord God, miss them!* In the flash before the collision, she thought she saw someone in the car. The horrific screams of steel on steel, or were some of those screams people, both cars swapping ends, her headlight beams going all directions. Until silence.

Get out of the car and go see how they are. Silence out there in the blackness. What if...? Thoughts pummeled her, jabbed her behind the eyes and through her brain. *Leave! Get out of here! NOW!*

She must get out; at least see who they are. She can't! Do it! I can't! She cranked the key. Her car started right up. She spun the wheel and tore around the other vehicle, something clanking in the front end. How she made it without looking at the other car, she never knew.

"Esther! Esther!"

Ben's voice. "It's okay, Esther. You're safe. It's all right. Come on, look at me. You're going to be okay." He was kneeling in front of her, gripping her arms.

She shook her head. "No. No!"

He murmured, "I know a flashback when I see one. It's all right now. It's gone."

She jerked away. "You don't understand."

"Then talk to me."

"No! Take me home. Please! Now! I have to go home!" She wrapped both arms around herself and curled forward, anything to disappear. She must have been yelling all that—it was so loud.

Now they'd all know.

Chapter Twenty-Four

God, you have to help her, for she sure isn't letting me in." Ben felt like throwing his cell phone out the window or against a tree, or something. How about running over it with the SUV? Sure, kill the messenger. But if there were ever a time he needed a drink—it was now. Not just a drink but enough to become oblivious.

Esther, what are you doing? God, give me ideas. I know what she is going through. If only she would talk with me. Why can't she let loose and let someone help her?

If this was what loving was like...loving. When had he begun to feel that? He couldn't point to an hour and day, but the feelings were there. It wasn't exactly like the love he'd felt for Allie, but it was kind of the same thing. But Allie never had the horrible baggage that Esther carried.

They needed to have a serious discussion, and it better be soon.

He clicked off as soon as the call went to the message center. What if there was an emergency and no one could get hold of her? Or was she just screening his calls? That thought stabbed like a stiletto right into his heart. What else could he do to make her trust him?

Ever since he had brought her home from the dinner yesterday, she had not turned any lights on in her house. Was she a closet alcoholic drinking it off the way he wished he could? He was pretty good at picking up on the signs of alcoholism and drug use and had seen none in her. Maybe he should just break the door in to make sure she wasn't lying on the floor. Call the sheriff? On what grounds? What a hullabaloo that would cause! He'd just met her family. How would they react if he sent in law enforcement for help? The thoughts and fears kept stampeding through his mind.

Good thing he had to work today; he was glad for the distraction. Perowsky probably thought he was punishing Ben, making him work the day after Thanksgiving, although of course His Highness made sure he had his own entire weekend off, Wednesday through Sunday. For sure no one missed him. When Ben got off today, he would work with Ansel on his house, interior stuff, re-shingle the roof Saturday, and then after church on Sunday finish the outside work if possible. So at least he wouldn't be acting like a worried mother hen all the time. Just whenever he had a moment.

He cruised north along his favorite dirt road. The day after Thanksgiving, every hunter in the state turned out to bag that deer, but there seemed to be very little hunting activity up here today. A beater Honda. A couple of pickups with open beds. Smugglers didn't use teensy cars and open pickups. Let the hunters bask in the nonsense that they were smarter than your average whitetail. Ben started home.

Three miles outside town he slowed and fell in behind yet another beater Honda. Five miles an hour below the speed limit. It drifted slowly to the right, swerved to correct, began to drift again. He sighed. He hated traffic stops, especially at the end of his shift. But he was authorized to make them, he was expected to make them, so he flicked on his light bar and touched off his siren.

It took the driver nearly a quarter mile to notice him and pull over. Ben got out and approached the car with caution, standard procedure. The driver's-side window went down. His mouth dropped open.

Amber Harden was pawing through her purse for her driver's license. She fished out a small wallet, looked at him, and her eyes lit up. "Ben! Oh, I'm so glad it's you!" She tossed her purse aside and swung her door open. Before he could tell her to stay in the car, her feet were on the ground. She lurched erect and steadied herself by gripping the door and the roof edge.

Exactly what do you say in this situation? "Hello, Amber."

"I drove by your house yesterday, but you weren't home. Nobody was."

"Ansel and Beth and the kids went to his cousins' for Thanksgiving."

"And I drove by that doctor's, too, but she wasn't home, either."

Caution prevailed. "I believe she has family near Bemidji." His brain screeched to a halt, shifted gears. "How do you know where she lives?"

She giggled. "I asked Maizie. Maizie's Beauty Parlor. She's still there on Second Street, same as always. I got my hair done Wednesday. Do you like it?"

Tact, James. Tact. "I've always liked it."

"I had years of news to catch up on, just years, and the place to do that is the beauty parlor. Operators always know everything. You want to know anything, ask Maizie." Her voice slurred slightly.

He jerked a thumb toward her car. "I think I recognize this heap. Did you buy it from Donny Taylor?"

She cocked her head. "Yes. Why?"

"It got rolled a couple of months ago. The frame's probably sprung. Hope you didn't pay much for it."

"He didn't mention that. Hey, it was a good deal and it works for me."

"Keep an eye on your tires. They're going to wear quickly. Where is your baby? He's not in his car seat."

"Jenny is taking care of him this evening. She feels sorry for me. You feel sorry for me, too, don't you?" She moved in closer.

"I feel sorry for all of us. It was a tragic loss." He could smell the whiskey on her breath. "Out celebrating?"

"Dinner at the Walleye. Old times' sake, y'know? Still the same bartender."

Old times' sake. The Walleye? What a low-down dive. When Ben was dating her, they never went to the Walleye. For starters, they were both underage. So she must have taken up going there after he went into the marines.

He held out his hand. "May I see your keys?"

"Sure!" She twisted around to pull them out of the ignition and nearly spun out. She steadied herself on the steering wheel, paused, pulled her keys. When she stood up, she nearly spun out again. "Here y'are. Why do you want to see them?"

"I want to keep them. You're in no condition to drive."

"What...Ben..." She pouted. "I can get home okay." She brightened a bit. "Or you can take me."

For a moment he was totally torn. Here was a woman who'd come back to make peace with the father who dropped dead right in front of her. A woman who was surviving a hard life, so far. An old friend, a schoolmate, a former girlfriend. Arresting her now, in the midst of her terrible grief, was immoral. Un-Jesus-like. Just plain nasty.

But.

"I'm sorry, Amber. You're under arrest, driving while under the influence."

Her mouth and eyes went wide. "You wouldn't do that! You couldn't! I'm not that drunk!"

"Remember Dougie? Died our junior year?"

"He was an idiot. Always showing off. It's no surprise he wrapped his car around a tree. I'm not like that. I'm very careful. Very safe."

"I said I'm sorry and I mean it. But it's not just that you could kill yourself driving drunk, it's who you might take with you. An innocent stranger. Your own baby."

"Doesn't our past together mean anything at all to you?" And she squirmed in still closer.

"Yes. It does. You need help, Amber. This can get that help started for you." And he repeated it once again, because he meant it with every ounce of him: "I'm sorry."

Sunday evening already. The days were mushing together, the way they did on long holiday weekends. Esther should have gone to church today. Instead she had lain in bed until noon, feeling sorry for herself. She had heard of people blocking out unpleasant memories and had scoffed—until she realized she was doing exactly that. Well, trying to. But every time she thought she had those demons securely bound, they broke loose to torture her. Double torture. Sure, Jefferson was damaged to start with, but what she did...Why did God bring him into her life now, when the memories were getting worse, more intrusive? Was God so cruel? Ben called her demons flashbacks.

That's what soldiers got, not a physician's assistant. But it sure seemed he was right.

Now she sipped coffee and read through all the text messages and listened to the phone messages, too. So Ben had even come by the house. Maybe he didn't realize that when he hung up on the answering machine, his number stayed there.

She had just texted Ben the message, "I'm OK. I'll b at work usual time Mday. Sorry 2 cause u trouble."

Trouble? The whole weekend she had locked the door and refused to answer it. She'd called her counselor, but Dr. Phillips was out of town and had yet to return her call. Sort of like the cops; where were they when you needed them? Other than doping herself to sleep, she couldn't think of anything else to do. Nor did she wish to do anything else. She wasn't sure which.

What she was sure of was that she had to recover enough to be at work at eight thirty tomorrow morning.

She reread Ben's text messages. And listened to his phone messages. And the ones from her mother, her father, and Kenneth. No one could figure out what had happened and she wasn't about to tell them. Her mother did scold her roundly for ruining the nice holiday, but she expected that. She probably would have been disappointed if her mother had not reamed her. And in front of that nice young man, too.

Flashback, Ben said. It was more than a dream, more even than a nightmare. She felt the cold air, smelled the spilled gasoline, heard every nuance of the sounds and the silence. It did more than feel as if she were out on that black road on that black night, the scene with all its horror playing out for real, not in her memory.

She walked to the bathroom. "Get a hold of yourself!"

she ordered the ravaged face in the mirror. *What is going on? Am I in a new phase of PTSD? What's happening? Or...or what?*

The tears burst from the bonds she'd put up to fight further disintegration and ran rivers down her face. She threw herself back on her bed and let the pillow soak up the overflow. Would this never stop? She was no longer sure what was real, what the flashback had meant, or anything else. When she woke the clock said two and by the dark window, it meant two A.M. Her stomach complained, but finally her head felt clear. The stomach was easy to take care of.

Out in the kitchen she fixed a cup of herb tea and plopped a piece of bread in the toaster. When the toast was ready, she sliced cheese and let it melt on the toast so when she sat at her two-person table in the kitchen, she got some protein in her, too. When that one was done, she did the same again and refilled her tea cup with hot water and another tea bag.

It probably would not be a good idea to go out for a run now, but even the thought made her smile. If the people of Pineville had suspicions that she was going around the bend, that would convince them for sure.

Instead she fixed herself a lunch, showered, dressed, and let herself into the clinic at seven. At least here she could tune out the voices in her head. While the pile of paperwork from the storm had been gone through, she had other follow-up work that had been waiting patiently. Would it ever be possible to get totally caught up, let alone stay that way?

Sometime later a tap on her door caught her attention. She glanced at her watch. Eight fifteen. "Yes."

"Just checking on you."

"Come on in."

"My word, but you are early. Esther, what happened to you?" Barbara shut the door behind her and stared at Esther behind her desk.

"That bad?"

"Maybe not to someone who doesn't know you, but those bags under your eyes aren't smudges—you have black circles all around them. And they are swollen, too."

"I had a meltdown and some sort of a flashback."

"Yesterday?"

"No, Thanksgiving Day at my mother's house. I've been sleeping and hiding ever since. Woke at two this morning and could tell I was better again."

"Is that why Ben called me?"

"I don't know. I shut down everything and hid in my bed."

"He wondered if I had a key to your house. He was frantic."

"I left a text on his phone last evening, telling him I was all right."

"I think he cares for you, probably more than even he realizes."

"Yeah, well, he's probably so furious with me now, he'll never speak to me again."

"You want to talk about it?"

Esther shook her head. "I tried to call Dr. Phillips, but she was out of town and I didn't want to talk to whomever was taking her calls. Right now I want to get through today without frightening my patients with the zombie look."

"You want some coffee?" At the nod, Barbara headed for the door.

"Let me get some concealer around my eyes and some

coffee and I'll be ready. Thank you, Barbara." She headed for the bathroom with her makeup bag.

She could fix up the outside so that hardly anything showed. But the inside. Ah, the inside. That was a mess for sure.

Chapter Twenty-Five

Hadn't she just wondered if she would ever get the clinic records caught up? She just did, filing the last of the endless pieces of paper, and it was only nine fifteen A.M. Curiously, no patients had shown up as yet.

She wandered out into the hall, into the waiting room. Barbara sat alone, pondering a crossword puzzle.

"Sure is slow today," Esther mused aloud.

"Comes in bunches. You know that. New coffee's on." Absorbed, Barbara didn't even look up.

As Esther turned to wander back to the kitchen, Sarah Applegate entered the double doors. "Hi, Dr. Esther!" At last! A customer.

"Hi, Sarah!" Esther continued down the hall. Why did Sarah have an appointment today? she wondered. Oh well, she'd know soon enough. She liked Sarah, really liked her. Such a bright kid, but before she left home that brightness would no doubt be snuffed by her mom's distrust and negativity. Or maybe she'd escape before the light went out completely. Had Esther really escaped her mom's constant criticism? What would she have been like without it?

On impulse, Esther stopped at her office to grab her stethoscope. *Drape a stethoscope around your neck, and you're a doctor.* Ben's maxim. She smiled at the thought. The smile faded quickly, pushed off her face by the thought of that meltdown, by the thoughts of poor little Jefferson. And Ben. Right now her thoughts about him were confused and confusing. She continued down the hall to the break room and new coffee.

She stopped cold, gasping. Speak of the devil. Ben stood beside the vending machines in the break room, a half-eaten maple bar in one hand, coffee mug in the other. He waved a finger, his mouth kind of full. "Fresh doughnuts, courtesy Beth. Fresh coffee, courtesy Barbara." He didn't sound the least angry or frustrated with her.

She stammered. "Ben…" Licked her lips. "Ben…" Squared her shoulders. "Ben, I am so sorry. I don't know what to say or how to say it, but I am so very sorry."

He was smiling. "Remember a couple of times I said I've been there? I'll say it again. I've been there. Apology accepted but not necessary."

"You don't understand, but—"

"No, *you* don't understand. I do understand." Still that easy smile. "Let's start over. Fresh doughnuts from Beth, coffee from Barbara."

This was all just too much. She could…what could she do? The best way would be to go with the flow. He accepted her apology. Start from there. "All right. Let's." She chose a doughnut. "You're not in uniform today. I'm not used to seeing you in civvies."

He sobered. "Stopped by my office early for some files. His Majesty was there, said if I didn't show up on time and in uniform, I was fired. I said, 'Nah, I'm not that lucky' and left."

"You guys really *don't* like that temporary chief!" She took a bite of maple bar, paused to savor the first creamy excellence of the frosting in her mouth. She frowned, talked with her mouth full. "He can't really fire you, can he?"

"In theory, yes. But there are so many bureaucratic hurdles he'd have to jump through, it's not worth the effort. I'm safe." He popped the rest of the maple bar in his mouth and moved in close to her as he surveyed the doughnuts. She liked his closeness, but did she like the funny feeling it caused in her? Maybe she did. He chose a sticky bun, poured her a mug of coffee, and refilled his own.

The break room door clunked. She turned as Mr. Aptos entered pushing a wheelchair.

"Mr. Aptos! Why, Hannah! You're out of the hospital!" Esther laid aside her doughnut to cross the room and reach out to the lady in the wheelchair, both hands. She stopped, drew her hands back. "Oh, dear, I'm all sticky!"

Hannah laughed and grabbed her hands. "I do believe sugar washes off. It's so good to see you, dear!"

"How is your leg doing?" Esther eyed the cast, a huge white tube encasing the lady's leg from her ankle all the way up.

"My orthopedist says I'll be walking in no time. Actually, I have a walker when it's just around the house, but I don't use it out on the street." Hannah dropped her voice conspiratorially. "You know, an old woman charges down the shopping mall in a wheelchair with this cast sticking out, and the Red Sea parts, just like that!" She made a sweeping motion. "Teenagers, other shoppers, they all leap aside. I love it!" Her eyes twinkled. Esther remembered too well when they were dulled by pain.

Here came Sarah Applegate into the break room. Patients didn't come back here. And in walked Dr. Livingston! And Dr. Ho! Wait; and Ansel came in carrying Dawn, and here was Beth with her newborn. Roy Abrams doddered in but the door didn't close behind him, because that Culpepper boy was entering. What was his name? Gary. He held the door open, for Gramma Alma was coming through it.

Gramma marched straight as an arrow over to Esther, hugged her, and kissed her cheek. "You're looking good, Chicken Little!"

Chicken Little? Gramma hadn't called Esther that since she was six and started school. *Too old now for that nonsense*, Mom had decreed, and so it ended. Esther had always missed that nonsense, she'd missed it so much.

"Wait a minute!" She stepped back as sudden panic made her chest vibrate. "What's going on here?" She backed up against the counter, suddenly bobbing in a sea of faces crowding, smiling, watching her. "What are you all doing?"

Ben shrugged. "We just wanted the chance to tell you how much we care about you."

No! I'm out of here! She headed for the door.

No one blocked her way, exactly, but no one stepped aside, either. Dr. Ho leaned his back against the door, closed his eyes, and yawned elaborately, patting his gaping mouth with an open hand.

"No!" The panic multiplied itself inside her so strongly she was getting dizzy. She stepped back and gripped the counter behind her with both hands.

Beside her, Ben studied the floor. "Y'know, when a bunch of friends get together to wish you well, it's usually called a party, and you have a good time. You look panicked."

"Please! Just go! All of you, just go away! I can't—I can't do this!"

How could she stop this madness? And she realized in even greater panic that she could not. Whatever this pressing, churning, staring crowd was going to do, she couldn't change it.

Sarah stepped to the front. "Dr. Esther, I've decided what I want to be when I get out of school. I'm going to be a doctor, like you. You believed me when my own mom didn't, and you weren't afraid to stand up for me. There's a whole lot of kids I know who need someone like that, and I'm going to be that someone. It's tough to be—you know, okay—clean—when it seems like everyone else around you is—you know." She bit her lip, looked near tears. "Thank you."

Esther hadn't expected that. It slammed into her, stopped her thoughts cold.

Gary Culpepper stood tall near her. "And I think I'm going to do the paramedic thing. That night when we were all working all night was the most amazing night of my life. Dennis and Yvette have the fun job, but you were in there the whole time, and you never yelled at me, or anyone. I've been talking to Dennis, and he's going to sign me up for the training. Thank you."

"I was talking to Dr. Livingston a little while ago." Roy Abrams stood over by the side counter. "You couldn't save my Denise, he says nobody could have. But you tried. You tried so hard, even when you didn't have enough to work with. Thank you."

"You've been talking about a medical facility for years." Mr. Aptos stepped out from behind Hannah's wheelchair. "Nobody listened to you. But you kept at it. You're still keeping at it. People say I'm the one getting this thing moving, but it's not me. It's you. It's always been you. And because of you, people's lives are going to be saved, and people are going to get better medical treatment, the care they need. You've given this area a bigger gift than you can ever imagine, little lady. Thank you."

Her head was spinning. She steadied herself, tried to quell the panic.

Hannah wheeled forward a couple feet. "I didn't want to be one to complain, but I was hurting so bad. You gave me something to do, something important, and it helped me get through the night. Thank you."

Ansel stepped to the front with Dawn; people moved aside to accommodate him. "Ben was telling me how you managed to start a line in this beautiful baby, in her scalp. That's next to miraculous right there. You saved her life. Thank you."

And beside him, Beth was smiling. "Thank you for delivering my baby in the middle of all that chaos. You called it textbook. I call it miraculous. Thank you."

Sarah raised her voice from the back of the room. "Thank you again, Dr. Esther! See you later." She waved as she walked out, and Dr. Ho smiled as he held the door for her.

"Bye." Gary Culpepper waved, left behind Sarah.

Everything was swirling around like cotton candy in a cotton-candy spinner. One by one they left; Hannah rolled forward and kissed her hands, then let Mr. Aptos wheel her out.

Gramma Alma parked in front of her, squeezed her arms. "Your father and I have decided that you will never ever please your mother, because she cannot be pleased by anyone, not you, not me, not your father, not even your brother. That's her problem, not yours or ours, and it's sad, because she misses out on so much. Follow your heart, dear Chicken Little. You please us all, more than you know." Gramma walked out and Esther desperately wanted her to stay. But she couldn't find the words to call her back. She couldn't find any words at all. The panic was so intense she felt close to throwing up.

Ben took her arm, led her over to the chair at the table, pulled it out for her. She flopped into it, clunked both elbows on the table, and covered her face. She was sobbing, sort of, but it wasn't really; it was continual shuddering. "Go away. Please."

Chairs clunked as Ben sat down at her right. And there were Dr. Livingston and Dr. Ho sitting down, too. Meddlers.

"This was an intervention, wasn't it." She took a huge shuddering breath. "Isn't that what they call it?"

Dr. Ho's voice purred, gentle. "Not exactly, where people tell the subject how someone's addiction or alcoholism has negatively impacted their lives. Basic idea, but we changed some things. Like, we know how crowds of people can induce anxiety in post-traumatic people, so we asked that they leave after."

She raised her head. "In other words this was all carefully staged."

"No, it wasn't!" Dr. Livingston was emphatic almost to be the point of being angry. "We got them together, explained what post-traumatic stress is and how it has affected you, and asked them to say whatever was on their minds. Whatever was in their hearts. We didn't know what they would say. No one was directed or coached, except for the leaving part."

Dr. Ho smiled. "We are afraid you don't realize what a

positive force you are in this community, so we did this. And these people all care about you."

"Did anyone tell you why—" She changed course. "About when this started?"

"Yes." Dr. Ho was still smiling, compassion in his eyes. "Hit and run."

She gasped. How...?

He grinned mischievously. "I talked to your brother and father. You claimed your car damage was caused by a deer, but deer don't leave paint scuffs. They're certain you hit another car."

And rage welled up, burning away the confusion, the fear. Delicious rage. It burst out of her harder than she wanted it to. "So thank you so much, you just ruined my life! I was thinking of getting the full degree sometime. That's not going to happen now. They won't take a post-traumatic stress victim. And by the way, I would love to stay out of jail. That's not going to happen now, either. Hit and run is a crime, maybe you heard, and you just announced it to the whole world!" Curious, her fury in some way was dissipating her terror.

Dr. Livingston nodded. "So you were going to get past this problem on your own, and when you were stable again, you'd go back to school. Is that it?"

When he said it, or maybe the way he said it, it seemed foolish. "Yeah. Yes, that's what I was going to do. Except just a few weeks ago, I met the people I hit. Just by chance, a grandmother and a disabled boy. They were the people in the car I hit. Now I don't know what...I just don't know. I don't have the money to help them or anything, but...I don't know, but the boy was so..." And words failed her.

"So, in the intervening years, have you been recovering or getting worse?"

She crossed her arms on the table and dropped her forehead onto them. She was so sad and hopeless, she didn't even feel like responding.

Dr. Livingston leaned toward her. "Let me tell you some things, Esther, true things. One, you can recover from this, but not the way you're going about it. Two, this does not damage your chances to become a physician. Staying ill would. Three, I've discussed this with pretty good legal counsel, and this does not mean the end of the world or even jail time."

"Legal counsel. I can't afford a lawyer, at least not a hotshot." She raised her head to study him a moment. "Who?"

"I'm married to her."

And her brain went *zing* again. She felt hot tears coming. She didn't want that. After she had worked desperately for so long to keep her past silent, the world knew her most horrible secrets. She didn't want that. These powerful men controlled her life and she did not. She didn't want that. The harder she tried to salvage the future, the worse things got. She most of all didn't want that.

Ben gripped her arm. "You wouldn't talk to me when I brought you home, but you did say enough that I could dig out the old incident reports. The cops file things forever, you know."

You wouldn't dare. You couldn't! But no use saying that aloud. Of course he could.

Ben asked, "What color was the car you hit, Esther?"

She wasn't expecting that question. "Black. Like the road."

"What color car was Clara Holmgren driving?"

"I don't know. Black, I ... wait." The woman had said ...

But how...? "A white one. That she thought ought to show up in the headlights."

"There were two hit and runs, Esther, within twenty-four hours of each other. No one ever found out who hit Clara Holmgren. Your father and brother both mentioned that the paint scuffs on your car were black. The car you rear-ended was parked on the asphalt and its owner was half a mile beyond, headed for a gas station with a gas can; he had run out of gas, and he was also inebriated. No one ever found out who hit his car, either, but I don't think anyone tried hard. Pretty darn stupid, parking out on the roadway."

"You mean I...?" Jefferson, Clare, Ben, these men, that intervention or whatever: It was all coming at her way too fast.

And now Dr. Ho was speaking, his voice mist-like at the edge of her awareness. "As a first step, I want to put you on a serotonin reuptake inhibitor that I've found quite useful for my patients. I believe you will be amazed a month from now how much better the world looks. This seems to work better than some others."

"I don't need another antidepressant."

"Give it a couple months; if there's no change, you can go back off it. Now I want you to tell me—if you could do anything in the world, what would it be?"

"Mom wants me to go into obstetrics in an urban set—"

"Stop. Pretend for a moment that your mother doesn't exist; she's not a factor. Just pretend. You. What would *you* most like to do?"

She opened her mouth, closed it again. What did she want? What did Esther want? She had never really considered that. But *I don't know* seemed pretty lame.

She thought about the people whose lives she could not

save. Chief. Denise Abrams. And the people for whom she made a difference, sometimes even a life-and-death difference. And the babies. Wriggly little Nathan fresh from his mother's womb. Sweet Dawn, abandoned, alone, desperately fighting a losing battle to stay alive. And this morning, there they were right in front of her, both of them, unable to speak but telling her volumes anyway.

She drew a deep breath. "I think; I think, if it were just me, I'd like obstetrics anyway. Maybe after I get my loans paid off, obstetrics in a small-town setting. An area like this needs someone who enjoys the work. Or a general practitioner. That's good, too."

She happened to look up at Dr. Ho, the first real eye contact she'd made with the two physicians since all this went down. With these three; Ben sat silently beside her, carefully studying her. Not staring. Quietly, pleasantly studying.

Dr. Ho had tears in his eyes. They hadn't bubbled up over the lids yet, but they were there. He wasn't acting sorrowful or anything. He just...he just had tears. He smiled, glowed. "Esther, you do not know how happy you just made me."

This was surreal. This wasn't really happening.

Dr. Livingston explained, "Warren and I have had some long discussions about you. There's a critical short-age of doctors willing to work in rural areas, and yet they're desperately needed. The fact that you want to borders on the miraculous. We were hoping you would want to, based on your success as a practitioner here in Pineville, but we didn't know. We need you, Esther."

Dr. Ho picked it up. "So we have devised a plan, subject to your approval, of course. You recall we have recently re-turned from a symposium on just this question—delivering medical service to rural communities. There are a number of grants coming available, and George and I are ready to make up the difference, if your education requires more money than the grants will provide. You will not have to go into debt."

"But...!"

He raised a hand. "Please hear me out. The first step, of course, is to stabilize you emotionally. That can be done. Work on this post-traumatic stress problem. Meanwhile, let's get you started toward your degree. You can serve part of your residency here, and I can use a resident in Grand Forks, so your future is assured following the course work. Based on your grades when you earned your certification as a physician's assistant, there should be no problem there, either. When the new facility is opened here in Pineville, you should be about ready to step in."

"*Why?* Why are you two doing this?"

Dr. Livingston said, "Our interest is strictly self-serving. We desperately need you, we need anyone in a rural setting."

Dr. Ho said, "Even more important, you will be a splendid doctor. You have proven yourself. You are worth every effort to save."

Dr. Livingston stood up. "We of course will remain in contact, and I will give you the name of a reliable counselor who can work with you. We have several excellent counselors on the base, well practiced with stress disorders. Also, you're going to have to sit down with my wife and work out the legal ramifications."

"I've been working with a counselor for several years."

"That's good to know. The ones I am referring to have probably done more work with PTSD than most others. I think they can help you."

"Okay, I'll give it a try." *The legal ramifications. We need you.* It all swirled around inside her. She remembered standing and shaking hands with them as they left. She remembered Ben rising and shaking with them also. She flopped back into her chair, still terribly aswirl. Gobsmacked, Granny Alma would say. Nothing less than gobsmacked.

She looked at Ben, sitting quietly beside her. She wagged her head. "This is all too—weird. Are you responsible for this?"

"I helped some, since I know the people and the doctors don't. Helped set it up. And Barbara, she helped. The doctors orchestrated it, worked out the logistics."

She sighed a great, shuddering sigh. "Ben? What do you think I should do?"

"Marry me."

Chapter Twenty-Six

Marry me. Five hours later Esther still floated in a sort of shocked daze.

He'd never even said he loved her. He had never once kissed her. Weren't marriage prospects supposed to court?

Did she love him? She cared, that was for sure, but love him as in to marry him?

"You have a patient in room two." Barbara still had traces of a giggle in her voice.

"Would you knock it off?" Esther felt her smile lines crinkle again.

"All I said was..." There it was again.

"I know what you said. I'm on my way." Esther picked up the chart. *Marry me.*

She read the name again and glanced down the chart. Amy Klapton, one of her pregnant mommas. She tapped on the door and went in. "Good afternoon, Amy. How can I help you today?"

A pregnant woman with a little boy at her side waited in the chair.

"Joey has something caught up in his nose. He can't blow it out."

"I see. He's not the first little boy to come down with this syndrome. Come on, Joey, let's get you on the table so I can see better." She lifted him up so he sat with his feet dangling over the edge. "Now, what did you put in your nose?"

"A bean."

"I see. I'm going to have to look up your nose, so you lie back here and hang on to your mommy's hand. I know you are going to be a brave little boy, aren't you?" She nodded while she asked the question so he nodded back. She felt the bridge of his nose; just below that, in the right nostril, was something hard. "You sure did." Choosing the most delicate of her limited choice of forceps, she shone a light up to see a white dried bean waiting. "This will feel funny, but you lie real quiet and we'll be done in an instant. You only put one bean in, didn't you?"

"Yes." He hesitated. "The second one didn't fit."

She worked the forceps up there, managed to engage the bean, and pulled it out. "You were really brave all right. But I don't want you to put anything in your nose ever again, hear? Your nose doesn't like that. It's uncomfortable, and besides, it wastes beans."

He nodded. "Sorry."

Amy was obviously suppressing a snigger. "Me, too. Come on, Joey, let's go home."

"Ice cream?"

"No chance. Not when you did this. No treats." His mother rose and waited for him to scramble down. "See you for my appointment next week." Out they went.

Esther jotted down her notes and handed the file back to Barbara. "That's it for today?"

"It is. And what a note to end on. Beans up the nose. How come boys do that more than girls?"

"Girls are smarter."

"Esther, get out of here. Go, get ready for your big date."

Esther started to leave and turned. "How did you know you loved Ed?"

"No fireworks, more a slow burn. But I knew I wanted to be with that man and no other for the rest of my life. The fireworks came later."

"Hmm." Not much help. The weather had been perfect for fall, and it still was. She should have walked to work. The western sky was already catching the flames of sunset. The bundle of clouds gleamed gold around the upper edges, and where they parted, oranges flowed into vermillion, which faded into pinks. She caught the reflections in western-facing windows of the houses on her street. With so many of the old elm trees broken in the storm, the horizon was more obvious.

Ben had said he would pick her up at six thirty, and he'd called later to make sure she'd understood. He wasn't taking any chances. On the one hand, a tiny thrill rippled up her back. On the other, she dreaded telling him all that had happened, describing that night. But it wasn't Jefferson. A burden the size of Fort Knox had been lifted from her.

In the shower and out so she didn't have time to ponder the events of the morning. All those people, there just for her. That was the strangest intervention she'd ever heard of. And the message about her mother. Someone else had told her that once, but she'd blown it off. This came from Gramma Alma, and she had never lied to Esther or even stretched the truth. Gramma Alma loved unconditionally, more than anyone Esther had ever known. But she also had the gift of insight, a rare combination.

Instead of her usual jeans or khaki pants, Esther pulled out a black wool skirt and cowl-neck sweater. Then dug into her collection of good jewelry. A three-strand necklace of turquoise and silver, bangly bracelets, and a silver loop belt that hung just below her waist. Earrings finished it off. After fashioning her hair in a French twist, she studied herself in the mirror. She'd pass. Good thing Ben was tall, she thought as she slid her feet into black pumps with two-inch heels. No one would ever convince her that four-inch-and-up heels looked attractive, let alone sensible. She finished with eyeliner and mascara that made her blue eyes even more blue.

When she opened the door Ben stopped, his eyes widened, and he whistled softly. "Who are you and what did you do with Esther?"

She laughed and motioned him in. "I clean up fairly well, I take it."

He nodded. Maybe he figured sometimes silence was the wiser option.

He handed her a long, thin box. A single velvety red rose. He shrugged. "A dozen seemed kinda much."

"A dozen roses is too much. This is perfect. Thank you!"

"I hope you don't mind driving to Grand Forks. I made reservations at the Rogue on the River."

So, do we talk on the way down or way back? "Sounds delightful." She brought her leather coat from the closet and handed it to him. After helping her into it, he cupped his hands around her shoulders and turned her to look in the oval mirror above the half table in the entry.

"You look stunning."

Shivers radiated from under his hands and shot down her arms, ran circles around her heart, and tickled her lungs, making her catch her breath. She felt an urge to turn, put her arms around his neck, and see if his lips tasted as good as he looked.

"What?" His voice had dropped to a heart-pumping tone.

"I—ah..." Esther did exactly what she dreamed, turning in his arms and raising her lips to meet his. *I can't believe I am doing this. Nice girls...oh, hush.* As if they'd done this before, they deepened the kiss. She'd been kissed a few times in the past, but this was like no other. She felt her heart opening like the soft petals on a rose that yearned for the sunshine. Was this what love felt like? If so, she had a full-blown case of it and Ben seemed to be the only person in the world.

"Shall we go?" he whispered against her lips.

"Must we?"

"We must." He drew her arm through his and turned the lock on the door as they went out.

On the drive to Grand Forks, Esther dithered. She couldn't believe it. She was not a ditherer, but back and forth went her mind, totally out of her control. *Tell him now. No, tell him later. It would destroy this magical evening.* Wait. Did he really say "marry me" as an answer to her dilemma? That was no answer, that would only lead to more problems. But problems were far easier when halved with someone who loves you, they say. Just like joys are doubled with the same.

"So Bo is home caring for Dawn?"

"Yes, he makes sure Beth is aware when Dawn even squeaks her first indication of a need." He turned to her with a smile. "Biggest mistake I've made is tell him to guard her."

They talked about some of her patients, and touched

lightly on the progress of the bond sales and the coming clinic. When the young man in front of the restaurant tapped on his window, Esther rolled her eyes. Valet parking even? Another opened the door on her side. Ben tucked her arm through his and they strolled into the candlelit interior.

They were seated at the white-clothed table, their water glasses filled, and leather-bound menus propped in front of them. Music floated from the harpist in the corner with the silver and china clinking counterpoint. Fresh lavender in each table's bud vase added a subtle fragrance to the delicious odors emanating from the kitchen. Magical? More than magic.

Esther sighed and felt the tension drain away to be replaced by a quiet sensation of peace. Reading the menu was like a trip to Europe with French, German, and Italian recipes. The descriptions made making choices even more difficult.

The waiter in black pants and a white dress shirt returned to their table. "I can come back, *oui*?"

Ben looked at her and she nodded. She pointed at random to something.

"A fine choice, madame."

Ben ordered the prime rib, medium rare.

Esther eyed the bread basket with two kinds of rolls, a flat bread with sesame seeds and pencil-thin breadsticks. The butter came in small squares with a design imprinted on each. The whole picture looked too good to eat.

She enjoyed just sitting across the table from Ben. His smile warmed her midsection. "This is such a treat."

"Good. We all need a treat once in a while."

They shared growing-up stories as they made their way

through the marvelous meal. By mutual, silent assent, they stayed with funny stories, positive stories. From picture-worthy plates to service that came before being asked, the dinner created a warm memory that she was sure would stay around forever.

Back in the car, she heaved a sigh. "That was absolutely perfect."

"I thought so, too. I'm glad we could share that."

Now to ruin the evening, a thing she was so good at doing. "Were you serious this morning when you said 'marry me'?"

"As a broken leg."

She shook her head. "No. Then the answer is no. You're fighting alcohol, I'm fighting the past. We're two messed-up people. We can't; I mean, not yet; I mean…" She looked at him. "It wouldn't work."

He stared out the windshield, not exactly grim, but his mouth was firm. He nodded. "We're messed up. You got that right. But I think most of the mess is behind us, both of us. My whole life, everything was gold. Good athlete, good student, good marine, good patrolman. Good whatever I wanted to be. Then Allie got ripped away from me. She was pregnant. I lost the two most important things in my life at once. We'd been trying for years, and then…" He flung both hands wide, a gesture of hopelessness. "I'm not saying this right, but I can't really describe the emptiness. Sense of betrayal, actually. I couldn't imagine why God would do that to me, the golden boy. I did everything right, and He…anyway, the bottle helped at first. Then it enslaved me, then I got mad. You provided the reason to get off the booze, to get out from under, first with Dawn, then with you."

"Me?"

"I can't help you walk if I'm still crippled. I want to help you."

"Then you're not ready to say you're past it. You have to put alcohol behind you for you, not us." She laughed. "Listen to me! I can psycho-counsel everyone except my-self."

"Me too." He was smiling. "You see? We need each other." He twisted in his seat to look at her squarely, eye-to-eye. "I wondered for months why you were trying so hard to keep your stress disorder secret when the whole world could see it. I was watching your face as Ho and Livingston conducted that so-called intervention. I could see you melt. Terrified, then furious, then defeated. I mean, defeated in a good way. The brick wall was broken down. We can help you now. You can help yourself. We're both in a better position to think about marriage than we were even a month ago."

"And Thanksgiving. That was a flashback, yes. Clear as if it were happening then. I'd never had anything quite so—so vivid. We should get started back. It's late. I can describe it on the way home."

He twisted back to face the wheel and hit the ignition. "You don't have to if you don't want to, you know." They rolled out to the stop sign.

"I want to. For the first time since then, I actually want to. Even my counselor has never heard it. It's weird. I knew it happened, but I guess you could say I refused to remember. But I kept remembering parts of it anyway. And when Jefferson entered the picture I was devastated. Wiped. Interesting how your mind can block something it doesn't want to deal with."

It gave her the strangest feeling, almost a thrill only dif-ferent, to finally describe that horrible night when she hit and ran. "Ben, I was so scared when the PTSD started. Scared me to pieces. I had no idea what was happening. I had horrible dreams and finally went to a doctor for help because I couldn't study, couldn't concentrate, and I had no idea why. I thought I was going crazy. And now, well you saw what's happened. I've been seeing a counselor for several years but never could determine the cause of the depression. I've been on meds to help counteract that. But the PTSD has been getting worse instead of better." She ordered her hands to unclench their stranglehold on each other.

"And the feelings of inadequacy you mentioned?"

"Lived with that all my life. According to my mother, I never could do anything just exactly right. Dr. Phillips helped me see that, but it is near to impossible to let those things go." She paused, feeling drained. "At least for me."

He wheeled the vehicle into her driveway. She really admired his driving skill, so casual, so exact and careful. And most of all, she respected him. Maybe that was even more important than love. Respect.

He killed the engine; he was smiling. "A few weeks ago, had you told me this, I probably would have cut and run. But thanks to Ansel and Beth, God has fixed some things. My rage at Him had to go for me to heal. To think I was refusing to forgive God, who sent his son to die for me, so I could forgive Him. Can you beat that?"

"So you are saying I have to forgive my mother?"

He nodded. "And even more so, yourself."

"Ben, how could I have just driven off like that? It wasn't Jefferson, but it so easily could have been."

"Not hard to see. You were young and terrified. Never encountered a situation like that before, didn't know what to do, panicked. Not hard to see at all."

She could see he was right, but it didn't work. She was still torn up. "You said they never found out who hit the black car. What are the legal consequences, I mean, if I walk into the highway patrol office and confess?"

"Are you aware of the statute of limitations?"

"I heard the phrase."

"With a few exceptions, most crimes are forgiven, so to speak, after seven years. Or three, for some. Never for murder or manslaughter."

"So if I just wait a few years, you're saying."

"Talk to Dr. Livingston's wife. But you're not in serious trouble, as for example you would have been had you hit Clara's car."

"This is all coming at me too fast. I have no idea what will happen now. I know this. I sure have some hard work to do."

He chuckled. "It'll be worth it. Peace is always worth it. Let's both just bring God in on this, let Him do the worrying and fussing. Far easier on the body."

"I can't believe you are saying these things." She realized he had taken her hands in his.

"I can't either." His thumb stroked the back of her hand.

"Someone said that storms change things."

"Well, I guess. In our cases, our entire lives. And that will continue to happen. Look at all that has gone on."

Esther leaned her head on the back of the seat. "Do you wish you could see ahead?"

"Nope, not anymore. Have enough to do dealing with the here and now." He was studying her again. Not staring. Studying. Sort of exploring her face with his eyes. "I love you."

Love. More foreign territory she would have to explore. This exploration, though, should be much more delightful than exploring stress disorders. "I think I am learning what love feels and looks like. And if that's what I'm experiencing, I rather like it."

Ben leaned over, turned her face toward him with a gentle finger, and kissed her softly. "This is what love feels like."

Brand-new feelings, wonderful feelings, bubbled through her. She took a deep breath and drew back. "Ben, are you sure? I mean; about us. That this would work?"

"Absolutely. But then I've had more time to realize and admit my feelings than you have." He kissed her again.

"What about Dawn?"

"I want to adopt her. I want the two of us to adopt her. Beth and Ansel will keep her until then. And all will be well."

"You have it all mapped out."

"In my head at least. I've always been that way. Except when I was boozing. Another reason to steer clear of the bottle."

"So much work ahead." She wrapped her fingers through his and kissed the back of his hand. "So much is new to me. I—I would like to say yes. But..."

"That's a mighty small word with so much hanging on it." He squeezed her hand. "But we're not in a hurry. Do the work, both of us. Forgive ourselves, others, the past. When we marry we will rejoice in every day God gives us, just like I am planning on doing right now."

His expression suddenly changed, from pleasant to stricken. He made a funny sound, something like *argg*. "You know what I think this means? I have to forgive His Highness for being such a jerk. Forgive Perowsky!"

"Well, you said *work*." Esther started to giggle and

tried to stop. "Ben James, you are on your way to becoming a wise man. Go see Mr. Aptos, he's got wisdom to spare."

"By the way, are you a lark or an owl?"

"I wake the dawn—most of the time."

"Me too. Are you sure there isn't a heavenly edict about larks and owls marrying?"

"Nope. Together we'll wake the dawn and welcome in each new day. New days not only for us, but all of Pineville. Just wait and see."

Epilogue

From the roar of thousands of voices in conversation to a quiet, rustling mumble, to near silence. Thousands of faces turned toward this temporary stage. Two times thousands of eyes looked up here.

Showtime.

From the sidelines, Ben rolled Mr. Aptos's wheelchair out into the center of the stage near the mikes and set the brake. The crowd below and before them erupted in cheers, applause.

Mr. Aptos turned slightly. "Ben, if I die in the next five minutes, I'll die happy. I never imagined it would be this good."

"You spearheaded a lasting work that will save many lives. Betcha every speaker Lars lined up is going to say that."

"Do I have to hang around for all those speeches?" There was a twinkle in his eye.

"If I have to be up here, you can just suffer, too. Now shut up and smile at the folks."

Bill Aptos cackled exuberantly. And he smiled at the folks.

Had Ben taken bets, he would have won. The state senator, the state rep (election year), the state health and human services secretary, and the lieutenant governor all orated majestically, all extolling the role William Aptos had taken in forging a new future for Pineville. Or something. Ben got bored and quit listening even before the senator had finished.

He looked out at the faces, most of which he recognized. Crowds never bothered him. They terrified Esther, so she was down in front of the stage, the first of this vast crowd. Beth and Ansel flanked her, and Dr. Ho and Dr. Livingston stood behind her. Two years ago, they would have stationed themselves there to block her from bolting. No need to now.

Ben would have preferred that Mr. Aptos be free of his Parkinson's, of course, but at least he was still alive, still here to see his dream fulfilled. The old man chuckled and wisecracked, absolutely ebullient.

Esther was watching with a glorious, radiant, superlatively happy smile. It was the same radiant smile she'd worn on their wedding day four months ago, and on their honeymoon in Hawaii, and when together they had signed the final papers for Dawn's adoption. The radiance reflected what Ben felt.

Finally they got to the finale. About time, not that Ben was getting antsy or anything.

Behind them, a bright red satin ribbon stretched across the front doors of the Paul Harden Memorial Hospital. The lieutenant governor stepped forward and handed Mr. Aptos a pair of huge golden scissors.

Bill twisted and nodded to Ben. He nodded back. He released the brakes and rolled Bill over to Esther down front there.

Her mouth dropped open. Startled, she shook her

head. Too late. Ansel plunked a wooden stepstool in front
of her and was handing her up to Ben. She looked instantly terrified, but she held her own, gripped his hand,
stepped up onto the stage.

Mr. Aptos handed her the golden scissors.

She looked at Ben. But it was not an I'll-get-you-for-
this look. It was an I'll-do-this-because-I-love-you sort of
look. Behind her the crowd was clapping enthusiastically.

Mr. Aptos wrapped her hands in his. "You are the hero
here, Esther. God bless you. Go do it. You've earned it."

Her mouth moved but she said nothing.

Ben pushed Mr. Aptos along beside her as she crossed
to that big satin ribbon.

She took a deep breath. Ben wouldn't have believed it,
but she seemed to grow an inch. She squared her shoulders, stepped forward, clipped the ribbon, handed the
scissors to Mr. Aptos, and kissed his forehead. "Thank
you, Mr. Aptos, for making my dream come true."

He gripped her hands in his aged, trembling ones.
"Thank *you*, Esther. It was my dream, too. Now wave to
the nice people."

The hospital doors swung wide open.

Ben turned the wheelchair outward and Mr. Aptos and
Esther raised their hands toward the crowd in what was
called a photo op. There were cameras aplenty, too. Not
as much news coverage as the storm two years before, but
lots of coverage nonetheless.

As much as Ben hated meetings, this had to be one of
the better ones. For the next hour he pushed Mr. Aptos,
escorted Esther, and watched people pour into the hospital to tour the facility. When he finally took Mr. Aptos
back to the Creekside Rest nursing home, he was plain
tuckered out.

He pushed the wheelchair in through the double doors, the security doors, and took his leave. Apparently the party wasn't over, because as he left, the housebound residents started toasting Mr. Aptos, urging him to cut a decorated sheet cake.

Ben stepped out into quiet twilight and drew in a huge chestful of cool evening air. What a day. Where was Esther? She had been drawn aside for a news interview; apparently that shy young doctor would be the toast of the TV morning shows, whether she liked it or not. That's okay. She could handle it now.

"Ben?" She stepped out of the shadows beside the walkway. She had Bo on leash.

Grinning wide enough to eat a pie in one piece, he turned and took both her hands in his, gave Bo a brief scratch behind the ears. "TV interview, huh?"

"Not as bad as I thought it would be. The interviewer's really good at putting you at ease. Afterward, I snuck out the back. I needed some quiet. So I took Bo for a walk on that path down by the pond. Just Bo and me."

He was still grinning. He couldn't quit grinning. So good. This was all so good. He draped an arm over her shoulder and led her off toward the house. "Let's go home."

Reading Group Guide

1. Dealing with grief is something we all need to learn how to do. Ben went one way, Esther another. Have you ever lost someone you loved? What did you learn about the grief process? What could you share with someone else to help them along the grieving path?

2. Family secrets can really be destructive, and bearing a terrible secret alone can be just as bad. Do you know someone who was set free after their secrets became known?

3. How do you feel about keeping secrets?

4. Grief and secrets can both be destructive to not only one's mind but also one's body, as both Esther and Ben knew, and yet they couldn't let go. What triggered a turnaround for each of them? What does that say to you?

5. Natural disasters seem to do more to trigger community concerns for one another than anything else. What have you done to prepare should a disaster hit your area? What has your church or community done?

6. What characteristics do Ben and Esther share? What is different? What advice would you give them regarding their lives?

7. Hopefully we can learn things from the stories we read. What impacted you and your life the most from this story?

8. What would you like to tell or ask these characters if you were able to talk with them?

9. Who was your favorite character and why?

10. Have you ever known someone with PTSD? How has their problem affected your life as a friend or relative? What advice would you give someone who needs help?

Turn this page for an excerpt of
Lauraine Snelling's

One Perfect Day

Available now from FaithWords.

Chapter One

Nora

Gordon, where are you?
Betsy, a middle-aged yellow lab, looked up as if she had heard Nora speaking. The two had been best friends for so long that the twins frequently teased her about mental telepathy—with a dog. Betsy thumped her tail and gazed up from her self-assigned spot at Nora's feet.

Leaving the bay window seat where she'd been staring out at the moon lighting fire to the frost-encrusted winter lawn that sloped down to the lake shore, Nora crossed the kitchen to set the tea kettle to boiling. Tea always helped in times of distress. She brought out the rose-sprinkled china teapot and filled it with hot water. Tonight was not a mug night but a stoke-up-the-reserves night. If there had been snow on the ground, this was the kind of night, with the moon so bright every blade of grass glinted, when she would have hit the ski trails. An hour of cross country skiing and she'd have been relaxed enough to fall asleep whether Gordon called or not.

So, instead she drank tea. As if copious cups would make her sleep deeply rather than toss and turn. Perhaps she would work on the business plan if she got enough caffeine into her system.

Betsy's ears perked and she went and stood in front of the door to the garage.

Nora's heart leaped. Gordon must be home after all. But why hadn't he called to say he was at the airport? His business trip to Stuttgart, Germany, had already been prolonged and here they were trying to get ready with just four days until Christmas. The last one she could guarantee that the twins would still be home for. Her last chance for perfection. When he'd told her a week ago he had to fly to Stuttgart again, the word again had echoed in her head.

Betsy's tail increased the wag speed and she backed up as the door opened.

"Mom, I'm home." Charlie, the older twin by two minutes and named after his father, Charles Gordon Peterson, came through the door in his usual rush. "Oh, there you are." He paused to pet the waiting dog, grinning up at his mother. "Good girl, Bets, did you take good care of mom?" Betsy wagged her tail and caught the tip of his nose with her black spotted tongue. "Smells good in here." He glanced around the kitchen, zeroing in on the plate of powdered-sugar-dusted brownies. "Heard from Dad?"

"No." Nora cupped her elbows with her hands and leaned against the counter. At five-seven the raised counter fit right into the small of her back. When they'd built the house, she and Gordon had chosen cabinets two inches higher than normal since they were both tall. Made for easier work surfaces. "Go ahead, quit drooling and eat. There's a plate in the fridge for you to pop in the microwave."

"Where's Christi?" Charlie asked around a mouthful of walnut-laced brownie.

"Upstairs. I think she's finishing a Christmas present."

"Are we going to decorate the tree tonight?"

"We were waiting on you." *And your father, but somehow he always manages to not be here at tree decorating time.* While Gordon was not a bah humbug kind of guy, his idea of a perfect Christmas was skiing in Colorado. They'd done his last year, with his promise to help make hers perfect this year. Right. Big help from across the Atlantic. While she knew he'd not deliberately chosen to be gone this week before Christmas, it still rankled, irritating under her skin like a fine cactus spine, hard to see and harder to dig out. Charlie retrieved his plate from the fridge and slid it into the microwave, all the while filling his mother in on the antics of the children standing in line to visit Santa. Charlie excelled as one of Santa's elves, a big elf at six foot but with dark curly hair and hazel eyes that sparkled with the delight. Charlie loved little kids, so when this perfect job came up, he took it and entertained them all in his green and red elf suit. He could turn the saddest tears into laughter. Santa told him not to grow up, he'd need elves forever.

"One little girl had the bluest round eyes you ever saw." Charlie took his warmed plate out and pulled a stool up to the counter so he could eat. "She had this one great big tear trickling down her cheek but I hid behind my hands..." He demonstrated peek-a-boo with his fingers. "And she sniffed, ducked into Santa, caught herself, and peeked back at me. When he did his ho ho ho, she looked up at him with the cutest grin." He deepened his voice. "And what do you want for Christmas, little girl?"

Charlie shifted into shy little girl. "I-I want a kitty.

My mommy's kitty died and she needs a new one." He paused. "And make sure it has a good motor. My mommy likes to hold one that purrs." Charlie came back to himself. "Can you believe that, Mom? That's all she wanted. She reached up and kissed his cheek, slid off his lap, and waved goodbye."

"What a little sweetheart."

"I checked with Annie who was taking the pictures and got their address. You think we could find a kitten that has a good motor at the Humane Society?"

"Ask Christi, she'd know." Christi volunteered one afternoon a week at the Riverbend Humane Society and would bring home every condemned animal if they let her. She'd fostered more dogs and cats in the last year than most people did in a lifetime. She'd found homes for them too, except for Bushy, an older white fluffy cat with one black ear and one black paw. His green eyes captivated her, or at least that was the excuse for his taking up permanent residence. Wherever Christi went, Bushy followed.

"I will. Be nice if there was a half grown one with a loud motor."

"Loud motor for what?" Christi, Bushy draped across her arm, wandered into the kitchen, a smear of sap green oil paint on her right cheek, matching the blob on the back of her right forefinger. Tall at five nine with an oval face and haunting gray/blue eyes, she looked every bit the traditional blonde Norwegian. But as much as Charlie entertained the world, she observed and translated what she saw onto canvasses that burst with color and yet drew the eye into the shadows where peace and serenity lurked. Christi would rather paint than eat or even breathe at times.

"A little girl asked Santa for a kitty for her mother," he shifted into mimic, "cause Mommy's kitty died and she is sad."

"That's all she wanted?"

"Gee, that's what I asked too." Nora motioned toward the teapot and Christi nodded. While her mother poured the tea, Christi absently rubbed the paint spot on her cheek.

"There are three cats for adoption right now. I like the gold one, she loves to be held, the other two would rather rough house."

"You think it would still be there until after school?"

"I'll call Shawna and tell her to hold it for you. Are you sure you want to do this? What happens if she doesn't really want it?"

"Can anyone turn down one of Santa's elves?"

"You'd go in costume?"

"Why not?"

"I could paint you a card."

"Would you?"

"Sure, have one started. All I need to do is change the color of the cat. Luckily I made it white like Bushy here." She rubbed her cheek on the cat's fluffy head. "How long until we decorate the tree?"

"Give me five minutes."

"Okay, you two start on the lights and I'll finish the card. You want me to sign it for you?" Christi had taken classes in calligraphy and taught her mother how to sign all the Christmas cards in perfect script.

"You know, you're all right for a girl." Charlie bounded up the stairs to his room where all his herpetological friends lived. Arnold, a three foot Rosie Boa who should have been named Houdini, was his favorite.

Nora handed Christi her mug of tea. "Take a brownie with you."

"Thanks Mom. You heard from Dad yet?"

"No." Nora knew her answer was a bit clipped.

"Something must be wrong." Christi's eyes darkened in concern. "Did you call him?"

"I tried, cell went right to voicemail."

"So, he was on it?"

"Or he let the battery run out." As efficient as Gordon was, you'd think he could remember to plug his phone into the charger. The two women of the family shared an eye rolling.

"He'll call."

"Unless he's broken down someplace."

"You always tell me not to worry."

"Well, advising and doing are two different things." Nora set her cup and saucer in the dishwasher. "Want to help me unroll the lights?"

"I was going up to finish that card."

Nora checked her watch. "Ten minutes?"

"Done." Christi scooped Bushy up off the counter where he'd flopped and headed up the stairs, not leaping like her brother, but lithe and regal, the residuals of her years of ballet and modern dance.

Nora and Betsy headed for the living room but when the phone rang did an about face and a near dive for the wall phone in the desk alcove. "Hello."

"Nora, I'm sorry I didn't call sooner."

"There you did it again." She tried to sound harsh but relief turned her to quivering Jell-O.

"What?"

"Apologize. Now I can't be mad at you." His chuckle reminded her of how much she missed him when he was gone.

"Art and I got to talking and I didn't realize the time passing. I had to get some sleep. Is the tree up yet?"

"What, are you trying to outwait me?"

"What ever gave you that idea?" He coughed to clear his throat.

"You okay?"

"Just a tickle. Look, I should be on my way home this afternoon. I've got to wrap this thing up but I told them the deadline is noon and I'm heading for the airport at three, come he-heaven or high water."

"Well, don't worry about the tree." She slipped into suffering servant to make him laugh again. "The kids and I'll get that done tonight." It worked. His chuckle always made her smile back, even when he couldn't see her.

"They have school tomorrow right?"

"Right. Last day so there'll be parties. I have goodie trays all ready to take."

"You made Julekaka for the teachers again?"

Nora chuckled. "Gotta keep my place as favorite mother of high school students."

"Is that Dad?" Charlie called from the stairs. "Tell him to hurry home. I have to..." The rest of his words were lost in his rush.

"Charlie says to hurry home."

"I heard him. Give them both hugs from me. Mrs. Buchwalter is glaring me daggers."

"Do you need a ride from the airport?"

"No, I'll take a cab. I love you."

"You better." She hung up on both their chuckles. How come just hearing his voice upped the wattage on the lights? And after twenty-two years of marriage. As people so often told them, they were indeed the lucky ones. "Please Lord, take good care of him," she whispered as she blew him a silent kiss. She joined Charlie in the living room where a Blue Spruce graced the bay window overlooking the front yard where she and Gordon had festooned tiny white lights on the naked branches of the maple that burst into fiery color in the fall and the privet hedge that bordered the drive. Lights in icicle mode graced the front eaves while two tall white candles guarded the front steps. She'd filled pots with holly up the flagstone stairs and hung a swag of pine boughs, red balls, and a huge gold mesh bow on the door.

"Here." Charlie handed her the reel of tiny white lights and pulled on the end to plug it in.

"I already checked them all this afternoon. Just start at the top of the tree."

They had a third of the lights on the eight foot tree when Christi joined them, setting the finished card on the mantel to dry. "I didn't put it in the envelope yet, so don't forget this in the morning, or you are coming home before going over there. Shawna said she'll put your name on the golden cat. She's already been fixed so she is ready for her new home." Christi picked up another reel of light strings. "You need to put them closer together."

"Yeah right, Miss Queen Bee has spoken," Charlie mumbled from behind the tree.

"You don't have to get huffy."

"You don't have to be bossy."

"All right, let's just get the lights on." All they had to do was get through this drudgery part and then all would be well. Gordon always tried to skimp on the lights too. Like father like son. Silence reigned as they wound the lights around the tree branches, punctuated only by a "hand me another reel, please" and "ouch" when a spruce needle dug into the tender spot under the nail. Nora sucked on her finger for a moment to ease the stinging. Inhaling the intoxicating spruce scent brought back memories of the last years and made her grateful again for all the joys they'd had. One more thing to miss tonight, the rehash she and Gordon always did post tree trimming and when the children had gone to bed, like Monday morning quarterbacking, only with more smiles and laughter. Much of the laughter came because of Charlie's clowning around.

"What if she doesn't like the cat?" Charlie asked.

"Then we'll take it back." Christi said matter of factly.

"By back, I'm sure you mean to the Humane Society. Bushy would not like another cat around here." Nora's hands stilled. This she needed to clarify.

"Of course, Mom."

Nora looked up in time to catch a head shake from her daughter and one of the "I'm trying to be patient" looks Christi was so good at. Why was it so quiet? "Oh, I forgot to put the music on. Messiah all right?"

When both the twins shrugged, she knew they'd rather have something else but were giving her the choice. She crossed to the sound system, hit the number three button and waited a moment for Mariah Carey's voice to flow out. She'd play the Messiah after they went to bed. They'd all attended the Sing Alone Messiah concert the second weekend in December. At least Gordon had been home for that tradition.

A bit later they all three stepped back with matching sighs.

"All right, throw the switch." She looked at Charlie who had taken over that job years earlier. This certainly was a night for memories. When the tree sprang to light, they swapped grins and nods. The ornaments were the easy part.

By unspoken agreement, the ornaments they'd bought one each year on their annual family shopping trip and dinner out tradition, they hung higher in the tree to keep away from batting cat's paws and a dog's wagging tail. While the twins snorted at her sentimentality, she hung the ornaments they'd made through the years, some like the Santa face with a cotton ball beard, beginning to look more than a bit scruffy, but dear nevertheless. The ornaments their Tante Karen had given them through the years on their Christmas presents brought up memories and set the two to recalling each year and what their interest had been then.

Nora knew that her sister watched both the twins and the shops carefully through the year to find just the perfect ornament. When the twins had trees of their own, they already had eighteen ornaments to take with them. The thought made Nora pause. The home tree would look mighty bare. She hung the crocheted and stiffened snowflakes she had made one year and given for gifts. Then three little folded paper and waxed stars she'd made in Girl Scouts took their own places.

When they'd hung the final ornament, they stared at the box with the glorious angel that always smiled benignly from the top of the tree.

"Let's leave that for Dad." Christi turned toward her mother.

"I agree." Setting the angel just right with a light inside her to make her shimmer was always Gordon's job, for years because he was the only one tall enough and now because they wanted him to have a part, no matter what miles separated them.

Charlie shrugged. "I am tall enough, you know."

"I know." Nora gathered her two chicks to her sides

and they admired the tree together. "Thank you. I know it is late with school tomorrow but I really appreciate your helping the tradition continue." She tried not to sniff, but her body went on automatic pilot.

Charlie's arm around her back squeezed and Christi leaned her head against her mother's. Together they turned and surveyed all the decorations; the mantel was the only thing that Nora changed year after year, and all was done but hanging the Christmas stockings. The hooks waited. Charlie picked up the flat box that held the cross-stitched or quilted stockings and they each hung up their own. Nora hung hers and Gordon's while the kids hung the ones for Bushy and Betsy.

"Now Santa can come." Christi smoothed the satin surfaces of her crazy quilt stocking, with every satin or velvet piece decorated with intricate embroidery stitches, cross stitch, daisy chain, and feather. "When I get married, will you make my husband a sock to match?"

"I will." *Just please don't be in too big a hurry*. Not that Christi was dating anyone. She often said she left all the flirting up to her brother since all the girls were after him all the time.

But Nora often wondered if Christi was a bit jealous, not that she would ask. Her daughter talked more with her father than she did her mother. Unless, of course, it was a real female thing.

"Anyone for cocoa? The real thing? I can make it while you get ready for bed. I'll bring the tray up."

"And brownies?" Charlie asked.

"Fattigman?" Christi loved the traditional Norwegian goodies Nora made only at Christmas time.

"Of course, and since you'll be getting home early tomorrow, you can help me with the sandbakles."

Charlie groaned. Pressing the buttery dough into the small fluted tins was not his idea of fun.

"He who eats must press." Christi sang out her mother's line from their years of little and on up.

Nora watched her two swap shoulder punches as they climbed the stairs. No matter how much they teased each other or argued, the bond between them ran deeper than most siblings. Gordon called it spooky; she figured it was a gift from God.

Time to make cocoa as her family had called it. In her mind, hot chocolate came in a packet or tin. Good thing she'd picked up the miniature marshmallows. Betsy padding beside her, she returned to the kitchen to fix the tray. If only Gordon were here. Carrying the tray up the stairs was his job.

If you liked *Wake the Dawn*, be sure to pick up national bestselling author Lauraine Snelling's novel *Reunion*

"Inspired by events in Snelling's own life, REUNION is a beautiful story about characters discovering themselves as the foundation of their family comes apart at the seams. Readers may recognize themselves or someone they know within the pages of this book, which belongs on everyone's keeper shelf."

—*RT Book Reviews*

Every year, the Sorenson family has always gathered at Dagmar Sorenson's home in Munsford, where her children Keira and Marcus also live. This year, the first since Dagmar's passing, will be bittersweet. Keira dutifully sorts through Dagmar's belongings, desperately searching for her birth certificate so she can apply for a passport for a much-dreamed-about trip to Norway. Why did her mother hide the document? The fifty-year-old secret shakes her whole world. Who is she? Who is her father? And who was the woman she called Mother? How can she tell her family the truth?

Her brother, Marcus, and his wife, Leah, have a devastating secret of their own. Their college-bound daughter, Kirsten, is pregnant. Has she destroyed the bright future she's earned? Her father's trust? And what about his ministry?

"REUNION is a captivating tale that will hook you from the very start...Fans of Christian fiction will love this touching story."

—FreshFiction.com

You may also enjoy *One Perfect Day*

LAURAINE SNELLING
Bestselling Author of *Breaking Free*

"Snelling's captivating tale will immediately draw readers in. The grief process is accurately portrayed, and readers will be enthralled by the raw emotion of Jenna's and Nora's accounts."
—*RT Book Reviews*

Nora Peterson is determined to make Christmas perfect. Next year her twin teenagers will be off at college, and their lives will never be quite the same. With her husband delayed on a business trip abroad, Nora's nerves are already frazzled when she gets the news of a car accident that will not only change the Petersons' lives forever, but also those of another family.

As a nurse, Jenna Montgomery has always struggled with balancing her personal and professional life. Her daughter, Heather, has suffered from a heart defect for most of her life. Now that Heather is twenty years old and still on the organ transplant waiting list, Jenna must find a way to accept that this is likely their last Christmas together. Then the miracle Jenna has desperately prayed for becomes a reality in an instant, and Heather's health is restored.

While Nora struggles with depression and grief, Jenna discovers that miracles aren't always easy to receive.

"Snelling, whose novels have sold more than two million copies, is sure to grab readers from the start of this holiday melodrama...[a] spiritually challenging and emotionally taut story. Fans of Christian women's fiction will enjoy this winning novel."
—*Publishers Weekly*

And don't miss Lauraine Snelling's national bestseller,
Breaking Free

Just get by. Those words have gotten Maggie Roberts through ten long, hard years after a tragic accident sent her to prison. There, she's kept her heart walled up and her head down, so when a chance to work in a high-profile retired Thoroughbred racehorse program is offered to her, Maggie is reluctant.

Nevertheless, her love of horses makes the opportunity too tempting to resist. Maggie finds new purpose working with Breaking Free, an abused blood-bay gelding who lashes out at anyone who tries to help him. Maggie soon learns he'll be put down if he can't be controlled, and she is determined to save him. But when a local businessman sets his sights on adopting the horse, Maggie may have to let go of the one thing keeping her afloat.

> "Reminding us that love can spring forth from ashes, that life can emerge from death, Lauraine Snelling writes a gripping and powerful novel that will inspire and uplift you."
> —Lynne Hinton, author of *The Last Odd Day*